Praise for MODEL HOME

"A nuanced and compelling portrait of a family

"To read Eric Puchner's debut novel, *Model*
dismay the unraveling of a family. Puchner has brought to bear his primary gifts
as a storyteller: startling language and the accretion of memorable scenes."
—San Francisco Chronicle

"I'm still trying to recover from reading about the pathos of the Zillers, which
thanks to the fine talent of Eric Puchner I will remember for quite a long while."
—Alan Cheuse, *Chicago Tribune*

"What's most impressive is Puchner's ability to keep his characters so relatable.
We'd gladly be the fourth child in the Zillers' dark, funny, completely human
story." **—*Elle***

"Puchner choreographs scenes of blazing hilarity and infernal despair, creating
an exceptionally well-plotted, caustically funny, and bracingly compassionate
novel of family lunacy and love." **—*Booklist*** (starred)

"With careful attention to nuanced and fractured perspectives, Puchner teases
a fragile beauty out of the loneliness that separates the members of this family."
—*Publishers Weekly* (starred)

"Puchner's prose is forthright, delightfully detailed, and the distance he strikes
from his characters seems just right: not so close that we can't see them in
social context, not so far that we don't feel for them deeply in their distress."
—NPR's *All Things Considered*

"Puchner's powerful first novel is much more than the sum of its deceptively
simple parts. Grade: A." **—*San Francisco* magazine**

"The Ziller family is utterly believable here. . . . There's a terrible shame involved if
you fail in America. But that shame is universal. That's what this estimable book
is about." **—Carolyn See, *The Washington Post***

Additional Praise for *Model Home*

"A compelling portrait of an oddly quintessential American family. Puchner gets the relationships among the family members just right."

—*The Dallas Morning News*

"The whole idea of family comes unraveled in Puchner's gloved and graceful style."

—*Los Angeles Times*

"Puchner knows how to bring home the ache, to let us feel with the characters that connection is only just barely out of reach."

—*The Rumpus*

"This novel, set with perfect pitch in the 1980s, nevertheless feels as immediate as Facebook postings. Puchner is a master of the telling detail and the delayed revelation."

—*Stanford Magazine*

"You know those novels about families where everything—I mean, *everything*—goes wrong, yet you can't stop reading? And laughing out loud amid the heartbreak? That's the kind of book Eric Puchner has created with his debut novel, *Model Home*."

—Books & Authors blog

"The subject of this marvelous novel is nothing less than the soul of the American family, in which love sometimes hides inside estrangement and survival can be a choice made under duress. All of it is played out in the California desert, land of false dreams, and yet the result is anything but arid: a searing, bitterly funny, achingly humane book by one of our most talented young writers."

—Ann Packer, author of *Songs Without Words* and
The Dive from Clausen's Pier

"Eric Puchner's *Model Home* is 1980s California in a nutshell: bright and frantic, giddy and broke, desperate and strong and always, always moving."

—Daniel Handler, author of *Adverbs*

"Reader, rejoice! Eric Puchner has given us a brilliant, unpretentious family saga of uncommon mastery and soul. *Model Home* is filled to bursting with wonderfully rendered love and heartbreak, hope and despair, triumph and travesty. Read this awesome novel. Read it now."

—Elisa Albert, author of *The Book of Dahlia*

"*Model Home* is a fantastic follow-up to Eric Puchner's remarkable story collection, *Music Through The Floor*. Puchner is such a tremendously skilled writer you barely notice how deftly he slips between points of view, how he creates characters that are so real their yearnings and failures become your own. This is a heartbreaking yet consistently funny novel that wraps its arms around all the beauty and tragedy of the unfulfilled American dream."

—Stephen Elliott, author of *The Adderall Diaries*

"Readers will feel the angst of teenage love, the frustration of plans gone wrong, and the heartbreak of the human condition. For anyone who likes fine writing on contemporary domestic crises."

—*Library Journal*

"Family love flickers capriciously throughout this fine domestic drama, which runs the gamut from hilarious to harrowing. A wild first novel that amply confirms the promise of Puchner's story collection, *Music Through the Floor*."

—*Kirkus Reviews* (starred)

"*Model Home* is Eric Puchner's first novel, and it shows loads of talent . . . The family might be a slightly older version of the Gladneys in Don DeLillo's *White Noise,* which combines comedy and catastrophe in a similar fashion."

—*The Mark* (Toronto)

"Compelling . . . In the grandest terms, it's a book about the failure of the American dream, not unlike its theatrical cousin *Death of a Salesman*. It's the California setting and the current economic crisis that make this well-crafted book all the more resonant."

—KPBS's Culture Lust

Also by Eric Puchner

Music Through the Floor: Stories

MODEL HOME

A Novel

Eric Puchner

Scribner

New York   London   Toronto   Sydney

Puc

The Southern California depicted in this book
is a blend of real and imagined geography.

Scribner
A Division of Simon & Schuster, Inc.
1230 Avenue of the Americas
New York, NY 10020

First Scribner trade paperback edition September 2010

SCRIBNER and design are registered trademarks of The Gale Group, Inc.,
used under license by Simon & Schuster, Inc., the publisher of this work.

For information about special discounts for bulk purchases,
please contact Simon & Schuster Special Sales at 1-866-506-1949
or business@simonandschuster.com.

The Simon & Schuster Speakers Bureau can bring authors to your live event.
For more information or to book an event contact the
Simon & Schuster Speakers Bureau at 1-866-248-3049
or visit our website at www.simonspeakers.com.

Designed by Carla Jayne Jones

Manufactured in the United States of America

1   3   5   7   9   10   8   6   4   2

Library of Congress Control Number: 2009038051

ISBN 978-0-7432-7048-9
ISBN 978-0-7432-7049-6 (pbk)
ISBN 978-1-4391-7034-2 (ebook)

Credit:
Stay Awake
from Walt Disney's MARY POPPINS
Words and Music by Richard M. Sherman and Robert B. Sherman
© 1963 Wonderland Music Company, Inc.
Copyright Renewed
All Rights Reserved   Used by Permission

For Katharine,

through love and loss

Items Checked Out Today:
Blasphemy
35101512054375   Due: 3/5/2018

Model home : a novel
35101512756466   Due: 3/5/2018

Sulfur Springs
35101513772652   Due: 2/26/2018

MODEL HOME

PART I

Summer 1985

PART 1

CHAPTER 1

Two days after his car—an '85 Chrysler LeBaron with leather seats and all-power accessories—vanished from the driveway, Warren Ziller crept past the expensive homes of his neighbors, keeping pace with his dog's limp. Buggy Whip Lane was shrouded in a mist that blurred his glasses. It was June, month of foggy mornings; vines of bougainvillea climbed the telephone poles and hung like tinsel from the wires. Warren tugged at Mr. Leonard's leash, trying to keep to the narrow horse trail skirting the road. The wood chips at his feet sent up a pleasing funk of manure. He passed the Hathaways' and Wongs' and Dunkirks', the Temples' and Starchilds', each house white as a tooth, distinguished only by a lone cactus or bronze deer in the yard or surfboard tipped against the wall. There was something very appealing about these surfboards. They looked doomed and precarious but never seemed to fall over. He'd lived here three years and the sight of them still gave him a thrill. When he tried to define California to himself, to reckon the fathomless miles he'd traveled from Wisconsin, Warren always thought of these beautiful toys on the verge of collapse.

Mr. Leonard stopped along the trail to inspect a rock and began to sing to it. A high, sorrowful croon, as if he might coax the thing into a duet. The mutt was old and arthritic, but it had never occurred to Warren that his mind might deteriorate. As dogs went, he'd always been bright and resourceful, sniffing out lost shoes or teasing doors open with his paws.

"Have you noticed anything funny about Mr. Leonard?" Warren asked when he got home. His children were sitting around the kitchen table together, most likely by accident. The house smelled of McDonald's and bare feet. Mr. Leonard limped to his bowl and stared at his meager ration of kibbles.

"You mean aside from him singing to rocks?" Lyle said, clipping her toenails into an empty sneaker on the floor. The sneaker was presumably her own.

"You've noticed?"

"Any rock. He can't resist."

"Maybe someone gave him some LSD," Jonas suggested.

"I don't think so," Warren said.

"Has he been jumping out of windows, thinking he can fly?" Dustin scoffed. "That's a myth."

"Dogs can't fly?" Lyle said, laying her clippers on the table.

Camille, his wife, looked up from the sink. "There's nothing funny about it."

"I think it's inspiring," Dustin said. "That he can find love so late in life."

"In Vietnam," Jonas said, "they kill dogs when they're no longer useful and use them for food. There's a dish called Dog Seven Ways."

"Boys! That's enough," Camille said.

"Yeah," Lyle said. "Mr. Leonard can hear you."

The mutt caught his name and came limping over to the kitchen table, tail thumping.

"How do I love thee," Dustin said, leaning to pet him. "Let me count the ways."

Camille walked over to Mr. Leonard and bent down to stroke his head, then looked up at them accusingly. "I hope you remember this, what a laugh riot you're having, when you're singing to rocks."

A guilty hush came over the table. In the silence, Warren had a chance to take in the spectacle of his children: Dustin, his college-bound son, shirtless as usual and eating an Egg McMuffin he must have picked up on the way home from surfing, preparing for another deafening day of band practice in the garage; Lyle, his redheaded, misanthropic daughter, sixteen years old and wearing a T-shirt with DEATH TO SANDWICHES stenciled on the front, her latest protest against corporate advertising; Jonas, eleven and haunted by death . . . what could he say about Jonas? Every morning he poured granola in his bowl and then spent five minutes picking out all the raisins and dates, only to *sprinkle them back*

on top. He liked to know where they were so "they wouldn't surprise him." Today he was wearing an orange windbreaker over a
matching orange shirt. Warren felt something brush his heart, a
draft of despair. He glanced under the table: orange corduroys,
and—glaring conspicuously above Jonas's Top-Siders—coral-
colored socks.

"Jonas, you're dressed entirely in orange."

Jonas nodded.

"He's exercising his individuality," Lyle said.

Dustin clapped Jonas on the back. "I admire you for making
the rest of us seem normal."

Warren watched his orange son picking raisins from his cereal.
He had enough on his mind already without worrying about the
boy's mental health. "You look like a carrot."

"Thank you," Jonas said politely.

Warren frowned. He picked up the front page of the newspaper
and was confronted with Mandy Rogers, the mentally retarded
girl who'd disappeared from school. It had been two weeks since
she went missing. There were signs hanging all over town: the flat,
porpoisey face grinning at you from under a cowboy hat. Eerie
and inescapable. Warren drove by the Rogerses' house, its squad-
ron of news vans, on the way to his office every day.

"I wish they'd just find that poor girl's body," he said.

"You don't know she's dead," Camille said. "I wish you
wouldn't go putting ideas in their heads."

"What do you think? She just wandered off?"

"Yeah, Mom," Lyle said. "She's waiting at the Lost and Found?"

"Maybe it's the same guy who stole the Chrysler," Dustin said.

"I doubt it. Car thieves don't generally abduct people."

Warren said this without batting an eye. There were surfboards
leaning undisturbed in all their neighbors' yards, yet Warren's
family had believed him when he'd said the Chrysler was stolen.
It dismayed him, how easy it had been. A fake call to the police,
a trip downtown to file a report. (The truth was he'd spent the
afternoon at the office.) He'd smoothed any wrinkles of doubt by
telling them there were bands of crooks who specialized in gated
communities, knowing that people left their keys in the car. "Sitting ducks," he'd called the families of Herradura Estates.

In truth, Warren had been in denial about the Chrysler. He'd
hoped—despite the fact that he hadn't made a payment in six

months, had ignored the bill collector's increasingly terse and belligerent notices—that the lender might just forget the whole business. Instead the men had come at night, while Warren was asleep. He'd gone out to the driveway with Mr. Leonard and found a dark drool of oil where his car had been. And the stain was only a herald of things to come. There was the furniture, the new Maytag washer, the house itself.

Dustin finished his breakfast, licking some grease that had run down his wrist. It was such a boyish gesture, so casually innocent, that the taste of fear eased back down Warren's throat. He would protect this innocence at all costs. If that meant lying to his family until he found a way out of this mess, so be it.

"How are the Deadbeats?" he asked Dustin, who'd gotten up to wash his hands in the sink. Warren loved to sit in the garage while they practiced, listening to their brain-throbbing music.

"We're not called that anymore."

"You're not?"

"It's a dumb name," Dustin said. "We're trying to think of a better one."

He turned his back to Warren, searching for something in the fridge. Warren was very familiar with this back. He had whole conversations with it. It was a strong back, beautiful in its gentle slopes and mesas: he'd gotten to know it the way you get to know a favorite view or painting. A back, even a silent one, was better than nothing. Still, there was a certain amount of faith involved: you had to trust it was listening, hunched over a guitar or a surfboard as if you weren't even there.

His wife had disappeared from the kitchen. Warren got up from his stool at the counter and went to find her. The hallway, like their room itself, was decorated with shell sculptures and turd-colored macramé things and paintings not unlike the splotch of oil staining the driveway. Camille had bought them all at a store called Creativity Unleashed, which sold art by mentally retarded people. Mandy Rogers's disappearance had inspired her to invest in heroically unattractive art. She'd wanted to hang it all over the house, but the kids had refused to adorn their walls with "retard paintings" and the bulk had ended up in their bedroom. When Warren objected, wondering if some types of creativity weren't better off leashed, Camille had called him hardhearted. He couldn't tell her it was the waste of money that frightened him.

Now he found his wife in the bathroom, tugging at her tennis skirt instead of getting dressed for work. He had to remind himself it was Saturday. Camille made educational videos for the public school system, and Warren often felt guilty for not taking it as seriously as she did. It was her goodness—her belief in higher rewards than money—that he'd always been attracted to.

"Where did Jonas get orange socks?" he asked, watching her put on some lipstick.

"He picked them out at Nordstrom's," Camille said.

"You bought them for him?"

"How was I supposed to know he'd dress up like that?"

Warren sat on the bed to untie his sneakers. "Given the choice between a slow kid and a genius who dresses like a carrot, I might have chosen the former."

"Any word from the police?" she asked.

"What?"

"About the Chrysler! Did they learn anything?"

Warren shook his head. "Probably scattered all over the state by now," he said.

Thankfully, Camille didn't seem to question this and began dabbing her lips with a Kleenex. A little pink T, like a cat's nose, stained the middle. She was still lovely: blond hair and the sort of wholesome, cheerleadery face, freckled and wide-eyed and slightly bucktoothed, that caused people to smile at her from their cars. She was a Midwesterner in the way Blackbeard was a pirate: iconic to the species. Even when she was angry at Warren she seemed hopelessly preppy, her face a cardigan pink. He wanted to tell her that his project in the desert—for which he'd sacrificed everything, his family's own future—was a disaster. Everything they had was in peril. If she knew, they could face down the debt collectors—the angry phone calls and investors—together. It would be like before they were married, when Warren was in law school in Chicago and they were living in a run-down studio in Rogers Park, so poor they'd been forced to eat a moose Camille's brother had shot in Michigan. They'd survived on ground moose meat all winter, using Hamburger Helper to mask the flavor. Moose Helper, they'd called it, laughing at the TV commercials they'd thought up as a joke.

Warren got up from the bed and kissed Camille's neck, holding the faint bulges that had recently formed at her waist. She turned around in surprise.

"Camille . . ."

The surprise on her face melted to concern. "What is it?"

"There's something . . ."

He couldn't meet her eyes. Last week, making love, she'd said something to him strange and terrible, a confession of despair. *I want to die.* Through the bedroom window, he could see Dustin waxing his surfboard in the backyard, kneeling on the lawn while Jonas practiced his fencing moves. The sun had broken through the mist, lighting the persimmon tree near the garden into a blaze of orange fruit. Beneath it, lunging in the sunlight, his fruit-colored son looked weirdly beautiful.

"Mr. Leonard," Warren said quietly. "Maybe it's time we had him looked at."

CHAPTER 2

Lyle's mother had to drive her to work, a universe of suck, because her dad's car had been stolen from the driveway and he'd had to borrow Lyle's Renault, which despite having the words "Le Car" stencilled on the door in bubble letters was infinitely less embarrassing than riding with her mom. They drove through the hills of Herradura Estates, slow as a hearse. An anemic-looking cyclist overtook them on John's Canyon Road. Lyle slid down in her seat. There were several things that embarrassed her about her mother's Volvo: (1) it had her mother in it; (2) there was a Post-it note on the steering wheel that said RECYCLE BOTTLES; (3) the stereo was typically playing something called "Come, Ye Makers of Song"; (4) they were often mistaken for people with special needs, because her mom insisted on signaling before pulling into a parking space. Worst of all were the slogans plastered all over the back bumper: NO APARTHEID, KEEP YOUR LAWS OFF MY BODY, GOOD PLANETS ARE HARD TO FIND, and the more bluntly confessional I BRAKE FOR SPOTTED OWLS. (Dustin wanted to replace it with I DON'T NEED TO BRAKE, BECAUSE I'M BARELY MOVING.) Last week her mom had added COMMIT RANDOM ACTS OF KINDNESS, which to Lyle perfectly summed up her psychotic brand of cheerfulness.

There was someone jogging on the wood-chipped trail that ran along the road. Jennifer Boone, a senior at Palos Verdes High who lived down the street. Lyle slid even lower in her seat. Her mother honked as they passed, which caused Jennifer to startle like a deer and veer dangerously toward the bushes.

"I can't believe Dad's car got stolen," Lyle said sullenly, hoping her mom was unrecognizable in tennis clothes. She was wearing a pink Izod, a skirt fringed with Lilliputian pom-poms, and a see-through visor that made her look like a bank teller from *Bonanza*. "Isn't that why we live in a gated community? To prevent theft?"

"This isn't a gated community, honey. It's an equestrian village."

"There are gates, right? They go up and down?"

"That's for the horses," her mother said. "Otherwise people would drive through all day and scare them."

Lyle squinted at her mom, wondering if she really believed they lived on a dude ranch in the suburban hills of L.A. An intriguing theory, since it might explain the visor. Lyle would not have been surprised if the horseback riders who occasionally ambled by their house were stooges brought in by Herradura Estates. She couldn't help being impressed by the marketing genius involved—just paint some horse crossings on the street, call yourself an "equestrian village," and rich people came running.

"This is all Dad's fault for moving us out here," she said. "The car getting stolen."

"In Nashotah, you always complained about how boring it was. I seem to remember you saying you couldn't wait to leave."

"Anyway, the guards don't do jack. They're rent-a-cops. All you have to do is give the name of a resident."

Her mom sighed, checking the rearview mirror. "Do you really have to be *so* negative? As long as people believe it, what does it matter?"

It mattered deeply. Lyle's mother, of course, was one of the deceived. She read books with "healing" or "mindfulness" in the title. She went on check-writing sprees to save various birds of prey. Once she'd bought a newborn calf for a poor farmer in Mali and was shocked to receive a picture in the mail one day, a wordless thank-you, showing the meat drying in lurid strips from the farmer's roof. She'd rushed to the bathroom in tears. *He's starving to death!* Lyle wanted to shout. *Of course he's going to eat it!* Most infuriating of all was her mother's optimism: whenever Lyle said she disliked someone, her mom looked at her with her eyebrows pinched into a V, head cocked to one side as if she were draining an ear. "You don't really hate that person," she'd say. "You just have different values."

But Lyle *did* hate people. Hating people was one of her biggest hobbies. Just last night, in fact, she'd started a list of things she despised:

1. People who call old women "cute"

2. People who talk about dead relatives as if they're happier now

3. Anyone who refers to herself as a "chocoholic"

4. DBCs (Dumbshits in Baseball Caps)

5. The adjective "hot" for anything except weather

6. People who use the term "110%"

7. Song titles with numbers in place of words

8. People who own Smiths records and don't know the lead singer is gay

9. Volleyball

10. Convertibles

11. Bob Marley

12. Anyone who uses the word "ganja"

13. Dogs small enough that they shiver when they take a dump

14. People who look at you funny when you use the word "ingratiate"

15. People who order in Spanish at Mexican restaurants (Mom)

16. People who say "Decisions, decisions" when looking at a menu

17. Bathroom graffiti that rhymes ("Wine me, dine me, 69 me")

18. The Beach Boys

19. People who check their car for scratches before getting in

20. People who refer to little boys as "boss" or "chief"

21. Anyone who says the sentence: "And WHO do we have here?"

22. Volleyball (x2)

23. CALIFORNIA

This last one she'd written in big letters and retraced again and again until the letters engraved several pages of her journal, fading gradually like a wound. She detested it, this land of Jeeps and joggers. The Golden State. What kind of stupid nickname was that? Perhaps it wasn't supposed to describe the place itself so much as a fascist condition. If you weren't golden, you had no right to exist. Lyle used to go to the beach when they first moved here, hoping she might get a tan like the Audras and Stephanies in her class, her skin turning brown and luscious. She lay in a deserted corner of the beach, sweating and miserable, terrified someone from school would see her and notice how pale she was. A circus freak: the Whitest Girl in California. She was determined to stay until she looked like the other girls, the ones with butterflies of sand stuck to their asses, running into the waves and twirling around with a squeal. Instead she burned herself so miserably she couldn't sleep. Her skin blistered and peeled off like Saran Wrap, leaving her whiter than before. After a month of suffering, she realized it was hopeless and gave up completely.

She'd been bored in Wisconsin, bored living on the same puny lake her whole life, but at least she hadn't felt like a freak of nature. She hadn't cried herself to sleep because some DBC had called her Vampira at school.

On their way out of Herradura Estates, Lyle's mother pulled up to the guardhouse and its red-striped gate, which lifted magically as they approached. She brought the car to a stop in order to say hello to Hector, the new gatekeeper. Lyle waited with mounting dread as her mother rolled down the window. Please don't speak Spanish, she thought. Please don't please don't please don't please don't please don't.

"*Hola,*" her mother said in a cheerful voice. "*Cómo estas?*"

"*Bien, bien,*" Hector said, smiling through his mustache. He looked vaguely amused, as though doing his best to conceal the fact that he spoke perfect English. "*Y usted?*"

"*Nosotros estamos yendo a la* shopping mall." Her mother actually said "shopping mall" in a Spanish accent.

Hector cupped his ear. "*A donde?*"

"The mall," Lyle's mother said. "The Perfect Scoop. For my daughter's job. *Ella vende helado.*"

Hector ducked down and smiled at Lyle in the passenger seat, as though she were six years old. She felt like flashing him her tits. "*Que bueno.*"

"*Le gustan los libros. Siempre.* How do you say it? A worm."

Lyle's mother stuck her finger out the window and began to wiggle it around. Hector squinted at it from the guardhouse.

"She still goes to work?" he said finally, looking concerned.

"*Claro que si!*" her mother said, smiling.

She said good-bye and Hector relaxed back into his chair, believing no doubt that Lyle had worms. Lyle wanted to murder her mother. She would strangle her slowly and then dump her out of the car and drive to New York, where she'd never have to wear shorts and where it was okay—sophisticated even—not to be tan. She'd never actually been to New York, but she was sure that paleness was a sign of cachet. Certainly there was no volleyball. If you tried to play volleyball in New York, people would throw things at you from the street. They would stone you with cigarettes and umbrellas.

At the mall, Lyle's mother dropped her off at The Perfect Scoop Ice Cream Parlor and then drove off to commit more random acts of Spanish. Lyle was surprised to find Shannon Jarrell already inside the store, sitting with her legs crossed by the tower of plastic tables and reading a *People* magazine. Shannon's being there on time was a miracle of Newtonian physics, but she lifted her eyes casually, as if it were an everyday occurrence. "Hey."

"How did you get in?" Lyle asked.

Shannon looked back at her magazine. "Jared. He gave me the keys."

Jared was the manager, who had a crush on Shannon and was always staring at her ass. Today she was wearing cutoff jeans to show off her tan, a direct violation of the company dress code.

Her legs were long and slender and glowed like hot dogs. She'd rolled the sleeves of her Perfect Scoop T-shirt over her shoulders, which had the same Oscar Mayer tan. A flip-flop dangled insolently from one foot.

"Did you cash in the register?" Lyle asked.

"No. I was waiting for you."

"Why?"

She shrugged. "You always do it."

Lyle swore under her breath and went into the back to get the cash drawer. She had to do everything. If the tubs were empty, Shannon would just tell the customers they were out of chocolate or vanilla chip or pralines-and-cream rather than get a new tub from the freezer. Not that Lyle gave two shits about the people who came in—but she couldn't afford to slack off like Shannon, because nothing would get done. And whose well-concealed ass would Jared fire?

She spun through the combination on the safe and retrieved the drawer of money. The back room was small and cozy, a home away from home, stocked for some reason with a shelf of cheap liqueurs. On slow afternoons, when she was working by herself, Lyle would sit back here with her feet up and sip Kahlúa from a mug, lost in whatever novel she was reading, so wrapped up in the vicissitudes of beauty and despair that she wouldn't notice the *bee-bong* of the door as a customer walked in. *Hello?* the customer would yell into the void. *Are you alive back there? Not exactly,* Lyle would yell back. Sometimes, if it was a good enough book, she'd put it down in a daze and wobble out to the front, greeted by a world—faces, movement, squares of sunlight on the floor—that seemed less real than the one she'd been reading about. It was as if God had decided to phone it in.

Locking the safe again, Lyle glanced at the corner of the room and noticed a sleeping bag rolled into a strudel, propped beside a pillow. A flash of proprietary anger went through her. She carried the cash drawer out to the register.

"Christ. You didn't *sleep* here."

Shannon smirked. "Me and Charlie."

"Your boyfriend?"

Shannon nodded, pleased with herself.

"Why?"

"We were playing Yahtzee." She laughed. "What do you think? His parents are cool, but not *that* cool."

So that's why she'd enticed Jared into giving her the key. Lyle started to refill the syrup dispensers, watching from the corner of her eye as Shannon unstacked the tables and dragged them to their places. How did she make screwing on the floor of an ice cream shop seem glamorous? If Lyle had done the same thing, it would have swept PV High that she was a miserable slut. It wasn't fair or just or randomly kind. Lyle watched the boys who came in for ice cream, how their faces changed when they saw Shannon: a wide-eyed slackening, as though they'd been conked in the head. It made Lyle want to tip them over like a row of bikes.

"You should give Jared the keys back," she said now, snipping open a bag of caramel topping.

"Why?"

"Otherwise we'll have to start charging by the hour."

A flash of outrage crossed Shannon's face before dissolving into a smile. As an object of male worship she could afford not to be angry, which drove Lyle crazy. Shannon picked the *People* off the windowsill and started to flip through it nonchalantly.

"You're a virgin, aren't you?"

"None of your business."

She narrowed her eyes, smiling. "You are, aren't you? I knew it."

Lyle ignored her, carrying the pillow-sized bag of caramel back to the fridge. For the rest of the morning, she tended to customers while Shannon inspected her nails or browsed through magazines or whispered to friends on the phone as if she were selling nuclear secrets. (*I work with a virgin!* Lyle imagined her saying.) Once two people came in at the same time and Shannon made no move to get off the phone, letting the second customer wait until Lyle was available. It was the sort of thing Lyle would have had fun complaining about to Bethany, her best friend, mocking Shannon's urgent whispering. Besides herself, Bethany was the only Californian she knew who didn't like the beach. It was Bethany's idea to make T-shirts with fake slogans on them, thinking up the brilliantly inspired PLEASE BUY THIS SENTENCE. Now that she'd moved to France for eight months, because of her dad's business, Lyle had no one to complain to but herself. She'd failed to anticipate the depth of her loneliness. Her old friends in Wisconsin had betrayed her after she left, falling in love with football players or pimple-faced tenth graders; they'd stopped writing very much, and then altogether. Now the same thing was happening with Bethany. Only a month and a half had passed, but already her letters had grown shorter: last week she'd sent a single paragraph and a picture of her "sort-of *petit ami*," a boy with large ears and Dickensian teeth.

Eventually, when she'd exhausted all sources of leisure, Shannon went out to get something from her car. Lyle knew she'd be gone for thirty minutes but didn't care. It was a relief. She sneaked into the back room and picked up where she'd left off in *Tess of the D'Urbervilles*. She felt a certain affinity for Tess. Actually, she couldn't help being a little attracted to Alec D'Urberville's "black mustache with curled points." Just as Tess was baptizing her dying son by candlelight, the door chimed; Lyle slipped the book back in the drawer, pained that she was too embarrassed to read it in front of Shannon.

It was the gatekeeper. Hector. He looked startling outside of his little guardhouse: a real person, rigid and wiry, his uniform ironed to a crisp. He looked like the inside of a closet. She smiled at him uncertainly, and he lifted his finger and wiggled it like a worm. She laughed.

"I was wondering if I could get some ice cream."

"Sorry. We only sell corn dogs."

He seemed flustered. "I mean, I'd like to get an ice cream cone."

"Never mind. A joke." She frowned. "What flavor do you want?"

He looked at her closely, studying her face instead of the tubs of ice cream displayed in front of him. His mustache, impossible to describe, reminded her why she only liked them in books. The word that popped into her head was "illegitimate." If mustaches had parents, this was definitely an orphan. "I don't know. What's your favorite?"

Lyle shrugged. "Pistachio?"

"I've never tried it."

"Here. Have a taster."

She grabbed a spoon and handed him a fluorescent green smudge of ice cream. His face fell. He eyed the smudge suspiciously and then sucked it from the little spoon, wincing for a second before he could recover.

"I'll have that," he said. "A sugar cone."

Lyle bent over the tub with her scoop, curling the ice cream from the sides and then packing it into a green snowball. By the end of the day, her arm would ache so badly she'd have trouble sleeping. She glanced up and was surprised to discover Hector looking at her breasts. She stood up straight, pressing the snowball into a cone. For the first time, it occurred to her that he hadn't just wandered into the store by accident.

He didn't leave, which surprised her as well. He sat at one of the plastic tables in the corner, eating his cone. He hunched on his elbows, closing his eyes to swallow. It was like watching someone eat his own shoe. Lyle took a weird delight in watching him suffer. Heroically, he licked the scoop down to an eroded-looking dune and then crunched through the cone, finishing the last bite without looking up. Lyle walked over.

"You've got green in your mustache," she said, offering him a napkin.

Hector blushed. He was younger than she'd thought: nineteen or twenty, though it was hard to tell with the hair on his lip. While he wiped his face, dabbing the ice cream from his mustache, Lyle stood patiently in the sunlight from the window. It was a feeling like being onstage. She knew that if she waited long enough, something would happen. The air was filled with glittering specks, like snow. Gravely, he asked if he could have her phone number.

"Yours," Lyle said, surprising herself.

She wrote his number on her hand and then went to hide in the back. Her heart was pounding—not from nerves but from a cold rush of power. He was still there; the door hadn't chimed. Lyle retraced the number in darker pen. She wanted Shannon to see it, but also wanted Hector to take off before she saw who it belonged to.

CHAPTER 3

"How about the Turpitudes?" Biesty said.

"What the hell does that mean?" Tarwater asked.

"My poor coxcomb." Biesty shook his head. "Think depravity, but times ten."

Band practice. Sunday morning. They were standing in Dustin's garage, trying to come up with a name that would reflect the intelligence of the band while defining its commitment to rocking one's ass back into the womb. So far in their six-month history, the perfect one had eluded them. (They'd been happy with the Deadbeats, or at least communally okay with it, until some hippie at a party had asked them if they covered Grateful Dead songs.) Dustin shot a weary look at Biesty, his best friend, whose glasses were perched on top of his head like a tiara. Biesty was the only person he knew who could quote Heidegger while tripping on three hits of acid. As a summer project, he'd decided to read *The Riverside Shakespeare* in its entirety while smoking large amounts of Royal Afghani, a project that had started to affect his sanity. Now he grinned at Dustin, as if the Turpitudes was really the best name since the Sex Pistols.

Dustin sighed. The garage was cluttered with bikes and ski equipment and at least one dartboard, which Starhead—their drummer—had placed on his stool to make himself taller. One of Starhead's tom-toms refused to screw tight and drooped from its stand like a giant flower. Then there was the issue of Tarwater's bass, which still had Twisted Sister and Def Leppard stickers on it from his formative musical years, circa last year. Occasionally, when they were tuning up, he'd break into the bass line of "Rock of Ages." At times like this Dustin wondered whether they were really destined to write the next chapter in punk history.

"Turpitude is singular," Starhead said. True to his nickname, he'd shaved a star into the top of his head, which he ducked down to show people whenever he introduced himself. "You can't just add an *s* to it."

"Who says?"

"It's like being called the Friendships. Or the Moneys."

Biesty shrugged. "You can say that. 'Moneys.' If you have different kinds of currency."

"All right," Dustin said, trying to avoid an argument. It often occurred to him that his main function as bandleader was keeping the peace. "So we've got the Turpitudes, Viet-Nun, and Toxic Shock Syndrome. We each get two votes, the rule being you can't choose the same name twice."

"What about mine?" Tarwater said. The fact remained that Tarwater was a good bassist, so you had to take his suggestions seriously no matter how stupid they were. If you pissed him off, he might threaten to leave the band or refuse to turn on his amp until you performed one of the dreadful ballads he'd written, perhaps "Despair Is My Silent Angel" or "Brothers Won't Be Shackled (White, Red, or Brown)."

"Okay, Tarwater," Dustin said equably. "What's your idea?"

"The Butt Hawks."

"The Butt Hawks?"

"Yeah." He smiled proudly, despite the silence.

"What signifies this breed of hawk?" Biesty asked.

"What do you *think*?" Tarwater said.

Dustin cocked his head, trying to look encouraging. "Is it, like, a hawk that flies out of your butt?"

"No. Jesus."

"I'm just trying to get my mind around it."

"A bunch of guys who like women's butts?" Starhead offered.

"No, you fuck-brains." Tarwater paused, perhaps for emphasis. "It's a *mohawk that grows out of your butt*."

"Wow," Dustin said.

"That's disgusting," Biesty said. Dustin shot him a glance over Tarwater's head. "Disgusting, but ambiguous."

"How about Asshawk?" Starhead suggested. "Just for, like, brevity."

To settle things, Dustin shredded a piece of paper into little pieces and then handed them out. Everyone wrote down their top two choices and stuck them in a baseball cap. Dustin had a sense of something historic in the making. He tallied the votes. In the end, Toxic Shock Syndrome won out narrowly with three ballots. (The Butt Hawks got two, which could only be explained by illegal voting.)

So began the first official practice of Toxic Shock Syndrome. Dustin tuned his Stratocaster with a feeling of long-awaited departure. He'd worked all spring at Randy's Audio Emporium so he could have enough money to take the summer off, his last before college, and steer the band toward greatness.

"Are you going to tell your dad our new name?" Starhead asked, twirling a drumstick.

"Why?"

"He's our number one fan."

Dustin frowned. "He's not a fan. He likes barbershop quartet records. I think he's just had a head injury or something."

"It's pretty weird," Biesty said, wedging a cigarette between the strings of his fretboard. "The way he veges on those steps. I'm waiting for him to shotgun one of those Cokes and start slamming."

They warmed up with some covers—"Los Angeles," "TV Party"—but the image of his father, nodding along to the beat and tapping his foot, kept messing with Dustin's groove. Who'd ever heard of a punk band whose biggest fan was a forty-three-year-old real estate developer in boat shoes? He was impossible to avoid, because you never knew when he was going to be home anymore. If Dustin turned up the amps to an ear-blistering ten, his dad would just shut his eyes and lean his head back against the wall. The louder they played, the more he seemed to enjoy it.

Today, sure enough, he wandered into the garage in the middle of "Mandy Rogers," Dustin's paean to loss and suffering in a godless universe. *(You prayed to Him at night like a good little nun, the one person, you thought, who wouldn't shun or make fun.)* As usual, his dad got a Coke from the fridge and then sat on the steps with that lost look on his face, as though he were waiting for a life-changing message to wash up on the beach. Biesty grabbed the mike from its stand and began prowling the garage while he belted the chorus, as though searching for Mandy or God or both; normally Biesty's stage antics inspired Dustin, but now they seemed dumb and overwrought. It was his father's fault. Somehow, just by sitting there, he had a way of making everything seem ridiculous. Why couldn't Dustin just have a normal dad like Biesty's, who never took any interest in anything and jerked off in his bedroom all the time to his ten-year stash of *Hustler*s?

"Would you play that one song you wrote?" Dustin's dad asked while they took a cigarette break. He didn't care if they smoked, which—despite Dustin's griping—gave him a measure of respect with the band. "About the shit hitting the fan?"

"Dad, this is practice! We don't do requests." Dustin glared at his father's polo shirt. "Anyway, that's the Circle Jerks. We didn't write it."

"The Circle Jerks?"

This had always seemed to Dustin like the perfectly irreverent name—but now he began helplessly to doubt it. Wasn't it a bit juvenile? Before Dustin could stop him, Biesty turned to his father with a courteous expression.

"It's when you stand in a naked circle of men," he explained, "and masturbate the participant in front of you."

"Are they homosexuals?"

"*No*, Dad. Jesus."

"Do you have a recording of it?"

Dustin shook his head.

"I've got it at home," Tarwater said. "I could tape it for you, Mr. Ziller."

"Thank you, Brent. That would be great."

"You might like the Ramones, too. They're more middle-aged."

Dustin raised his voice. "Look, Dad, do you *have* to be in here?"

"It's chill," Starhead said. "He's only listening to us practice."

"It's *not* chill. Christ. What are we going to do next? Invite the neighbors over for juice and cookies?"

The way his dad stared at his Coke, smiling as though he had indigestion, gave Dustin a twinge of guilt. Still smiling, his father hunched up the stairs—the back pocket of his khakis pulled out like a rabbit's ear—and disappeared inside the house. Dustin remembered the Halloween when he was seven, how some teenagers had run by on his way home from trick-or-treating and stolen all of his candy. He'd come home in tears. Dustin's father had taken him out later in the dark, carrying him on his shoulders under the strange high buzz of the streetlights, through the clumsy swooping of bats, knocking on people's doors and rousing them out of bed in their pajamas, until Dustin had filled three bags of candy. But what was he supposed to do now, start doing whippits with the guy? Going on double dates?

"Finally," he said. "Safely locked up."

After band practice, Dustin drove to the beach to meet Kira, who'd been there since eleven working on her tan. He would have liked to be going straight to the beach, since the vision of his beautiful girlfriend lying in the sun—that sexy, inviting dip at the small of her back, like somewhere a kitten might curl up—was giving him a hard-on. It was bad enough to have a hard-on with your sister in the car, but he had to drive all the way to Miraleste to drop her at the library. He couldn't even blast the stereo, not with Jonas sitting in the backseat next to the only speaker that worked, gazing out the window at God knew what. How Dustin's mom had convinced him to drag the kid along with him to Rat Beach, he did not know. Somehow it had to do with the car shortage. Dustin got a kick out of Jonas, he was strange and hilarious and dressed for the second day in a row entirely in orange, but this did not mean he wanted to show up at the beach with an Oompa-Loompa.

Still, it was hard to be bummed out when you were driving basically beachward and the air would soon sting of salt and the fog had burned off into a spectacular California day, the sky so blue you had to remind yourself it was real, like those textbook photos of the Earth's atmosphere. They drove past the Courtyard Mall, which made Dustin feel sorry for the consumer zombies inside. He felt sorry for dead people. He felt sorry for anyone not from California (perhaps the same thing). He felt sorry for his bandmates, who were holed up in Starhead's house, high on his mother's Percocet and watching *The Decline of Western Civilization* for the zillionth time.

"Something weird's going on with Dad," he said, glancing at Lyle, who was wearing a T-shirt that said MURDER IS A FAUX PAS. She hadn't bothered to wash her hair, which hung over her eyes in greasy red strings. "He's always, like, hanging out in the garage."

"Maybe he misses the Chrysler," she said.

"No. I mean, he just sits there with this stupid expression, like he wants to hug me or something."

"Mom's the same way," Lyle said. "Especially when she looks at endangered sea otters."

"I'm being serious."

Lyle nodded. "Actually, I saw him last night. Doing the laundry."

"What?"

"Uh-huh. A big load of whites. It was three in the morning."

"Are you sure it was him?"

"Well, he was wearing boat shoes."

"I can't imagine him doing the wash at all," Dustin said.

"Exactly! A pod person!" Lyle peered into the backseat. "Jonas, you're the genius. What do *you* think's wrong with Dad?"

Jonas shrugged. "He's addicted to heroin and his veins have collapsed?"

"Where does he get these ideas?" Dustin said happily.

"Gee, I don't know. I'm sure Mom's videos have nothing to do with it."

Lyle pretended to shoot a needle into her neck, tongue lolling from her mouth. Dustin laughed. They had fun at home, giving their mom a hard time or pretending their dad had gone deaf, talking to him sotto voce, but he and his sister never hung out together for real. It amazed Dustin to think how close they'd been as kids in Wisconsin, playing Pounce for hours on the bed or making tape recordings of made-up poems or selling Country Time lemonade to their neighbors in Nashotah, palming it off as homemade and making a killing. One summer they spent hours at a time inside the pink, echoey, breezeless cave of a flipped-over raft in the lake: it was like being behind an eyelid, or in the same luminous, too-loud brain. It was there, hidden under the raft, that they'd started playing Cats vs. Dogs. It was World War III and they had to decide what things to let into their bomb shelter; for every thing they saved there was something else they had to leave out, dooming it to extinction. Frogs were safe but not toads. Milkshakes but not banana splits. The Beatles but not the Rolling Stones. Lyle loved the game and insisted on playing it every chance they got. Dustin couldn't imagine playing anything like it with her now. She hated everything; there'd be nothing, no one worth saving.

At the library, Lyle got out of the car without saying good-bye and strode off in her baggy T-shirt, eager to get to her books. His friends called her the She-Yeti. What bugged him more than the nickname was that they used it in front of him, as though his sister was so white and abominable he wouldn't possibly object. Dustin had stuck up for her more than once, surprised by his own anger. Though he'd never tell her this, Dustin sort of admired her: she dressed the way she pleased and didn't worry about being tan or popular.

At Rat Beach, Dustin parked the car in the shade of a euca-lyptus and walked down the dirt trail with Jonas, who hadn't brought a bathing suit with him or for that matter even shorts. As usual, the beach itself was nearly deserted. He loved everything about it. He loved parading down to his favorite spot, skirting the breakwater where the sand wouldn't fry his feet to a crisp, the sexy-looking moms glancing up from their kids to watch him laze by. He loved the soreness in his face from the salt. He loved the lifeguard stand boarded up and gone to rot. He loved, when he walked, the way the sand fleas rose in front of his feet before he stepped, psychically attuned to his stride, as if there were an invisible person walking in front of him. He loved the seagulls, the mellow swells, the sun top-browning the water into three feet of delicious warmth.

He found Kira's radio and towel and then saw Kira herself, walking back from the Snack Shack with a frozen Snickers bar, its wrapper torn down like a banana peel. Her long brown hair was frizzled from the ocean. She smiled at him and Jonas, a rabbity two-teethed grin that drove Dustin crazy and often haunted his dreams. They'd been seeing each other for close to a year.

"Who are you supposed to be?" she asked Jonas, staring at his clothes. Jonas had laid his towel in the sand and was standing beside it, like a butler awaiting a command.

"A human being," he said.

"Right. Stupid me. Do you always go to the beach in cordu-roys?"

Jonas thought about this—or seemed to. It was hard to know. "No," he said. "Sometimes I go to the mall."

Kira looked at Dustin, who raised his eyebrows to indicate they'd entered the Jonas Zone and all present dispatches were use-less. She really seemed to like his weirdo brother, a first in terms of his romantic history. "Do you think we'll have freaky kids?" she asked, leaning into Dustin's ear.

"Like deformed ones?"

"Ha ha." She kissed his cheek. "I just pray they get my brains."

"Good thinking," Dustin said. "If they were too smart, we wouldn't be able to sell them to the circus."

She punched his shoulder but couldn't help laughing. Just for kicks, Dustin imagined what their marriage might be like, how he'd be a lauded figure in the history of L.A. punk and they'd live in a bungalow in the Hollywood Hills, where he'd write his critically acclaimed songs in the bathtub. And being married meant they could screw whenever they wanted. That was one thing, to be honest, he could really get into. Right now their sex life was a little bit *unfulfilled*. Actually, it was an exercise in major suffering. They'd be going hot and heavy in the backseat of the Dart or on the Shackneys' living room couch or on the dewy black tarp of their trampoline, dry-humping until Dustin's dick was chafed, until his pain and pleasure zones were thoroughly confused, but when it came to the magic moment—the unfastening of Kira's jeans—there was always the Grip, the hand that came down to stop him with a gentle, proprietary squeeze. That would be that, end of story, go back to Dustinville. Other girls had aimed the Grip at him before, and he'd protested with a fierceness that surprised even him. But Kira was different. She was the real thing, maybe the love of his life, and he was willing to wait until she was ready.

Now, perhaps to torture him, Kira stripped down to her bikini bottoms, bending over to pull her gym shorts leisurely down her knees, a sight that should be in *The Guinness Book of World Records* for most incredible boyfriend perk. She squirted some sunscreen on her arm and started to rub it into her skin.

"You look like a corpse," she said to Jonas, who was lying fully clothed on his towel with his eyes shut.

"Thank you," he said. Kira glanced at Dustin. "Actually, corpses don't think."

"If you're not a corpse, what are you thinking?"

"Don't start," Dustin said.

Jonas opened his eyes. "Do you really want to know," he said suspiciously, "or are you just making small talk?"

"I really want to know."

"I was thinking about whether it was worse to be eaten by sharks or to get picked apart by vultures, I mean if you're too weak to move and not fully dead."

Kira frowned, snapping the lotion shut. "Jonas, you're eleven years old. You should be worrying about, like, if gerbils go to heaven."

Jonas chose to ignore this. Nearby, beyond a raft of seagulls, Dustin could see two kids about Jonas's age playing in the sand. One was buried up to his head like a mummy while the other constructed a towering penis at his crotch, running down to the water and bringing back cups of wet sand to gigantify its length. "Holy crud!" the buried kid was shouting. "She's gonna collapse!" Dustin loved Jonas as he was but wished sometimes he'd build sand penises and say things like "holy crud" instead of worrying about being eaten to death. Lately he'd begun knocking on Dustin's door at odd times of the day, asking if he would help him practice a fencing move or decorate some pointless card to Mandy Rogers. It made Dustin sad, that Jonas seemed so alone, but he didn't have time to be the kid's parent.

Kira tuned the radio to her favorite station, which was playing "Peace Train." Dustin hadn't told his bandmates about Kira's secret penchant for Cat Stevens and Fleetwood Mac. Nor had he told them the other things that, in a future wife, he found faintly troubling. Last week they'd gone to see a play in downtown L.A., one that Biesty had told him about, and during the performance an actor had unzipped his pants onstage and pissed into a bucket. Afterward, it was the first thing that Kira mentioned: *Was it really necessary that he take a whiz in front of everyone?* It wasn't even her objection that bothered Dustin but that he'd foreseen it so perfectly even before the actor had zipped up his pants, right down to the word "whiz." He couldn't shake the feeling that everything she did was utterly predictable. He knew that she'd close her eyes for a second and take a deep breath before entering a party; that she'd eat the edges of a Peppermint Pattie first and save the gooey center for last, asking jokingly if he wanted a bite; that she would stare at him sometimes when they were watching a movie and say, in the middle of the best scene, "You're so adorable when you're serious."

The problem was he had a different vision of himself. In this vision he was not adorable at all. He was strange and spontaneous and did charismatically delinquent things, like piss in a bucket for a crowd of strangers.

"I made you something," Kira said now, reaching into her

purse. Always, as soon as he saw her beautiful, heart-melting face, any reservations he had immediately vanished. She pulled out a cassette tape and handed it to him. Slanting across the case, in embossed letters, was a label that said THIS OBJECT IS DESIGNED TO MAKE NOISE. "It's those songs you recorded at Biesty's house. I made ten copies."

"You did?"

"I thought we could sell them the next time you play."

Dustin was moved. She was always doing things like this, helping to set up gigs or sneaking into the teachers' lounge at school to Xerox flyers. Her belief in his talent stunned him sometimes. It was like having a fantastic dream about yourself, then waking up to find that someone else had had it too.

"Shit," she said, sitting up on her towel. "There's Taz. She saw me. The Witch of Endor."

Kira's sister trudged up the sand with a cigarette in her mouth, trailed by a shirtless boy in Elvis sunglasses. She had a streak of white dyed into her bangs. For some reason, the cigarette made her seem even younger.

"I need some money," Taz said without even glancing at Dustin. She was wearing a saggy bathing suit and a pair of cutoff jeans that seemed to be biodegrading. She looked like Kira but wasn't half as pretty; it was nice seeing them together because it made Kira seem even hotter. Her friend with the Elvis sunglasses stood there quietly, observing Jonas as if he were maybe a mesmerizing speed bump.

"Didn't Mom give you any?" Kira said.

"I spent it already."

"On cigarettes?"

Taz scowled. "What is this, the Inquisition? Like you don't smoke all the time in your bathroom."

"Is he dead?" the boy in the Elvis glasses said, nudging Jonas with his foot.

"Waiting to get picked apart," Dustin said.

The boy stepped back.

"What are you going to buy with it?" Kira asked Taz.

"Some angel dust. At the Snack Shack."

"Christ, just take some," Kira said, pulling a five out of her purse. Her sister stuffed it in the pocket of her cutoffs without saying thank you and headed off down the beach, stranding her

friend in a lizardlike trance. "Boo," Jonas said, opening his eyes.
The boy started and jogged after her.

"Little slut," Kira said, watching them leave. "I guarantee you
she just met that creep an hour ago."

Dustin kissed Kira's neck and made her squirm, because it was
a beautiful day and you had to make your girlfriend forget about
her bitchy sister, who'd been kicked out of ninth grade and sent to
a "therapeutic boarding school" in Northern California for troubled teens. Something told him it was going to be a long summer.
"Maybe she's changed. You haven't seen her all year."

"Yeah, right." She kissed him, smiling. "You're too nice, that's
your problem."

Dustin frowned. He took off his shirt and jogged down to the
water, more swiftly than he'd intended. Some guys he knew—
surfers—waved at him from the other side of the lifeguard tower,
giving him the hang loose, their boards jutting from the sand in a
Druidic-looking circle. All bro-ness and sunshine. Sometimes he
wished people didn't think he was so friendly. It was an annoying
misunderstanding. For one thing, the thoughts running through
his head weren't always very kind. They were nasty and irreverent. He wasn't sure how the misunderstanding had happened, but
it had. He wasn't particularly nice to his parents, but no one ever
got to see that and it did him no good.

He swam in the ocean for a while, bodysurfing on the close-
to-unrideable waves, avoiding the little-kid surfers wiping out
and getting sand facials. He gave up after a while and decided to
head in, catching a puny swell that walled off into a sandy wash
of foam. When he surfaced, Kira was standing waist-deep in the
water in front of him, her face damp and somber. A bubble of
foam clung to her hair before withering in the breeze. *She's going
to break up with me,* Dustin thought miserably.

"What is it?"

She started to say something and then trailed off, blushing
through her tan. "I think we should just . . . you know. Do it for
real."

He kissed her happily. "When?"

"I don't know. Before you go to college."

His heart sank. "That's, like, three months away." He waded
backward into the surf, so no one would see his hard-on. "Anyway, what difference does college make?"

"Everything will be different."

"UCLA's forty minutes from here. It won't change anything."

She frowned as if she knew more than he did about college life, even though he'd visited UCLA three times and even spent the night in some crazy art major's dorm room. "July thirtieth," she said quietly. "A month from this Thursday. It's our year anniversary."

Dustin nodded. She hugged him, smiling now, and they walked up the beach together in the sun, the water shrinking from his back like silk. A month! He'd waited this much time; in the history of the universe, a month was no more than a blip. But there was something about having sex for the first time on your year anniversary that seemed hopelessly conventional. *Nice.* They walked by an elderly woman in a beach chair, tan as a waffle, who smiled at Kira as they passed. *What a lovely couple,* he could see the woman thinking. Dustin glanced at his girlfriend's face, smiling sweetly in return, and felt a surprising twirl of revulsion.

Ahead of them, over by their towels, some kids were messing around in the sand; Dustin was astonished that his brother seemed to have made some friends. And then he saw Jonas. Or rather, Jonas's scrawny-looking ass: he was naked from the waist down and lunging at the kids, who were throwing his orange cords back and forth and dancing in little triumphant hops. The penis-builders from earlier. Dustin yelled at the kids and they took off running, ditching Jonas's cords in the sand. He wrapped a towel around Jonas's waist.

"Where's your underwear?"

"I wasn't wearing any," Jonas said.

"Jonas, *why?*"

"I don't have any orange ones."

Dustin glanced down the beach at Kira, who was retrieving Jonas's pants. He saw how his brother's life would be an endless trial of humiliations that he was too orange and clueless to avoid. Jonas dropped the towel to put his corduroys back on, his shriveled little penis darker than the rest of him.

"They're lucky I didn't kick their asses," Dustin said.

"Yeah, right." Kira put her arm around him. "Like you could ever hurt a fly."

CHAPTER 4

Dawn. Warren lay in bed, listening to the cries of wild peacocks echoing in the canyon. After three years, he still hadn't gotten used to their eerie feline racket. He'd been up since four o'clock, waiting for the world to materialize again. It had been a long and eventful two hours. There had been fear, self-pity, vertiginous despair. There had been thoughts of deserting his family. There had been fury and remorse. Warren had lain there in the dark, wondering if the sun would ever come up.

Now, the light from the window bathed the room in a bluish glow. Everything was just as they'd left it last night: the bowfront dresser, the bowl of potpourri perched on the TV set, even *The Joy of Sex* stationed in the middle of the bookcase, its spine covered with masking tape. (This clever bit of subterfuge was Camille's, who thought the kids would be uninterested in a conspicuously large book whose title they couldn't read.) And still there, too, was the painting named "Pac-Man in Heaven," one of the pieces she'd brought home after Mandy Rogers disappeared. Not a painting, actually, but a furry, king-sized Pac-Man cut out of brown shag carpet and then glued to a background of Crayola clouds. What had possessed Camille to buy it he could only imagine. It was not only hideous but disturbing. Who would identify with Pac-Man enough to imagine his afterlife?

Warren stared at the furry brown circle, its mouth permanently ajar, as though its hunger had survived the grave.

He sat up in bed, careful not to disturb Camille. She was fast asleep beside him, facing the wall so he couldn't see her face. From the back, the first streaks of gray in her hair concealed by the blue light of dawn, she looked like the girl he'd fallen in love with. Warren watched her from above, admiring the delicate rise and fall of her back. He used to admire her this way that winter before they were married, when she was still finishing up college and he was at the University of Chicago for law school. On the weekends, Camille would take the train down from Madison to see him and they'd walk the bitter streets together, huddled against the wind, the skyscrapers twinkling in the sun like swords. They were hopelessly, helplessly in love. He remembered sitting with her in the Amtrak station one Sunday afternoon, miserable at the thought of parting again even for a week, Camille crying into his parka as if she were leaving him forever. There was no question about her getting back: she had an exam the next day and would fail the class if she didn't take it. The train to Madison came into the station but she didn't move from the bench, didn't look up, gripping Warren's hand until it hurt. The train pulled away and they looked at each other for the first time, Camille's face ragged with relief. The joy was like nothing he'd ever felt. They bought a bottle of cheap champagne and spent the rest of the day in bed, giddy at the thrill of what she'd done, as if the world—its trains and exams and scheduled intrusions—were merely a nuisance to their love.

They had lost this feeling, the way you might lose a favorite gift you were no longer attached to. It had not seemed an important loss at the time: Dustin was born, and if anything a deeper, more devout-seeming love took its place. Once, while they were bathing Dustin together in the sink of their apartment, washing his scabbed-up belly button and tiny, heartbreaking penis, Camille had turned to Warren with a look of such stunning affection that he had actually lost his breath. *I will never be happier than I am now,* Warren had thought. Seventeen years later, he realized how sadly prescient this was. He did not know how he and Camille had ended up like this, so stranded in their own lives that they could barely wish each other good night, but it was one of the several ways in which love—so persuasive in its innocence—had betrayed him.

Warren climbed out of bed and sifted through his dresser, placed strategically on the left side of the room. He always slept on the left half of the bed, Camille on the right. It was one of those agreements they'd reached years ago without ever discussing it. Once, when Camille was out of town, he'd tried sleeping on her side and found himself inching back to his own spot, a homesick traveler. It occurred to him they would sleep this way until they died.

He got dressed quietly and walked down the hall. Stopping at Dustin's room, Warren cracked the door and was confronted once again with his son's naked back. He was lying on his stomach, covers kicked into a tangle at the foot of his bed. There was something alarming in the way he slept: limbs thrown out, like the victim of a crash. Once, when Dustin was a toddler, he'd fallen asleep in the middle of the airport, spread-eagled on the floor as though he'd dropped from the ceiling.

Dustin's headphones had slipped from his ears and lay upright on the pillow, perched atop his head like a halo. Warren had tried his best to support him, to give him everything he needed—this kid who was more interested in the Circle Jerks than speaking to him. Really, Warren had done it all for him. He'd dropped out of law school after Camille got pregnant, gone to work for her father in Milwaukee so they wouldn't have to eat moose meat. He'd dreamed of being a judge, using his degree to rise up the ranks, but ended up getting into real estate because Camille's father had a connection. And he'd done well with it, developing condos and resort homes on the same lakes he'd fished as a kid. If there'd been any regrets or second thoughts, those first years, they'd vanished as soon as Warren got home from the office, as soon as he saw Dustin's face go brainsick with delight. They used to dance around the living room together, Dustin clutching his shirt in his tiny fists. He'd never expected his ambition—his dreams of greatness—could be so easily trounced by a baby's grin.

It was his single accomplishment, providing for these beautiful, snot-faced creatures that Camille had brought into the world. He'd moved them to California and bought a larger house than they needed, seduced by the idea of giving them even more. How proud he'd been showing them the big lawn and persimmon tree, the famously expensive views of L.A. He'd filled the extra space with overpriced furniture, leasing it until he had the money to buy it outright. He wasn't worried—in a year or two they'd be as rich as his neighbors. Now it was all disappearing: this room, this house, this life he'd built from scratch.

Creeping closer, Warren lifted the headphones gingerly from Dustin's head and bent down to listen. He longed to hear something, to catch the soundtrack of his son's dreams. But there was nothing. Silence.

After walking Mr. Leonard, Warren went into the kitchen and poured himself some Grape-Nuts, searching the Frigidaire for blueberries before remembering what Camille had said yesterday about their being five dollars a carton at the grocery store. "They think we're the Shackneys" were her exact words. Warren wondered if she was on to him. He was still looking into the fridge when the scuff of slippers surprised him from behind.

"You're up early," Camille said. She was wearing pink pajamas, thin enough to show the lovely shadow of her breasts. Warren found he could not look at his wife without being reminded of his failure.

"I couldn't sleep," he said, pouring milk into his Grape-Nuts.

"Did you take a pill?"

He ignored this eminently practical question. On the counter was their long-distance bill from last month. He took it to the table with his cereal. "You called Nora Lundy eight times last month."

"So?"

"Doesn't she have any friends in Wisconsin?"

"We grew up together," Camille said. "Anyway, what does it matter?"

"It just seems . . . I don't know. Excessive. You don't see me calling my friends from Wisconsin every day."

She opened the dishwasher. "Which friends are you talking about?"

"What do you mean?"

"Nothing. I just didn't know you kept in touch with anyone, is all."

He looked at her angrily. "Maybe because you erase my messages from the machine."

Camille sighed. "That was one message. A year ago. And it was on the machine for a month."

"That's not the point."

"Did you ever even listen to it?"

"Christ, I'm up to my neck in work! I can't drop everything just because an ex-neighbor calls!"

"Please don't yell at me," Camille said.

She never lashed back or used bad words. Once, when they

were playing doubles with the Hathaways and he kept stealing her shots, she'd called him—bafflingly—a "fud." It occurred to him that they hadn't played tennis with anyone for months.

"Warren, what's going on?" she said sadly. "Is there something you need to tell me?"

Warren bent over his Grape-Nuts, avoiding her eyes. It was her calmly disappointed face, so pale and reasonable, that drove him crazy. The bird clock over the stove chirped like a summer tanager. Camille's parents had given it to them years ago, when they'd moved into the lake house in Nashotah. Warren couldn't hear the clock go off without thinking of the creaky, ant-infested house, wondering why they'd ever left.

After breakfast, he walked out to Lyle's Renault and squeezed behind the wheel and tried once again to move the seat back, his head touching the roof so that he was forced to stoop in front of the rearview mirror. He looked to himself like a giant mosquito. A half-naked Barbie doll dangled from the mirror, twirling from a shoelace noosed around her neck. The Barbie doll had on a T-shirt that said SAVE THE PARAMECIUM. Warren turned the key and the ignition squealed, jolting his fingers. He cursed. He tried again and the engine turned over, accompanied by a noisy, tailward rattle.

The rattling persisted as he drove up High Street. Warren wondered if the muffler was going to fall off. He slowed at the stop sign before John's Canyon Road, the brakes whining loudly enough to hurt his ears. The Shackneys' house loomed from across the street. It was the biggest house in Herradura Estates, a Spanish Revival with an indoor pool and a dopey ranch sign at the end of the driveway that said HACIENDA DE SHACKNEY in lariat-style script. The sign had been weathered to look antique. Standing beneath it, clutching surfboards, were the Shackney boy and a kid with hair slanting diagonally across his face. They had the invincible look of eleven-year-olds who didn't dress all in orange. He could not imagine what blissfully untroubled parent would pick them up at this hour to take them surfing.

"Nice car," the Shackney boy said.

"What?"

"Are you, like, French?"

"No," Warren said. It dawned on him, too late, that they were making fun of him. He pointed at the ranch sign. "Are you, like, Spanish?"

"You should get your brakes checked," the kid with slanty hair said.

"Why don't you kids mind your own business," he said angrily.

"Is that your Barbie doll?"

Warren stuck his arm out the window and gave them the finger. It was remarkably satisfying. Pleased, he looked up at the house and saw Mitch Shackney—the father of Dustin's girlfriend—watching him from the top of the driveway.

Warren touched the gas and the Renault rattled off, sending a desolate chime back from the canyon. He wondered if his mind was betraying him, like his own father's. When Warren was seven years old, his dad had ushered him onto the roof on Christmas Eve and told him he was going to kill Santa Claus. This was in Oconomowoc, the town in Wisconsin where he grew up. His dad, an avid hunter, had grabbed one of his 12-gauges before leading Warren out of the attic and setting up watch on the hip of the roof. "We'll wait here and then get him when he's going down the chimney," his father said. Warren, stiff with terror, sat there and waited for the far-off jingle of Santa's sleigh. His father held the gun in his lap and combed the sky, as though he were scouting for ducks. They hunched there in the freezing moonlight for nearly an hour. Warren's hands were numb, he had to take a pee—but he didn't dare move. Finally, without a word, his dad sighed theatrically and led Warren back inside the house, his shoulders sagging in defeat.

Until that night, Warren's dad had been a sober, hardworking man known for his friendly good nature. He owned a sporting goods store downtown and Warren remembered the constant huddle of men at the checkout counter, the smell of sweat and Brylcreem and sauerkraut. His dad's only vice was poker, which he played every Saturday night at the Rotary Club, making sure to go home if he lost his five-dollar buy-in. He was unswervingly frugal, perhaps to a fault. After that night on the roof, though, he started to give things away to baffled customers or lock up the store whenever he felt like it, showing up at the house in the middle of the day to take a nap. One time, he came to dinner with one of Warren's sock puppets, a dog with floppy ears and sewn-on buttons for eyes. He refused to talk normally, using a deep, woofy voice to ask for the salt. Warren thought it was funny at first, one of his dad's jokes, but then his mom began crying and his father started to make the puppet cry as well, mimicking her quiet sobs.

The next day, Warren's mom made his dad go to a doctor in Milwaukee, where they ran some tests and discovered he had a brain tumor. ("A sore in his head" was how she explained it to Warren.) He died a few months after that. They'd never been rich, but now Warren and his mother struggled to survive. The store was in a shambles; in his madness, his dad had given away half the merchandise and ordered three times what they needed from distributors. A rent increase crippled them further and the store went bankrupt. Warren's mom, who hadn't worked a day since she got married, ended up cashiering at the Exxon and waitressing at a German restaurant downtown four nights a week. Warren was left alone most of the time and developed a seepy warmth in his chest that he identified as shame. He was ashamed of the tiny apartment they'd moved to, ashamed of his mom's gas-smelling hands, ashamed of the unfashionably wide ties she picked out for him at the Lakeshore Thrift. Oconomowoc was a vacation town, and every summer rich kids from Milwaukee descended on the lake for a summer of waterskiing and badminton and reckless sunburned drinking. Warren got a job at the Seven Seas Club, working as a dishwasher—what the old cooks there called a "pearl diver." After lunch, he used to do yard work as well and see the kids lying down by the marina or drinking beer on their floatboats or rigging their C-boats for the weekend race, the lake cracking with gunshots. The girls were tall and willowy, with pageboys curling up their necks. They'd lie on the diving raft for hours at a time. Warren would watch them sunbathing with their slender legs crooked up, a row of lovely triangles, as he mowed the lawn in his uniform. He was proud of his tan Mediterranean skin and used to wear his shirt unbuttoned all the way down to his pants. He had some vague idea that he looked like James Dean. Once, while he was raking the easement down to the dock, he saw one of the boys with his shirt unbuttoned like his. The boy was raking the asphalt with a shuffleboard broom, the girls all giggling through their hands.

Warren kept his shirt buttoned after that, avoiding the dock as much as he could. At school that fall he devoted himself to his classes; he knew that his only chance was to work, to take advantage of the ethic he'd inherited from his father—that whatever romantically exotic attraction people felt for poor boys in movies was not to be found in real life. Sure enough, he got a scholarship at the University of Wisconsin, where he worked his ass off and stayed more or less with the other scholarship kids until he met Camille, identifying her immediately as one of the girls with willowy arms. She was as rich as the vacationers in Oconomowoc, the daughter of a businessman. But she was different, too: she blushed easily, she didn't drink, she was shocked by some of Warren's language—not like the wild girls he saw at the lake. Even in college, she was always volunteering at soup kitchens and nursing homes around Madison. He didn't notice at first how beautiful she was, but it revealed itself gradually the more he looked, like one of those pictures that invert mysteriously into something else.

Still, walking across campus sometimes, Warren would think of the boy with his shirt undone, the girls giggling, and his face would flush with shame. He'd hear the bright, piano-y laughter, afraid to look up from the grass. It wasn't until after he and Camille were married, when they were living on their own and Warren was making more money than his parents—his father—ever dreamed of, that he'd been able to squeeze the memory from his mind.

Now, pulling up to the office in Lyle's Renault, Warren tried to ignore the Barbie doll beaming at him from her noose. Larry's Alfa Romeo was parked under the only strip of shade. Larry was his old friend and partner, the man who'd helped spell his ruin. He'd coaxed Warren out to California, seducing him with the promise of "easy millions." Those were his precise words. He'd shown him the sun-bleached acres of hardpan desert, the forest of contorted Joshua trees, and said, "This is the future of California." If he hadn't said that, if he'd said something along the lines of *This is the future of toxic waste*, Warren wouldn't have fallen in love with the fucking place and invested his life's savings in it. He wouldn't be down to a single credit card, a gravely wounded American Express, the others having been snipped in two by trembly cashiers.

Larry was waiting for him in the receptionist's chair, one foot propped on the desk. He preferred to work in the lobby, where he could catch the morning rays through the window. (They'd laid off the receptionist weeks ago.) Besides time and energy, he hadn't invested much in the project—it was Warren's baby, right down to the name on the deed. Anyway, Larry had two other projects in the works near Palm Springs. Retirement communities, miles away from anything toxic.

"I talked to the bank," Larry said, fiddling with a Band-Aid on his toe. "The lending officer." As usual, he was wearing a Hawaiian shirt and flip-flops, his legs brown and muscular below pleated shorts. Mr. California. In college, he'd been pale and sickly, always missing class because of the flu. "They're going to call the loan at expiration."

"They'll foreclose on us."

"That would be my, um, prognosis."

Warren's legs felt unnaturally heavy. He had not told Larry about the direness of his own predicament. "I've been stringing the GC along for six months. He's going to take me to court."

"Unless we move some of these units." Larry stood up and walked into Warren's office without asking, as though they were under surveillance. Warren followed him into the sour-smelling room. His desk, a heap of papers and brochures, seemed living proof of something. "Look," Larry said, lowering his voice, "there's no legally binding reason we have to tell them about the dump."

"Jesus, Larry. Does the word 'cancer' mean anything to you?"

"Astrologically?"

Warren put down his briefcase. "Did you lose your conscience, or was it surgically removed?"

"Look, this whole cancer thing's a racket. Every day it's something else. Now they've got this thing against grilled chicken. The black stuff's bad for you." He laughed. "I mean, we've been cooking meat since, like, early man. Neanderthals? You don't think their woolly mammoth was charred at the edges?"

"They weren't dumping toxic sludge in the Stone Age."

"True. They were too busy bashing each other's heads in."

"Have you ever smelled one of these landfills?"

"Hellacious," Larry said. "Like rotten eggs."

Warren sat down. They'd been close in college, but their friendship had long since been whittled away by the stress of Auburn Fields. Warren wondered if Camille was right, if he'd truly lost all his friends. "And you wouldn't feel guilty?" he asked Larry. "Selling houses nearby?"

"Why? Because the government decides to dump its crap next to our property?"

"I just don't understand how they could do this to us," Warren muttered.

"Exactly because it's just *us*. We're the only suckers around. Anyway, they've got a PR team that could get the pope to suck his own dick. Industrial sewer sludge, and they're calling it 'biocake.' I mean, you've got to hand it to them. Sounds like a granola bar." Larry actually laughed. "I'm sure the city of Palmdale's getting kickbacks to beat the band. Ben Blyskal on the planning commission told me they're donating twenty grand to the school board."

Larry flip-flopped over to the wall and inspected the bulletin board that said AUBURN FIELDS at the top. There was a brochure thumbtacked to one corner; the cover showed a Latino family opening presents on Christmas, their eyes wide with wonder and delight. Below the picture, in Edwardian-looking font, was a quotation by Henry David Thoreau: *Go confidently in the direction of your dreams. Live the life you have imagined.* The quote had been Warren's idea. At the time, before the county announced their plans, it had never occurred to him that building affordable homes in the desert would bankrupt him. It had seemed like a brilliant, even a noble, idea: first homes for Californians squeezed out of the market. The "drive-till-you-qualify" crowd, as Larry put it. Who wouldn't want his own house? Besides, the market was booming: Japanese investors were foaming at the mouth. Their pals at Sakamoto Investment had jumped at the chance. Even the infrastructure was a relative snap. They'd coaxed the county into declaring it a Mello-Roos District, so they were able to run the sewage and water and electricity out there on a municipal bond. Everything had seemed to fall magically into place.

At least that's the story Warren told himself. In truth, even before the dump issue, he'd had a chance to pull out. When Larry started to get cold feet after the feasibility study came in—when the estimate was far more than they'd expected—Warren had insisted they go through with it. He could have gone back to Wisconsin, could have eaten the cost of the study and saved his family from impending doom, but he'd convinced the folks at Sakamoto Investment that it was worth the risk. It had been Warren's idea, too, to build twenty houses before they'd sold the lots. "Create the supply," David Stockman had told the country, "and the demand will follow." It was a formula too seductive to resist. He could blame Larry for the mess he was in—he gave in to the temptation more and more—but in truth Warren had brought it on himself.

Now the dump had become the nail in the coffin. You could see the construction crew breaking ground from the Auburn Fields gate: less than a mile away, a cloud of ominous dust blooming from the earth.

"Look," Larry said, "if you really want to stop this sludge from being dumped, we should get as many families as possible in there. Nobody gives a flying fuck about two developers. But twenty families: they could form a coalition, go to the papers with it. Raise a real stink. See what I mean? It's in everyone's best interest to sell these houses."

"Are you forgetting our man jumped ship? It's against his 'professional ethics.'"

"Fuck the broker. We'll do it ourselves."

Warren closed his eyes. It had not occurred to him to lie to people. It was morally indefensible, so why did the heaviness in his legs seem to lift? Even the room itself seemed slightly bigger, as if someone had pushed back the furniture.

"Ourselves?"

"We'll hit the phones. The streets. Whatever it takes. For Pete's sake, enlist your fucking family."

Warren pretended he hadn't heard this. "You're forgetting about the view."

"People like construction. It's a sign of growth. If they ask, we'll tell them it's a shopping mall. Honestly, it could be just what we need to sell them on the desert."

Warren stared at the papers on his desk. "Even if we could sell the things," he said after a minute, "how are these 'twenty families' going to band together if they don't know about the dump?"

"Word will spread. Believe me. These things have a way of getting around." Larry cocked his head toward the phone. He was no longer smiling. "This isn't Wisconsin, Warren—it's the desert, kill or be killed. Survival of the fittest."

Warren stood up and walked to the bulletin board on the wall. Larry was right: it wasn't their fault the county had decided to dump sludge near their property. Why should Warren and his family suffer? It was wrong to lie to people, in a fair and righteous world—but this was not a fair and righteous world. It was a world where you could work for twenty years to give your children

something, a life you never had, and then see it whisked away by
some fucking bureaucrats living off your tax dollars.

Warren stared at the twinkling Latino family pictured in the
brochure. Desperate straits required desperate measures. He
would do whatever he could—lie, swindle, bust his ass—to save
his family. He pulled the Yellow Pages from his desk and picked
up the phone.

"I need your credit card," he said.

"What are you doing?" Larry asked.

"Ordering some business cards." Warren untacked the brochure from the bulletin board and flipped it over so the faces
weren't visible.

CHAPTER 5

Camille stood in the bathroom in her underwear, waiting for her endometrium to shed. By now, the corpus luteum should have stopped producing estrogen, which in turn should have caused the tiny veins and arteries in her uterus to pinch themselves off. Bad news, of course, for the endometrium. Good-bye, nothing there, *degeneration*. A week ago, it should have begun its clotty, bright red trickle from her body. She remembered the animated sequence from *Look, Ma, I'm Only Bleeding,* one of her best productions, in which the endometrium melts into little rainy droplets.

She closed her eyes and took a deep breath. She'd heard about women with IUDs getting pregnant. It was definitely possible. *Actual failure rate: 4 percent.* Once, at a party, someone had told her about a baby being born with a Copper T in one hand: he'd come out of the womb that way, clutching it like a rattle.

Camille squatted until she was nearly sitting on the tiles and slipped a finger inside herself, reaching through the warm folds to the dimpled hardness of her cervix. The strings were still there, small and whiskery. She glanced at herself in the door of the shower. She couldn't remember the last time she'd checked: the squatting, the single finger, felt crudely automotive.

She washed her hand carefully and went into the bedroom, surprised to find Warren sitting on the bed. He was wearing running clothes, a dickey of sweat darkening his T-shirt. All summer he'd been keeping unusual hours at work; she never knew if he was going to be lurking around the house or hanging out in the Chrysler for no reason, listening to some god-awful tape of

Dustin's. Well, the car had been stolen—he wouldn't be doing that anymore, at least.

"What are you doing home?" he asked, tugging at his shoelaces. Maddeningly, he always tied them in double knots he couldn't undo.

"I've got my presentation today," she said. "I wanted to change clothes."

"Presentation?"

A sizzle of anger ran through her. "For *Earth to My Body: What's Happening?* Remember, I told you yesterday. I've got to present the script to the advisory committee."

Camille went into her closet and surveyed the piles of carefully stacked sweaters, all pink or green or periwinkle. The kids made fun of her sometimes, calling her "the Stepford Mom." Was it her fault if she looked good in pastels? "Did that thing with the broker go okay?" she asked.

"What?"

"The broker. You said you were meeting with him this morning."

"Oh. Right." He paused. "Yeah, everything's great. There's a lot of interest."

She came out of the closet, but he was sitting on the far side of the bed so she couldn't see his face. *Everything's great:* it was the extent of their conversation these days. Camille wanted to believe that this was true. Sometimes, in fact, she did believe it: when you looked at all the starving people in Angola, or the four-year-olds tied to rug looms in Pakistan, sold into bonded slavery by their own families, things were comparatively very good indeed. Other times—when she examined their marriage, how little they seemed to confide in each other—she wanted to drop what she was doing and grab Warren by the shirt, to scream into his face like one of those hysterical victims in a disaster movie: *We're lost! Danger! Our lives are in peril!* She wanted to save them before the engine room filled with water. Instead, she couldn't even tell him about her period. She was too nervous—frightened—of what it might reveal.

Warren disappeared into the bathroom and turned on the shower. Camille put on her favorite outfit—the blue skirt suit with a teal bow-collared blouse—and immediately felt frumpy and self-conscious. Perhaps it was only Herradura Estates, but something about the way women looked at her here, their eyes drifting magnetically to her shoes, made her feel like an Amish person. It had not been this way in Nashotah, where people wore sweatpants out to dinner and couples walked around the lake in matching windbreakers, beaming dowdiness and goodwill. She could have fetched the mail in her pajamas and no one would have cared. Camille had not wanted to leave the lake but had done so for Warren, so he could pursue his dream project in California. In fairness, she'd been surprised at first by its virtues. She liked her job, there was tennis all year round, she had to admit the weather was glorious—but after three years in Herradura Estates she could not say she'd made any true friends. Not that people weren't nice to her. In fact, they were perfectly kind. But that was the problem: their kindness was *perfect*. It had none of the goofy, shambling warmth her friends in Wisconsin had given off. She could spend hours on the phone with her best friend, Nora Lundy, chatting about the silliest things. It pained Camille to think about how many of her other friendships had dried up or dwindled to Christmas mailings, simply because she'd moved halfway across the country. Lately Warren had been bugging her about the phone bill, hinting she should limit her calls to Nora, as if she hadn't sacrificed enough for him already.

Camille tripped over his running shoes on her way to get some earrings from the dresser. She blamed her clumsiness on Warren—or rather, blamed it on the annoying hunch that he was having an affair. The idea had occurred to her last week. Not that she believed it really—it was just a hunch—but why else would he be acting so strangely? He was distracted all the time, lost in a daze at the dinner table or else staring at the kids without speaking, as though regretting something he'd done. The other day, after Dustin's green-eyed girlfriend had come over for dinner, she'd overheard him tell Dustin that he'd always had a thing for them. Green eyes. Warren, her husband of nearly twenty years. Who used to tell Camille that her own eyes were his favorite color, "blue as Lake Michigan."

Other times he seemed about to speak, staring at her shyly before looking away, as if he was on the verge of telling her something but had decided not to at the last minute. It had happened last Monday in the bathroom. He'd actually begun to tell her something; she was sure it was a confession.

Camille looked at herself in the mirror above the dresser, studying the soft, motherly bulges at her waist. She wondered if Warren no longer desired her. "Erotic fatigue," they called it on TV. Men were particularly prone to it, supposedly—something about the survival of their genes. Certainly she and Warren made love much less than they used to. Camille had confessed this to Nora Lundy, who'd admitted to having similar problems with her husband; to get in the mood, they'd started watching pornographic movies before bed. Camille had thought Nora was joking until she'd offered to send her a tape. She'd said no but an envelope had arrived in the mail anyway, empty except for a videotape with the label scratched out. Camille had slipped it in the VHS player when the kids weren't home and was so dismayed by the threesome taking place in a dentist's office that she'd ejected it after five minutes. What had shocked her more than anything was the woman's nipples: one was much larger than the other, smearing her breast like a glob of food. *Harder,* the deformed woman had moaned, *fuck me till I die.* Camille tried to use the line that night with Warren, to see if it would excite him as much as the tattooed men in the movie, but she couldn't bring herself to use any bad words. What had come out—confusingly, no doubt—was "I want to die."

It must have been that night when her Saf-T-Coil failed to destroy his sperm. If that was in fact what had happened.

Camille went into the kitchen, which smelled sweet and unwholesome. Her children were eating Pop-Tarts with snowdrifts of icing on top. She tried to get them to eat three square meals, to make their daily way up the food pyramid, but it was a hopeless cause now that Lyle and Dustin could buy their own food. "Remember," she told them, "you're only supposed to have one serving of sugar a day."

"How many Pop-Tarts in a serving?" Jonas asked.

"Pop-Tarts are fruit," Dustin said. "You can have four servings."

"They are *not* fruit."

Dustin checked the box. "Says here 'real strawberry flavoring.'"

"That's not fruit," Camille explained. "Wouldn't you rather have a nice bowl of real strawberries?"

They looked at her in disbelief.

"Is that a joke?"

"Could we put strawberry flavoring on them?"

Camille sighed, looking at the unnaturally pink filling inside Jonas's Pop-Tart. It *did* look delicious. To her chagrin, she found that her mouth was watering. "You may not care now, but later in life you'll regret polluting your body."

"How would you know, Mom?" Lyle said. "You've never done anything wrong in your life."

"That's not true, honey."

Lyle and Dustin looked at each other. "Name one bad thing you've done," he said.

"Well, let's see. Let me think."

"You forgot to recycle the bottles," Dustin said.

"You drove over fifty?" Lyle suggested.

"Once, when we lived in Milwaukee, I got a two-hundred-dollar parking ticket for blocking a wheelchair ramp. Downtown. I protested the ticket and lied about it. I went back the next day and parked legally . . . then I, um, took pictures of the bumper so that it looked like it wasn't in the red part."

Lyle and Dustin seemed stunned, clutching their Pop-Tarts in midbite. Then they burst into hysterical laughter, their mouths pink as flowers. Jonas laughed too.

"You're a regular menace to society, Mom," Lyle said.

Camille turned to get some yogurt from the fridge, her face stinging. She knew they were just trying to be funny; still, it bothered her, their ganging up on her like this. She could have told them about Bobby Wurzweiler and the things they did to each other in his boathouse, all when he was supposedly engaged, his hands cold and strange and skittery on her breasts. She'd been seventeen to his twenty-one. To this day she remembered it perfectly: the calluses on his hands, rough from waterskiing; the stale, smoky, rotten-dessert taste of his mouth. He'd given Camille her first cigarette ever, rolling it from a crumpled-up bag in his pocket. They'd spent the whole summer down there in the Wurzweilers' boathouse, making love on the mildewy floor and smoking Bobby's homemade cigarettes and talking about running off together without telling their parents, picking leaves from their tongues as they smoked. He vowed to leave his fiancée, a girl from Madison, and Camille believed him. He was doting and persuasive, the heir to a beer fortune. He didn't leave the girl, of course, but deserted

Camille as soon as the summer ended; when she called his house finally, reckless with despair, he hung up at the sound of her voice. It was only through the newspaper that she'd found out about his plane crash, a week before the wedding, his body dragged from Lake Michigan with his father's.

Camille spooned some yogurt in a bowl, watching her daughter get up to toast another Pop-Tart. It was a beautiful day, eighty degrees out, but Lyle was wearing jeans and a sweatshirt tied around her waist. Camille wanted to tell her only daughter that this was a mistake, that she should enjoy being young while she could, that soon enough the world would break her heart in ways she couldn't begin to imagine.

No, of course, she didn't really believe that. What was wrong with her today?

"Can I have some money?" Jonas asked her. Amazingly, he was not dressed in orange but in the blue Izod he insisted on calling a "crocodile shirt," since the reptile on its breast had a triangular snout. Camille was relieved before remembering that all three of his orange shirts were in the wash.

"What for?"

"I want to buy a *People* magazine."

Lyle and Dustin looked at each other. "You read *People*?"

"I'd like to read about Mandy Rogers. The untold story. She's on the cover."

"The untold story," Dustin said, "is that she's chopped up in someone's fridge."

"Dustin!" Camille said. "What did your father say? Don't give your brother ideas."

"Mom, Christ. He already has ideas. Ask him about getting eaten alive by sharks."

Camille dug two dollars from her purse and handed them to Jonas, wondering how on earth she'd ended up with such a morbid child. Distressingly, he could not seem to make friends. There had been someone from his fencing class for a while, a shy girl named Sheila with a red rash encircling her mouth. She'd come over one Saturday and left after an hour, insisting that Camille drive her home. Later, Sheila's mother had called in a pique, explaining that Jonas had told her daughter there was no such thing as heaven. "A crock," he'd called it. Camille talked to her son about his language but did not know how to address the larger problems he faced as an eleven-year-old atheist in orange pants. She had suspicions about the afterlife herself. Also, she felt in some troubling way responsible for his friendlessness. He was her last child, the least miraculous-seeming, and Camille sometimes wondered if she'd been a more devoted mother to Dustin and Lyle. Even as a toddler, Jonas hadn't been particularly needy or affectionate, more interested in playing by himself than in winning her love. Camille had more or less obliged. Not that she loved Jonas *less* than his siblings: it was only that he made it easier to remember those parts of the world that demanded her attention. Sometimes she'd catch herself at one of his fencing meets, startled by the clamor of white-jacketed children finding their parents, and discover that she had no idea whether he had won or lost.

She wanted a cigarette. Something about the Pop-Tarts. She hadn't smoked one for years—but suddenly she wanted to feel the dark, feathery warmth in her lungs.

The feeling persisted at work. There was something about the PV County public schools office—the bare walls, maybe, yolk-yellow and studded here and there with thumbtacks—that made the craving more pronounced. She found Mikolaj, her camera-man, sitting by himself in the recording studio, blond hair hanging in a ponytail down his back. She hoped it was damp from the shower and not greasy. Mikolaj had been a filmmaker in communist Poland; Camille didn't understand the details, except that he'd been involved in the Solidarity movement somehow and had fled the country when a warrant went out for his arrest. His dream was to make an allegorical zombie film about Polish history. Instead, to support himself, he was making videos about family planning and the PVCPS payroll system. Camille would have liked to find him an inspirational figure.

"Hello, Camille," he said. His right eye was bloodshot, a nebula of red spreading from one corner. He had the weedy arms and bedtime squint that Camille associated with hitchhikers. She always felt nervous around him, shy and staticky, as though she were tuned between stations. "Today's the big day for presentation."

"I'm sure everything will be fine."

"I don't know," he said bitterly. "These parents are worse than communist. They want to make law against sex."

"It's understandable. McMartin Preschool and everything, and now Mandy Rogers."

"Mandy Rogers?"

"The girl who was abducted."

"Oh, yes. Very sad. Boo-hoo." She smelled something on his breath, a whiff of mouthwash. "On every news show, this one girl."

"Did you go over the new script?" she asked, to change the subject.

"This is your important news. A girl with no brains, the whole world should pray for her!" Mikolaj leaned forward in his seat. "I can ask you a question, Camille? About my film?"

"Well, honestly, I don't have much time right now."

"Do you think this is good title?" he said. "*Hunt the Mists Slowly?*"

Camille glanced at his untucked shirt, one tail of which was stained with a ring of coffee. She wondered if he'd used it for a coaster. "I think maybe just one 'mist' is better. *Hunt the Mist.*"

He looked at her for a moment. "Yes, of course," he said gratefully. "They hunt for one mist only, the mist of freedom. The big mist that is never in touching distance."

Camille walked back to her office. Perhaps he wasn't drunk, as she suspected, but demented with homesickness. Or—the most likely explanation—he was both. Last week, searching for a slide, Camille had rummaged through a box under the light table and come across a suspicious-looking bottle, empty except for a heel-tap of liquid. There was a square of downy white on the bottle where the label had been peeled off. And two mornings ago she'd found a strange note in the top drawer of her desk: *YOU ARE BEAUTYFUL*, it read, followed by a string of words she couldn't decipher. She'd hired Mikolaj out of charity and felt betrayed by these developments.

In her office, one last time, Camille went over the script to *Earth to My Body: What's Happening?*, skimming carefully through each scene, which she'd storyboarded in colored pencil next to an accompanying narrative. She slowed down for the section titled "Conception, or What a Long Strange Trip." This was the part the committee had objected to the first time around. She'd planned on using actual stock footage of sperm invading an egg, filmed under a microscope, but several PTA members and

Father Gladstone from the Roman Catholic archdiocese had protested. They were concerned about the footage having been taken in a lab. "This is the miracle of life," Father Gladstone said. "We don't want these kids thinking they can duplicate it in their basement."

Camille's brilliant idea was this: she'd get actual children to participate, dressing them in T-shirts that said SPERM and EGG on them. She'd videotape them on the old soccer field behind the art department. The sperm—ten of them—would run across the field and "invade" the egg, which would consist of five girls holding hands in a circle. Only one of them, the Chosen Sperm, would be let in. It would be fun, and the kids would be able to relate to it.

When she explained all this later, however, standing behind the podium and addressing the "concerned citizens" of the advisory committee—including several representatives from different faiths—she was met with a disconcerting hush. The auditorium was large and windowless, which only amplified the silence. Camille's eyes drifted to Rabbi Silverberg, who was staring at her rather than the Xeroxed script in his lap. He liked to sit in the fourth row and scowl at her ominously through his beard. In front of him sat Wendy Felsher, a community educator from Planned Parenthood. Camille tried to imagine Rabbi Silverberg in his underwear, as someone had once advised her to do, but picturing the religious dignitary in his briefs made her feel indecent.

"Which kids do you plan on using?" This came from one of the teachers, Narmada Khan, normally an outspoken defender of Camille's work. The committee was supposed to be a perfect cross section of the public but in fact had been more or less randomly appointed by the school board.

"I thought we'd use the ACCESS kids," Camille said, adjusting the microphone. "I talked to Sue Kaufman already, who's running the summer program. We'll need permissions, of course."

"Isn't that the gifted program?"

One of the other teachers snorted. "Hoo, boy. Good luck."

"I'm worried about exposing these kids on videotape," Carl Boufis said. He was the only father in the PTA and most people believed he was gay. "Who's going to be doing the filming?"

"Mikolaj Czarnecki," Camille mumbled. "My cameraman."

Mikolaj stood up from the front row and did a Shakespearean bow, rolling his hand in a long flourish of gestures, as though he were shaking out a sprain. He seemed a bit lost afterward and sat down in a different seat than before. Camille smiled at the audience.

"What's going to happen to this so-called egg?" Father Gladstone said, squinting at the Xerox in his lap.

"Nothing," Camille said. "I mean, it's just a demonstration."

"Could we follow up with a birth scenario somehow? Just, um, thinking out loud here, tell me if I'm overstepping, but could the girls in the egg hold up a banner maybe? One that says BABY?"

"Good idea," Wendy Felsher, the Planned Parenthooder, said. "Let's thoroughly confuse the viewers."

Father Gladstone ignored her. "It's the sense of continuity I'm worried about. We don't want to give a false impression, like this egg's going out with the trash."

Wendy Felsher scowled. "I don't think we need to politicize this, Father."

His face hardened. "As long as it feels like a permanent choice, that's all I'm asking. We're not playing God here."

"And what if this is a rape?"

"This is not a rape," Camille said. "It's an educational video."

"Father Gladstone's just trying to be accurate," Carl Boufis said.

"In that case," Wendy Felsher said, "why don't we have someone come in with a coat hanger T-shirt?"

"Ha ha ha ha!" Mikolaj said from the front row, slapping his knees. "This is much more interesting!"

Camille's cigarette craving deepened. She looked up at the back row and found Lexie Cross, an eighth-grade teacher and the only member of the committee besides Father Gladstone who was wearing black. She'd moved here six months ago from London, which seemed—at this moment—like the epitome of sophistication.

"Ms. Cross," Camille said, "do you have any input?"

Lexie lifted her head slowly, as if wishing not to disturb the silver scorpion pinned to the lapel of her jacket. "I don't know," she said in her well-dressed British accent. "This whole idea. Isn't it a bit, um, silly?"

"Silly?"

"I mean, kids dressed as sperms?"

"They're not dressed as sperms. They're wearing T-shirts."

"Well, I don't know. It still seems a bit juvenile." She pursed her lips. "These are fifth graders, right?"

Camille frowned. "Well, I don't think 'juvenile' would be the right term. 'Interactive,' maybe. 'Educationally hands-on.'"

"Have you asked the kids what they think?"

"What?"

"The kids. How do they feel about the video? Do they fancy the idea?"

Camille blinked. She looked at the other committee members, who seemed to find this a reasonable question. "Well, I'm not sure their input's relevant. I mean, I think we're better equipped to demonstrate the ins and outs of conception. As adults, I mean."

Lexie Cross smiled. "I'm not sure we should go so far as filming the ins and outs."

The auditorium rippled with laughter. Even Rabbi Silverberg seemed to enjoy the joke, his beard twitching up and down in the fourth row. Camille did her best to ignore the blaze in her cheeks, wondering how she was ever going to please such a ridiculous group of cretins. She was about to give up, resigned to go back to the drawing board, but the mood seemed to have shifted. With a few concessions to Father Gladstone, Camille's script was half-heartedly approved, if only because no one could think of a different one. She was too humiliated to feel victorious. She slipped away after the meeting and ducked briskly to the exit. Wasps rose from the *Passiflora* and buzzed at her face, their hind legs dangling like twigs. Dodging these hideous creatures, she felt like she might cry. Strangely, it was not the laughing faces of the committee members that she pictured but those of her children, their mouths pink with filling.

She touched her stomach. Even if Warren wanted to start over, a new beginning, she couldn't imagine going through another love affair with a baby, setting herself up for rejection.

Someone called Camille's name, and she turned to see Mikolaj running to catch up with her, panting for breath. The nebula in his eye had spread into a galactic event. Camille glanced around the deserted campus, wondering if anyone could see them.

"These committee people are very bourgeois," Mikolaj said with disgust. His breath no longer smelled of mouthwash but of something stale and wonderful. Tobacco. Camille searched his body for evidence of a pack. "Don't worry about these mentally retardeds and their jokes."

"Can you picture me doing something bad?" Camille asked him.

"What?"

"Something bad. Anything. Running off with somebody's fiancé."

Mikolaj closed his eyes. "Yes, I picture. Very easy. We are all bad people. The dangerous is the leaders who tell us always they are good." He opened his eyes, staring at her with a curious look. "I make you happy?"

CHAPTER 6

Lyle couldn't sleep. She was sick, crazy, a living girl wreck. She checked the clock radio by her bed: 5:02 a.m., the enormous numbers buzzing in her face. That was something to add to her hate list (clocks that buzzed), but she couldn't muster much contempt because visions of Hector kept clogging up her thoughts. All night long she'd dreamed of him. There was Hector, kissing her with his sad-looking mustache. Or Hector again, playing a song on the piano—"Tiny Dancer"—while Lyle did a striptease onstage. Or Hector and her little brother, Jonas, hiding out in the woods and waiting for vodka-slamming Soviet mercenaries to attack them with rocket launchers.

The Soviet mercenaries were from the movie they'd seen last night at the Courtyard Mall. Hector had met her there after work. (She'd insisted on seeing something with rocket launchers, because they'd be less likely to run into any of her classmates from PV High.) Hector had fidgeted throughout the movie, his girlish hands resting on his knees. During the sex scene, a brief glimmer of breasts, he'd yawned from nervousness. Lyle began to despise him. He wasn't attracted to her; why had he asked her out? She wondered if he was gay. Earlier, on the phone, he'd told her he wrote poetry. Afterward, walking back to the parking lot, he'd grabbed her by the arm and kissed her ferociously on the lips, pinning her against the wall as though in a fever. His mustache felt large and petlike. When he stopped for a breath, Lyle had rushed to her car before anyone could see them together, telling him she had a ten o'clock curfew.

She was ashamed at her shame. Why did she care what her

classmates thought? Justifying it now, she decided it was the kiss itself that had frightened her.

Lyle opened her bedside table and took out the poem he'd given her before she ran off. It was still crinkled from his pocket. She'd already memorized it, but there was something about seeing the actual words on paper, the earthquakey wobble of Hector's handwriting, that was like a drug.

bones

she is beautiful, when I see her in the light
skin the color of clouds
the color of my bones

she hides inside her clothes
she makes me laugh
her body is serious: breasts hips freckles

we are serious, laughing
my favorite thing to be

i want to take off her clothes and burn them in a fire
i want to count her freckles like stars
i want to eat her for dessert and then spit out the bones

lick them clean

It was a bad poem, but Lyle didn't care. She read the last two lines again, an agreeable sort of fear kindling in her chest. It was exactly the way the boys looked at Shannon Jarrell, the ones who wandered into The Perfect Scoop—as though they could eat her for dinner. But would they spit out Shannon Jarrell's bones and lick them clean? Lyle doubted it. That was another thing entirely. It wasn't enough to devour her: Hector wanted to taste every morsel, like a dog.

It was useless, trying to sleep. Lyle got up, bleary-eyed, and padded to the bathroom in her DEATH TO SANDWICHES T-shirt. She flipped on the light and squinted at herself in the mirror. Miraculously, she looked the same as always: red hair, Vampira skin, arms a warp-speed blur of freckles. The word she thought of was "plain." Not ugly or hideous. Plain. When she was younger, fourteen, she used to pray to God to get rid of her freckles. She'd made outlandish promises: *I'll chop off one of my toes* or *I'll dress like my mother for a year.* But the freckles were still there, and now someone wanted to count them like stars.

She was suffering physically. She wanted to touch herself. She wanted to lie on top of her stuffed giraffe, Giggles, like she used to do when she was four.

Lyle closed her eyes and pictured herself as an X-ray, a blue window of bones. Once, at The Perfect Scoop, she'd overheard a boy with bad acne bragging to some of his friends: *I was eating her out and she went, like, totally haywire.* Such a dutiful way of putting it. Eating her out. There were other expressions: "munching carpet," "dining at the Y," "yodeling in the valley." Inventive, maybe, but not very illuminating. They were about the yodeler and not the yodel. They did nothing to unravel the mystery—the exquisite torture—of what it would actually feel like.

By the time Hector called, after his shift, Lyle had convinced herself that he was going to back out of their plans to get lunch. She'd spent the morning imagining him in the tiny guardhouse, alone with his thoughts, the truth of her ugliness flowering in his mind. "Your parents need to put my name on the visitor list," he said on the phone. "I can't get through the gate."

"What?"

"Bud's right here. In the guardhouse."

Lyle laughed. "But you work there!"

"It's the rule."

"I'll walk up and meet you."

She was secretly relieved. Her parents were at work, but she hadn't figured out how to explain Hector to Dustin should he emerge from the garage unbidden. Hector met her by his truck, a little pickup that shone like a limousine. He was still dressed in his guard uniform: pinned to his breast, like a toddler's toy, was a sheriff's badge that said CARTER SECURITY. Lyle looked away, embarrassed. She was dismayed to see that his license plate said KAMELION. Perhaps it wasn't his car—he was borrowing it from a sorority girl.

She climbed into the truck, which smelled like the inside of a sandwich. Hector pushed a tape into the stereo: a mad crunch of guitars, slow and furious. They drove for a while without talking.

"Why does your license plate say 'KAMELION'?" Lyle asked finally. She had to shout over the music.

"They're my favorite animal."

He seemed serious. She retied one of her Doc Martens. "Where are we having lunch?"

"I'd like to change, do you mind? I forgot to bring my street clothes." He eyed her sleepily, though not so sleepily that the carnivorous look had gone from his eyes. She felt like a pork chop: Bugs Bunny, stranded on an island and changing into the fulfillment of Elmer Fudd's fantasy. "I was thinking maybe I'd fix something at my place."

"Cook at your place?"

"If that's, um, cool with you."

He frowned, chewing one end of his mustache. It had never occurred to her that he lived somewhere. They took PV Drive North toward the freeway, coasting down the great green hill of Palos Verdes until they reached the mini-malls and gas stations along Anaheim Street, descending into a smoggy world of derricks and smokestacks and oil flares flickering like candles. Glowing through the grayness was a tremendous orange tank painted like a jack-o'-lantern. A painter was hanging from a rope, whiting out a giant pyramidal eye. Lyle had driven this way many times, to get to the freeway, but soon they passed the on-ramp and entered an area she'd never been, a neighborhood of Spanish billboards and Mexican taquerias and stores called Pepe's Pants and Car Aroma Supply and Food 4 Less Carniceria. There was some graffiti on the side of a Laundromat that said CHRIST JESUS IS YOUR ONLY HOPE. Lyle wondered if it was a mistake but was too embarrassed to ask Hector.

Eventually they turned onto a smaller street lined with stucco houses, nestled behind fences and painted bright as Easter eggs. Even though it was the middle of summer, Christmas lights hung in squiggly vines from many of the houses. There were wet clothes draped over the fences and dogs sleeping on the sidewalk and signs on the telephone poles that said CASH FOR YOUR HOUSE or SUPER BAILAZO. Hector kept his eyes glued to the street, driving on the wrong side because everyone's trash cans were pulled mysteriously into the road. As they turned north, he pointed at the nearby hill with its Mediterranean haze of red-tiled roofs.

"We're neighbors, basically. You can almost see your house from here."

"Really?"

"If it wasn't for the smog." He turned down the music. "Did you know Wilmington was this close?"

"No."

Actually, she hadn't even known it existed. At Hector's house, they pulled into the driveway and parked next to a weight bench covered in clear plastic and surrounded by neatly stacked disks. The blinds were drawn in all the windows, like a serial killer's. Lyle's palms were sweating. For the first time, she wondered if his poem wasn't intended as metaphor: perhaps he really wanted to eat her. He'd kill her first, then dine on her flesh. She thought of Mandy Rogers, her oblivious gnomish grin. Lyle's throat felt dry. She glanced behind her at a trash-strewn alley, wondering if she could make a dash for it in her Doc Martens.

Hector cut the engine, which guttered to a stop. Surprising herself, Lyle grabbed his uniform and pulled his thistley mustache toward her mouth. They kissed like blind people, knocking teeth. He pulled back, glancing at the house.

"My mother's here," he said apologetically. He blushed. "I'm going to get my own apartment. Soon as she sells the house."

Hector's mother met them at the door, impossibly old, brown scalp visible through a scorch of hair. She was holding a bouquet of wilted sunflowers. She grinned rapturously and yelled something in Spanish: *"Estoy casi muerta!"* I'm almost dead. Lyle stepped backward.

"Hola, Abuela," Hector said calmly. He turned to Lyle, tapping his head. "She's not totally in charge."

The old woman handed Lyle the flowers and ducked into the kitchen, where she began pulling things out of the refrigerator and sniffing them theatrically. Hector ushered Lyle inside and then went to answer the phone. The living room was small and dark. Hanging on the walls, like an exhibit, were pieces of religious memorabilia: a sculpture of the pietà, a naked saint calling for help from a sea of fire, a framed picture of John Paul II waving Miss America–style from the Popemobile. A man's photo stood on the fireplace behind a wall of prayer candles, their glass containers Brailled with wax. The place gave Lyle a sludgy, unreal feeling, as though she were watching soap operas on a beautiful day.

Another woman appeared—Hector's mother, she realized

with relief—and Lyle introduced herself. The woman was much stouter than Hector and surprisingly beautiful, her arms clinking with bracelets. She had Hector's same dainty-looking hands. She squinted suspiciously at the sunflowers in Lyle's fist, which were gray and droopy, their petals crinkled into little flames.

"Thank you. You don't need to bring flowers."

"These aren't . . . I didn't buy them," Lyle said.

"We have some just like."

Hector's mom took the dead flowers and stuck them in a glass of water on the kitchen table, arranging them as best she could. She ignored the old woman, who was unwrapping a stick of butter like a candy bar. Lyle wondered if she'd be forced to watch her eat it. At the last minute, Hector's mom snatched the butter from the old woman's hands and put it back in the fridge.

"She eats them like Popsicle," his mom explained, unembarrassed.

Hector returned and said something to his mother, a brisk stream of Spanish. They seemed to be arguing. Outside of her name, Lyle couldn't follow a word. Hector smiled awkwardly and then showed Lyle his room, a dark, cockpitty space at the back of the house. The walls were covered in posters, mostly of chameleons: satanic-looking lizards, perched on branches and eyeing Lyle like pinups. The colors made her eyes swim. Even the window had been postered over, a blood-red chameleon glowing translucently in the sun.

Hector sat on the bed next to a little cage made out of wire mesh in the corner. It was filled with leafy branches. She couldn't see anything inside, but then he pointed at a gaudy, tie-dyed creature basking under a lightbulb, its tail curled up like a rope of Play-Doh. Its eyes were looking in different directions. Lyle laughed out loud: it was preposterous, like something God had cooked up after a head injury.

"This is Raoul," he said, as though introducing her to a buddy.

"Your chameleon's named Raoul?"

He shrugged. "He's a veiled chameleon. You can tell by the crest on his head."

"How many kinds are there?"

"Over a hundred." He checked the thermometer hanging in the cage. "I used to have a terrarium, a glass one, but it was driving him crazy. Kept attacking his reflection."

"Really?"

"They can't stand looking at themselves."

Lyle was liking the creature more and more. Hector reached into his bedside table and pulled out a little ziplock bag filled with suspicious white powder.

"Want some?" he asked.

Lyle's heart tripped in her chest. "Okay."

"I was joking. It's vitamins for Raoul."

Walking to his dresser, he opened a Tupperware container filled with crickets and then jiggled a few of them into the bag of powder. He shook the ziplocked bag in one hand. Then he dumped the powdered crickets, white as snowflakes, into a bowl at the bottom of Raoul's cage. The lizard clung to his branch without moving. Just when Lyle decided he was uninterested, perhaps even dead, his tongue swelled into a bubble and spat across the cage like a spurt of tobacco and flew back into his mouth, all before you could blink, the hind legs of a cricket squirming from his lips.

"He can snag a cricket from thirty centimeters away," Hector said proudly.

"Wow." Lyle felt a little queasy. "I thought he might, you know, *chameleon* himself. Camouflage."

"They don't camouflage themselves," Hector said. "That's a myth."

"They don't change colors at all?"

"Only if they're angry or emotional. Or sick."

Someone—his grandmother—yelled from the other room. If it was Hector's name, Lyle didn't recognize it. He got up finally and then returned a minute later, carrying a pair of sunglasses.

"Sorry. I've got to hide these or she'll stand there by the door like a movie star. I usually take her to the beach on Fridays. She likes to watch the seagulls." He looked at Raoul, who was still gnawing on the cricket. "Maybe you could come with us sometime?"

"I hate the beach," Lyle said. He seemed disappointed. "I'm not much for sunbathing."

"Me neither. God. Mostly I just sit there and write poems."

Hector reached under the bed and pulled out a stack of notebooks bound by a rubber band. There must have been four or five notebooks. Lyle wondered if he'd forgotten about lunch.

"Are they all love poems?" she asked suspiciously.

"No. I mean, they're mostly about me."

"Why do you keep them under the bed?"

He laughed. "My mom's, like, the youth director of her church. She thinks I'm going to hell already."

"I like the one you gave me," she said, meeting his gaze.

He glanced away again. She could tell that he was going to give her another poem to read; perhaps, like "bones," it would mirror her own erotic lunacy. He opened one of the notebooks and handed it to her. "The Piranhas of Time," the poem was called. Her heart sank. It had all the dopey anguish of a heavy metal song. In growing desperation, she latched on to a couple lines near the end:

5 a.m., a circus in my brain
my juggler vein exposed to you

"I like how you use 'juggler vein,'" she said. "After 'circus.' That's really clever."

"What?"

"Instead of 'jugular.'"

He blushed crimson, grabbing the notebook from her. "I'm going to go to veterinary school. As soon as I get my bachelor's. I'm taking night classes at Harbor College."

She hadn't meant to humiliate him: there was none of the dark thrill she'd felt watching him eat the ice cream cone at The Perfect Scoop. Something was happening to her. It had to do with the posters, with his pet chameleon, with the weird, touching fact that he'd wanted to show her his room to begin with. Hector wouldn't look at her. Lyle touched his leg, feeling the pleasant crease of his pants. Someone—his grandmother again—yelled crazily from the living room. They both stared at Raoul, who'd changed from his greenish, tie-dyed swirl into a deep, miraculous blue.

"He's jealous," Hector said, clearing his throat.

CHAPTER 7

"What are they going to do?" Biesty said. "Trash the place?"

Dustin smiled. "I wouldn't count it out."

They were on their way to a party in San Pedro, one that a guy had told them about at an X show. Some girls were being evicted from their duplex apartment and so they'd decided to throw a farewell party. The "farewell" was for the apartment, not the girls. The guy had laughed when he explained this, flashing them a mischievous grin. Dustin had never met any kids his age who were living by themselves, in their own duplex. Let alone being evicted.

He was nervous but enthralled. The steering wheel of the Dart stuck to his hands. He generally felt like something great and exciting and revolutionary was taking place nearby, if only he knew the right people.

The duplex was down by the harbor, near a field of deserted loading bridges. Dustin parked at the curb, wondering if he'd dressed in a way that would make him look less surferlike. After some deliberation, he'd decided to wear the new octopus belt buckle he'd bought at a record store in Hollywood, even though it poked him in the stomach whenever he sat down. If you looked closely, you could see a bottle of whiskey in one of the tentacles. To shore up their courage, Dustin and Biesty shared a Corona in the car. They'd been friends since the first week of tenth grade, when Biesty had shown up to chemistry in a pair of enormous black glasses taped together at the bridge. Dustin had assumed he was special ed, one of those guys who wears shorts every day even in December, and so was astonished when he'd taken off his sweater to reveal a Ramones T-shirt. The next day he'd let

Dustin try on his glasses. No prescription. Even the tape, it turned out, was a hoax. Dustin had always been popular without trying; the idea of making it more difficult to attract friends had never occurred to him.

It wasn't until a week later, though, when Biesty played him a song on his Walkman, that Dustin knew they were going to hit it off. "TV Eye," by the Stooges. Dustin had never heard such music: it was like someone had smashed Elvis's face with a hammer and told him to sing it off. It was a primitive thing, sound more than song, and it made you feel as cool as it was. Like you could destroy a girl's sleep. In line at the cafeteria, listening through Biesty's headphones, Dustin realized that his dick was hard. He'd confessed this to Biesty sometime afterward, when they were both drunk on Mr. Biesterman's liquor, and his new friend did not laugh at him or call him a faggot. He said, "I always want to fuck my favorite songs." If ever asked to explain their friendship, why they were going to UCLA together in the fall, Dustin would point to this one canonical remark.

"Are you sure this is cool?" he said now, staring at the curtained windows of the apartment. There were shouts from inside, punctuated by a scream. Biesty grinned from behind his wire-rim glasses. Sometime last year he'd traded in his special-ed look for something brainier, perhaps to compensate for the amount of dope he was smoking.

"If anyone messes with us, I'll beat the knave into a twiggen bottle."

"What the hell does that mean? 'Twiggen'?"

Biesty shrugged. "Do I look like a Shakespeare scholar?"

"Yes."

"Here. Have some more twiggen."

Dustin gulped at the Corona. "When we get to college, you'll have to stop talking like this. I mean, if either of us are going to make friends."

"Friends are overrated. Anyway, once Toxic Shock hits it big, we'll have hordes of groupies. Groupies are a hundred times better than friends."

Biesty smiled, as if it were all a big joke. But it was not a joke to Dustin. Fame seemed as inevitable to him, as uniquely destined to be his, as a Christmas present he'd glimpsed in his parents' closet. His current life was merely the prelude before Christmas.

UCLA was a way for him and Biesty to get out of the house, to leave behind the petty distractions of family so they could focus on assembling the band that would make them famous—he had no intention of graduating. Their first step would be to find a bassist who could actually spell "syndrome." Kira would become famous as well, a Yoko to his Lennon, someone to help him down the lonely path of stardom.

"Will we get vaporized tomorrow in a nuclear holocaust?" Biesty asked, shaking the Magic 8 Ball he'd found by his feet. It had been in the Dart since Dustin bought it. Biesty held the ball up to the window. "'Outlook not so good.'"

"Jesus," Dustin said.

"Better than 'Without a doubt.'"

"Let's go find some more twiggen."

They rang the doorbell of the apartment, a sour tang of beer creeping up Dustin's throat. The guy who greeted them was wearing suspenders without a shirt and an old top hat, green as the iridescent coat of a fly. He doffed the hat like a butler. His pants were cut off below the knees, one leg longer than the other.

"What's your, ahem, meager power?" he said to Dustin.

"Meager power?"

"Like a superpower. But not so super. Something you can use for daily things." He put the top hat back on, twirling it once in his hands. "Mine's, ahem, always having the right change."

"The power, ahem, to suck my own cock," someone said behind him.

"Is this Suzie's place?" Biesty said. "Someone invited us last night."

The man in the top hat stepped aside. *Tu casa es Sue's casa.*

Dustin and Biesty squeezed past him into the apartment, which reeked woozily of Magic Marker. Crowded around the living room were people drawing on the walls, scribbling graffiti or obscene doodles or beautiful strange animals with human feet. A few of them were very good artists. Above the couch, on the far side of the room, someone had written MANDY ROGERS PHONE HOME. Dustin followed Biesty into the party, impressed by the general ugliness of the guests. In particular, he was impressed by the girls, who looked like refugees from a nursing home. They wore granny glasses and cardigans and witchy striped stockings pulled up to their knees. He found them sexy in a way he couldn't explain. Contributing to this ugliness was the music, a swarm of noise and backward lyrics that made the Stooges seem like Donny and Marie.

There was a dead lobster in the middle of the floor. Dustin wondered if the music had killed it. The lobster appeared to move, infinitesimally, and he realized it was engaged in a catatonic crawl. Saddled to its back, like a rodeo rider, was a naked GI Joe, one arm raised in the air.

"What's this music?" Dustin asked loudly.

"Butthole Surfers, I think."

"Wow." He'd never heard them before, but the name had always filled him with a vague sense of awe. He felt weirdly like his father.

"I was hoping we'd get to sledgehammer some walls," Biesty said, depressed. "Something more aerobic."

Dustin nodded, though actually he liked the party better the way it was. Like some wonderfully deranged kindergarten.

Biesty perked up when he spied a girl in leopard-print creepers smoking by herself in the corner, the scorched, caramelly smell of hash drifting from her direction. He sniffed his armpits and went over to greet her. Dustin roamed off to see if he could find something to drink. He bumped through a knot of skinheads with homemade tattoos, asking them if they knew where the beer was. They paid no attention to him. He found this keenly attractive. He wandered into the kitchen, which was stripped of belongings except for a tower of boxes beside the refrigerator. Leaning against the wall was a poster-sized chart showing a black couple with Afros illustrating different sexual positions. It struck Dustin as racist, but then he decided he might not be hip enough to appreciate its irony. It was easy to be liked, but it had never made anyone famous.

He nodded at a group of people sitting across the room. One of them—a wasted-looking girl racooned in black eyeliner—seemed to have a wire sticking out of her mouth. She had her head against the wall, as if she were asleep. Sitting beside her was a boy in a plaid shirt with the sleeves cut off, his arm thrown around a beautiful girl in a cowboy hat. The boy was wearing a dog tag around his neck. Dustin recognized immediately, the way you might see your own face in a dream, that he'd always wanted to be like him. The boy oozed the sort of coolness—predatory and smoke-wreathed and as physical as breath—Dustin only felt in the garage with his guitar.

"It's deep in the night and I'm lost in love," the girl with the wire sticking from her mouth said.

"Pay no attention," the boy said. "She only speaks rock and roll."

He introduced himself to Dustin, explaining with a straight face that his name was Breakfast. The way he said the word made it seem like the coolest name in the world. "And this sorry husk of a girl is Suzie, evictee."

"What's up with the wire?" Dustin asked.

"You'll have to ask Miss Orthodontist over here."

"It was her idea," the girl in the cowboy hat said. "She's all, 'Take them off! Right now!' Then I bring out the pliers and she's like, 'Oooh, quit it, you're hurting me.'"

"Now I'm gonna be twenty-two," Suzie said. "Oh my, and a boo-hoo."

The girl in the cowboy hat scowled. "She's getting on my nerves."

"Yeah, Suze. Shut up or we'll rape you."

"Goody gumdrops," Suzie said.

The other girl giggled. "You wouldn't even."

Breakfast seemed to contemplate this. "I might make love to her by force," he said thoughtfully.

"What about you?" the girl said, looking at Dustin. "Would you rape her?"

Dustin didn't know what to say. There was something witty or dangerous to express, but the exact words eluded him. "I have a girlfriend."

The girl looked at Breakfast, and they both laughed. Dustin wanted to tell them that he'd rape her anyway, but it wasn't true and he felt conversationally out of his element. He'd been to some wild parties in Herradura Estates, but nobody ever tried to take off each other's braces. He walked over to the fridge and opened it: an old can of olives, the sag of an empty twelve-pack. On the inside of the door, someone had Magic Markered REAGANOMICS MAKES ME HUNGRY. The same person, perhaps, had drawn the picture of a lobster on the lone carton of milk, doodled under the words HAVE YOU SEEN ME? Dustin felt a surge of happiness. This was what people did if they didn't care about refrigerators:

they defaced them. They dropped out of the refrigerator game altogether. Lobsters, lost and unheeded, roamed their apartments.

. A girl with a white streak dyed into her hair opened the back door, clutching the handle for balance. She looked familiar. She was wearing a plaid skirt and saddle shoes, which made her appear even younger than she was. After sliding the door shut again, a two-handed endeavor, she glanced up and caught Dustin's eye.

"Oh my God," she said.

"What?" Breakfast said.

"It's my sister's boyfriend."

"We were just talking about her," the girl in the cowboy hat said.

"Fucking bitch," Taz said. "I'm going to destroy her with voo-doo."

"What are you doing here?" Dustin asked, staring at Kira's little sister. The happiness he'd been feeling had evaporated.

"What am *I* doing here? Fuck. That's a good one."

"You know these people?"

"We met at a Flag show," Breakfast explained. "Greg Ginn was trying to get in her pants."

"Actually," the beautiful girl said, "he'd already taken them off."

Taz looked at Dustin's belt buckle. "Yucko, bucko. That's one ugly belt."

"She and Suze have been doing PAM snorts," Breakfast said apologetically.

Dustin didn't ask what a PAM snort was. Taz wobbled over to the fridge, the lightning bolt in her hair bisecting her eyes; he was only beginning to figure out that the saddle shoes were an ironic gesture. Both of her ears were covered in little jewel-like scabs. Dustin frowned. Somehow, through no fault of his own, he'd gone from being a guest at this party to an unwitting accomplice in the drug use of his girlfriend's sister. His girlfriend's fifteen-year-old, *mentally disturbed* sister. He'd either have to risk getting in deep shit with Kira or call her and look hopelessly uncool in front of Breakfast and his friends.

He was relieved when Breakfast suggested they go on a beer run. Dustin offered to do it himself and bring Taz along for company. He needed to figure out if he could be held responsible. He checked for Biesty on the way out, but he'd disappeared somewhere with the hash smoker.

"You *like* this shit?" Taz asked, pointing at the tape deck. Getting her in the car had been psychologically complex, achieved in the end by the promise of cigarettes.

"It's X. The best band in the world." He turned it up.

"It's, like, stomping on my buzz."

"What do you listen to?"

She shrugged. "The Buttholes."

"The Butthole Surfers?" He laughed. "You just heard that at the party."

"Probably because it was my tape."

Dustin wondered whether she was telling the truth. They stopped at a red light, under the glow of a streetlamp. She was definitely less attractive than Kira. She had fuzz between her eyebrows and there was a little mole, like an errant crumb, on her upper lip. Plus the scabby ears, which she kept picking at with her fingernail. There was something about her face—its unreadable smirk—that made him unhappy.

"Is there, like, an unperverted reason you keep staring at me?"

"What's that in your hair?" he asked. "Peroxide?"

She turned her face away quickly. "It's a witch's forelock."

"What?"

"I thought Kira only dated smart guys." She kept her face turned. "Like a birthmark. They used to burn people at the stake if they had it."

"Does your family know you're here?" he asked.

"Right. Ha-ha. They packed me a lunch."

Dustin frowned. "Just so they don't think I have anything to do with it."

"I won't tell a peep. A person. Don't get your panties in a wad." Taz tried to roll her window down, struggling with the lever. It came off in her hand. "Piece of shit," she said, tossing the lever into the backseat.

"Hey!" Dustin said. "That's a hundred-dollar part!"

"And it doesn't work? I'd say you got majorly ripped off." Her eyes surveyed the front seat before settling on the steering wheel in Dustin's hand. It was his favorite part of the car, wine-colored and big as a yacht's. "Do you have some of those, like, fuzzy dice?"

"No."

"I thought only people with fuzzy dice drove cars like this."

At the 7-Eleven, Taz insisted on coming inside to pick out her cigarettes. Kira was right: she was a major pain in the ass. Who did she think she was? Girls loved the Dart; just last weekend someone on Hollywood Boulevard, a chick with a *mohawk*, had asked him for a ride. The 7-Eleven was as bright as a toothpaste commercial. Sweating on their little Ferris wheel, the hot dogs looked sad and immortal, as if consigned to hot dog hell. Dustin found himself wishing he had never left the house. He glanced at the mirror above the beer section and saw a friendly-looking surfer kid in a ridiculous belt buckle. A guy wearing one of those travel vests with all the pockets on them came over and stood beside Taz.

"To beer or not to beer," the man said, "*that* is the question."

Taz looked at him. "Did you really just say that?"

"What?"

"'To beer or not to beer, that is the question'?"

"I'm trying to decide." The man winked at them, checking his watch. "It's getting late."

"Congratulations," Taz said, shaking his hand. "That's the stupidest thing I've ever heard."

Dustin bought the beer with his fake ID, annoyed at his envy. He wished he had the balls to tell someone they were stupid. They headed back to the party, cruising down Western with its grubby-looking mini-malls, all of them the same Pepto-Bismol pink. He'd have to remember to put that in a song. "Pepto Abysmal," he'd call it.

"Kira said you got kicked out of boarding school."

Taz scowled, lighting one of the cigarettes he'd bought her. "Kira doesn't know anything."

"Actually, she's very smart. She's worried about you like your parents are."

"*Actually,* they couldn't give two shits."

Dustin shrugged. What did he care? "If that's true, then you must be a real fuckup."

"Or maybe they're just, like, total hypocrites." She yanked up a sock. "Everyone knows Kira smokes dope. She's going out with *you,* for crap's sake. She smokes out, screws to her heart's content, but of course they treat her like some virgin-ass Teen for Christ."

"Well, they're half-right," Dustin mumbled.

"What?"

"Nothing." He felt his cheeks go warm.

Taz laughed. "Kira's a *virgin*?"

"I didn't say that."

"I don't believe it!"

"Hey. I never said that."

"Holy crap," Taz said, grinning. "She must be, like, the only one in her class."

This wasn't true, of course. How could it be? And yet he had a vision of the rest of the incoming seniors at PV High, doing it all over campus while he groped and fondled under the maddening threat of the Grip. Dustin began to drive recklessly for no reason, whipping between lanes and braking suddenly at a red light. They rocked forward in their seats, the beer clinking at Taz's feet. "Whoa," Taz said. The light changed and Dustin veered onto a side street, fast enough that the tires squealed. "Big man," Taz said, raising her hands in mock fright. Dustin felt ridiculous but couldn't stop himself. He flew down the narrow street doing sixty; a man stepped off the sidewalk into a strip of hydrangeas, shaking his fist like someone in a movie. "*Very* impressive," Taz said as they screeched up to the party.

He couldn't look at her. His face burned. When he finally did glance at her, gripped by loathing, he was surprised to see that she was no longer smirking. Or rather, she was still smirking at him but it was as unpersuasive as a mask, her eyes big and childlike. He'd actually frightened her.

Inside, there was something going on. A group of people were huddled in the living room, cheering at the floor. Dustin nudged into the circle to see the attraction. The lobster was backed against the wall, reared up with its claws raised like boxing gloves, cornered by a hissing gray cat standing a few feet away. The cat was arched into an omega, as though being sucked helplessly to the ceiling.

"Get some Raid," the guy next to him said.

Dustin went into the kitchen to put the beer in the fridge. He did not like this party quite so much anymore. Biesty was hanging out by the poster of "Afrosexual Positions," writing something on the wall; Dustin looked closer and recognized the lyrics to "All Tomorrow's Parties."

"Can't you see it?" Biesty said, shaking him by the shoulders. His eyes behind his glasses were red as a rooster's.

"What?"

"The writing on the wall!"

Ordinarily Dustin would have laughed, but he kept thinking about Kira's sister. Somehow she'd made everything he did seem like a joke. It wasn't only the smirk: just the thought of that witchy streak in her hair, dangling stupidly into her eyes, was enough to make him feel like a fraud. Dustin drank one of the Budweisers he'd bought while Biesty worked on a hash-inspired rendering of a Keebler elf. The girl named Suzie was passed out against the wall, in the same position as before. On the wire sticking from her mouth, threaded like beads, were several olives. Dustin's heart sank. There was some elemental contradiction in his dream of himself. He wanted to live in a world where people did drugs all day and said what they were thinking and took off each other's braces if they felt like it, but where doing these things never seemed bleak or depressing. He could have his beach and his fucked-up parties, too.

Breakfast came in the back door, grabbing a beer from the fridge. He failed to offer Dustin any money. "You better tend to your girlfriend."

"What?"

"Taz le Raz."

"She's my girlfriend's sister."

Breakfast shrugged. "Whatever. She's out there entertaining the guests."

Dustin went out to the back deck, where Taz was standing near a potted cactus, several people watching her with the same guilty enthrallment he'd seen on the faces cheering the lobster inside. The only one not watching was the guy in the top hat, who sprayed some PAM into a plastic bag and then stuffed it up to his face. He blinked his eyes wide when he was finished, like something hatching from an egg.

"You're fucking AWOL," the beautiful girl in the cowboy hat said to Taz. The girl turned to Dustin, laughing. "Tell her it's not funny."

"What?"

"She's got some glass in her mouth. She's going to swallow it."

"It's her meager power," the guy with the top hat said.

Taz grinned at Dustin and stuck out her tongue. Sure enough, there was a shard of glass on it, green and hooked like a claw. Part of a beer bottle. The word EXTRA was written across it in white letters. Dustin tried to grab Taz's arm, but she flinched and backed away, clenching her teeth.

"I'm a witch," Taz said. Her voice was strange, lispy and garbled. "It won't hurt me."

"She's already eaten a little piece," the girl said.

"An appetizer," the guy with the top hat said. "As it, ahem, turns out."

"You'll slice up your throat," Dustin said, stepping closer.

Taz looked at him through her creepy forelock. "What are you going to do about it?"

He had no idea. Frankly, he was beginning to understand why they historically burned witches at the stake. Taz flipped the forelock out of her face, like a dare. Without thinking, he snagged the sleeve of her T-shirt and she sprang toward him suddenly and mashed her face into his own, trying to force his mouth open with her lips, not a kiss so much as a retaliation, a physical attack, Dustin opening his lips until he could feel the glass at the end of her tongue, the cool claw of it, smooth and warped and razory, and then she was pushing it into his mouth, transferring it like a harmless bit of candy. They pulled away. Dustin plucked the shard from his mouth with two fingers, as if it were alive. His hand was trembling. He could taste some blood on his tongue. Taz smirked at him triumphantly, ignoring the other people on the deck. Only then, seeing that she was trembling as well, did it occur to him she wasn't as crazy as she seemed: she'd been planning her attack, waiting for him to come and find her.

"Who is this guy?" someone asked. "You know each other?"

"My future brother-in-law," Taz said.

CHAPTER 8

At Nordstrom, Camille wandered the aisles with the vague feeling of oppression that always accompanied her visits to the pleasantly air-conditioned department store. The handbags were particularly oppressive. Something about their sleek leather forms, displayed like jewels in their little glass cubbies, made her feel lost and frumpy and unloved. The man playing the piano nearby seemed to understand this, tinkling out "The Lady Is a Tramp" to the arriving shoppers. Even the salesclerks, who smiled dutifully at Camille but failed to approach her in any way, seemed to wonder why she was here.

She wondered this herself. She was supposed to be at the post office, sending in her check to Oxfam International. There was a famine in Ethiopia; close to a million people had died. Instead she was wandering around a store selling $400 purses, drawn here mysteriously after dropping Lyle off at work.

She was preparing to leave, heading through Coats toward Beauty and Fragrance, when she saw it. The shawl. It was black and elegant and exotically Western-looking, fringed with little tassels. Even the mannequin it was draped over seemed more glamorous than the rest, one hand raised in the air as if hailing a cab. Camille touched the lovely black fabric, soft as down, hanging from the mannequin's arm. Before that moment, the word "shawl" had been a powerless clump of letters. She checked the price tag dangling from its shoulder: $295.

"Gorgeous, isn't it?" one of the saleswomen asked. She was smiling politely, though her eyes simmered with boredom. "Would you like to try it on?"

"It's awfully expensive."

"Well, it's cashmere. From Italy. That's actually a fairly good price."

Camille stared at the tassels. "It's not the sort of thing I usually wear."

The saleswoman glanced at her mint green shirt, embroidered at the hem with tiny pink and blue flowers. Camille recalled that the precise color was "seedling." Turning to a rack near the mannequin, the saleswoman removed an identical shawl from its hanger and held it out to Camille. Camille shook her head and fled the store. When she got to the Volvo, taking refuge in its leathery heat, she found she was actually trembling.

She took the pack of Camel Lights from her purse and lit up a cigarette. She hadn't known what kind to buy at the Shell Station, so she'd asked for the brand she'd once found shoved in the back of Lyle's underwear drawer. The first puffs put a stitch in her throat, the tremor of a cough, but soon enough the stitch seemed to loosen and the smoke filled her lungs as naturally as breath. She blew a cirrus stream of it out the window. She'd smoked three cigarettes from the pack already. She blamed the family planning clinic for her nerves: if they'd fit her in earlier today, instead of asking her to wait until four, she wouldn't be in such a state. She'd know one way or another. Instead she'd had to pee in a jar first thing this morning, as per their advice, and then hide the still-warm sample at the back of the fridge.

If she were actually pregnant, the cigarettes would be unforgivable.

A jet climbed the sky like a rocket, spinning a long thread of smoke that feathered in the sun. She thought of Bobby Wurzweiler and his callused hands, touching her in his boathouse. All week, she hadn't been able to see a plane without thinking of his face.

When she'd smoked the cigarette to a nub, Camille slipped the Volvo into drive and headed by the post office, wondering what Warren would say if she came home in a glamorous shawl. She wondered if he was really at the office, as he claimed, or tangled in the sheets of some hourly motel, his lover's bra hanging from the doorknob. She felt sick inside, an actual blow. She pulled over on the side of the road to catch her breath. Cars whooshed by her window. She stayed there for a long time, staring at the trash-strewn ice plant lining the shoulder. How surprised her family would be to see her like this. She thought of a painting she'd seen once in a book, by that Mexican artist with the eyebrow: two duplicate women with their veins exposed, one slowly bleeding to death while the other looked on.

Enough was enough. Camille would confront Warren about the affair, the next time they were alone. How had they reached the point where she couldn't even bare her suspicions? This wasn't being married to someone. It was being married *away* from him, an estrangement by degrees.

Her resolve foundered a bit when she saw the Renault parked in the driveway. Steeling herself, Camille got out of the car and entered the house. Warren was sitting by himself at the kitchen table, the coffeemaker gurgling on the counter. He didn't notice her at first, pinching the bridge of his nose. Whatever strange woman he was seeing, it didn't seem to be making him happy. Camille thought of how Warren used to fix her coffee every night, back when she was breast-feeding Dustin: she'd get the baby to sleep finally and meet Warren in the kitchen, where he'd be waiting with a mug of Folgers. It was the only time she could drink it and not affect Dustin's sleep. So exhausted were they, so happy in their mutual caretaking, that she'd actually sit in Warren's lap rather than retrieve the second chair from its evening post by the bathtub. They would drink out of the same mug, passing it back and forth until it cooled in their hands.

"Where have you been?" Warren asked, not unkindly. His face looked old without his glasses, the skin under his eyes beginning to pouch. He picked his glasses off the table and put them back on.

"Dropping Lyle at work," she said. "Then I had to stop by the post office, to send a check to Oxfam. I wanted to make sure it was certified."

"Oxfam?" He seemed suddenly nervous. "How much did you send?"

"Five hundred dollars. I doubled it this year because of the famine."

He winced. "For Christ's sake, Cam!"

Camille stepped back. "What's the matter?"

"You're sending money to *Nigeria*? Do you ever think about your own family for a change?"

"You're one to talk about family! Anyway, it's Ethiopia. A million people have died. If you watched the news occasionally, you'd know about it."

"Ethiopia."

"There was a whole song about it, too. On the radio. 'Do They Know It's Christmas?'"

He looked at her in disbelief. "That's the name of the song?"

"Yes. By the Band Aids."

"That's the stupidest thing I've ever heard," Warren said.

"It's not stupid! It's famous! *At Christmastime, we let in light and we banish shade.*"

She was actually singing. Mr. Leonard hobbled out of his doggy bed and began to sniff her shoes. Incredibly, Warren burst into laughter. "Isn't that exactly what they need? More shade?"

Camille did not have a rejoinder for this. The fact that she didn't made her too angry to speak. The coffeemaker piddled to a stop. She walked around the counter and stared at the pot of swamp brown liquid.

"Are you sending back our furniture?" she asked.

"What are you talking about?"

"Someone called this morning. From Flegel's Home Furnishings. They said they'd been authorized to come pick up the stuff we'd leased."

Warren swore under his breath but then seemed to catch himself. "I'm ordering a new living room," he said after a moment. "It doesn't make sense to renew the lease for another year."

"You're ordering new *furniture*?"

"Yes."

"You weren't going to consult me about it?"

"Christ, Camille! What do you want me to do? You're always off storyboarding *Earth to My Vagina*!" Warren looked at her. "I'm sorry. I didn't mean that." He glanced at his watch and then stood up, touching his hair. "Shit. I'm showing the property at five. A couple from Riverside. Do you think—I mean, if you're not too busy right now—could you trim my hair a bit? So it's presentable?"

He handed her the scissors from the phone table. For a second, Camille imagined stabbing him in the back with them. She needed something to drink. Ignoring him, she laid the scissors on the table and then rounded the counter to the fridge, staring into its rotten-smelling depths until she heard Warren pick up the scissors and retreat to the bedroom. She could not find the orange juice. She was rummaging through the shelves with a growing sense of rage, realizing the kids must have finished it—just once, *one time* in their sheltered, go-lucky, beach-bumming lives, they could bother to make a new pitcher—when she knocked over a can of maple syrup at the back and discovered the jar she'd hidden there this morning. The urine sample. Camille felt the itch of an idea, a sly tingle of revenge. She removed the jar from the fridge and held it in her hand, the coldness of it numbing her fingers. It did nothing special when she opened it. The smell was stale and carroty, pungent enough to make her eyes water.

Surreptitiously, she removed the half-filled pot from the Mr. Coffee by the sink and then poured in the jar's contents, watching them vanish without a trace. Then she got a travel mug from the cupboard and filled it from the coffeepot. The mug awaited Warren when he returned. He was dressed in a coat and tie, his hair combed damply over his ears in a failed attempt to make it look shorter. She'd wasted her sample—they'd no longer be able to test her today—but Camille felt drunk. Tipsy with badness. She held out the mug, like an offering. It was only after Warren had received it in surprise, lowering his lips gently to take a sip, that she realized she was grinning.

"You're a good person," he said to her.

CHAPTER 9

"You know that the owner of Baskin-Robbins died at fifty-four?" Shannon said. "Heart attack."

Lyle took another bite of coffee chip with hot fudge and chocolate sprinkles, ignoring the worrisome cramp lodged in her ribs. No doubt she was following Burt Baskin to an early grave. Still, what business was it of Shannon's? Lyle never griped about the Diet Cokes she slurped down like a junkie. She used the same cup for hours, refilling it thirty times a night. There was something fascinating in watching the straw's transformation from pristine, pin-striped tube to mangled, sorrowful reed.

They were sitting in the back room of The Perfect Scoop, listening to KROQ on the radio and waiting for the *bee-bong* of a customer to snatch them out front. Shannon watched Lyle finish the sundae with her lips pursed in disgust. At least she could no longer call her a virgin. Or she could, but Lyle would know the truth: last night she'd done it with Hector, a nineteen-year-old man, who was older than Shannon's boyfriend and had his own pickup truck. She'd seen him twice since visiting his house, dates that had ended in the cramped cab of his truck—some impromptu necking, more squashed than exciting, aborted at critical junctures because of her curfew. But last night had been different, planned shyly in advance. They'd arranged to meet during his graveyard shift. She'd sneaked out of the house in the middle of the night and through the yards of her neighbors, avoiding the streets for some reason, crossing a moon blue savanna of grass, sprinklers *shk-shk-shk*ing over her legs, so that when she got to the guardhouse her jeans were heavy as curtains. She'd tapped on the window, waiting for Hector to let her in. He'd held her for a while, to warm her up; it took Lyle a minute to realize he was shivering as well. They wobbled into a corner, knocking the clock off the wall. "If a car comes," he said, "I'll lose my job anyway." It had hurt a little bit, not badly, and then it was over. If she had to choose a word it would be "pragmatic." The best part, unexpectedly, was afterward. They'd held each other for a long time, as if they might shatter like the insides of the clock, watching the trees outside the guardhouse swoon gently in the floodlight.

"There's an owl living in that hollow pine," he'd said.

"A *spotted owl*?"

"A barn owl. I watch him all night. Oscar. He hunts for mice in the canyon."

Lyle looked at him. "You named it Oscar?"

"Oscar Valentino," he said. "Like Valentine. His face looks like a heart."

Besides that, what she remembered most was Hector opening the condom wrapper with his teeth, like a McDonald's ketchup.

Of course, Lyle wasn't about to tell all this to Shannon Jarrell, and certainly not the part about Hector's befriending a bird. She tried to read *Adam Bede*, which she'd just started, no longer caring if Shannon thought she was a nerd, but every time she picked it up Shannon sighed and fidgeted and asked her some stupid question about what kind of tattoo she should get on her ass. The choice was a rose or a scorpion. Lyle suggested the words STORE IN A COOL DRY PLACE, which was met with a look of such profound and humorless disgust that Lyle figured her opinion wasn't exactly in high demand. But each time she returned to her book, Shannon would somehow forget about Lyle's irrelevance and ask her something else.

Finally, Lyle gave up and dropped *Adam Bede* on the counter. Though she hated that it was true, some secret part of her was flattered by Shannon's attention. For the hundredth time, she tried to pinpoint the cryptic arrangement of features that made her coworker beautiful. The face itself was thin and elflike, tapering into a perfect triangle. Lyle had seen a chart somewhere depicting the ten different shapes a person's face could come in; she'd identified her own, depressingly, as "oblong."

"I've got an idea," Shannon said.

"What?"

"There's a bottle of tequila in the cupboard. From when Charlie and I spent the night."

"You *left* one here?"

"Jared's down with it." She shrugged. "Probably thinks I want to party on his cock."

Lyle glanced behind her. "What if a customer comes in?"

"We'll just have a shot or two."

Shannon got up and opened one of the cabinets over the sink, rummaging behind the boxes of straws and plastic spoons to find a half bottle of Jose Cuervo. She placed it on the floor in front of them. Lyle didn't feel like drinking on the job, at least not with Shannon Jarrell, but she didn't want to seem like a pussy for refusing either. That was the thing about the Shannons of the world: if you didn't feel like doing what they did, it was never because you didn't secretly *want* to.

"I wish we had some limes," Shannon said.

"There's lemon sorbet."

"Gross," she said. Nevertheless, she went into the front and came back with a cone topped with a lopsided scoop of sorbet. Shannon took a swig from the bottle, scrunching her face into a failed impersonation of ugliness. She licked the sorbet, careful not to smear her lipstick. "Nasty."

She handed the bottle to Lyle, who glanced toward the front of the store and then took a sip that made her throat burn. She bit into the sorbet, and the burn moved to her head.

"What do you think?" Shannon asked.

"Hard to say exactly." Lyle sniffed the bottle, like one of those wine creeps on TV. "It's delightfully complex."

To Lyle's surprise, Shannon laughed. A goofy giggle, almost human. Shannon wiped the mouth of the bottle with the end of her Perfect Scoop shirt and then took another swig, closing her eyes this time and chugging a few gulps. When it was Lyle's turn, she watched carefully to make sure Lyle drank the same amount.

"A hint of, um, cat piss, don't you think?"

Lyle sniffed the bottle again. "With a bouquet of jockstrap."

"Bouquet. Ha."

"Its opulent nose recalls a men's urinal."

Shannon giggled again. "Jesus. Is that one of your book words?"

"Urinal?"

"Fuck you, too." She scowled at the floor. There was something in her face, a softness, that resembled shyness. "'Opulent.' Does that mean big?"

Lyle shrugged. "Like lavish, I guess."

Shannon rummaged through her purse and took out a lab notebook. A long list of words, coupled with their definitions, ran down the inside cover. Shannon printed the word "OPULINT" under "STULTIFYING," following it with Lyle's definition.

"I'm trying to improve my vocabulary," she explained. "Any word I don't know."

"It's an *e,*" Lyle said, pointing.

Maybe she'd misjudged Shannon after all. They took turns on the tequila, taking longer and longer glugs. Lyle noticed that Shannon had stopped bothering to wipe off the bottle with her shirt. The door *bee-bong*ed and they stayed where they were, covering their mouths to avoid laughing, until the customer had left. Thoughtfully, Shannon asked Lyle if she had a boyfriend.

"From school? Is it Dudley Silverberg?"

"No. God." Lyle felt her heart beat faster. "He's older."

Shannon leaned forward. "What? How old?"

"Nineteen."

"Man," she said, leaning back again. Lyle couldn't tell if she believed her or not. "What does he do? I mean for a living?"

"He's a writer. A poet."

"Wow. I bet he's all intellectual, right? You read to each other from books?" She seemed impressed. "Do you fool around at his apartment?"

"He's got a house."

"Fuck. I'd kill for that. With Charlie, it's like planning a major event."

Shannon handed the bottle back to Lyle, who closed her eyes before taking a swig. The tequila seemed to have lost its flavor; or rather, it tasted bad as ever, but her throat was no longer interested in her mouth's opinion. When Lyle opened her eyes, she was shocked to see there wasn't any left.

Shannon appeared to be rummaging through the cabinet. Her contours, vague already, had become even fuzzier. Laughing, she pulled something out: a box of hairnets. She stretched one over her head so that Lyle was confronted with the visual oxymoron of Shannon Jarrell in a hairnet. Remarkably, she still looked beautiful.

"My cousin found one of these in his burrito once. Can you believe that? He was cutting into it and pulled out an entire hairnet with his fork." She stuck out her tongue, which made her look like a ravishing turtle. "Someone must have, like, wanted to sabotage the place."

"Could have been an accident," Lyle said.

"No, sir. How could it be an accident?"

"One cook's folding up a burrito? And another's leaving at the same time? Juan and Carlos? Carlos whips off his hairnet and tosses it at the trash, *adios,* and it lands in the burrito right when Juan's looking up. To say good-bye, I mean." She mimed Juan's oblivious folding of the tortilla. "Boom. I mean, bam. Folds it right in."

Shannon liked this apparently. Loved it. Was maybe even getting a hernia from laughing so hard. The hairnet had slipped to one side of her head, perched jauntily like a beret. Lyle laughed, too, amazed at herself: Had she really just said Juan and Carlos?

"You're fucking funny, you know that?" Shannon said, catching her breath. She wiped her eye with one knuckle. "Why are you always, like, hanging out by yourself?"

"Maybe I'm a leper."

Shannon closed her eyes. "Shit, I'm wasted. Bugfuck."

The door chimed again. Shannon burst out laughing and pointed at her hairnet. Lyle stood up, lurching to one side before finding her balance. When she turned her head, she was aware of the wall needing to catch up with her eyes, wobbling into focus like a slide. She emerged from the back room to find a middle-aged couple huddled over the display of ice cream tubs. The woman was wearing a sweatshirt that could only be described as "deciduous": an embroidered tree covered the front of her chest, its branches drooping suggestively down her breasts and shedding a blizzard of rainbow-colored leaves.

"How's the macadamia nut?" the woman asked, smiling.

Lyle stuck a finger in her mouth, pretending to throw up. The woman stopped smiling. She studied the other tubs uneasily and then insisted on trying it.

"Well, I think it's quite good," she said. "Delicious."

Lyle laughed. "Please."

"Excuse me?"

"We call it Macadamia Butt."

"What about the cheesecake?" her husband asked from the far end of the case.

Lyle glanced at the woman. She walked over to where the man was standing and leaned over the counter, addressing him in private. "Tastes like sperm," she whispered.

The man looked at his wife. Lyle had no idea what sperm tasted like, only that some girls in matching sorority shirts had tried the flavor once and claimed a resemblance, nearly peeing themselves laughing. The woman dressed as a tree stared at her. Perhaps she was retarded. After struggling with the macadamia nut for several minutes, Lyle scooped some water from the little trough by the register and dumped it into the tub, smooshing some of the sludgy mess onto a cone. A trickle of sludge dripped down the side, and she bent down and licked it clean.

"You just licked my cone!" the woman exclaimed.

"I did?"

She turned to her husband. "That girl just licked my cone."

"Oh, for Pete's sake, shut up. I'll make you a new one."

The man's face reddened. "Is there a manager here? Someone in charge?"

"No," Lyle said. "I mean, yes. Shannon!"

Shannon poked her head out, still wearing the hairnet like a beret. The man seemed to have lost his sense of outrage, dumbstruck by her beauty.

"This girl licked my ice cream cone," his wife said indignantly.

Shannon turned to Lyle, her face stern and managerial. "Did you lick this woman's ice cream cone?"

"Only with my tongue."

"Please. Take this," Shannon said, pulling a gallon tub of mint chip from the case and offering it to the woman. "Eat yourself bulimic."

"You're both drunk!" the woman said.

Shannon looked at her sweatshirt. "You'd better rake your tits."

"We'll call the actual manager. The owner. What are your names?"

"Mildred," Shannon said. "With an *M*."

"Me too. With an *H*."

When the couple had left, Lyle and Shannon collapsed on the floor. They hugged each other, gasping for breath. Lyle told her about the sperm comment. She knew Shannon was as wasted as she was, that only yesterday she might have made a snide comment about Lyle's having no idea what sperm tastes like. No doubt they'd be fired; Lyle was supposed to get her two-month raise next week. Still, a voice in her head was saying: *I'm hugging Shannon Jarrell.*

CHAPTER 10

The hair salon was bright and barren and smelled like lathered dog. Warren wrote his name on the list at the counter and sat down in front of an intimidating display of hair products. The words "Shear Magic" were printed on every bottle. He did not like these bottles. Or perhaps it wasn't the bottles themselves so much as the fact that someone was buying them. So far, since his meeting with Larry, he'd failed to sell a single house. Six appointments, and not so much as a nibble. Warren's face was starting to break out, his first pimples in years. So far only one couple had been interested enough to ask about the machines breaking ground nearby, but Warren had not managed to tell them it was a shopping mall. Instead he'd shrugged enigmatically, hoping to seem unconcerned. But the husband had sniffed something out: he'd turned courteous and withdrawn, his interest retreating like a mirage. Warren had cursed himself the whole ride home, punching the Renault's AM radio so hard it no longer switched on.

It would not happen again. Yesterday he'd driven out to Van Nuys and lurked in front of a Century 21 office, handing his card to everyone who walked out, but had yet to receive a call.

"How would you like it?" Warren's hairdresser said, lowering his chair with a hydraulic *shunk*. The guy had large hoop earrings and a wild nest of hair, white as a dandelion puff. Aside from an Asian woman cleaning the floor, sweeping a voodooey assortment of locks into a pile, they were the only people in the salon.

"Short," Warren managed.

"Clippers?"

"That's fine."

"Tapered on the side?"

Warren frowned. "Whatever you think's best."

The hairdresser—whose name was Mick—looked at him con-
temptuously. He wasted no time with the clippers, lifting one side
of Warren's hair with a comb and shearing the brown tussock
poking through its teeth. Watching this strange man clip his hair,
submitting like an infant to his contempt, Warren thought how
nice it would be to come to work every day knowing you'd have a
steady stream of customers. Demand-side economics. No one ever
got their hair cut in advance.

The phone rang, and Mick put down his clippers to answer
it. His face in the mirror hardened to a scowl. "Mom," he said
angrily, "I'm not talking about it anymore. Do you understand?"

He did not mention that he had a customer. Warren's hair was
half-gone, the left side shaved close enough to see the scalp. He
was spending fifteen dollars on this haircut—money from Dustin's
T-Bond, intended for college. He spun his seat so he wouldn't have
to look at himself and stared at the muted TV in the corner. They
were doing a segment about Mandy Rogers. Her face filled the
screen, eyes puckered into tiny slits. It was the bags under them,
the dark puddingy circles, that startled Warren. They didn't belong
on a fifteen-year-old girl. They belonged on a prime minister, or
someone who'd survived a drought. Perhaps it was an illusion—a
trick of the lighting—but the eyes seemed to zero in on him from
across the room.

"Mom, you're driving a wedge between us. Capital 'Us.'"

Warren checked his watch, hoping the hairdresser would see
him. He felt the top of his head, touching the jagged frontier
where the crew cut sprouted into hair. On TV Mandy Rogers had
been replaced by a fleet-footed bulldog; the caption at the bottom
said *I'm long for my kibbles, I'm long for my bits.*

The hairdresser turned his back, his voice shrunk to a whisper.
"You ungrateful bitch! How many lawn chairs did I return for
you last week?"

Warren stood up. He might punch someone or break into
tears. He unsnapped the nylon cape cinched around his neck and
walked out of the salon, heading to the Renault without looking
back. He sat in the driver's seat for a minute, catching his breath,
transported for a moment to his mother's funeral. He could recall

it all perfectly: the coffin creaking in the wind; the gray snow of the cemetery seeping into his shoes; the endless skein of geese that interrupted the service, honking and honking overhead, causing the scattering of mourners to look even smaller. His mother's few acquaintances, amassed from a lifetime of work. For a long time Warren had supported her financially, but in the end he had not been able to erase the dutiful solitude of her life.

Warren glanced at the rearview mirror: if he turned to the left, where his hair still fell shaggily past his ears, he looked only slightly deranged. He flipped on the radio before remembering it was broken and then pulled out of the parking lot, ignoring the old woman in a cartwheel hat ogling him from the curb. The car was stifling. He thought about stopping somewhere to finish his haircut, but the idea of walking into another Mane Event or Wish You Were Hair filled him with dread.

Warren drove down Crenshaw Boulevard, bordered on both sides by identical mini-malls. The sun blazing off the pink and green buildings only magnified their grubbiness. The real question— the one that hounded Warren at night, disrupting his sleep—was why he'd left Wisconsin in the first place. They'd been happy there, well-off by most standards: thanks to the white flight from Milwaukee, there was no shortage of home buyers wanting a piece of lake country. And their house in Nashotah had been bright and crowded and happy, alive with the sound of acorns dribbling down the roof, the living room windows opening to the summer breeze off the lake. Warren had built the place himself. It wasn't as lavish as the vacation homes he developed, was perhaps even a bit small, but he liked the sense of warmth it conveyed, its crowded, hivelike sense of communion. The house was a minefield of shoes, and he could identify his children by the creaks they made in the floor above him. Mostly he loved the lake itself, the knowledge that he owned a small bit of shore. He liked to wake in the morning with the first streaks of sun and take the canoe out by himself, the motorboats quiet as alligators in their slips, steam curling from the water as he paddled past the dew-slick docks. His father had taken him fishing on this very lake, once a week in the summer, and they'd marveled at the rich people sleeping in their houses. They'd fished in the cattails between docks. It had felt wrong somehow, like stealing. Alone in his canoe, years later, Warren would scan the shore on his way back home and feel a jolt of pride when he spotted their house, the windows so bright they hurt his eyes.

Somehow, though, it hadn't been enough. Ever since he was a kid, he'd imagined leaving Wisconsin: his father's illness, the smell of gas that lingered on his mother's skin, even in the mornings—they seemed to be a part of the landscape itself, as inescapable as the lakes and moraines and snow-flattened cornfields. The westerns he'd watched while his mother worked the swing shift had proffered another world, one filled with sun and dust and violence, a life of monumental dreams. He remembered the day Larry had invited him out to California. It had been the middle of a bitter winter—he'd spent the day before shoveling the driveway in zero-degree wind—and Larry had called him from the car phone in his Alfa to tell him about the "golden egg" he'd found in the desert. Warren had thought he was shouting through a blizzard before realizing the top was down. When Warren landed in L.A., groggy from an in-flight nap, he was amazed to see that the baggage handlers were wearing shorts. He had to shake his head to make sure he was truly awake. He had the same feeling touring Herradura Estates for the first time, seeing all the sprawling ranch-style houses, their corrals and barns and glacier blue pools, the horse trails twining through a canyon of scarlet flowers. For the first time Warren understood the difference between being well-off and being rich. The real estate agent showed him the cheapest house on the market, well beyond what he could afford. Warren didn't care. He raided stock intended for their retirement, a taste of the pillaging to come. That his family hadn't dreamed of such a life was further incentive to give it to them.

At home, Dustin and his friend Mark Biesterman were blocking the driveway, hosing off their surfboards. Dustin's beautiful girlfriend sat on the lawn in shorts and a bikini top. The two of them were so clearly in love that it flooded Warren with nostalgia. They blinked at him as he got out of the car. The hose drooped in Dustin's hand, a stream of water gushing down one leg.

"Wow, Mr. Ziller," Kira said.

Mark Biesterman nodded, impressed. "I like your do. I mean, it really interrogates the whole notion of 'hair.'"

"It was a mistake," Warren explained.

"No sense regretting it. To thine own self be true."

Through the carport, jutting beyond the corner of the house, was the open end of a truck. The mud flaps of the truck said FLEGEL'S HOME FURNISHINGS. Warren looked back at Dustin, who was still drenching his own leg with the hose.

"Dad, what happened to your head?"

"You let men into the house?"

"They said they're here for the furniture. I opened the garage for them." Dustin shrugged. "Did Mom buy some new stuff?"

Warren went inside the house, ducking through the front door. The foyer smelled like cigarettes. Near the living room he found two men in baseball caps, corseted in weight belts, carrying the leather sofa toward the garage. The man facing Warren started. He studied Warren carefully and then lowered his end of the couch, as though trying not to disturb a predator.

"That's my sofa," Warren said.

This seemed to boost the man's confidence. He reached into his back pocket and flourished a folded piece of paper, a medical bracelet sliding up one wrist. A tattoo on his biceps said DEATH BEFORE DISHONOR. "Warren Ziller? We have authorization here to retrieve five items of furniture. One Stewart sofa in Bookle Mushroom, one Boone recliner in Leisure Mocha, two Ezra chairs in Whispy Bronze, and one Noguchi cocktail table."

"Get out of my house," Warren said quietly.

"This isn't bouclé," the other guy said, looking at the sofa. Warren could see his belly button, tumescent as a pregnant woman's, peeking above his weight belt.

"What?"

"It's black leather."

"Says here Stewart in Bookle Mushroom."

"Must be a mistake. Only Pattersons come in bouclé."

"Excuse me. Boo-*clay*." The guy with the bracelet snorted.

"It's French."

"Forgivez-moi, Monsieur Sofa Expert."

Warren stepped forward, raising his voice. "I said, get out of my house."

"We'll be out of your life forever, Mr. Ziller. Soon as we clear this up."

The man with the bracelet glanced around the hallway before going into the living room and picking up the phone that was sitting on the floor. Warren did not remember leasing the phone table. He stared at the man's tattoo as he dialed. It seemed profoundly inaccurate. He sidestepped the couch and headed for the garage. The door was open, the Flegel's truck backed up to the line of shade crossing the driveway. Feeling ill, Warren squeezed past the Deadbeats' drum set and a forgotten pogo stick and edged into the cluttered reaches of the garage. Cobwebs tickled his face. He stopped at the metal cabinet fastened with a rusty padlock in the corner. He had to try the combination twice; his hands were shaking too much to find the numbers.

His father's guns were leaning in a pile. Carefully, Warren took one out, laid it on the ground, and unzipped the leather case. A Browning. It smelled of mildew and something worse, like urine. The barrel was corroded with rust, but he recognized the 12-gauge from when he was a kid. He used to watch his father clean it after hunting trips, hunched prayerfully over the parts, polishing each bolt and O-ring with a rag. Kneeling, Warren took the shotgun out of the case and hefted it in his arms. Some pellets fell out of the barrel and littered the ground. Mouse turds. How resourceful, to live in a gun. It made a kind of sense. Warren opened the breech of the Browning and looked inside. It wasn't loaded, of course, but the men in his house wouldn't know that.

He remembered something from law school, the Castle Doctrine: if a stranger broke into your home, you could lawfully respond with deadly force.

Warren closed the action of the Browning and then stood up. His head felt clear, empty with purpose. He looked up and saw Jonas watching him from the middle of the garage, his eyes shifting between the gun and Warren's haircut.

"Dad, what are you doing?"

Warren lowered the shotgun, blinking at his son. Jonas was not dressed in orange but was wearing his Izod inside out, the crime-scene outline of an alligator on his chest. Warren had the sudden, abysmal feeling that he'd left nothing of value in the world. From the living room, he could hear the man with the tattoo talking on the phone.

"Nothing," he said. "Just looking at your grandfather's guns."

Jonas regarded him skeptically. "There are some guys in the house."

"Yes. There are."

"What are they doing?"

"Taking the furniture back."

"What's wrong with it?"

Warren frowned. "They believe it belongs to them."

Jonas seemed to accept this. Warren had an image of his own father sitting on the roof, gun cleaved to his lap, casing the sky for Santa Claus's sleigh. He took his finger from the Browning's trigger.

"Are you going to kill them?" Jonas asked.

"No."

He seemed disappointed. "You'll have to dispose of the bodies. There's an old incinerator behind the Hathaways' barn, but I don't think it works."

"I'm not a murderer, Jonas."

"Are they going to take Mom's car, too?"

Warren stared at his son. The boy knew much more than he pretended. Warren wondered if it was lonely to be so strange. He felt strange and lonely himself. Not for the first time, he wondered why he was so much more wrapped up in Dustin than in this macabre and friendless child. Maybe it was the charge that Dustin gave off, a crackle of power; watching him in the garage, basking in the cockiness of his music, Warren couldn't help feeling that everything would be okay. Or perhaps this was a rationalization: he'd been smitten with Dustin from the day he was born. The truth was Jonas had never evoked the same woozy wonderment. Warren wanted to hug the child in front of him, to say something that would make everything all right, but couldn't imagine what on earth that would be.

He told Jonas to go outside and then locked the guns in the cabinet. All around him were bikes and boogie boards and barely scuffed skis. The waste of money appalled him. Inside again, Warren walked to the living room, where the two movers were cinching their belts. The guy with the belly button was grinning about something. They paid no attention to Warren. Through the panel window beside the front door he could see Dustin goofing around with the hose, cracking bullwhips of water in his girl-friend's direction.

"It's the Stewart in Bison Leather," the guy with the bracelet said sulkily. "Frank here was right."

"Listen," Warren said, taking out his wallet. "The boy out there. The handsome one with curly hair. Will you tell him some better stuff's coming? Furniture? It just got delayed for a couple weeks?" He took a ten-dollar bill from his wallet. "Make it sound that way? Like we're trading it in?"

The man stared at the ten-dollar bill, his lips thinned into a line. He glanced at his partner. Warren couldn't look them in the eye.

"Sure," the guy said, taking the money. "No problem."

Warren went to his room and shut the door. He lay in bed, staring at the hideous Pac-Man yawning at him from the wall. Noises echoed down the hall, a din of scrapes and thuds and voices: the sound of his house hemorrhaging around him. He felt cold and helpless but also somehow relieved, as if the worst were finally beginning.

CHAPTER 11

Dustin drove down the street with Kira, headed to her house for dinner. He wished he could swing by Starhead's place and buy a gram of weed, just to get him through the night. He was happy to be ten dollars richer but still wondering why the hell the furniture guy had given him the money. "Your dad needs help," the man had said, handing him the folded-up bill. It was strange, but then again a lot of strange things had been happening lately. The best strategy, Dustin had decided, was not to think about them too much. Case in point: he'd spent all day at the beach with Kira, knowing they were having dinner at the Shackneys', but was only now admitting to himself that Taz might not confine herself to her room.

"Is your sister going to be there?" he asked now. He was careful to avoid saying her name, not wanting to appear overly familiar. Why Kira insisted on inviting him to these family dinners he didn't fully understand, though he suspected it had something to do with impressing her parents. She'd had some bad boyfriends in the past and this was her chance to show Dustin off, like a report card. Normally, he was happy to indulge her.

"Who cares. The little bitch keeps leaving her retainer in the bathroom. In the same cup as my toothbrush."

"She has a retainer?"

"She does it on purpose. She knows how disgusting it is."

Dustin stared at the road. "When did she get her braces off?"

Kira frowned, uninterested in her sister's dental history. "My mom thinks she's 'emotionally disturbed.' Sure. As long as they think she's nuts, she can do whatever she wants."

He nodded, though he believed that "emotionally disturbed"

was probably an understatement. What kind of fifteen-year-old swallows glass to impress people? Of course, he couldn't tell Kira about the glass incident. Certainly he couldn't tell her that Taz's face had begun to disrupt his dreams, smirking at him while she squirted PAM up her nose or yanked his car apart piece by piece, smirking at him even as she kicked off her saddle shoes and began to unbuckle his eight-armed belt, engaging him in an act of statutory proportions. This particular vision had appeared to him last night. She had touched him expertly with two hands. He'd hoped, of course, never to see her outside of his dreams again—but that was clearly a fantasy.

"Anyway," Kira said, "I think she's been sneaking out. She's always sleeping till two in the afternoon."

"What's wrong with her ears?" Dustin asked casually. "I noticed these scabs all over them. At the beach."

"That's one of her issues."

"Issues?"

"She picks at them until she bleeds. Her therapist says she's got a parasuicidal condition." They slowed for a stop sign and Kira turned to him, squeezing his thigh. Her front tooth was smudged with lipstick. "Let's not talk about her. I've been so happy lately. Thinking about our anniversary."

Only a madman, a drunken pervert, would tarnish the purity of Kira Shackney's love by fantasizing about her little sister. Her underage sister. Who wore, he was just beginning to fathom, a *retainer*. Those things that kids wear. Those things that collect disgusting bits of food and which you occasionally see little boys licking after lunch. The party, the beer, the Butthole Surfers—all of it had conspired to make him temporarily insane. How else could he explain it?

At the sign for Hacienda de Shackney, they drove through the Old West–style gate and pulled up the long shaded driveway to the extravagant portico of the Shackneys' house. Mr. Shackney met them at the door, wiping his hands on his slacks. He had a Band-Aid on one cheek. Dustin looked at the floor so he wouldn't stare. It was one of the things he'd noticed about California, these Band-Aids on people's faces: he did not remember seeing them in Wisconsin.

"Man of the hour," Mr. Shackney said, clapping Dustin on the back.

He led them into the kitchen, which was as large as a restaurant, and pulled out two St. Pauli Girls from the chrome Sub-Zero fridge. He handed one to Dustin, winking at him as though they were involved in some kind of shady investment. Dustin knew what was coming: the Trial by Sports. Somehow, purely by accident, he'd led Mr. Shackney to believe he was an avid sports fan. Dustin knew almost nothing about sports, but somehow this misunderstanding had persisted and it was too late to correct it. The key, he'd discovered, was to slip in the word "powerhouse."

"What'd you think of the game last night?"

"I couldn't watch all of it." Dustin waited, perilously, for some hint of what sport Mr. Shackney was talking about.

"When Denver missed it. Jesus. I thought that they were goners."

"Me too."

"Know what they need?" Mr. Shackney lowered his voice. "Someone like Noll. An X's and O's coach."

"Yeah. You're right."

"Miami, though. They're starting to make some noise."

"I don't know," Dustin said. "Denver's a powerhouse."

Mr. Shackney slapped him on the back again, beaming. "You said it, kid. You. Said. It."

While they waited for dinner, Dustin and Mr. Shackney sat in the living room sipping their beers, staring out at the crisply mown backyard that sloped to a tennis court at the bottom of the hill. Mr. Shackney wanted to know how his father's real estate venture was doing; Dustin tried to concentrate, but his attention kept drifting to the hallway that led unstoppably to Taz's room. It was a dark hallway, with lights that went on automatically as you made your way to the bathroom. It reminded Dustin of the reptile house at the zoo. Unless you were stoned, the effect was merely irritating. As Dustin tried to make small talk, the back door opened and Kira's little brother came clattering in with his skateboard, wearing one of those surf-wax T-shirts that said THE BEST FOR YOUR STICK. Unlike Jonas, he would never lack for friends or have to worry about being pantsed.

He greeted Dustin with a nod. "Why does your father have such a crappy car?"

"Brent Alexander!" Mrs. Shackney said, poking her head into

the living room. She had bionic hearing, which seemed to turn on magically like the lights. "That's completely out of line."

"His real one got stolen," Dustin explained.

"Sucky," Brent said.

Mr. Shackney seemed relieved. "I'm betting that's why your dad seems a bit . . . on edge."

Dustin felt a vague tremor of alarm, as though his dad's car loss was suckier than he'd realized, but he was too worried about Taz to investigate it. He was still clinging to some small shred of hope that she wouldn't surface. His heart sank when they sat down to eat in the dining room and he noticed six place settings at the table. Plunging his heart further was Taz herself, who emerged from the kitchen in a hooded sweatshirt and black jeans shredded at both knees, yawning as though she'd just woken up from a nap. The rips in her jeans opened and closed, like little mouths, when she walked. She flopped into her chair at the table and smirked when her eyes reached Dustin's. The witch's forelock was still there, dangling between her eyes; Dustin was hoping it would have miraculously disappeared.

He stared at his plate, focusing on the giant molar of salmon in front of him. He wanted to wipe her smirk away with his napkin.

"So Kira tells me your music is really taking off," Mrs. Shackney said, two fingers pressed to her neck. She was a marathon runner and constantly checked her pulse. "What's the name of your band?"

"Toxic Shock Syndrome," Dustin said.

Taz laughed. "That's the name of your band?"

Kira looked at her. "So what?"

"Don't you get that from tampons?"

"It's a very serious disease," Kira said. She smoothed the napkin in her lap. "People die from it. Don't they, Dust?"

Dustin nodded, staring at his salmon. A bead of sweat trickled down his forehead, but he did nothing to wipe it from his face. He'd decided the only way to survive the evening would be to talk—to move—as little as possible.

Mr. Shackney looked at him suspiciously. "So it's, like, a public service sort of thing? Raising awareness?"

"Well, I think it's terrific," Mrs. Shackney said. "Everyone should know about these problems. Have you been playing at the public schools?"

"It's not really about that," Dustin explained. "I mean, we're socially conscious—but it's more about conspicuous consumption. Stuff like that."

"What's conspicuous consumption?" Brent asked with his mouth full.

"You know. How everything's about shopping and stuff you don't need." Dustin happened to glance at the brightly lacquered didgeridoo balanced on a stand in the corner, a souvenir from one of the Shackneys' "little trips." Hanging on the wall nearby was the branding iron that Mr. Shackney used to monogram his steaks. Dustin's eyes caught Taz's: her smirk widened, as though he had a blob of salmon stuck to his chin. "Not just shopping. Everything. Like, we have a song about Mandy Rogers."

Mr. Shackney dropped his fork. "It disgusts me. These perverts. We should send them all to an island, castrate the bastards."

"Mitch, please. Can we not be so graphic?"

"I just think if it was one of my own kids. That poor girl being raped."

"You don't *know* that's what happened," Taz said, picking at her food. "Anyway, what if she went off with some guy on purpose?"

"Oh please," Kira said. "She's mentally retarded."

"What? Retards don't like to get laid?"

"Taz! I swear, I'm about at my limit." Mrs. Shackney checked her pulse. "Even if she weren't handicapped. She's just a girl."

Taz snorted. "She's the same age as me."

"That's young enough!" Mr. Shackney said. He wiped his mouth. "If I ever got my hands on one of these sickos, I'd cut his balls off myself."

"Mitch!"

"Could I help, Dad?" Brent asked.

"Sure. It'd teach you a thing about justice."

"Are you okay?" Kira said, looking at Dustin. "Your face is all sweaty."

"I'm just going to use the bathroom," Dustin said.

He walked down the telepathically brightening hallway and locked the door behind him, inspecting himself in the mirror above the sink. His face was redder than usual. Slapping it with cold water, he closed his eyes and pictured Taz's sneering lips, the stupid smirk that seemed to accentuate the little mole on her lip. Why did it piss him off so much? It made him feel like a loser. A *fraud*. But he wasn't a fraud. He was a talented guitarist who would one day make her extremely sorry, when Toxic Shock Syndrome—or maybe Viet-Nun, they could still change their name—became a household word. The Shackneys were right: she was a nutcase, mentally unstable. Probably she was tortured with jealousy over Kira's beauty. She wasn't worth wasting a second's thought over.

There were some bars of soap lined up in a dish on the sink, blue and speckled and identical except that each one was larger than the one before, as though laid out for the Three Bears. He thought of the lobster wandering through the party in San Pedro. He rearranged the soaps, putting the smallest one in the middle, but it didn't make him feel any better.

After a while, he gathered his courage again and opened the door. Taz was standing in the hallway in front of her room. She was frowning, her bangs covering her eyes. She saw Dustin and the smirk returned, as if of its own accord.

"What are you doing?" he asked.

"They sent me to my room."

"Why? Did you try to eat your glass?"

The smirk didn't change. "Actually, I told them I thought you were an alcoholic."

You're completely insane, Dustin thought. Ignoring her, he brushed past and walked down the still-bright hall and took his place serenely at the table. Or rather, he did this in his mind. In reality, he grabbed Taz by the arms and mashed his lips into her smirk, leaning her against the wall in a noisy, unpleasant kiss. He could taste the lemony glaze of salmon on her tongue. He half-expected some witchy thing, sharp and hazardous, to end up in his mouth. The light down the hall flicked off. Before he could stop himself, they began to press together with their hips, a slow, Lego-like push, his breath thinning to a shiver, the promised snap eluding them as they stumbled sideways and the light went on again, reminding them—or Dustin, at least—where they were.

He let go. She was no longer smirking. A dribble of blood rolled down her neck, seeping from her earlobe. She wasn't a witch, of course, but a miserably lost girl.

He rushed past her for real this time and returned to the dining room. The Shackneys were hunched over their plates, talking in low tones, involved in a conversation they'd clearly had before.

He could tell it was about Taz. When they saw him return to his seat, everyone straightened. Dustin realized he had no idea how he looked.

"*There* he is," Mr. Shackney said, winking. "Better watch your drinks."

"Feeling better?" Mrs. Shackney asked.

Dustin nodded, surprised to discover that he actually was. Kira put her hand on his leg. Her smile was so different from her sister's smirk, so affectionate and admiring and filled with love, that he felt indecent. He ate the rest of his salmon, trying to forget what had happened in the hall. Kira told her parents about some of his songs, gushing about how talented he was, but Dustin was having a hard time looking her in the eye. It was only partly out of guilt—there was something, too, about the way she sat there, all dressed up and polite and at home with the didgeridoo standing behind her.

"Why are you looking at my ears?" she asked, blushing.

"I'm not."

"Ugh. They stick out, I know."

Mrs. Shackney patted her hand. "You have beautiful ears, honey. They're perfect."

Dustin agreed with her, forcing himself to smile. It was true. There was nothing wrong with them.

CHAPTER 12

Warren sat in the driveway, studying his head in the rearview mirror. He'd taken his electric razor to it and shorn it to a military buzz. He'd had the same head for forty-four years but was only now getting to know it. There were little divots, worrisome black freckles, a tiny, trapezoidal window over his ear where no hair would grow. Dustin, approvingly, had told him he looked like a skinhead. Warren did not know what this was but suspected it was not a resemblance that would help him move houses.

Warren's throat was dry. An unquenchable thirst. It had been there a week, ever since the Flegel's men had emptied out his living room.

He went inside the house, unable to keep from glancing down the hall at the barren rug. His mouth turned to cotton. He walked to the kitchen and grabbed one of Dustin's Cokes from the fridge. Several pots burbled away on the stove, filling the house with a syrupy, dispiriting smell. The kids called their mother Pyrex, goddess of casseroles; Warren couldn't complain in the same way since she was generally the one who cooked. He used to justify this by their differences in income: he worked harder, supported the family, it made a certain amount of sense. Now, thinking of her rushing home from work to get dinner on, he felt guilty and obsolete.

Mr. Leonard limped through the back door followed by Camille, who was wearing what appeared to be a poncho, black and armless and fringed with little tassels. When she saw Warren, she blushed self-consciously and busied herself with Mr. Leonard's leash. Lately she seemed perpetually angry and alert, as if she were waiting for him to say the wrong thing.

"New jacket?" he asked timidly.

"I bought it today, before picking up Lyle." She glanced at him before hanging up the leash. "How does it look?"

"Fine. I mean, great."

"You don't like it."

"I do," he said. "Just I've never seen you in black before. Or a, um, poncho."

Her eyes narrowed. "It's not a poncho," she said, walking to the sink.

"What is it?"

"It's a shawl. It's cashmere."

The word alarmed him. "Did you put it on your American Express?"

"Why does it matter?" Her face and ears were pink: with anger or humiliation, Warren couldn't tell.

"No reason. Just wondering. I mean, we should be careful, with Christmas coming up."

"It's July!"

Warren waited for her to ask about their finances, steeling himself for the third degree, but she seemed uninterested in pursuing the matter. Whether this was denial on her part or something more dangerous, he couldn't tell. He took a swig of Coke and the motion startled Mr. Leonard, who stiffened on his doggy mat as though he'd just seen a ghost. There was something oddly curatorial about him. Camille dropped something in the sink—perhaps on purpose—and he jerked his head back and forth, like a bird.

"What's up with Mr. Leonard?" Warren asked.

"He got into the chocolate-covered espresso beans."

"What? How many did he eat?"

"The whole bag."

"Jesus," Warren muttered. "Why don't we just throw our groceries down the toilet?"

Camille studied him for a second, as though he'd lost his mind. While she was turning off the stove, Dustin came in from the yard, slamming the screen door behind him. Mr. Leonard shot up like a jack-in-the-box.

"Whoa," Dustin said. "Those dog vitamins don't screw around."

"He's heavily caffeinated," Warren explained.

"Are you sure that's a good idea?"

Lyle stepped into the kitchen, joining Dustin by the counter. Camille regarded them angrily. "Which of you left the espresso beans out?"

"Mom," Lyle said, staring at her shawl, "are you in a play or something?"

She turned a deeper shade of pink. "What do you mean?"

"It's cashmere," Warren said, defending her.

"They make ponchos in cashmere?"

Jonas came in from the hall with one of his toy guns and immediately sprung it on his mother, twirling it Old West–style from his hip. She turned to Warren, as if the shawl's poncholike qualities were his fault. Her eyes seemed to fill with tears.

"You're wearing tennis shoes with your suit," she whispered, staring at his ketchup-stained sneakers.

"My loafers were giving me blisters."

She turned back to the sink, refusing to look at him. How could he tell her that he'd been trolling the neighborhoods of San Pedro on foot, handing out business cards to anyone who looked solvent? It had been hard enough to explain the living room: in the end he'd told her it was an early birthday present, that he'd wanted to surprise her with new furniture but that there'd been a mix-up with the order. The new stuff wouldn't get here for a month. She was skeptical at first, but he reminded her how long she'd been pining for a gray chenille couch to replace the leather one. He did not want to lie to her, but every time he considered telling her the truth—that he'd lost their retirement funds, the kids' college funds, and every fund in between—his tongue dried up like paper and he couldn't speak. When he managed to get Auburn Fields off the ground, he reminded himself, he'd be able to put the money back in.

As for the kids, the fact that the living room furniture had disappeared hardly seemed to faze them. They'd accepted Warren's explanation as easily as they'd accepted his lie about the Chrysler. It was only Jonas who gave him looks, but even these were hard to interpret, more conspiratorial than accusatory.

"How's Kira Shackney?" Warren asked Dustin at dinner, trying to make conversation. His son seemed startled.

"Fine."

"I ran into Mitch Shackney, while I was walking Mr. Leonard

yesterday. He had his other girl with him, the younger one. What's her name?"

Dustin fidgeted in his chair, perhaps out of boredom. "I don't know."

"I guess she's been going to school up near Santa Cruz. Doesn't really know anyone here." Warren poured himself some more water from the pitcher on the table. "I said it might be nice if all you kids got together sometime. Jonas, too. I mean—I know she's a bit older."

"Oooh, Jone," Lyle said. "Maybe you can score some action."

"Okay," Jonas said.

"She's fifteen!" Dustin said. "Anyway, she likes to eat glass."

"What?"

"Did you know that lions sometimes get confused when they're licking their cubs and end up eating them instead?" Jonas said.

"What?" Lyle said. "By mistake?"

"Their brain circuits get crossed. I read it in *National Geographic*."

"That's ridiculous," Warren said.

Lyle turned to Camille, who'd walked in with a casserole, Mr. Leonard trembling at her heels. She was wearing oven mitts designed to look like cow heads. "Mom, did you ever feel like eating us?"

"No, honey," she said quietly. "It never crossed my mind."

Everyone passed their plates to Camille, who served them dinner. Warren looked at the night's offering, identifiable from past incarnations as Polynesian pork: chunks of meat and pineapple swimming in a brownish goop, topped with Chinese noodles, steaming next to a bowl of leftover Spanish rice. He tried to imagine what they'd be eating if they went truly broke. He guzzled the water in front of him. "I wonder if for once we could have a normal dinner conversation? One that doesn't involve cannibalism?"

"What's eating *him*?" Lyle asked.

"He left his loafers somewhere," Camille said mysteriously, missing the joke. She picked up her knife and fork and began to saw ineptly at a cube of pork.

"Mom, you're still wearing your oven mitts."

"Just once," Warren said, "I'd like to have a normal dinner. One time in the history of this family. Is that too much to ask, just to sit down and talk about our day for once?" They were all looking at him. Perhaps he was shouting. He lowered his voice. "I mean, something could happen to us."

"Like what?"

"I don't know," Warren mumbled.

Camille glared at him, close to tears again. "Yes. Why don't you tell us."

"We could get crushed by an earthquake."

"Our whole bodies?" Jonas asked. "Or just, like, our limbs?"

"If there's an earthquake, can we live in a hotel?" Lyle said.

Camille snorted. "Your father would like that."

"How about a nuclear winter?" Jonas said excitedly. "We might freeze to death and get eaten by rats."

"Dad, are you all right?" Lyle asked. "That's, like, your third glass of water."

Warren dropped his fork. Mr. Leonard jerked upright, sitting on two legs like a gopher. "I just want to have *one normal conversation*! *Please!*" Warren's family stared at him, mouths stuffed with food. The clock in the kitchen caroled like a rose-breasted grosbeak. He turned to Lyle. "How was school today?"

"It's summer, Dad. Vacation."

Dustin waved his hand near Warren's face. "Traditionally falling in the months between May and September?"

Warren knew it was summer. It was simply that the words "summer" and "vacation" had momentarily uncoupled in his brain. The stress was making him senile. He reached up to loosen his collar before remembering that he'd already unbuttoned his shirt. He'd vowed not to involve his family in Auburn Fields, it was the one promise to himself he hadn't broken, but he saw now that this was a luxury he couldn't afford and pulled out the wad of business cards he kept in his suit pocket. AUBURN FIELDS, they said, then below it: LIVE WELL . . . FEEL INSPIRED. He rolled off the rubber band and handed a stack of cards to each of his children.

"What are we supposed to do with these?" Dustin asked.

"Since it's *summer* and everything, I thought you might like to help me out. With work."

"Help you out?"

"For instance, Lyle, if you see anyone at the ice cream parlor. You know, who looks old enough to retire." Warren frowned. "Or Dustin. When you're at the beach."

"You're building a retirement community?"

"No. I mean, it could be. Like Palm Springs, but for unrich people."

His children studied the cards skeptically, as though this was further proof of his craziness. Perhaps it was. If he was crazy, he would no longer be responsible for his behavior.

After dinner, they all gathered on the rug in the living room for a screening of Camille's new movie, crowding onto the faint, coffin-shaped shadow where the couch used to be. Jonas was in the film, his first role, and for a moment—watching his children joke about agents and paparazzi—Warren almost forgot his troubles. Lyle brought out the popcorn and a moldering box of Milk Duds. It was a family tradition, to watch Camille's latest opus before it went out to schools across the county. Historically, the children were a receptive audience, hissing at the sight of a joint in *Drugs: Get Lost!* or cheering when Peggy, the criminally shy misfit in *Square Peg,* got a date. It was rowdy and affectionate, and made Camille happy. Now, crowded around the TV, the cozy nest of children reminded Warren of happier times. The days of warmth and furniture. Camille used to sit between his legs, feeding him popcorn over her head.

He reached out to touch Camille's hand on the floor, but she flinched and scooted away from him. He recalled, vaguely, that she'd had some trouble with the movie—something to do with the advisory committee, maybe—but to be honest he didn't remember what it was she'd told him. Nor had he remembered the title: *Earth to My Body: What's Happening?* Like all Camille's movies, it was a frantic pastiche of styles. There was a brief scene from *Rebel Without a Cause,* which cut to a still of Bugs Bunny dressed up in drag, which cut to an animated illustration of a young girl's breasts growing larger, shown in stages like a balloon. The voiceover proclaimed, "The areola enlarges and becomes darker."

"Nice buds," Lyle said.

"Hubba hubba," Dustin said. He frowned. "I'm just joking."

Eventually—after a caption titled "Where's the Stork?"—the narrator began to speak of bolder subjects, such as the man inserting his penis into the vagina. Jonas appeared on-screen with some other kids. Dustin and Lyle cheered and stamped their feet, throwing popcorn at the TV. The kids were all wearing same-colored shirts, standing in front of some goalposts. It seemed to be some sort of soccer team. Could they really be named *The Sperm*? As the narrator intoned about "the long journey to fertilization," the soccer players began to run toward the camera, perhaps responding to a goal kick. The camera pulled back and Warren could see a second team as well: a group of girls with THE EGG printed on the back of their T-shirts, clasping hands in a circle. It wasn't soccer at all. It was a coed game of rugby. The Sperm's offense battered the Egg, trying to get at the ball. Jonas fought his way inside the circle while some kids from a third team—the Electrical Signal—began to beat up on Jonas's teammates. One of the boys fell to the ground, clutching his shin. The sequence ended, mystically, with the winning team holding up a victory banner on which someone had stenciled the words THE MIRACLE OF LIFE.

The room was uncharacteristically silent. Jonas, the star of the sequence, seemed as nonplussed as everyone. Warren glanced at his wife, who seemed to be waiting for some kind of affirmation.

"Where did you learn to play rugby?" he asked.

"Rugby?"

"It was football, right, Mom?" Lyle said. "That's why they were in a huddle."

Camille turned red. "Those were the egg!"

"I get it," Dustin said. "Like they were trying to protect it from getting smashed."

"*Trying* to," Jonas said proudly. Dustin held up his hand, and they high-fived.

"You didn't smash anything," Camille whispered.

"The football was the egg?" Warren suggested, trying to help out.

"It's metaphorical! Weren't you listening to the voiceover?"

"I was confused by the Cervical Mucus," Lyle said.

"I like that he actually had mucus," Dustin said. "Nasal, I mean."

Camille stood up. Her face was strange and ugly, lips tucked in as though she were trying to whistle through her teeth. "It would have made perfect sense, but you were too busy fucking cheering."

She stomped out of the room. Warren sat there, unable to speak. He looked at his kids: they were speechless as well, Lyle's hand clamped over her mouth as though she were the one who'd said a bad word.

Warren got up and followed his wife down the hall. He found her in the bedroom, standing by the window so he couldn't see her face. There was something erotic about her that he couldn't place. He looked closer and realized—to his astonishment—that she was smoking a cigarette. He'd only seen her smoke once before, on the day of their wedding. She'd disappeared in the middle of the reception and he'd found her outside near the Dumpster, dragging on a cigarette and watching a plane blink slowly across the sky, a look of inscrutable sadness on her face. Then, too, he'd been bitten with lust. He'd asked her what was wrong and she'd thrown her arms around him before he could see her face—overcome, she'd told him later, by the force of her love.

It seemed unlikely now that she was having similar thoughts. The windows were open and a breeze ruffled the curtains, sending bright ribbons of sunlight over the bed. Camille turned around. Her eyes were smeared with mascara, and for a moment he didn't recognize her, so distant were her thoughts from him.

"It's a good movie," Warren said, as gently as he could. "Very original."

"Please," she said. "How dumb do you think I am?"

Later, unable to sleep, Warren lay in bed counting his heartbeats. Camille was curled into a cannonball on the left side of the bed; she'd inched to the edge of the mattress, as though she'd rather imperil herself than accidentally touch him in the middle of the night. Listening to his wife's breathing, as familiar to him as his own heart, Warren thought again of their wedding. He'd been so nervous getting ready that he'd forgotten to snip the price tag from his tie. Calmly, in front of everyone, Camille had reached down and bitten through the plastic fastener with her teeth. She hadn't wanted to spit on the floor of the church and had kept the plastic twig in her mouth, tucked under her lip, for the duration of the ceremony. Afterward, glowing with triumph, she'd pulled it out of her mouth like a salmon bone.

At one point, this had been an anecdote they'd shared at parties, acting it out to make people laugh.

Warren went into the kitchen for a glass of water and flipped on the lights. Mr. Leonard was sitting on his doggy mat, still as a statue, staring at the wall ahead of him. He looked like he might jump out of his skin. Warren said the dog's name, but his eyes didn't blink. They began to frighten him. Could he be asleep? Treading softly, Warren walked over and put his hand on Mr. Leonard's head, which barely filled his palm. The poor mutt was trembling. Warren knelt in Mr. Leonard's bed and put his arms around him, trying to soothe the shaking from his bony ribs, holding him like a child.

CHAPTER 13

"Don't look at me," Lyle said, pulling up her jeans. "I hate my ass."

"I think it's beautiful," Hector said.

"It looks like a turnip."

He shrugged. "Some vegetables are very attractive."

"Is that supposed to be a joke?"

"I like the way you look." He grew serious, the way she preferred him. "You're like . . . I don't know. An angel or something."

They were in the guardhouse, listening to Hector's dopey, doom-smitten music. Lyle watched him straighten the name pin on his uniform, which had tipped up-and-down so that the little horseshoe insignia was spilling its luck. They'd had sex against the wall again: less frantic this time, but still briskly navigational. There was the sense of wanting to get home after a long day of hiking. *That was amazing*, Hector had said afterward, though she'd barely moved a muscle. It seemed to her there were some pretty low standards at work. It was like the Presidential Fitness Test she'd had to take in fifth grade: she hadn't done well, in fact had managed only a single pull-up, and they'd given her a certificate anyway. As for the craving itself, the one Hector's poem had aroused so torturously, they might as well have been doing actual pull-ups.

What she'd come to look forward to was this: the time afterward, when they sat together in the warm guardhouse and listened to the slow whoosh of the wind and watched the trees shiver in the floodlight. Sometimes they gave each other back rubs; Lyle would rub the soreness from his skinny shoulders, feeling the Braille of pimples on his skin. The street was deserted at 3 a.m., and it seemed to her that they were the last ones on earth. The clock was still broken from before, stuck permanently at 3:37 a.m. She punched the stop button on the boom box.

"Hey," he said. "That's a good song."

"I like it," she lied. "I just have a headache. From last night, I guess."

"You're hungover?"

"Shannon Jarrell and I got drunk again. After work."

He turned and looked at her. "Shannon? I thought you hated her."

"She's not so bad."

"This is the one who almost got you fired? Who's always staring at her legs?"

"We waited till closing this time. There wasn't anyone there." Lyle sat down on the floor, pulling her LIKE A STURGEON T-shirt over her knees. "She's smarter than she seems. She's got this list of words she keeps to improve her vocabulary. If you look like her, everyone just assumes you're stupid."

Hector smiled, his mouth pinned up at both corners. There was something about this smile that annoyed her. A smugness. *No matter how hard you try,* it seemed to say, *you'll always be rich.* He sat down beside her, the dank, walnuty smell of sex rising from his uniform.

"How come you haven't told your parents about us?" he asked casually.

"They'd shit a brick."

"I'm only nineteen."

"In California, that's statutory rape."

Hector frowned. "It's just weird seeing your mom at the gate. Like she has no idea. Yesterday we were talking in Spanish, and she told me you were pregnant."

"What?"

"*Embarazada.* I think she meant embarrassed." He looked at the silent street outside. "You've been to my place twice."

It was the first time Lyle suspected there was some hidden motive there, that he hadn't just invited her over for the hell of it. It was some kind of competition. She wondered if it was partly this that attracted her.

"Anyway," he said, "I thought you didn't care what your parents thought."

"I don't."

"So what's the big deal?"

"What do you want me to do?"

"You could start by letting me see your house." He laughed. "Or how about the garage? I hear it's really nice."

It was the first time she'd heard him be sarcastic. "All right," she said quietly. "Let me tell them first."

"When?"

"I don't know. Soon."

She expected—*wanted*—him to pin her down further. Instead he seemed to trust her, which made her feel worse.

"Some clown was shot on our corner yesterday," he said.

"Really?"

"A drive-by."

"Jesus." She put her arm around him, scooting closer. "Why do you say he's a clown?"

"That's what he was. An actual clown. Makeup and everything. He was on his way to a birthday party—this little girl that lives down the block."

"Jesus. Who would shoot a clown?"

"Lots of people, I guess." He shrugged. "The weird thing is, they still had the party. One of those big inflatable moonwalk things? You could see all the kids bouncing inside of it, screeching like crazy. It was shaped like a castle."

He was a lousy poet, but there was something sad and perplexing about him that reminded Lyle of a poem written maybe by someone else. She looked at Hector's truck in the floodlight, the word KAMELION spelled out on the back. Suddenly, it seemed impossibly touching.

"My mom's freaking out," he went on. "She wants to sell the house and move to the country."

"Why doesn't she?"

"She's been talking about it, like, for years. *El campo, el campo.* She's convinced she can't afford it."

"She can?" Lyle said.

"There's money in the bank. She's been saving up for it. It's why she won't put my grandmother in a nursing home. She wants

to make sure there's enough for a house, too. Meanwhile, Abuelita keeps sneaking out and getting glass in her feet." He flexed
one arm like a bodybuilder, cradling his elbow in the palm of his
hand. "Mexican for 'cheap.' It's what my dad used to do, whenever Mom bitched about money."

Lyle didn't have problems like this. Her problems were all
related to wishing people dead, not worrying about getting killed
herself. She had an idea, suddenly, that she would help Hector's
family. It wasn't a thought-out plan but a hazy impulse to actually
do something randomly kind rather than just drive around with a
stupid bumper sticker on your car. She reached into her jeans and
took out the business card her dad had given her, which was still
tucked into her front pocket. "My father has these houses. You
know, that he built. He told me he's selling them really cheaply."
She handed Hector the card. "Here. You could give him a call if
you want. At his office."

Hector laughed. "What? Houses around here?"

"No." She tried to remember what her dad had said. "They're
out in the desert somewhere."

"They're really that cheap?"

"He said they're, like, way below what they should be."

Hector stared at the card. He grew quiet, holding it between
his thumb and finger like a slide. Lyle felt a misty pride, as though
someone were watching her from an audience. The someone
looked like her mother but was smoking a cigarette and wearing
tall zippered boots. Lyle flipped the little switch on the boom box
to RADIO: a staticky pop, then the gooey strains of "I Just Called
to Say I Love You."

"God, I hate this song," she said.

Hector wasn't listening. "I think I'm in love with you," he said
softly.

"From the bottom of your heart?" she joked, lolling her head
like Stevie Wonder. She was making fun of a blind person.

"No," he said. "More than that."

Lyle's heart was pounding. "Don't be stupid. How can it be
more than that?"

"I don't know. From the underness of my heart."

"The underness?"

"You know. Below the bottom."

She wrinkled her nose, showing how moronic he was. Secretly, though, she imagined a hole under the earth, dark as a bomb shelter, his love hunkered down there in case the world got blown to pieces. A devotion that would survive anything. Lyle liked the idea of this. She touched Hector's hand, picturing Shannon Jarrell's face when she told her.

CHAPTER 14

Camille watered the agapanthus, trying to figure out why Warren's shirts were spread out across the rosebushes. They'd been put out to dry, six of them in a row, like a chain of paper dolls. Evidently he'd washed them himself. It wouldn't have upset her so much, except that he'd been taking his shirts to the cleaner's for fifteen years. It was a beautiful day, clear and breezy, eddies of darker green moving through the lawn. Camille dragged the hose farther through the grass and watered the shirts, one after another, watching them darken under her spray.

Sometimes she doubted it—her suspicion that he was having an affair—but then Warren would come home from work with his sneakers on, flashing her those exhausted, frightened, shame-ridden looks, rushing to the phone before she could answer it. Last Sunday at dinner he'd drunk five glasses of water. Whatever he was hiding, he could barely look her in the eye. He'd ordered new furniture for her, but if this was meant to soothe his conscience it didn't seem to be working.

Inside again, she took off her cashmere shawl and hung it on the peg in the kitchen. She'd begun wearing the thing defiantly, even when it was warm out. Let the kids make fun of her: What the hell did they know about fashion? They could whistle like moronic cowboys, but the girl at Nordstrom had called it "gorgeous." When Camille had gone back, days later, the girl had remembered her, wrapping her in the shawl and showing her off to the other salesclerks as if she were a vision of glamour.

Camille went to the bathroom and changed her tampon, dropping it in the trash. Stress must have messed up her cycle. She should have been ecstatic, or at least wonderfully relieved. Hadn't she spent the last few weeks puffing cigarettes, praying that the problem would go away, gulping smoke like poison? Or at least, isn't that what she'd been doing unconsciously? And lo and behold, she wasn't pregnant after all, her problems on the embryo front were solved.

She was mysteriously, savagely disappointed.

She wandered into the kitchen, where the kids were sitting at the table. It seemed like they were always in the kitchen. Didn't they ever use the other rooms? Camille stepped over Mr. Leonard, who was staring miserably at the bag of Cool Ranch Doritos being demolished by her children.

"Why were you watering Dad's shirts?" Lyle asked her.

"Because he left them in the garden."

Lyle seemed to accept this. They all did, in fact. Since she'd cursed that night in the living room, they'd regarded Camille with a leery sort of awe. She pointed at the bag on the table. "What does that mean exactly? Cool Ranch?"

"Means delicious," Dustin said.

"Means they can't call them Powdery Gunk," Lyle said.

Dustin closed his eyes. "There's a ranch, and it's cool, and you're, like, kicking back with all the other Doritos."

Camille nodded and began to wash out the pot to the coffee-maker.

"Hey," Dustin said. "Aren't you going to tell us about the food pyramid?"

"You're old enough to make your own decisions."

They seemed disappointed. Camille wondered if she'd been wrong about them, if maybe on some level—deep down—they actually looked forward to her nagging. Jonas seemed particularly forlorn. He was dressed head to toe in orange again, the third time this week. She'd forgotten to buy him more orange socks at Nordstrom. Perhaps this was why he seemed angry, refusing to catch her eye or even look up from the table.

Lyle got up, as if annoyed by her presence, and Camille made up an excuse to follow her, trailing her into her room. She had an overwhelming desire to confide in her daughter, not only about Warren's being in love with another woman, but about her quaky, unexpected grief over not being pregnant. Lyle ignored her, leaning into the bathroom mirror to put on some lipstick. Camille was amazed to see that it was pink.

"Where are you going?"

"Out."

Camille nodded. The bathroom smelled like a fashion magazine. Makeup was strange enough—had she begun wearing perfume? "What's the matter with Jonas? Is he upset for some reason?"

Lyle shrugged. "Maybe his feet hurt."

"What are you talking about?"

"You were supposed to pick him up from fencing today. At two. He waited for an hour and then walked home by himself, all the way from the rec center."

"Oh shit." Camille shut her eyes. "I've had a lot on my mind. I'm rewriting *Earth to My Body,* the voiceover. It's been a bad week."

"Don't you mean *summer?*"

She opened her eyes, trying to dispel the image of her son trudging up Portuguese Bend Road in his fencing jacket. "Does Jonas feel that way?"

"Why do you think he dresses in orange?"

"I haven't the faintest idea," Camille said.

"God, Mom, wake up. He's sending up a flare. The other day I dropped him off at the mall, and he kept talking about how he might get abducted like Mandy Rogers. He sounded *excited.*"

"Why would he want to be Mandy Rogers?"

"Are you kidding? It's like a lovefest. Have you driven by her house lately?"

Camille's heart lodged in her chest. The thought of Mandy Rogers's lawn, covered in prayers and toy cowboy hats and WE LOVE YOU spelled out in flowers, made her want to cry. She couldn't drive by the place without thinking of Lyle. What would she ever do if she disappeared? Camille tried to pretend that her sons meant just as much to her, that losing them would be exactly the same, but deep in her heart she knew this wasn't true. Once, when Lyle was a baby, Camille had locked her in the car by accident. She'd been utterly undone, trapped outside the window as Lyle screamed and flailed and kicked, trying to escape the plastic prison of her car seat. It was like watching someone drown. Camille had no choice but to leave Lyle where she was and run to find a phone. She still remembered them vividly, the worst fifteen minutes of her life: waiting for the police to arrive, Lyle wailing so hard she'd begun to claw at her face, Camille weeping hysterically outside and trying to pry bricks from a wall to smash the window.

She wanted a cigarette—a deep, ferocious craving—and then was ashamed of thinking of it. There was a radio sitting on the shelf, plugged into the wall near the bathtub. Noticing the stupidity of this arrangement made her feel slightly less awful. "Lyle, for heaven's sake. Please don't put the radio there."

"I like to listen to it in the shower."

"You'll electrocute yourself." Camille squinted at the radio, which had a sticker on it that said PANTERA. "Where did you get this anyway?"

"Someone gave it to me."

"Who?"

"Hector," she said quietly.

A boy. Camille felt happy for her—also strangely bereft. "Someone from your class?"

"No. He's older." Lyle fiddled with her belt. "Actually, you know him."

"I do?"

She turned to Camille, as though craving her approval. A pale, awkward girl in lipstick. Was it possible that all her hostility, her inscrutable annoyance, was actually fear? "Hector?" Lyle said. "The guy who works at the gate?"

Camille laughed. "The one with the mustache?"

Lyle's face turned red. It was an awful face, her lips sucked in like an old woman's. Camille stared at her daughter's lipstick.

"He doesn't speak English."

"He speaks perfect English," Lyle said, slamming the door to the medicine cabinet. "They came here when he was four. Anyway, what difference would it make?"

"There's a Spanish sticker on his radio," Camille said lamely.

"That's a *band*. Jesus. Why am I even talking to you?" Lyle narrowed her eyes, her face red now but not from embarrassment. "We're having sex, Mom. I'd know if he spoke English, wouldn't I?"

"You're having *sex*? With a man you barely know?"

"I know him perfectly well."

"Is he here legally?"

"Oh Jesus. Wow. I knew you were full of shit with your acts of kindness, but I didn't know you were racist."

"I'm not racist. Please don't say that. I just don't think you should be having sex with some strange man."

"You mean a *Mexican* man," Lyle said. "Who works in a guardhouse."

Camille ignored this. "Do you even know where he lives?"

"Jesus. I've been to his house."

"He owns a *house*?"

"Mexican-Americans can't own houses?"

"That's not what I said. I'm just wondering how he can afford one."

"He lives with some roommates. They own it together." Lyle looked at Camille, her pink mouth pressed into a smile. "We go there to fuck."

Camille couldn't speak. She left Lyle in the bathroom and went into the kitchen and turned on the sink, picturing some men with grubby baseball caps watching her daughter through a peephole. She shook this racist, disturbing image from her head. Who did the bastard think he was? Maybe he'd preyed on other girls as well. It would be a good job to have, if you wanted to sleep with people's daughters. Trembling, Camille flipped through her Rolodex and found the number for Herradura Estates management. She picked up the phone, wondering if she could control her voice, but couldn't bring herself to dial. It was too much—the thought of Lyle despising her for the rest of her life. Perhaps Warren would know what to do. He'd said he'd be at the office all day, working on some elevations. A twang of love went through her. She dialed his office, longing to hear his voice.

Music thudded up the driveway. Pantera? Camille peered out the window, poised for attack, but it was only a beautiful blond girl slouched behind the wheel of a convertible Bug. She was wearing a tank top and sunglasses. Lyle came out of the house in one of her gigantic T-shirts, sweatshirt wrapped around her waist, laughing at something Camille couldn't hear. Her face in its garish lipstick looked like a woman's. Camille started to cry. She stood there while the convertible backed down the driveway, listening to the phone ring and ring and ring.

CHAPTER 15

On his way out to Antelope Valley to meet the Granillos, Warren kept the Renault in the slow lane in case the muffler decided to fall off. The view from the freeway was soothingly apocalyptic. Go Kart World, Toyota Planet, Land of Sheet Metal—he'd seen the names so many times that they failed to alarm him. Watching cars overtake him and zip back into his lane, steady as water around a rock, Warren ran through the spiel he was going to give Mrs. Granillo as he showed her Durango number 4, the house of her dreams. It seemed, from her voice on the phone, that he might actually have a shot. He would not make the same mistake he'd made with the couple from Riverside. If she asked about the dump, he would tell her it was a shopping mall. He would talk it up, sing to her of the Mojave International Galleria, tell the struggling woman about all its beautiful, air-conditioned, unbeatably priced amenities.

For the first time in weeks, his panic began to lift. It felt just like that: the lifting of a weight. He'd sell the house; word-of-mouth would spread. He'd get his furniture back, his Visa, maybe even his car. Of course, they'd have to leave Herradura Estates—but his life, his family, would be saved.

Rounding the San Gabriels, Warren got off on Highway 14 and began the long descent into the valley, an endless, moon-stark desert stretching into the distance, spiked here and there with Joshua trees poking up from the dirt. Their arms branched haphazardly in the sun, like the thoughts of a lunatic. The trees, the Mojave, seemed to appear out of nowhere. Warren still found it beautiful—breathtaking even—though he regarded it with the begrudging respect you might have for an enemy.

He searched for the poppy preserve that had once been a selling point, trying to spot a few dreamy flashes of orange in the hills, but the summer drought had rendered them as brown as their surroundings.

He pulled off the highway and followed the long dirt road to a block of brand-new homes, his very own ghost town, parking in front of the strip of grass meant to evoke images of croquet matches and Fourth of July picnics. Warren couldn't afford the astronomical water bill, and now the grass had turned to a crunchy brown stubble more befitting the desert. The words AUBURN FIELDS glared at him from the engraved rock sitting in the stubble. The name had been Larry's idea. "Fields" implied living grass, even auburn ones, but when Warren had mentioned this to Larry recently he'd laughed in his face. "You're right," he'd said. "We should have called it Brown Dirt."

Warren took a deep breath. The Granillos were there already, parked up at the gate. The sun cuffed his face as he got out of the car to greet them. Mrs. Granillo was short and attractively dressed, wearing high heels and a sleeveless dress that showed off the dimpled drape of her arms. Her wrist, heavy with bracelets, clattered when he shook her hand. She introduced her son, who was nervously touching his mustache. He didn't offer his hand.

"I recognize you," Warren said, surprised. "Do you work with Lyle?"

"I'm a security guard. At Herradura Estates."

"Right!" Warren realized he was frowning. "Wow. Who knew. She's really been working the neighborhood."

The son reddened. "We're friends."

"Of course. I didn't mean—"

"My son like her very much," Mrs. Granillo said.

Warren looked at them, a ray of sadness spoiling his optimism. In doing his dirty work, had Lyle pretended to befriend this sullen-looking kid? Now here they were, mother and son, imagining some deep connection to his daughter.

Mrs. Granillo wandered over to the red-striped gate, inspecting it with a look of reverent mistrust. Larry had had it installed first thing, before any of the houses were built. Just having a gate out front raised your equity by 15 percent. According to Larry, it was the "honey that drew the bees."

"I never live with a gate before," Mrs. Granillo said, glancing around. "No person?"

"It's automatic." To demonstrate, Warren pulled a key card out of his wallet and stuck it in the little slot. The gate went up with a lurch. "There's a video camera right in here. It feeds to a monitor, a security company, who watch for any suspicious activity."

She laughed. "Don't say to my son. He'll be out of work."

Warren walked them through the gate and into the paved block of nearly identical tract homes. It had amazed him, when they were first choosing the colors, to discover there were so many shades of brown. Mountain Elk, Fedora, Olive Leaf. The idea was to match the natural hues of the desert. Like the desert, too, you could walk into any of the houses and hopelessly search for life. Beyond the small clump of houses stretched a vast clearing of dirt, empty lots graded for no purpose and stacked with framing lumber still bound with metal cord.

"*Mira,*" Mrs. Granillo said, entering Durango number 4 and pointing at the plastic chandelier dangling from the ceiling in the front hall. "I never imagine one day I have a *candelabra.*" She glanced at her son, who was inspecting the chandelier with a skeptical look. "I wish Jorge were here."

"Jorge?" Warren asked politely.

"My husband. He died three years ago. It was his dream for life—to own a house."

They walked into the living room. Mrs. Granillo wandered toward the fireplace and began to talk about her husband again, how he used to reminisce about the fires they had growing up in Chiapas. Warren failed to explain that it was merely decorative. He showed Mrs. Granillo and her son the air-conditioning and recessed lighting, the panel doors and stain-grade cabinets. Each time he showed her something new, Mrs. Granillo mentioned her husband and how she wished he were there to see it.

"Oh, Jorge would have so much love the bathroom," she said, her face lighting up. "He always sweared at the bathtub because it leak. But what I can do? I have to wash my mother every day."

"Your mother lives with you?"

"Yes, *claro.* This is for each of us." She looked around for her son, who'd disappeared into another room. "She is sick in the mind. How do you call it? *Está un poco tocada.*"

"Alzheimer's?"

She nodded. Warren had started to sweat from his armpits. A strange sort of sweat, cold and silvery, as if it belonged to a different climate. Mrs. Granillo's son met up with them in the kitchen, his face still pinched into a frown. He said something to his mother in Spanish. Ignoring him, Mrs. Granillo went over to the sink and inspected the InSinkErator, flipping the switch on the wall. It moaned on cue. She tested the pullout sprayer, hosing the window by accident.

"Look," she said to her son, "I no longer have to hunch over for dishes."

"I don't know. It's pretty far from everything."

"*Eso es!* No one will bother us."

"How are you going to look after Abuelita if you have to drive forty miles for food?"

This was Warren's cue. He looked out the window at the construction site in the distance and watched a backhoe materialize from the gigantic cloud of dust, buzzing like a mosquito in the empty desert. The dinosaurian neck of a crane loomed over the haze. Surely he was imagining it, the whiff of sourness already in the air.

"They're building a supermarket," Warren said, avoiding Mrs. Granillo's eyes. "A big one. A shopping mall as well."

"Where?" Mrs. Granillo's son asked.

"Right there. You can see it." To get a better view, Warren led them to the sliding doors that opened on the deck. He felt okay— less nauseated—if he directed his words at the glass. "Breaking ground as we speak."

"All the way out here?"

"Well, it's a high-growth area. Very in demand."

The son looked at him skeptically, picking up on something in his voice. Warren did his best to look him in the eye. It was his family or theirs, he reminded himself. Mrs. Granillo opened one of the cabinets and began swinging it back and forth.

"That's solid-wood construction," Warren said. "Maple."

"Very nice," Mrs. Granillo said.

Her son said something in Spanish, peering inside the cabinet. Warren thought he heard the word *barato.*

"What did you say?"

The young man shifted uncomfortably. "I said it looks like particleboard. The cabinet box. I installed cabinets one summer for my uncle."

"Lots of them use particleboard," Warren said, frowning. "What you want to watch out for is MDF, I think. Fiberboard."

"Actually, they both sag over time. You should have seen some of the carcasses we replaced." The boy opened one of the drawers under the counter. "Looks like the joints are glued, too," he mumbled to himself.

"I don't think is so bad," Mrs. Granillo said. "You should see what I have for fifteen years. The paint at least doesn't peel, with lead for babies."

Her son walked over to the sink and turned on the hot water faucet, which groaned obstreperously. "The faucet isn't sealed properly."

"I can get the plumber out here tomorrow."

"Very agree of you," Mrs. Granillo said.

"*Y esto es plástico,*" the boy said to his mother, touching the dish towel bar.

Warren turned to him with hatred. The kid's face was flushed, his chin raised as if anticipating an insult. For the first time, Warren saw that the boy's pride was on the line. The sale was slipping away out of some mystifying need to prove his own power. Warren wanted to beg or scream or kiss the boy's shoes. In desperation, he grabbed the plastic bar and yanked it easily out of the wall. The two sets of nail holes, poorly aligned, looked like startled faces.

"We can replace the fixtures. Chrome. Whatever you'd like."

Mrs. Granillo and her son stared at him. Warren fantasized about trashing the whole place, starting with the fixtures in the kitchen and then moving on to the walls and carpets and plastic chandeliers. He laid the bar gently on the counter.

"Look, honestly, I know that some of the finishing is . . . cost-effective. That's how we manage to keep the price low. But I guarantee you the construction is better than sound. We don't skimp when it comes to essentials." Warren turned to Mrs. Granillo. "With the money you save, you could install five new kitchens in here if you wanted."

Mrs. Granillo looked at her son, who seemed to have relaxed a bit. Perhaps it was all that he wanted: for Warren to admit the kitchen was cheap. They moved on to the bathroom, but the boy did not mention the plastic towel racks or vinyl floor curling at one corner from the heat. For the first time, Warren noticed he was wearing a homemade T-shirt that said I ♥ THE BERING STRAIT. A vague premonition crept across his scalp.

"We'll think about it," Mrs. Granillo's son said at the end of the tour.

Warren felt a tug of hope. "Yes. Please. But don't mull it over *too* long. You're the sixth family I've shown a Durango to this week."

"Do they build a cinema with the mall?" Mrs. Granillo asked, staring at the crane in the distance. "And a pharmacy?"

"I'm betting yes," Warren said.

"Ly didn't tell me it was so far out in the boonies," the boy said.

"Ly?" Warren asked.

"Lyle." The boy blushed, checking his watch. "We can find out for sure, Mama. Stop on the way out and talk to the construction crew. They ought to be able to tell us what they're building."

CHAPTER 16

Rat Beach was calm and almost deserted. Lyle strolled along the beach with Shannon, skirting the tidewater and feeling warm lumps of sand under her arches. There were no waves to speak of but a few surfers were out in the water anyway, their hair dry from the sun. Walking with Shannon, Lyle felt a shy flush of excitement, as though she were escorting a celebrity. Sunbathers dropped their books or adjusted their sunglasses, pretending not to stare. Not that Lyle blamed them. Shannon's body in a bikini was tall and perfect, marred only by a dark mole just below her belly button. Somehow it seemed less like a flaw than a public service: the YOU ARE HERE dot on a map. Lyle kept her own stomach bandaged in a towel, which she'd tied scrupulously around her waist. If she forgot about the towel, if she stared at the sand fleas in front of her and avoided looking at her pale and veiny feet, she felt almost beautiful, as though the sunbathers were ogling her as well.

Shannon had asked Lyle to the beach. Actually, what she'd said was: *I bet you could get a tan if you tried.* Lyle hadn't known this was an invitation until much later, while she was Z-ing out the register for the night and Shannon had asked casually when she should pick Lyle up for their "tanning session." She'd started to make up an excuse, but the allure of going with Shannon Jarrell to the beach, of basking in the flattering light of her beauty for a day and absorbing some of it herself, was too powerful to resist.

They chose a spot near the lifeguard tower. Shannon took off her baseball cap and actually shook out her hair, like someone in a beer commercial. Lyle sat down without taking off her towel.

"Aren't you going to lie out?"

"In a minute," Lyle said. "I'm just resting."

"Here," Shannon said, handing her a bottle of sun stuff. Lyle took off her sunglasses. It was Hawaiian Tropic Dark Tanning Lotion, SPF 4. *For the Natural Tan of the Islands,* the label boasted. This seemed racist or overly egalitarian, Lyle wasn't sure which. She handed the bottle back.

"I can't wear that. I'll fry to a crisp."

Shannon frowned. "No, you won't. I use it every day."

"I've got my own," Lyle said.

She rummaged through her bag and took out her SPF 15. Shannon shook her head in disgust, smearing a greasy glob of Hawaiian Tropic into her shoulder. It smelled sweet and dangerous, like a piña colada.

"That stuff's like for little kids," Shannon said. "You might as well wear a blanket. Don't you want to get tan?"

Lyle did want to get tan; she'd even bought a bikini at the mall. She watched Shannon slather herself in Hawaiian Tropic and then rub it into her skin, working slowly down her body—chest, stomach, legs—greasing each part to a buttery shine before moving to the next. It was like watching someone turn blissfully to glass. Maybe Shannon was right; maybe Lyle was just paranoid. Maybe she'd underestimated her ability to tan like an islander. If Shannon could use SPF 4, why couldn't she? After all, it was *four* times her natural skin protection. If you thought about it mathematically, four times was a lot. Lyle would have paid good money to be *twice* as unghostly as she was. She put the SPF 15 back in her bag. When she asked for the Hawaiian Tropic, Shannon seemed almost proud of her, nodding in approval before offering to rub the warm, coconuty grease into her back.

Fully greased, Lyle undid the towel at her waist and fixed herself a bed in the sand. She'd been too embarrassed to bring a book, so now she had no choice but to lie there like Shannon, the sun roasting her face. It was sort of relaxing at first, living the life of an islander, but before long she began to sweat. Or rather, began to melt like a glacier. Liquid streamed from her armpits. It puddled in her neck. It stung her eyes and trickled down her temples. It filled her ears, gradually, until she could hear the distant *swoosh* of her heartbeat. She peeked at Shannon, who was lying perfectly comatose. She seemed content to lie there forever. Lyle closed her eyes again and tried to think of how tan she was going to get, to ignore the sensation of being roasted on a spit, but her body seemed to expand against her will, inflating to three times its size, getting bigger and bigger until she felt like the Michelin Man in the Rose Bowl parade, untethered and monstrous. She opened her eyes again, trying to get rid of the feeling. A little hot tub of sweat had formed in her belly button. She could feel herself getting burned—horribly, irrevocably—but perhaps this was just in her head as well.

She wondered what Hector would say if he could see her. The thought filled her with shame.

A boy with scraggly wet hair was jogging in their direction, carrying a surfboard under one arm. Lyle put her sunglasses on but did not have time to cover her thighs. The boy walked up to Shannon and shook his head like a dog, drizzling some water on her face. Shannon sprang onto her elbows, scowling. The boy had little coronas of hair around his nipples.

"You're killing me," he said. "I can't sleep."

"Don't be stupid," Shannon said. She was laughing.

The guy scrunched his forehead, as though in pain. "I'm like a Jewish kid at Christmas."

"Who was that?" Lyle asked after he'd left.

"Some stoner. He goes to Miraleste."

"Does Charlie know about him?"

"Kidding?" Shannon said, making a face. "He's jealous enough already."

Lyle watched the stoner jog up the beach and seek out a crowd of other surfers. The four boys all glanced at Shannon, like a meal they couldn't afford. Maybe that was what it was like to be beautiful: overpriced. You flirted with whomever you felt like, because you knew they didn't have the money.

"What are you doing this weekend?" Shannon asked. "I'm thinking of having a little party. Just some friends. My 'rents are going to be in Ireland."

Lyle was too flattered to speak. The strength of her pleasure embarrassed her. "Ugh! I can't. We're going camping."

Shannon shrugged. "No biggie."

"Joshua Tree. My family does it every year. Four hours in the car with my mom, it's a real fucking blast."

"Your mom's a drag?"

"No. Just a racist bitch."

Shannon looked at her, visibly impressed. "I'm burning up," she said. "Let's go in the water."

"Go ahead. I think I'll stay here."

"Suit yourself."

From her towel, Lyle watched Shannon amble down to the water and wade out into the ocean before diving into a delicious-looking wave. She surfaced as a floating head, sleek and seal-like. The truth is, Lyle wanted to go swimming more than anything. She wanted to dive into the water like Shannon and escape the misery of heat and boredom. But she was too embarrassed. It would mean walking down to the beach with her white stomach and tuberous ass. She knew it shouldn't matter, that no one really cared who she was, which made her hate herself even more.

Later, Shannon wanted to head down to the Snack Shack for a frozen Snickers bar. Lyle put her T-shirt back on, cinching the towel carefully around her waist. She'd hoped that lying on the beach for an hour would somehow make her less self-conscious, but it had only increased her feelings of ugliness. Not only was she freakishly pale, she smelled bad from sweating so much. A group of junior lifeguards were gathered on the beach, chasing one another with a mammoth entrail of seaweed, and Lyle and Shannon had to hike up the beach to get around them. The boys looked in their direction and giggled. Lyle imagined they were laughing at her appearance. As they neared the Snack Shack, the beach grew more crowded, a maze of bodies: it seemed like everyone was staring at her and Shannon, wondering how in the hell they could possibly be friends.

Under the cliffs, near the chain-link fence, was a skinny man sitting in a beach chair and fiddling with a boom box at his feet. Hector. He was with his grandmother. Lyle's first reaction was relief. A burst of heavy metal drifted down the beach. When he turned to face the sun, she saw that he was wearing cutoff jeans and a belt, wet from the water. A delta of black hair glistened on his chest.

Hector looked in her direction, starting in surprise before bursting into a smile. He waved at her. Damp, his mustache looked dead and stringy. His grandmother was wearing a down vest the color of antifreeze, sprinkling sand on her feet, oblivious to the music roaring from the stereo. Lyle put her head down and kept walking.

"Who was that?" Shannon said.

"Who?"

"That guy that just waved at you."

"I don't know."

Shannon looked at her strangely. "Does he work on your house or something?"

"I've never seen him before."

"Wee-*yerd*." Shannon glanced behind her. "He's staring at us. What a perv." She leaned toward Lyle, pretending to whisper in her ear. "I think you should fuck him."

"What?"

"Go over there and fuck his brains out."

Lyle tried to laugh. "Yeah, right."

"Watch this."

Shannon turned around so that she was walking backward and pulled down one side of her bikini top, flashing a breast in Hector's direction. A triangle of white skin, almost as pale as Lyle's legs. She flipped around again, laughing.

"Now we're screwed," she said, tugging her baseball cap over her eyes. "He's going to rape us."

There were over seven thousand nerve endings in each of your feet. Lyle had read this somewhere. She tried to feel them as she walked. She wondered if it was a form of protection, to have so many nerves in such an impractical place.

"Are you all right?" Shannon asked.

"Yeah. Just a headache."

At the Snack Shack, Shannon ordered a Snickers bar from the cashier, who had bad skin and owly glasses steamed into bedroom winks. He looked like the guys at school who wore trench coats in spring and played D & D in the quad every afternoon. "Five dollars for the potentate," he said in a fake British accent, when Shannon handed him her money. He snapped the bill with two hands. "Not much of a ransom, but he's not much of a king!"

"What a dork," Shannon said afterward, sitting at a picnic table. "What does that mean anyway? Potentate?"

"Like a ruler," Lyle murmured.

Shannon sucked some chocolate from her fingers and pulled her lab notebook from her bag. Lyle watched some kids playing paddleball in the breakwater, feeling sick to her stomach. When she glanced back at Shannon, she'd added a word to her list:

POTINTATE. For some reason, it made Lyle feel even worse. She told Shannon she'd spelled it incorrectly.

"Doesn't matter. I just have to recognize it."

"What do you mean?" Lyle said.

"On the PSATs. It's multiple choice."

The sickness wobbled up her throat. Shannon put the notebook back in her bag. She smiled and then touched Lyle's hand. "Let's go find our friend the stoner. I bet he's got something to wash down this Snickers."

"Go ahead," Lyle said. "I think I left my wallet by our stuff."

She sloped up the hot sand again toward the fence. It wasn't too late. She could go back and apologize, she could kiss him on the lips, she could explain somehow that she hadn't recognized him through the tint of her sunglasses. Perhaps he'd believe her. Lyle's towel fell from her waist but she didn't stop, jogging toward the cliffs, though she could see already he was gone.

That evening, in the living room, Lyle sprawled on the lounge chair her dad had dragged in from the backyard. Her skin was on fire, radiating from every pore. It was like a machine she couldn't turn off. If she moved an inch, if she tried to lift an arm to scratch her nose, her body responded with a torturous ripple. She wondered if you could actually die from sunburn. It was a comforting idea. Her legs were particularly bad off. Visually, there was no way to describe them. They were "red" in the way that the universe was "large." Lyle closed her eyes and dreamed of shedding her skin like a snake, slithering into the cool, cool grass, leaving it in a burning puddle on the floor.

She was shivering. Which was weird, since she was pouring out heat. There was a contradiction there, but Lyle couldn't think clearly enough to resolve it.

On the TV, Mr. Roarke was talking to a little girl whose parents had been killed in a plane crash. Tattoo, that lovable midget, stared poignantly at his feet. She'd thought a *Fantasy Island* rerun might distract her, but the tropical sun and bikini-clad tourists were making her feel even worse. The remote control lay on the rug near her feet, where it had fallen off the armrest. For the past twenty minutes, she'd been trying to reach it with her toes, managing only to further its migration across the room.

She closed her eyes again. Her heart was beating more quickly than usual, actually stinging the sunburn on her neck. She tried to distract herself by thinking of a time when she could still move. In an earlier life, when her skin was cool and touchable, she used to sit at the foot of the couch, shirt pulled up to her neck, while her mother wrote delicious things on her back. First the touch of her fingernail, gentle as an ant, then the mysterious back-sized line that formed into a letter, fading like a secret as soon as it appeared. They did this for a whole summer when Lyle was small. It was better than talking, because her mom said things she never would have spoken out loud: not just I LOVE YOU, but MY BEAUTIFUL DAUGHTER IS FIVE and LOVELIEST GIRL IN THE GALAXY LIVES HERE. It was as if her mind was talking and not her mouth. But Lyle's favorite sentences were the ones she lost track of or couldn't follow, the words turning strange and doodly and complex, containing her whole mother inside of them. When the sentences ended—a gentle poke for a period, as though her mom were pressing a doorbell—Lyle could never be sure they'd happened at all.

Beyond the velvety lilt of Mr. Roarke, Lyle heard the back door open, a tumble of boys entering the kitchen. Their voices rang with good health. Mr. Leonard made some fainthearted attempts at a bark before the voices floated into the locality of Lyle's head.

"Jesus. What happened to you?"

She opened her eyes. Dustin, munching on an apple, was standing there with Mark Biesterman and Brent Tarwater. They looked impossibly vertical.

"Please leave me alone," Lyle whispered.

"UV exposure," Biesty said. "Leading cause of skin cancer."

"You shouldn't keep this on the floor," Tarwater said, picking up the remote and placing it conscientiously on top of the TV set. "Someone might break it."

"Wow, you really are bad off," Dustin said, squatting next to Lyle. His eyes widened in pity or alarm, she couldn't tell. "Your face is all, like, swollen. Haven't you heard of sunscreen?"

"Will you please please all just fuck off and leave me alone?"

"What's with you lately?" Dustin turned to go. "Some guy called earlier. I came in to tell you, but I guess you don't care. Victor or something."

He signaled to Biesty and Tarwater, who flicked off the TV on his way out. The screen fizzed in the silence. Alone again, Lyle outlined the steps of her mission. Operation Roomward Advancement. If she made it to her room, she could call Hector and ask his forgiveness. She would explain the situation—basically, that Shannon had brainwashed her, that she hadn't recognized him at first and then was too humiliated by Shannon's behavior to say hello—and he would understand and continue to love her from the underness of his heart.

First, though, she had to move. She had to decamp from the chaise and make her way through the kitchen, risking the perilously feeble attacks of Mr. Leonard. She gritted her teeth and tried to sit up in the chaise, arms stinging with pain. She did this twice before chickening out. Even though it wasn't His specialty, she prayed to God for a random act of kindness and tried a third time and managed to work herself into an upright position, shivering with pain, feeling as though an enormous Band-Aid had been ripped from her body. Her teeth were chattering. She waited to catch her breath. Haltingly, she shimmied on her ass to the edge of the chaise, feeling a vague sense of triumph. The feeling grew as she stood up and began to walk. The meagerest steps seemed like a victory. Maybe she wasn't an atheist after all. She minced her way to the kitchen, an excruciating voyage, shorts scraping like sandpaper against her thighs.

Luckily, Mr. Leonard was fast asleep in the sunlight from the window, twitching his ears and whimpering into the pillow of his doggy bed. Lyle crept past him and tiptoed across the deliciously cool tiles until she reached the safety of her room, closing the door behind her. Panting, she sat on the bed and looked out the window. A peacock was roaming the backyard, hobbled by feathers, dragging its glamorous carpet of eyes through the grass. She listened to its demented meows, feeling an affinity for its plight.

Before she lost the nerve, she picked up the phone and called Hector's house. It took her a long time to punch in the number. It rang five times, an eternity. She was about to hang up when Hector answered the phone, breathless as usual. For a second, she imagined he'd already forgiven her.

Lyle tried to explain everything—the beach, Shannon, how miserable she felt—but it just came out in a jumble of words. Hector's breathing had stopped. Static on the line, a distant mouse patter of voices.

"Hector? I don't know what I'm doing. What I'm trying to say." Her plan for blaming Shannon had deserted her, vanished as soon as she'd heard his voice. She had to keep herself from crying. "I guess I wouldn't blame you. If you hated me."

His grandmother yelled in the background, ranting at the TV. Something about the police and their ugly sunglasses. He'd be eating dinner right now, getting ready to go to work.

"I'm scared. I'm so sunburned I can't move." Hector's breathing returned, faint as a whisper. "My arms are swelling. They're going to blister, I think. I think maybe I need to go to the hospital."

"It hurts?" he said finally, in a tender voice.

"Yes."

"Your whole body?"

She felt a voluptuous relief. "Everywhere. I'm like a beet."

"Good," he said. "I hope you die of sunstroke."

He hung up. She put the phone on its cradle, thinking he might call back. Anything was possible. She was shivering, nauseated, unfathomably thirsty. She needed to take a bath, a cold one, but how could she possibly wiggle out of her clothes? Lyle opened the drawer of her bedside table, pulling out the pair of scissors she used to make decals for her T-shirts. Gingerly, she began to cut off her shorts, starting at the waist and snipping down each leg like a paramedic. They were her favorite shorts, but she didn't care. She did the same to her T-shirt and bikini bottoms, leaving them in a Lyleless puddle on the bed.

Naked, she walked to the bathroom. She still had the scissors in her hand. She had them, strangely enough, when she stepped shivering into the cold water of the bath. The water soothed her skin at first, cooling it for a minute or two before the burning came back again, patient as a shark. She opened the scissors and touched one of the blades against her thigh. She wished her mother would come home. She was always at work, making those ridiculous videos. Lyle remembered the scene in *Depression Hits Home* when Jill, the troubled teen who "just wants to disappear," pours the bottle of pills plaintively into her hand. It was one of Lyle's and Dustin's favorites: they still watched it sometimes when her mom wasn't around, shouting, "Do it! Do it!" at the TV.

But Lyle did not want to disappear. If this were *Fantasy Island,* she would tell Mr. Roarke what she wanted: to be around afterward. To watch her family pull her out of the blood-marbled water, sobbing like children. Understanding, for the first time, what they'd lost. Wasn't it everyone's fantasy? She imagined the grief, ugly and delectable, of her mother's face. And Hector. Hector would never recover. *I hope you die,* he'd said. He would love her forever, crippled with remorse.

But this wasn't *Fantasy Island.* No supernatural hoteliers would bring her back to life so she could savor her revenge.

She put the scissors on the rim of the sink, where she wouldn't step on them.

On the shelf over the toilet, still plugged in from yesterday, was the radio Hector had given her. She'd forgotten to turn it on. Lyle slid diagonally in the tub, groped one foot up the wall, and then pushed the power button with her toe. The music blared on, startling her. "I'll Tumble 4 Ya." She'd considered it to be a new low in the Culture Club oeuvre, but listening to the lyrics for the first time—*Downtown we'll drown, we're in our never splendor*—the song seemed intriguingly apocalyptic. Experimentally, she slid down to her chin in the water and walked her other foot up the wall as well, seeing if she could grip the radio between her feet. It was a game called Pinch the Radio. Object: to pinch the radio with her feet. By sinking to her earlobes, Lyle managed to grip the radio on either side with her toes, raising Boy George's voice an inch or two off the shelf.

Then she began to nudge it. It was an extension of the game, to see how easy it would be. Just for kicks. She wasn't serious or anything. She just wanted to get a taste, like the tiny spoonfuls they gave out at The Perfect Scoop. She nudged the radio until it peeked over the side of the shelf. This didn't seem to do much—no bells or alarms—so she nudged it again. Cyndi Lauper was conjugating the verb "bop." Lyle nudged the radio farther and farther, an inch at a time, until it was nearly halfway off the shelf, perched thrillingly over the tub.

It started to tip. In the tub's direction.

Lyle straightened her legs, pinning the radio to the wall. She'd managed to trap it with her feet. It hung there perilously, tilted like a seesaw. Lyle's heart was racing. She tried to think calmly. She considered maneuvering the radio somehow to her hands, but she was so deep in the tub that she couldn't reach up without bending her knees. Too risky. The other solution was to push it, ever so gently, back on the shelf. She tried to tilt the radio upright with her feet, flexing her knees the tiniest bit, but the radio began to slip even farther and she pinned it to the wall again, legs quivering with fear.

She was trapped. Like the radio. In the Hollywood showdown of life, they were taking each other with them. A briny bead of sweat trickled into her eye. Cyndi Lauper's chipper voice faded into the sultry thwunk of "99 Luftballons." Lyle wasn't sure what "luftballons" were exactly, but somehow they seemed like the solution to her escape.

She yelled for help. Screamed and screamed. Dustin was probably in the garage, practicing his ear-melting songs.

Her legs began to throb in a way unconnected to her sunburn. A trembly sort of muscle ache. Water dripped from her calves into the tub, *plink*ing ominously. She wondered how long she could remain like this. Ten minutes? Fifteen? Her feet were falling asleep: if they went completely numb, as they seemed to be intending, she didn't know whether she could keep her grip.

She knew something, though. She wanted to live. She wanted to jump through a sprinkler. She wanted to try cocaine. She wanted to smell a towel fresh from the dryer, to rewind a cassette tape with her pinkie, to drop snow on unsuspecting skiiers from a chairlift. She wanted to read *Ulysses*. She wanted to rot her brain with Billboard hits. It didn't matter that the songs were terrible. She wanted to hear the next one, and the next, and the next.

Her mother came home during "Cruel Summer." Lyle heard the lock turn in the back door, her legs limp and Jell-Oey. The radio had slid into a perpendicular axis to the tub. For a second, listening to Mr. Leonard scrabble to his feet, she was so relieved she almost dropped her legs by accident. She called her mother's name. After a long minute, Lyle's mom appeared in the doorway of the bathroom, wearing her absurd-looking poncho with little fringes on it.

Her eyes shifted from Lyle's naked body to the radio and then back again. In the first moments, before the gravity of the situation had presented itself, Lyle thought she saw an untamable *I told you so* cross her face.

"Could you get the radio, please? Before I die?"

Her mother snatched the radio from Lyle's feet, yanking the plug out along with it. Lyle's legs collapsed. She was really shivering, an all-out spasm. It was only now, saved from certain death, that she remembered her sunburn. Lyle hobbled from the tub, her fingers white and croneish from the water. How could she describe her mother's face? It was alarmed and lonesome and wonderfully momlike. It wasn't until she saw the tenderness of this face—a face that would never wish her dead—that Lyle felt the tears on her cheeks. She stepped into the poncho, her mom's arms spread like wings. Tightly, Lyle's mother held her to her body, squeezing her without knowing—not even the slightest clue—how much pain she was in.

CHAPTER 17

"I'm not really a witch," Taz said.

"What are you?"

"Good question."

They were sitting outside of the Sea View Condominiums, waiting to go into a party. The name of the place made Dustin laugh. Not only were they in Torrance and nowhere near the sea, the only view to be had was of a lopsided Dumpster overflowing with pizza boxes, a rusted bicycle frame chained to its foot. There was something depressing about it that made Dustin feel unwholesome. Actually, he felt wonderfully despicable. He'd just had sex with his girlfriend's sister, despicably, in the back of his car. He'd helped her sneak out of the house behind Kira's back, waiting down the block while Taz climbed out the window and then making a strategic getaway through the streets of Herradura Estates, Taz crouched in the front seat of the Dart like a convict. The whole plan had been his idea. He'd called the Shackneys' house while Kira was out shopping with her mom, hoping Taz would answer the phone. When she'd told him about the party being thrown by one of Breakfast's friends, he'd offered to give her a ride. Dustin didn't know where this ranked in the annals of bad behavior—he was too happy to quantify it—but it was certainly up there.

Now they were parked outside a condo, in a beautifully shabby part of L.A. Taz's eyeliner was smeared under one eye, like a bruise. They'd done it quickly, fumbling at each other's pants and then attacking each other so ferociously he almost forgot to get a Trojan out of the glove compartment, so intent was he on getting rid of her smirk. But something had happened afterward. She had clung to him without letting go, so fiercely that it hurt, cinching her arms around him like a boa constrictor. He'd worried at first that she was trying to kill him. He'd done something wrong and she was trying to break his ribs. It was only when she stopped squeezing and let go of him, looking almost surprised to see him on top of her, that he realized she wasn't angry. Ten minutes later, his ribs were still sore to the touch. He had never felt anything like this from Kira, who hugged him as though he'd be around forever.

Dustin lit a cigarette and rolled down the window so he wouldn't stink up the Dart. There was an uneasiness in his chest, a thickening haze of guilt, but he was choosing to ignore it. "How did you get sent to boarding school?" he asked.

"You really want to know?"

"Yeah."

Taz shrugged, blowing the white forelock away from her eyes. "I pulled my fingernails out."

"What?"

"With pliers." She shook a cigarette from Dustin's pack and then plucked the one from his mouth in order to light it. "They had to take me to the ER."

"Jesus Christ."

"Kira doesn't even know that."

The haze in Dustin's chest grew thicker. "You pulled out all ten of your nails?"

"Only my left hand. I'm not ambidextrous." She laughed, as if it were all a big joke. "It took me a week—I didn't do it all at once."

"Why the hell did you do it in the first place?"

She shrugged. "Fashion statement. Who the fuck knows."

"You're bleeding right now."

"What?"

"Your ear. Shit. I wish you wouldn't do that."

Taz scowled, dabbing her ear with the collar of her shirt. "You sound like Kira. She's always on my fucking case about it."

Dustin looked at the used condom, bloated and forlorn, on the metal floor by his feet. He couldn't imagine wanting to pull out his fingernails. It occurred to him that "wanting" was not an applicable verb. "It's our anniversary tomorrow," he said, trying to change the subject.

"You and Kira?"

"A year."

Taz looked at him, a flash of anger. "Do you want a fucking *present*?"

She got out of the car, tugging her shirt down before trekking off to the party. Dustin was amazed. He'd imagined she'd enjoy knowing how she was fucking up her sister's life. He finished his cigarette and then followed Taz into the party, which smelled like cookies. Taz, Suzie, and some other people were hanging around the living room, drinking Milwaukee's Best from cans. A girl about Taz's age sat in front of the couch, her face bent toward the floor as though in prayer. Behind her, a guy with tattooed arms was crouched over her neck with what looked like a pen attached to a melted toothbrush; a sewing needle poked out from the tip of the pen, which he kept dipping in a little saucer of ink. There was something—a little motor—taped to the other end.

"Did you make that yourself?" Dustin asked the tattooed guy, trying to break the ice. No one had spoken to him since he'd walked in.

"No. I found it on the sidewalk."

Dustin couldn't figure out if this was meant to be a joke. He laughed, deciding to hedge his bets. A guy with a bloodstained cotton ball in one nostril asked him who he was.

"We're, um, friends of Breakfast's."

"Just don't steal any records," the guy said.

"Look," Suzie said, pointing. "Porn Man's at it again."

Dustin peered out the window, which afforded an open view into the darkened condo across the way. A big TV flickered at the back of the room: two women on their knees, giving someone a blow job. Dustin had the weird desire to shield Taz's eyes. In front of the TV, visible in the murky blue light, was the back of an empty couch.

"I see his hand!" the guy with the cotton ball said. "We have a sighting."

"There's someone in there?" Dustin asked.

"He lies there naked on the couch," Suzie explained, "fast-forwarding to the good parts."

Dustin walked into the kitchen. Breakfast was hanging out by the sink, sharing a bottle of Old Crow with the beautiful girl. She introduced herself as Yissel, as if she'd never seen him before. In the corner, hunched over an old typewriter, sat a guy who looked to be in his thirties. He was wearing a motorcycle jacket and no shirt. There was a hollow place in the middle of his chest, a bony, cavelike dent below his sternum, large enough to wedge in a tennis ball.

"Want a misfortune cookie?" Yissel said.

"Sure."

She reached into a bowl on the kitchen table and handed Dustin a yellow fortune cookie. He broke it open and pulled out an asymmetrical strip of paper, which said YOU WILL DIE BÆFORE YOUR PARENTS. Dustin laughed. He grabbed a chocolate cookie from a plate on the counter and popped it in his mouth. It tasted like mud. When he looked up, everyone in the kitchen was watching him.

"Did you just eat that whole thing?"

"Yeah." His scalp tightened, a quiver of fear.

"Ho, man," the guy in the motorcycle jacket said. "He's going to, like, end up in the fetal."

"Happy trails."

Breakfast looked at him with concern. "Just remember. It's only hash."

Dustin nodded, to show he wasn't worried. He'd smoked hash plenty of times before. Yissel smiled in a friendly way, touching his shoulder and explaining that they were all going to have one, too. Nothing to worry about. When she picked up her own cookie, though, Dustin couldn't help noticing that she barely nibbled it.

He went into the bathroom to wash his face. He thought about making himself puke, but the idea of sticking his finger down his throat made him squeamish. Anyway, they were probably exaggerating. How could they know he was an experienced drug user? He walked into the adjoining bedroom, which someone had painted purple. The walls were decorated with kitschy Jesuses and taqueria calendars and black velvet posters of nudes with supernaturally large breasts. Two futons, stained with muddy footprints, covered most of the floor. There was a pistol on the dresser, a little price tag dangling from its trigger. It looked like a real gun. The tag said IN CASE OF ABJECT MISERY, PULL. Dustin walked across the futons and went back into the living room, where Taz was getting a tattoo on her biceps.

"Whoa, hey," he said. "Are you sure you want that?"

Taz looked at him sweetly. "You said, Daddy. If I ate everything on my plate."

The other people in the room laughed.

"Tell him what it is," Suzie said. "A Gorgon!"

"It's a Gorgon," Taz said.

"Fuck," the guy giving the tattoo said. "I thought you said 'organ.'"

"What?"

"You know. Hieronymus Bach."

Taz frowned. "Like a fucking *instrument*? In a church?"

The guy shrugged. "If you want a Gorgon," he said defensively, "you should speak clearly. Enunciate."

"Let's get out of here," Dustin whispered, leaning into Taz's ear. The party—the whole place—was beginning to remind him of a foreign film in which nothing happened but everyone was subtly deranged.

"Why the fuck are you whispering?" Taz demanded.

Dustin sat on the couch. On the other side of the room, near the stereo, the guy with the cotton ball up his nostril was making a mess of the records in the bookcase, pulling them one by one off the shelf and flinging them from their sleeves onto the floor. His eyes were big as quarters. Soon the carpet was covered in records, a shimmering pond of vinyl. He walked onto the records, crunching them carefully with his boots, stepping in a freaky, robotic way as though he couldn't bend his feet but had to rock inflexibly from heel to toe.

"What the fuck are you doing?" Suzie asked.

"Literally or metaphorically?" He peered around the room, as though surprised to find anyone there. "Literally I'm destroying all my records."

"What are you doing metaphorically?"

"Wearing ski boots."

"Grand Funk Railroad," Breakfast said, watching from the kitchen. "*E Pluribus Funk*. That was my favorite record in fifth grade."

They were an American band, Dustin thought, looking at the broken LPs on the floor. He'd meant to say it out loud, but a pluribus funk had entered his brain, causing him to mistake his desire to do something with the doing itself. His throat was dry, and he was beginning to feel uncomfortable. "They were an American band," he said, aloud this time.

"We heard you the first time."

"Who invited this asshole?" the guy with the cotton ball said.

"He's Taz's asshole," Suzie said.

Taz snorted, inspecting the half-finished tattoo on her arm. "No, he isn't."

"She doesn't have one. It's a miracle of science."

Dustin did not want to contemplate this. He was feeling worse and worse. Chiefly, his feet were suffocating to death. They weren't indigenous to his shoes, a man-made habitat. Carefully, he tugged off his Chuck Taylors and tossed them on the rug. It didn't seem to help. He pulled his socks off, too. This relieved the feeling of suffocation but gave rise to new concerns. He couldn't help noticing that his toes weren't equally evolved. Sprouting from some of them, black and weedy, were apelike vestiges of hair. He looked up, realizing that everyone in the room was staring at his feet.

Yissel began to tell a story about finding a cyst on her back when she was thirteen. The story was wiggly and hard to follow. As far as Dustin could tell, the cyst had hair and teeth in it and had to be removed before it got any clever ideas.

Dustin decided to step outside for a smoke. This implied a single step but in fact involved a series of challenging human maneuvers. Outside, it had begun to rain. You could see the swimming pool trembling under the lights. The rain made no noise and in fact lacked a certain credibility. In this way it was similar to the porno playing across the street, which in its sped-up form suggested a pair of emaciated, hyperactive clowns brushing their teeth with the same toothbrush. Dustin couldn't see the person watching: just a flabby arm sticking out over the couch, manning a remote control. Horrified, Dustin realized the owner of the arm was himself. By some trick of fate he was staring into his own future. He'd screwed his girlfriend's sister, but this only proved what a joke he was. Everyone hated him; he had no talent; he would never become famous. Hadn't a roomful of people just called him an asshole? There wasn't a person in the world who loved him. Even his parents, who'd raised him from birth, could care less if he lived or died. They knew the truth: he'd end up in a condominium by himself, watching porn with the blinds open.

Condominium. It sounded like a flower. He imagined a humongous lily, actually saw it materialize in front of him and begin to take on the gloomy features of his father.

His heart had begun to race. He couldn't control it. A cartoon version of itself, wacky and unhinged. Dustin sat down on the damp walkway and put two fingers to his neck, checking his pulse like Mrs. Shackney. He'd learned how to do it in grade school. Measure for ten seconds, then multiply by six. He checked his watch, trying to follow the minuscule hops of the second hand as he counted the beats.

Two sixty-four. Was that possible?

Bravely, he went back inside and faced the partygoers, who looked smaller and less anatomically feasible. They stared at him in an expectant way. There was the sense that he would have to say something. If he could say something normal, anything to win them over, they might be moved to save his life.

"What's going on out there?" Breakfast said.

"The condominiums are in bloom."

Taz's friends seemed to like this. In fact, they laughed so hard that one of them—the tattooist—spilled beer all over the carpet. It stayed on the surface for a moment, a stupendous dewdrop. Taz asked if Dustin was okay, staring at the fingers he was still holding to his neck. To his amazement, she seemed genuinely concerned.

"No," he said. "Actually not. I'm having a heart attack."

This was less popular. Dustin thought he heard someone boo.

"Whoa. Uncool. Death would be really uncalled for right now."

"Dude," the guy with the motorcycle jacket said, "you are *not* having a heart attack."

"I'm not?"

"I've had one before," he said proudly. "I think I'd know one when I see it."

"How many of those space cookies did you eat?" Suzie asked.

"Space?"

She looked at Breakfast. "We have a problem."

"Is your left arm numb?" Breakfast asked.

Dustin nodded. In truth, he'd forgotten it existed. What mental powers remained were focused on his heart, which was drumming so fast he'd stopped counting beats. It had turned into an alien creature. This was not his loyal, laid-back, intimate companion, but a stranger with a name tag. *MY NAME IS:* YOUR HEART.

Dustin left the room, in search of a phone. He'd have to call 911 himself. But if he called 911, they would discover the drugs in his system and he'd be arrested for drug possession, even if his heart was attacking him. He was nauseated and afraid and his feet were bare. After a long and eventful search, he found a room with some futons in it. It seemed to be a different bedroom than before. Bizarrely, it was nearly identical to the other one, right down to the gun on the dresser. Dustin ignored the gun and picked up the phone, which bore no instructions.

He decided to call Kira. She'd know what to do. She was a genius in times of crisis. He loved her desperately; she was the only person who understood him; how could he possibly have thought Taz was worth the risk of losing her forever? He dialed the Shackneys' number. The phone rang several times in his ear, so slowly that Dustin wondered whether he would die before anyone picked up. Just as he was giving up all hope, the answering machine came on and Mr. Shackney's prerecorded voice barked into his ear, telling him to leave a message.

"Kira, are you there? I'm having a heart attack. My pulse is, like, off the charts." Silence. He could hear himself breathing, panting into the darkness of the Shackneys' kitchen. He could hear it, too—the Shackneys' kitchen—breathing on the other side of the line. The sleepless hum of their Sub-Zero refrigerator. He realized that these might be his last words. He would have no other chance for forgiveness. "Kira, I have to . . . oh God, please forgive me . . . Taz is here. We're at a party. There's something . . . I can't even say it. The word. We did it. Your little sister. There's something wrong with me. A day before our . . . our anniversary."

Dustin hung up and closed his eyes, waiting for death. His teeth were chattering. His soul was unburdened, but he didn't feel any better. He sat on the floor and hugged his knees. He wanted to walk out into the front yard and lie down in his father's leaf pile. He used to do this as a kid. He'd crunch into the warm pile and then burrow into the cooler leaves, toward the damp and nougaty center, which smelled of sweetly rotting spinach. He'd stay down there, waiting for his father to find him. It was dark and cold and scary, but you knew that he was coming for you. It was part of the game. He would rescue you with his big hands and pull you out of the dark, your sweater stuck all over with leaves, shaking you softly like a present.

Dustin opened his eyes: someone was standing over him in the purple room, one sleeve rolled atop her shoulder. Taz. It seemed possible that her face was turning purple as well, adapting to its environment.

"Please," he said.

"Please what?"

"Help me."

She looked at him unhappily. It occurred to him that the unhappiness was not solely because of his death. He had the distressing sensation that she was in love with him but would rather let him die than see it. But he was probably imagining this. It was the one inarguable feature of being human: you never knew what people thought, and then you died.

Dustin waited for her to leave, then picked up the phone and called home.

CHAPTER 18

Warren drove through the rainy streets of Torrance, Dustin perched beside him in the front seat. There was something peculiar happening to his son. He was staring at the shuddery arc of the wipers, pupils full as moons, leg bouncing up and down in hummingbird time. Now and then his eyes would snag on Warren—a wild, amusement-park look—before returning to the road. Hash, was what Dustin had told him. Warren found this hard to believe. He'd smoked hash once in college, before he'd met Camille, and the only effect was a persistent tingling in one foot. This was a different thing entirely. Dustin had babbled into the phone about his heart rate, something to do with cardiac arrest, but when Warren had finally gotten there—breathless and alarmed—Dustin claimed it had been a mistake. Warren had checked Dustin's pulse himself, just to make sure: seventy-two. He might have taken him to the ER anyway, but Dustin had gripped his sleeve so earnestly, flashing him such a desperate, pleading look, that Warren couldn't resist the chance to please him.

"I wish I was a dog," Dustin said now, still perched at the edge of his seat. The overhead light was on, making it difficult to see the road; Warren had tried to turn it off, but his son had yelled at him in a strange voice.

"A dog?"

"You can do whatever you want. Everyone forgives you. You even get your own door."

"I like you as a human being," Warren said.

"Doggy door," his son said, frowning. The term seemed to impress or offend him, Warren couldn't say which. His eyes drifted to Warren's slippers, as if noticing them for the first time. "Did I wake you up?" he said nervously.

"No. We were playing Monopoly."

Dustin looked at the clock on the dashboard. "At one in the morning?"

"Lyle can barely move. Jonas and I had to distract her." The rain had turned to a drizzle; Warren switched off the wipers. "Your mother's pulling an all-nighter at the office."

Dustin stared at his bouncing leg. He seemed hurt. It was something Warren and the kids used to do when Camille was gone: stay up late playing Monopoly, sometimes for hours. They'd keep the money in their wallets, pulling it out with hammy, tortured looks. Warren could feel the candy-colored bills there now, swelling his back pocket: a wonderful, meaningless lump.

"Was Lyle the dead Scottie?" Dustin asked.

"What?"

"That was always her special piece. She'd put the little dog in the wheelbarrow, legs up." He looked at Warren, as though he were discussing something of grave importance. "Don't you remember?"

"Son, listen. I want to tell you something."

"I can't believe you don't remember that," he said angrily.

They rattled around a curve, sharply enough that the naked Barbie hanging from the mirror canted to one side. What did Warren want to tell him? Everything? Drugged out, helpless, his son was less likely to hate him. Perhaps he wouldn't even remember in the morning. Dustin was making a strange noise, like an animal; it took Warren a moment to realize his teeth were chattering.

"Actually, Dad? I need your help?"

Warren eased up on the gas. "What is it?"

"I really, um, *did* something. Fucked-up."

He began to tell a story, his words jumbling together. Warren had trouble following it, except that Dustin had mistakenly believed he was dying and had told Kira's answering machine that he'd slept with her little sister. Kira was going to hear it in the morning and break up with him. He needed Warren to help him steal the tape before the Shackneys found out.

"That's true? You had sex with Kira's sister?"

"No."

"Then why did you say that?"

Dustin closed his eyes, slumping back in his seat. "Fuck," he whispered. "Can't you just *help* me for once?"

"What are you suggesting we do? Break a window and sneak in there while they're asleep?"

"No! Don't make any noise!" He explained that Kira's sister kept her window open in order to sneak out at night. She was still at the party, probably wondering where he was and vandalizing the Dart. Warren could go through her window and no one would know. "I'm just too . . . fucked-up to do it."

"Dust," Warren said. "I'm a grown man. I can't break into someone's house."

Dustin glanced at him for a second, that same wild look, before returning his eyes to the dash. Despite the absurdity of the request, Warren felt an odd flush of happiness. He wished—*longed*—for the opportunity to help him. Amazingly, the boy started to cry. A distant, murmury sound, like something from another room. Warren hadn't heard this murmury sound since Dustin was a child. The crying grew louder. Besides the persistent rattling of the muffler, it was the only sound in the car. There was real fear there, panic or distress.

Warren decided to answer its plea. Whatever it was, Dustin needed him.

They entered Herradura Estates; at the top of the canyon, Warren flipped off his brights and turned down John's Canyon Road toward the Shackneys'. The rain had cleared, and the damp streets shone noirishly under his headlights. Warren parked by the curb where no one would see him. Floating above the HACIENDA DE SHACKNEY sign, half-hidden behind the branches of a pepper tree, the gibbous moon looked like a spoon-cracked egg. He asked Dustin where the sister's room was, trying to remember what he'd said.

"Around back," Dustin mumbled. He was no longer crying, his face pale and listless. The skin under his nose gleamed with snot. Warren waited, but this appeared to be all the intelligence he was getting.

He got out of the car and crept up the driveway, stepping past a drowned worm wiggling on the asphalt. His T-shirt fluttered in the breeze. He passed a sign on the lawn that said PROTECTED BY NORCO; Warren imagined this Norco, a Spanish thug with a gold tooth, patrolling the grounds with a tire iron. Except for the kitchen-bright glare of the porch, the house was dark. Warren went through the side gate and crept his way along the brick path skirting the house to the swampy grass of the backyard. The wetness seeped into his slippers and soaked his feet. Warren didn't care. His mind was sharp, free of the usual burdens. He felt almost spry. He tried to imagine Dustin's expression when he showed up with the tape, the glow of gratitude on his face.

The backyard was immense, a battlefield of toys, the moonlit trampoline glazed like a pond. Warren rounded it as quietly as he could, almost tripping over a croquet wicket hidden in the grass. He lowered into a crouch, heart beating in his neck. It took him a while to find the sister's room. Slowly, like a burglar, he waded through a thicket of butterfly bush to the open window, ignoring the icy crunch of a snail under one slipper. He peered into the moonlit room. Empty. Warren stepped through the window—a brief, painful pirouette—and entered the Shackneys' house. The room could have been Dustin's: the same spectacular mess, clothes everywhere, dirty dishes in the bed and T-shirts lolling from the dresser. There was a familiar smell of rotting apple. They even had the same poster on the wall, the spiky-haired fellow who looked like he was clubbing a seal with his guitar.

Warren picked his way through the clothes on the floor, opened the door as quietly as he could, and crept into the hall. A light went on and he froze in his tracks, petrified. No one. He squished down the hall and the light went out again, shrouding him in darkness.

By the time he'd felt his way into the kitchen, dimly beckoned by a light over the stove, any similarity to his own house had ended. The room was enormous. There was a built-in wine cooler and a Viking stove and a refrigerator that looked like it could house a side of beef. Warren opened the fridge, and a peach tumbled at his feet. He tried to put it back in, but the fridge was so stuffed with meat and produce and subtle variations of mustard that he couldn't find a place to put it. He turned around, still holding the peach. On the counter was a bottle of Châteauneuf-du-Pape, a price tag stuck conspicuously to its neck: $64.00. Warren did not know what Châteauneuf-du-Pape was, but the mellifluous words seemed to invoke everything that was lovely in the world, utterly at odds with the harsh Germanic syllables of his boyhood. He thought of those girls at the Seven Seas Club, sunbathing in their swimsuits, their legs crooked into perfect *châteauneufs*.

He crept across the tile and peered into the family room, which was lavishly furnished, a showroom of matching leather merchandise. He squished into the room in his soggy slippers and sat down on the edge of the couch, staring at a gigantic television set housed in an Oriental cabinet crowned by an intricately carved peacock. It was the biggest cabinet Warren had ever seen. The Shackneys must have commissioned it. Warren sat there for a minute, eating the peach in his hand and letting the juice run down his arm. His feet were cold, but he did not feel like getting up. His face stared back at him from the TV screen, darkly, like a ghost's.

Warren closed his eyes and sank into the couch. He could have been anywhere, in a church or a palace, so silent was the sleeping house. He had the odd feeling that he belonged there, that he could drift to sleep and be woken with a kiss.

Returning to the kitchen, oozing rain from his slippers, he found the answering machine blinking calmly on the telephone table. He laid the gooey peach pit beside it. All he had to do—to win his son's love and gratitude—was steal the tape. He pushed EJECT, but the button wouldn't work. It seemed to be jammed. He tried prying open the cassette cartridge with his fingernail, but it threatened to snap his nail off at the root. He did not want to bleed all over the Shackneys' kitchen. Warren shook the machine, hoping it would magically dislodge the tape. No luck. A bead of sweat trickled down his nose. The imprisoned tape mocked him, leering at him with owlish eyes. He thought about trying to erase the message, but couldn't find the volume and didn't want to wake anyone up.

He'd have to steal the whole thing. There was no other option. Reaching behind the telephone table, feeling his way down the cord, Warren unplugged the answering machine from the wall and tucked it under one arm.

He stood there for a second, gripping the machine like a football. Something about the deepening stakes, the responsibility of holding his son's future in his hands, made him not immune to his own heroism.

He turned around. The bottle of Châteauneuf-du-Pape, beautifully labeled in Art Deco script, sat on the counter. Warren grabbed that, too. On his way to the sister's room, fleeing the automatic light, he tripped over the runner tacked to the hall and nearly dropped the wine on the floor. He looked up after regaining his balance and saw a child standing at the far end of the hallway, face doughy with sleep. The Shackney boy. He was naked except for his briefs. In the harsh light of the hallway, he looked gentle as a fawn. The boy blinked at Warren a couple times before noticing the plunder in his hands, his gaze sliding from the bottle to the answering machine, a look of fear crossing his face.

Warren dashed into the sister's bedroom and scrambled through the window, losing a slipper in the mucky grass of the backyard. His foot slapped against the driveway. In the car, he jammed the ignition and spun away without looking back, pulling a U-turn on the rain-slick road and hydroplaning for a second before the wheels caught, the tailpipe rattling enough to wake the Dunkirks' Labrador, whose yapping Dopplered into woofs as they passed. Warren's eyes stung; he was panting; an angina-like pain clenched his chest. The bottle of wine rolled around at his feet. When they'd gained a safe distance, Warren rescued the answering machine from his lap and held it out to his son, who lifted his eyes from the bottle on the floor and gazed at the machine with a look of astonishment, recoiling in the dim light of a streetlamp.

"Jesus, Dad. Christ. Are you trying to fuck up my life forever?"

CHAPTER 19

The recording studio was small and dank. Mikolaj leaned over the microphone, doing his best—in gawky, imperfect English—to recite the new script Camille had written, clarifying that the kids in T-shirts weren't actually on sports teams. He was having trouble with "fallopian." The accent was a problem, but she thought it would be less distracting than if the voiceover switched to a woman's voice for no reason. Camille hunched over the mixing board, trying to synch Mikolaj's words to what was happening on the monitor. Even though they were sitting across from each other, separated by a few feet of table, she could smell the Listerine on his breath.

"'These children *re*-present the sperm, swimming up the Philippine tube.'"

"Not '*re*-present,'" she said. "'Represent.' Like 'rescue.'"

"What rescue?"

"That's how you pronounce it. The first syllable."

She was ready to give up on the whole thing, to quit her job and burn the movie before anyone could see it. Friday was the deadline for submitting it to the board. It was well past lunch already; she'd been here since yesterday, rewriting the script, catching a few hours of sleep on the break room couch. Her only ally, a Polish alcoholic, thought "fallopian" was a nationality. What's more, it was unseasonably cold and half the office seemed to be out on vacation. She realized now, worrying the fringe of her shawl, that the situation was grave.

Her eyes burned; she was so exhausted that she was beginning to question her own pronunciation. Annoyingly, Mikolaj grinned.

He leaned into the mike again, clutching his chest and emitting a hair-raising shriek from his throat. It took a second before she realized he was singing. "*I come to* your. *Emotional* re*scue.*" Camille laughed.

"I make you laugh," Mikolaj said. "This is a day of brave new thing."

"I laugh all the time," she lied.

"I was thinking you're like communist. Too busy making sure you are happy."

Mikolaj's ponytail had come undone, fanning his shoulders in greasy squiggles. His forehead, Camille noticed, was stippled with tiny scars. Even bloodshot, his eyes were strangely beautiful, green as could be, like something from the insides of a rock.

"Do you mind it if I smoke?" he asked.

Camille shook her head. Happily, Mikolaj pulled a bag of tobacco from his jeans pocket and rolled a cigarette. His lighter's flame genuflected toward the tip as he sucked on the other end.

"Why do you look at me?"

"Nothing," she said. "You just remind me of someone."

"I am the reminder of no one," he said proudly, smoke curling from his nostrils. "Would you like I make you one?"

"No, no. I have my own." Camille reached into her purse. There were only two cigarettes left in her pack. She pulled one out and let Mikolaj light it for her, and immediately felt more relaxed.

"We are the only smokers who work in this place," Mikolaj said casually.

Camille was queerly flattered. "My family doesn't like it."

"Why not?"

"I don't know. It doesn't fit their image of me, I guess."

"Ah, okay. Your true self is in secret place." He stared down at the table. "Just like I want to make movies, famous ones, but I am here speaking of tubes."

Maybe he wasn't drunk. Maybe Polish people were always like this: they spoke of true things, secrets, all the embarrassing gunk on the surface. She'd heard about babies being born with hearts outside their bodies. There were specks of dandruff, like ceiling dust, in his eyebrows.

"Is something wrong?" he said kindly.

Camille had an overwhelming desire to confide in this unem-

barrassable stranger—perhaps even to talk about Warren's affair—
but then remembered the note in her desk. "My daughter almost
electrocuted herself," she said instead. "With a radio. I told her
not to keep it by the bath, but she wouldn't listen."

"This daughter, how old?"

"Sixteen."

He leaned back again, leaving a haze of smoke between them.
"Well. She is at not-listening age. This is her specialty."

"When she was little, I thought we had a special connection.
More than most mothers and daughters, I mean. I used to sing
to her all day long, everything that we were doing, like an opera.
What's the word? *Besotted.* She would just watch me with those
big blue eyes. *Thing to me, thing to me,* as if it wasn't really happening unless I turned it into a song." Camille took another puff
of her cigarette, the smoke warm as sunlight in her lungs. "Did
you know that lions sometimes eat their own cubs? By accident?
They go to lick them and get carried away and end up eating
them."

Mikolaj looked at her strangely. "You wish to eat your daughter?"

"No. Ha. I just mean that's how I felt sometimes."

"Wow."

"*Feel.* Even when she's making fun of me."

He seemed impressed. "In Poland we never eat our children.
Only symbolically."

He dunked his cigarette stub in a cup of old coffee, a pleasant sizzle. Camille stood up to cue the video again. She was worried Mikolaj might start confessing things, too: she didn't actually
want to know anything about him. It might interfere with the
fantasy she'd constructed. In the fantasy, Warren lurked jealously
outside the window, watching her smoke a cigarette with a sad-
faced European who left her tragic love notes.

"I like you in this jacket," Mikolaj said when Camille returned
to the mixing board, nodding at the shawl.

"You do?"

"Very much. You are like fashion cowboy."

She decided to interpret this as a compliment. "My husband
hates it."

"Ah," Mikolaj said sadly.

She blushed. "It was too expensive, I think."

"Your husband should move to USSR. He does not know what money is for."

Camille frowned. "We should get back to work. It's nearly five."

"Okay. Yes. American way. No time to be dust collector."

He pounded his fist on the table, like a gavel. It was a big hand, tense and lonely as an animal. Without thinking, she reached down and touched it. Mikolaj seemed startled, the lines in his forehead raveling together. He looked upset. She hadn't thought of what to do next. Earnestly, Mikolaj edged around the table and grabbed her squarely below the shoulders, lifting her like a bookcase. He pressed his lips against hers, his mouth strong and hard and blundering, tongue bumping into hers like a fish, a taste of mouthwash giving way to something stale, white wine left too long in the sun, as unsteadying as the knobs of the mixing board jabbing in her rear—was she sitting? falling?—and then he pulled away and the kiss was no longer there, gone as quickly as it had come, the fierce squeeze of his fingers still burning in her arms.

They were breathing quickly. She glanced down and saw the childish bulge in his jeans. There was a smell, suddenly, of singed wool.

"Your cigarette!" he said.

"What?"

"It ruins your jacket."

Camille jerked her hand away, dropping the cigarette to the floor. A hole, big as a nickel, had burned through her shawl. As if to underscore the moment, the phone rang next door in her office. She hurried from the studio to answer it. The empty hallway seemed different than she remembered, a brighter shade of yellow, though the walls didn't smell of paint.

"I have to go," Camille said, returning a minute later. She gathered up her things without looking at Mikolaj. "My husband's in jail."

CHAPTER 20

"One thing I've never figured out," the man sitting across from Warren said. He was slurping at a miniature box of Frosted Flakes, which he'd filled with milk from one of those school-sized cartons. He'd requested them—both the milk and the cereal—from one of the officers on duty. Drunkenly, the man flashed the box at Warren, Tony the Tiger grinning maniacally over a bowl of corroded-looking flakes. "Why's he wearing a bandanna around his neck?"

"Who?"

"The tiger. I mean, who the fuck wears a bandanna around their neck?"

"I don't know," Warren said, directing his gaze to the steel toilet in the corner. A pubic hair sat on the rim, coiled like a tiny spring. He wanted to enjoy his arrest—the nadir of his life thus far—in peace.

"Fuck me," the man said. He thrust the box at Warren, as though he were showing him a photo of his wife. "It's mono-grammed! Tell me that isn't a little *T-O-N-Y* I'm seeing."

The man seemed to be waiting for a response, a trickle of milk leaking down his chin. Warren had no choice but to look: sure enough, the tiger's name was sewn into the bandanna, proof of his aristocratic tastes. Clearly, he was imparting a message to the less privileged of the world. If we all knew our place, we wouldn't pretend to be rich or break into our neighbors' homes and steal their belongings. *Burglary in the first degree.* That's what the guy taking Warren's fingerprints had typed into the booking sheet. When Warren asked why it was first degree, he'd looked at him as though he were a dim-witted child and said, "If you'd wanted second, you should have broken into a Radio Shack."

Warren had had plenty of time to ponder his crime. He'd worried the cops would come last night, scared they'd find Dustin on drugs and arrest him, too—but they hadn't shown up until this afternoon. Twelve hours of sleepless jitters. Mercifully, there hadn't been a scene at the house. They'd asked Warren to come down to the station, politely, and led him out to the squad car without making a fuss. On a scale of degrading events, it could certainly have been worse. There could have been tears or guns or handcuffs. Still, degradation was one of those things, like coffins, that didn't need a lot of extras. Walking down the driveway, slumped and frightened, he'd glanced back at the house in time to see Dustin emerge from the garage, gripping his guitar by the neck, a guitar pick glimmering in his teeth. Behind him were Lyle and Jonas, watching through the living room window like strangers. Warren's consolation was that the cops didn't know the full truth: he'd hoped that once he explained the whole story—the absurdity of stealing an answering machine from his son's girlfriend's parents—they'd let him off with a warning.

But when he got to the station and saw Mr. Shackney and his son waiting there as well, their faces stern and weary, he realized his mistake. This wasn't the principal's office. On the desk in the booking area, sealed in a plastic bag marked EVIDENCE, was Warren's ancient slipper—the same one Mr. Leonard had once peed on as a puppy. Beside it, a little chart titled CHAIN OF POSSESSION had been meticulously filled out. This, more than anything, had alerted Warren to the seriousness of things. In hindsight, he couldn't really blame Mr. Shackney for pressing charges. Probably it sounded worse than crazy: What kind of father would break into a man's house at the behest of his son, a drugged-out boy who couldn't stand his company?

The man with the cereal box got up to take a piss, forcing Warren to listen to the splash of his urine. Warren tried to imagine how he'd face Camille and tell her the truth. She would be on her way by now, probably seeing about bail at one of the gloomy places across the street. He dreaded the explanation he'd have to give, but it was also something like relief: the verifiable bottom. He could own up for good.

By the time Warren was released—an hour? two?—his cell mate had slipped into a flatulent sleep. Camille was waiting for him in the booking area. Her face looked pale and troubled, eyes rimmed with fatigue. The left corner of her mouth was smeared with lipstick, a faint blur of pink, as though she'd been kissing someone. Under different circumstances, the idea would have made Warren laugh. He could no more imagine her having an affair than he could her taking her clothes off at a party and doing the Hustle. Out of shame, he didn't offer to hug her.

They climbed into the Volvo, Warren's few possessions gathered in a paper bag in his lap. He felt oddly like a boy again, those dreary mornings at dawn, after his father's death, when his mother would drive him to school in an exhausted daze. Somehow the day had turned to night, the streetlights glowing through a bank of fog. The fog thickened as they climbed into the hills of Palos Verdes. The arraignment had taken only a few minutes; Warren's court date was set for September, a little over a month from now. Camille pulled a cigarette from her purse with one hand and lit it with the car lighter, blowing smoke out the open window, her mouth piped to one side like a seasoned smoker. She was stiff as a rod. She didn't look at him but stared straight ahead at the spectral cone of the lights.

"We're broke, Camille. Everything's gone."

She glanced at him, less alarmed than perplexed.

"The Chrysler wasn't stolen. It was repossessed." He stared out the window, the familiar street signs lost in the fog. "Our savings are gone. Everything. I invested every penny."

There was a release to it, the words tumbling free. He waited for the reckoning to begin. The anger and blame and cavernous contempt. He glanced back at Camille, but she seemed to be in denial, still watching the road.

"We're bankrupt," he explained, more slowly. "We'll have to move. Sell the house. God knows what else."

Inconceivably, she laughed, a Tourette's-like bark. They pulled up to the guardhouse, the gate opening as soon as Bud recognized them through the fog. It was so thick you could barely see the road; the houses, the toy-sprinkled lawns, seemed to have vanished. The soggy mist blew through Camille's window and tasted like salt. Her cigarette seemed to have gone out. As they rounded a curve of John's Canyon Road, Camille punching the car lighter in with her thumb, a shape loomed out of the fog in front of them, large as a child. Warren shouted. Camille slammed on the brakes: they bucked against their seat belts, skidding to a stop amid the tarry stench of rubber.

A peacock. It was standing, fully fanned, in the middle of the road. The green eyes of its feathers shone in the headlights, gorgeously amazed. From up close, the crown on its head looked like a tiny grove of trees. The peacock ruffled its feathers, twitching its fan back and forth before collapsing into a more plausible creature and sauntering off, dragging its long train into the fog.

Warren unclenched his hands from the bag in his lap. He'd forgotten how beautiful the birds were; when they'd first moved to California, he and Camille used to watch them breathlessly from the house, crowding the window, as if they were visitors from another planet. Now the birds had become pests, eating his flowers.

"I'm sorry," he said to Camille. He meant for everything.

She didn't respond. The car was in the middle of the road, but she seemed uninterested in moving it. The lighter on the dashboard popped, sounding faintly in the dark. "Are we still going camping on Saturday?" she asked.

"What?"

"The desert. Our annual vacation. Are we so broke we can't afford oatmeal?"

Warren felt something within him lift and scatter, like birds from a tree. He could barely see her face. "I don't know."

"We're still a family," she said. "Even if we don't act like it."

He didn't dare move, in case she'd startle to her senses. *I'm going on trial for burglary,* he wanted to say, but was too grateful to speak. The fog where the peacock had been seemed to move in the headlights, as if haunted by its presence.

"The other day I forgot to pick Jonas up from fencing. He had to walk home in his uniform."

She looked at him, a hank of hair dangling over one eye. There was a sadness in her face that had nothing to do with him. He touched her knee. Relaxing under his touch, her body seemed to fill with light, a miraculous brightening; only when high beams flooded the car did Warren realize there was someone behind them.

Camille pressed the gas, and they moved forward through the fog. At the house, she pulled up the driveway and stepped out of the car, standing there for a minute in the pale glow from the windows. She did not seem to want to go inside. A coin of pink turtleneck showed through her poncho on one side.

"There's a hole in your poncho," Warren said, joining her by the lawn.

"I know."

"Sorry," he said, catching himself. "Shawl."

Camille lifted her arms, spreading her tasseled sleeves as if to show off their poncho-ness. She shot an imaginary gun in the air. A joke, Warren realized in amazement, though she seemed as serious as can be.

CHAPTER 21

Jonas stood in front of the bathroom mirror. He raised his jacket in the air behind him and stretched it out like a cape, trying his hardest not to look like a four-legged prey animal. If you looked like a four-legged prey animal, you were doomed. Mountain lions were ravenous and not very good at counting legs.

"What the hell are you doing?" Dustin said. He was standing in the door to the bathroom, wearing flip-flops and a plain brown T-shirt. He might as well slather himself in blood and limp around like a wounded deer.

"Practicing for mountain lions."

"We're going to Joshua Tree," his brother said. "To roast marshmallows."

Jonas pointed at Dustin's flip-flops. "If you fall down, a mountain lion will ambush you from behind and sever your spinal cord."

"Don't get my hopes up."

This was typical of his brother's attitude lately. His entire family seemed to be having some sort of meltdown. Despite the fact that Dustin hoped to get eaten by a mountain lion, despite the fact that his dad had been arrested for a mysterious reason no one would talk about, despite the fact that his sister was still covered in blisters and would have to stay in her tent to avoid the hundred-degree sun—despite all this, they were going to spend the weekend in the desert *because they did it every year*. His mother had explained this to him several times, as if trying to convince herself it was a good idea. Jonas wondered if perhaps their family were a dying organism. It was like those praying mantises who end up getting eaten by their partners but keep mating anyway, out of habit, despite the fact that they were missing a head.

His family thought he was strange, a weirdo, but it was everyone else that was crazy. Why did people take trips into the desert, where there was no water or electricity and you were even more likely to feel like someone's imaginary friend? Jonas had a hard enough time believing in himself at home. Sometimes he'd spend all day around the house, practicing his fencing moves or watching TV while his family swerved around him, barely glancing his way as they rushed to the phone or slammed out of the house. It was as if the real Jonas had been picked up by a stranger and whisked away for good, locked up somewhere nobody could find. It was a feeling he could not explain to anyone, because he did not understand it himself. His mother had begun to kiss him lately, as if to make sure he was still there, but her need to keep proving it all the time only made him feel more like a ghost.

Jonas went into the kitchen, where Lyle was filling water bottles in the sink. A bag of marshmallows sat untended on the counter. After ripping the bag open with his teeth, Jonas impaled one of the marshmallows on a skewer and turned the stove up all the way, the burner sparking into a squiggling blue jellyfish. There was a real science to marshmallow roasting. The trick was to turn the thing ever so slowly, ten to twelve inches from the fire, so that it bruised magically but never crisped. He glanced up at his red-skinned sister, hoping to impress her, but she was already staring at the browning marshmallow. There seemed to be a connection between them. Jonas inched the skewer closer to the flame, and she winced. To get her attention, he was not above inflicting mental distress.

"Do you *have* to do that in here?" Lyle asked him.

"The stove's in here. I'm practicing my technique."

His mother popped into the kitchen, Mr. Leonard limping at her heels. She eyed Jonas's marshmallow with lovely spellbound interest before bending to kiss him on the head. Jonas waited for his mother to look at him that way, so that his missing self would return. Instead she grabbed a marshmallow from the bag on the counter and stuck it in her mouth, chewing it like a horse. Lyle and Jonas stared at her.

"Did you just eat a marshmallow, Mom?" Lyle said. "For *breakfast*?"

"Big whoops." His mother grabbed the bag off the counter, turning to Jonas before heading back outside. "We're leaving in five minutes. Don't forget to turn the stove off."

Jonas nodded, returning his attention to the marshmallow. It had gone black on one side, hopelessly crinkled.

"Did Mom just say 'big whoops'?" Lyle asked.

"I think she meant one whoop," Jonas said. "Singular."

Lyle left the kitchen, slow as an astronaut, and he sat down with his burned marshmallow at the table. As he ate, tears of marshmallow dripped onto the open newspaper in front of him. Jonas closed the newspaper, trying to hide his mess, and a stillness uncurled around him. On the front page was Mandy Rogers's father, a bouquet of microphones pushed into his face. He was standing in front of his house, holding a photo of her in his hand. The headline said: MANDY ROGERS FOUND DEAD IN ANAHEIM; MAN ARRESTED FOR FIRST DEGREE MURDER. Below the picture of Mandy's father was a quote, a single sentence, that read: *I hope they kill this sick animal even if he's the last man on earth.* The house was perfectly quiet. Jonas glanced at his orange cords and wrinkled orange Izod and felt a sudden desolate click, like a door being locked. He went into his room to change his clothes, his legs strange and flimsy, afraid to glance at the mirror in his closet. The air seemed to pass through him, a trickle of dust. Someone honked from the driveway. He parted his curtains and looked outside, where his family was waiting for him to appear.

CHAPTER 22

Lyle's idea of infernal punishment was riding in the backseat of the Volvo, still hobbled with sunburn, while the Boys of Killarney piped from the stereo. Even in her wildest imaginings of hell, she'd failed to incorporate any elbow horns. She'd failed to include a tin whistle performing the vocal line to "Hotel California." She recalled her near-death experience in the bathtub, wishing now that the radio had fallen in the water and fried her like a doughnut. She could have spared herself the Boys of Killarney, not to mention a weekend in the Mojave Desert.

"Can we listen to the news?" she asked, interrupting a jiglike rendition of "Go Your Own Way." Her mother was still snacking from the bag of marshmallows on the dashboard. Perhaps no one had informed her that they were made of sugar and pork skin.

"It's all Mandy Rogers," her mom said, wiping some marshmallow dust from her fingers. "I don't want Jonas listening to that."

"It's so awful to think about," her father said. "That poor girl being—"

"Warren!" her mom interrupted him. She turned up the stereo.

"Being what?" Lyle asked.

"*D-I-S-M-E-M-B-E-R-E-D.*"

Dustin laughed. "Hate to break it to you, Dad, but Jonas can spell."

"What does 'dismembered' mean?" Jonas asked.

Before Lyle could answer him, her mom twisted around in her seat. "Like when you, um, stop remembering something."

"Right," Dustin said. "Like 'I dismembered my old teacher today.'"

Jonas frowned, as though forgetting about Mandy Rogers was somehow worse than anything. "They don't know for sure it's her."

"Her clothes were buried in the guy's yard," Dustin said. "Who else would it be?"

"She might have escaped. A long time ago."

"Get real," Dustin said. "They found garden shears with blood all over them."

"Dustin!" their mom said.

"Sorry. *S-H-E-A-R-S.*"

A patch of sunlight was resting on Lyle's pants, scorching her like an iron. The Boys of Killarney launched into a Gaelic version of "Feelin' Groovy" that could only be described as avant-garde. Mr. Leonard began to yowl along from the back. After the bathtub incident, Lyle had briefly entertained the thought that she loved her family, that she might even go to college within a hundred-mile radius of them. Her best friend was in France; Hector despised her; she would never be Shannon Jarrell no matter how much Lyle pretended to like her. Her family was all she had. This had turned out to be a fit of lunacy. They were indeed all she had, but this was by no means a comforting thought.

By the time they pulled off the freeway for lunch, the Boys of Killarney had been replaced by *Sharing the Light: Hits from the Sofia Orphanage Children's Choir.* Lyle's father veered into a McDonald's and stopped at a life-sized statue of Ronald McDonald. The statue was missing one of its arms, which had done nothing to diminish the psychotic grin on its face. "Be with you in minute, please," it said in a Mexican accent.

"*Gracias,*" her mother said, leaning over her father's lap.

"Mom," Lyle said. "Do *not* speak Spanish."

"Why not?"

"Because you're talking to a machine. It's ridiculous."

"It's not ridiculous. This is a Latino area. Eighty percent of fast food employees in California are Latino."

Lyle stared at the amputee clown preparing to take their order. "Ronald McDonald is *not* Latino!"

"How do you know?" her mother said.

Lyle looked at her, incredulous. "Does 'Ronald' sound Spanish to you?"

"I don't know," Dustin said. "Ritchie Valens changed his name."

"It might have been Ronaldo in his country," Jonas said, nodding.

"That's not the point!"

Her father shook his head. "McDonald. Sounds Scottish to me."

Lyle got out of the car. She had no idea where she was going but knew that another second with her family would result in violence. The sun was so hot she could feel her skin through her clothes, a slow sizzle of pain, linked in her mind with the smell of french fries. She crossed the parking lot without looking back, her eyes tearing as she walked. There were no sidewalks and she had to walk along the shoulder of the road. People stared at her as they whooshed by in their trucks. If she could find a pay phone, she would try Hector. She would call him for the eleventh time this week. Maybe if there was the roar of traffic, if she were homeless and roaming the streets, he'd feel a prick of concern and not hang up at the sound of her voice.

She found a pay phone outside a store named Cigarettes Cheaper! and called Hector's house, only to get a recorded voice telling her to deposit sixty more cents. She began to beat the receiver against the phone. Just as she realized it wouldn't break, Lyle looked up and saw Dustin walking toward her in the shimmering heat, brandishing a red-and-white-striped arm. The hand at the end was raised in a wide-fingered salute.

"Look what I found," he said, holding up Ronald McDonald's arm.

She couldn't help laughing. Or rather, a laugh came helplessly out of her. "Where was it?"

"In the Dumpster behind the parking lot. Poking out like a zombie's."

Dustin threaded a cigarette between two of the yellow fingers and held it up to his mouth to light it. He passed the arm to Lyle, like an offering. It was surprisingly light. They passed the arm back and forth for a minute, smoking the cigarette in Ronald McDonald's hand, pressed against the wall in order to keep to the shade.

"Remember when I taught you to smoke?" Dustin said.

"You never taught me to smoke."

"Are you kidding? I showed you how to blow smoke out your nose, without choking to death."

"I don't know what you're talking about," Lyle said.

Dustin frowned. He looked at the arm he was holding. "Look at the size of that hand, will you? I bet the Fry Girls are psyched."

A man in a cowboy hat came out of the store and Dustin waved at him with the plastic arm. For a second, Lyle couldn't believe that she and Dustin were teenagers. It seemed like yesterday they were playing Cats vs. Dogs under a flipped-over raft, or working feverishly in their room on *The Land of Underwater Birds,* the book they'd written one summer when she was seven. She could picture the cover almost perfectly: strange birds swimming in the ocean or squatting in underwater nests, a flock of fish soaring through the sky above them. What a blast they'd had together, thinking up a world where everything happened in reverse. They'd spent a whole month poring over the details, giddy with creation, thinking up an endless litany of facts. *In the land of underwater birds, skydivers leap into planes. People sing "Miserable Birthday to You." Movie stars have terrible faces.* How lovingly they'd written it all down, diligent as monks, illustrating every page like a textbook. Lyle could not remember ever having so much fun.

Now, of course, she and Dustin would never be able to write a book together, it wasn't something teenagers did—just as in a year or two, probably, they would no longer be able to pull things from a Dumpster and use them as cigarette holders. Whatever was happening to them, it seemed unbearably tragic.

"Who were you trying to call?" Dustin asked.

Lyle looked at her feet. "A guy. Who despises me."

"Are you in love with him?"

"I don't know," she said. "He's got a mustache."

Dustin passed her the arm. "I've got one of those, too."

"A guy with a mustache?" she said, suddenly interested.

"Kira, I mean. Someone who won't talk to me. Dad stole their answering machine, and now Mr. Shackney won't even put her on the phone. Told me never to call again or he'd have me arrested, too. The actual words were a bit more graphic."

"I thought Dad broke into their house because you left something there. Your wallet."

Dustin laughed. "Is that what Mom told you?"

Lyle frowned, feeling foolish. Frankly, she'd been in too much pain to care about the details. It occurred to her she knew almost nothing about her brother's life.

"I'm sorry about your sunburn," he said.

"It's okay."

"Does it still hurt?"

Lyle nodded. She was sweltering in her jeans, sweat trickling down her legs. The car, at least, had air-conditioning. It was starting to seem marginally better than homelessness and starvation.

"We'd better not let Mom see this place," Dustin said, looking up at the Cigarettes Cheaper! sign buzzing over the entrance. "Dad pulled into the 7-Eleven. I think so she could buy more marshmallows."

"Not really."

"Really. She's in there right now. It's like a scene from one of her movies." He hunched down like a drug addict, teeth chattering, pulling a pretend bill from his pocket. "*Dame mas* marshmallows, *por favor.*"

"Stop," Lyle said. "You're hurting me."

At the campsite, Dustin helped his father put the tents up before dark, pounding stakes in with a rock. This was part of family tradition. You were supposed to find a rock in the desert and heft it back to your campsite, risking a fatal scorpion bite, rather than bringing along the perfectly good sledgehammer you had in the garage. You were also supposed to pretend to enjoy yourself, taking frequent breaks to admire the view, which—as far as Dustin was concerned—consisted of a bunch of ugly, squidlike trees, their branches all squidding in the same direction.

He knelt in the dirt to finish off a stake, wishing he were back home in the garage with a Budweiser. On the far side of the bathrooms, a rock climber crept her way up a boulder, dangling from one arm as she dipped her hand into a chalk bag. Her ponytail hung down like a plumb line. Something about the way she balanced there, inadvertently beautiful, reminded him of Kira. He didn't know how much Kira knew; since she hadn't called him, though, he figured she had a pretty good idea. It was a mystery how his depravity had emerged. He'd erased the message itself, well before the police had confiscated the answering machine. He didn't even know how Taz had managed to get home the night of the party, though it was easy enough to imagine the scene: the

Shackneys awake when Taz arrived, cornering her in the kitchen until they'd forced out the truth. Her little brother's pleased-as-shit face, grinning from the hallway.

Dustin had woken up the next morning, so stung with remorse it hurt to breathe. It was his punishment for betraying Kira. He'd believed that until he looked under his arms and saw the faint gray bruises on his ribs.

"Man, I'm parched," his father said, wiping his hands on his blue jeans. He always said this when they went camping, as though they were lost in the Sahara and hadn't brought ten gallons of water with them. To complete the impression, he was wearing a safari hat that cinched around his chin like a bonnet. He nodded toward the next campsite, where some kids were cranking AC/DC from their pickup. "Is that good music?"

"If you like arena rock," Dustin mumbled.

"Who's that? The lead singer?"

"*Rock and roll*. Played in a sports arena."

Dustin glanced at Lyle reading in the backseat of the Volvo, wishing Jonas and his mom would get back from wherever they'd gone with Mr. Leonard. Two days ago, when Mr. Shackney had called the house to tell them he'd phoned the cops, Dustin had found himself hoping his dad would get arrested. He'd wanted him to pay for screwing up so royally and ruining his life. But when he'd actually watched him getting hauled off to jail, his dad ducking into the back of the squad car, small as a criminal, his face dazed and frightened and toddler-like—when Dustin had seen all this he had not felt particularly good. He'd felt crumpled and small, as though he'd just killed something by mistake.

Later, describing to Biesty what had happened, he'd had a different feeling. A surprising twinge of pride. There was something about his dad being hauled off to jail in the middle of the day that sounded like an X song. Biesty had seemed impressed, though not nearly as impressed as when Dustin showed him the bruises under his ribs and explained how they'd gotten there.

"Think they, um, have any beer over there?" his dad asked now, eyeing the pickup truck. The musty smell of pot hung in the breeze.

"I don't know," Dustin said.

"How about I investigate."

Dustin shrugged, crouching down to fix a flip-flop. His father—

out on bail—wanted to drink a beer with him. Dustin followed him past the Volvo, where Lyle was still hiding from the sun, and into the next campsite, stopping at a large cooler sitting by the fire pit. A pair of woman's underpants, pink as a kiss, was laid out on a rock to dry. Affably, Dustin's father approached the truck and knocked on the roof over the driver's seat before leaning down to talk to the kids inside. The truck roared to life and took off in a cloud of dust, rooster-tailing to the road, wheels spinning for a moment before catching dragster-style on the asphalt.

"I didn't even get to introduce myself," Dustin's father said, returning.

"It's the hat," Dustin said. "They must have thought you were a ranger."

His dad walked over to the cooler and peered inside for a minute before pulling out a dripping six-pack.

"You're going to take that?" Dustin asked, incredulous.

"They won't miss it. Anyway, I've got a record already."

They walked back to the campsite, scrambling up a rock overlooking the tents. At the top, his father handed him a beer and they sat side by side in the hot sun, staring at the giant, egg-shaped boulders spidered with climbers. The wet can numbed Dustin's hand. It was the sort of thing you didn't tell your friends about: how the best part of drinking a beer sometimes was holding it, your fingers going old and creaky with the cold.

"It's beautiful, even with all the mountain climbers," his dad said, sipping his beer.

"Rock climbers, you mean."

"I guess I really screwed up your life," his dad said finally.

Dustin shrugged. "It was already pretty screwed-up, to be honest."

"Did you and Kira Shackney break up?"

"Probably."

"I'm sorry."

His father seemed genuinely eaten up, holding his Pabst Blue Ribbon with two hands. Dustin didn't tell him that it was not Kira he thought about all the time but her fifteen-year-old sister, the same girl who'd taken over his dreams. Last night she was naked and tied to a stake, surrounded by a mob of angry witch-hunters. Dustin had rescued her on a horse and then galloped off with her to the woods, where the nights were so cold they had to kill the horse and slit open its belly, sleeping inside of it to keep from freezing to death. It had been romantic, not bad at all. By the end of the dream they were both old people, in their forties, Taz's hair as white as her forelock.

Down below, Jonas and his mom were returning to the campsite, their arms laden with thorny twigs. Mr. Leonard hobbled over to the ring of rocks surrounding the fire pit, crooning at them and pacing in circles, determined that none be neglected.

"Is he in heaven or hell?" Dustin's father asked.

"Hard to say."

Lyle emerged from the Volvo, watching Jonas and his mother stack kindling. "We're drinking beer!" his dad called down, lifting the six-pack, and the three of them looked at Dustin, expecting him to be embarrassed.

Warren sat by the fire, watching his family roast marshmallows. Was there anything so mysterious as their motley approaches to this simple task? Camille poked hers at the fire, browning it in quick, vigilant stabs; Lyle sat as far away as possible, roasting hers with a four-foot stick; Jonas, epicure of marshmallows, held his high above the flames, turning it like a boar on a spit; Dustin dunked his right into the fire and pulled it out when the whole stick was aflame, letting it drip into the dirt—the last gasp of a sparkler—before blowing it out.

"Your father has something to tell you," Camille said, in between marshmallows. Warren had hoped, against reason, that she might let him off the hook. He did not want to disturb the trip. The beer he'd stolen had only made him fumbly and sentimental, more besotted with the faces of his children waiting for him to speak.

"Remember the Chrysler?" he said slowly, unable to look at them. A spark popped off the fire, and he batted his hair. Possibly he was a little drunk.

"Do you have a drinking problem?" Lyle asked.

"It wasn't stolen." Warren went on to explain about the Chrysler. He told them about the furniture, the empty accounts, the snipped-up credit cards. The toxic waste dump and doomed investment of Auburn Fields. The fact that Camille's salary, $20,000 a year, wouldn't so much as cover their mortgage. Once he'd begun, he couldn't stop. It was like sledding down a hill. He spared them nothing. He told them, to make sure there was no confusion, no false hope on anyone's part—including his own—that it was only a matter of weeks before the house was foreclosed.

When he was finished, Warren felt hungry. Dustin's and Lyle's marshmallows had caught fire and bubbled away to nothing. Insects chirred all around them, as unmoved as the rocks and trees.

"Where will we move?" Jonas asked.

"I don't know. Somewhere less expensive."

"How about Torrance?" Dustin said.

Warren couldn't speak. Perhaps his son didn't understand.

"I haven't had a very good summer either," Lyle said.

Warren blinked at her. "You haven't?"

"I saw Hector at the beach and pretended not to know him. My boyfriend. Hector Granillo, who works at the gate. I was ashamed of him, I think." She nudged the fire with her stick. "So I drove him away on purpose."

There was a respectful silence.

"Is that the guy with the walker?" Dustin asked.

"No!"

"I thought his name was Hector."

"Herman, I think," Camille said. "He's got rheumatoid arthritis."

"Yeah, well, I slept with Kira's sister," Dustin said. "Taz Shackney."

"You *did*?" Lyle said. "The one who's Jonas's age?"

Dustin scowled. "She's not Jonas's age. She's almost sixteen. The Shackneys found out and now Kira hates my guts."

Camille looked at Warren. "Is that true?"

"I left it on the answering machine," Dustin explained. "That's why Dad got arrested."

Warren threw some more kindling on the fire. He was too overwhelmed to react. Everyone looked at Camille, whose fingers were white with marshmallow.

"Mom," Lyle said, "what about you?"

"Besides making a video no one understands?" She frowned, scratching the dirt with her stick. "I thought I was pregnant for a while, and then I thought your father was having an affair when he wasn't. I put some urine in his coffee."

"You *peed* in it?"

"No. It was a urine sample."

"Holy shit," Dustin said, laughing.

"Wow, Mom. That takes the prize."

"It's not funny," Camille said to the kids, dabbing her eyes with her sweater. Whether she was laughing, too, or crying, Warren couldn't tell. Drinking his wife's urine seemed like small punishment.

"Mahatma Gandhi drank his own urine," Jonas said. "I saw it on PBS."

"You thought I was having an affair?" Warren said.

"Yes."

"You've got nothing to worry about, Mom," Lyle said. "So long as he keeps wearing that hat."

Warren uncinched the chin cord of his hat. He hadn't realized he still had it on. Like Camille's shawl, it had been the cause of gleeful derision when he brought it home from the store.

"What about Jonas?" Lyle said.

"Let me guess," Dustin said. "You forgot to return to your home planet."

"Ha-ha," Jonas said.

"If you're part of this family, you're going to have to learn to fuck up."

Later, they unrolled their sleeping bags and slept outdoors, deciding to forgo the tents. Warren knew that his children's reaction was purely of the moment, that once the reality of their bankruptcy sank in there would be anger and blame, there would be fights and new schools and unthought-of losses—but nonetheless he decided to bask in the reprieve he'd been granted. Camille laid her bag next to Warren's, which surprised him. It was bright enough to see their children's faces. Stuffed peacefully in their bags, they looked like mummies. He thought of all the camping trips he'd taken them on when they lived in Wisconsin, a chronicle of suffering. The trips to Hidden Lakes. The "vacations" in St. Croix State Park. Quetico in Canada, when they'd put a hole in their canoe and hadn't caught a single fish, finally forced to survive on tapioca pudding for three days straight. Even on the disastrous trips, there were the skies at night, a wonderment of stars. The stillness of one another's company. It was his favorite time ever: to be outdoors with his children, the sky's dwarfing hugeness making them seem closer than they were at home. Warren inched toward his wife, waiting for her to stiffen or roll over to face the other direction.

"Left or right?" Camille asked.

"What?"

"Which side is your zipper on? Mine's left."

Warren's was right. They climbed out of their bags and zipped them together, taking care not to snag the material. There was some extra space at the foot of each bag where the zippers didn't reach; the results looked like a pulled tooth. They climbed inside and wriggled down, sharing the warmth of their bodies. Camille's hair smelled like wood smoke. The beer drinkers next to them had yet to return. Warren slipped his hand under Camille's thermal underwear and felt the lovely shoal of her spine, overwhelmed with gratitude and relief, waiting for their children's breathing to settle into sleep.

CHAPTER 23

Hector lay in bed, shivering for no reason. Something was happening to him. He was freezing to death, despite being fully dressed in jeans and a sweater. He'd climbed into bed that way, stumbling in from the truck at two-thirty in the morning, feeling too drunk and lazy to feed Raoul. Now he was shaking so hard he thought he might puke. More than hungover: he was actually sick. His body felt weak and feverish, an achy junkyard of limbs.

He got up finally to check on Raoul, head throbbing, and padded over to the mesh cage in the corner. The branches where Raoul usually perched were empty. Hector crouched down to get a better look. Scattered all over the floor of the cage, like a toddler's mess, were Cheerios and broken-up cookies and random bits of food from the kitchen. Hector closed his eyes for a second, thinking maybe he was seeing things, but when he opened them the mess looked worse than before. He found Raoul lying in the corner atop a snowy bed of Quaker Oats. He was gray as a seal, legs splayed out in front of him. His tail, furled at the very tip like a musical note, had unraveled halfway across the cage.

Hector picked him up gingerly with two hands and lifted him out. He was cold and stiff and toylike. Hector went into the living room, where his grandmother was watching two women in fur coats scream at each other on TV. She seemed amused by their fury.

"You killed him," he said, showing her Raoul.

"*Sí?*" she said, smiling.

"*Lo mataste! Está muerto!* What were you doing, trying to feed him?"

She grabbed at the dead chameleon as if it were a gift. Hector pulled his hands away, and his grandmother searched the room.

"Almost dead," Hector said mockingly, in English. "Why don't you die for real?"

He went into the kitchen and found a shoe box under the sink and laid Raoul inside of it, curling his tail gently so it wouldn't break, too sick at heart to feel ashamed. He sat down at the table, cradling the shoe box in his lap. Beneath his venomous sadness for Raoul, simmering with his fever, was a self-pitying desire that Lyle could see what she'd turned him into. He still couldn't quite believe she was in on her father's scam. *Honestly, I wouldn't live ten miles from this place unless you like the smell of shit*. That was what one of the construction workers had said, after telling him what they were digging in the middle of the desert. It had not occurred to Hector that Lyle knew about her father's treachery, but then he'd seen her at the beach and she hadn't even waved. She'd stared down at the sand, too guilty to face him.

Hector walked to the window and parted the blinds with two fingers, watching his mother hang wash on the clothesline. She leaned over the hamper and clutched her lower back, wincing with her eyes closed. The pain in her face fanned Hector's self-pity. His teeth chattered. He grabbed his jacket from the closet and put it on. He'd find some way to get back at the Zillers; it would come to him spur-of-the-moment, a gift from the gods.

"Where are you going now?" his mother asked in Spanish, catching him as he walked to the pickup. For the first time, the license plate embarrassed him. His mother glanced at the shoe box in his hands before fixing on his rumpled clothes. "When's the last time you had a shower?"

"Don't start."

"You're dressed like it's winter." She stepped closer and he recoiled, clamping the shoe box to his chest. "What is it, *mijo*? Did you break up with that girl?"

He laughed. "No. I killed her with Cheerios."

She stepped back. "Hector, what's wrong with you? You're scaring me."

Hector got in the pickup, driving up Anaheim toward the verdant hill of Palos Verdes rising like a volcano above the smokestacks. He was shivering so much he could barely steer. He hunched over the wheel, trying to decipher the blurry grid of stoplights. Though he'd promised to stop thinking about it, the instant on the beach flashed through his mind again. Hadn't there been something else, too, before Lyle's frown? A split-second smile? He'd driven himself crazy with it, trying to remember if she'd really brightened or not, if he'd imagined her face beaming happily when she first caught his eye. Sometimes, clinging to a thread, he imagined that he'd misinterpreted the whole thing. Perhaps she loved him; it was all a mistake; she hadn't recognized him for real.

No, she'd seen him clearly and hadn't even managed to lift her hand. Let her call and cry her eyes out—he wouldn't rise to the bait of making her feel better.

Near the entrance to Herradura Estates, Hector parked out of sight of the gate and crept along the shoulder of the road, clutching the shoe box with two hands. Bud was reading a magazine in the guardhouse. Hector thought about talking his way inside, but he hadn't been to work in a week and couldn't bear to show his face. The clock that he and Lyle had broken was still hanging on the wall, stopped at the time of their first fuck. It was like something you'd find in a dream, twinkling with menace. Hector crouched past the guardhouse and hiked along John's Canyon Road until he reached High Street, turning down the sleepy, tree-lined, untoxic road toward the Zillers' house. Soapberries popped under his sneakers. There were no cars in the driveway or parked under the carport. Something about the house, the unnatural quiet of it, told him the Zillers weren't home.

He decided to wait for their return. First, though, he'd take a look inside. He'd see the house once and for all, even if Lyle had never invited him over. The day was clear and beautiful, bees bounced on the rosebushes along the driveway, but he was too feverish to feel the sun's warmth. Hector rounded the garage until he was facing a window whose blinds were open to the sun. He rested his head against the glass. A bedroom of some kind, probably Lyle's parents'. A creepy picture of Pac-Man floating in some clouds hung on the wall across from the bed.

Laying the shoe box in a bed of azaleas, Hector picked up one of the decorative rocks at his feet, lifted it to his chest, and then heaved it through the bedroom window, which shattered in a rain of glass. He waited for an alarm to go off. It would almost be a relief. When nothing happened, he retrieved the shoe box and stepped as best he could through the window frame, avoiding the stalactite of glass jutting from the top.

The room was cold as a cavern. Hector could barely think. Still carrying the shoe box, he walked past the bed and down a narrow hall lined with puke-colored artwork and ended up in what looked like the Zillers' living room. Except for an old patio chair and a TV set, there was no furniture. One of the vinyl straps of the chair was broken, a blob of bird shit meringued to one arm. Hector bent down to pick up a piece of popcorn buried in the rug. A bit of anger unflaked from his heart. He wanted to curl up in the lounge chair and go to sleep but was worried he might not resurrect himself. He looked up at the windows over the TV. The curtains were neatly drawn, letting in a thin cord of sunlight. In the foyer, beside the front door, lay a jumble of old camping gear and what looked like a telescope still packed in its box. For the first time, it occurred to him that the Zillers were out of town.

He walked into the kitchen, where the curtains were drawn as well. A charred bagel, black as a fossil, peeked out of the toaster. On the counter beside it was a handwritten list titled THINGS TO BRING ON TRIP. Hector's teeth were still chattering. He wondered if he was dying. Laying the box on the counter, too feverish to think, he walked over to the stove and turned on the burner, trying to warm himself over the flame. It scorched his fingers but did nothing to thaw the coldness in his bones. On the back guard of the stove, lined up in a row, was an array of baffling teas. Lemon Zinger. Evening in Montana. Lotus Flower Dream. He glanced around for a kettle before grabbing a small pot hanging from a rack under the cupboard, filling it to the brim in the sink. Tea might help. Warm his fever. He shivered over to the burner again. By mistake he splashed a bit of the water on the flame, which hissed and sputtered and flowered again under the pot.

It would not boil. Not if he watched it.

Hector grabbed the shoe box and wandered down the hall. He recognized Lyle's room right away. The wall of paperbacks; the poster of Morrissey in a stupid-looking pompadour; the *calaveras* taunting him from the windowsill, dressed comically as bride and groom—everything she'd described to him on the phone. Even the smell, a mixture of cigarettes and perfume, was dizzily familiar. Gently, though his hands were shaking, Hector lifted Raoul from his shoe box and laid him on the pillow of Lyle's bed. He tried to roll his tail back into a spiral, but it was as stiff as a pencil. The chameleon seemed smaller than before, obscene in its stillness. Something about the way it looked—tiny, helpless, eternally dead—made Hector ashamed.

His head throbbed. He hobbled over to Lyle's desk. Clutching the chair with one hand, he opened the drawer and stared at the mess of tapes and letters and photographs, startled to see a piece of paper with his own handwriting on it. The poem he'd given her. It was crinkled and worn, a tear beginning along one crease. Beneath it was another sheet of paper: a different poem, written in Lyle's handwriting. It had no title and began in the middle of the page. Hector pulled the poem out, trying to control his shivering enough that he could follow the words.

Mustache
A word made up of two:
Must ache,
A command,
As though I'm supposed to hurt like this
A job I have to finish
Or a formula for missing you

Must + ache =

No bristles kissing me
A lizard on TV
A red pickup that isn't yours
An inflatable castle
A clock that's stopped on us
A second name for my heart

Hector's legs felt weak. *A clock that's stopped on us.* He read the poem again, lingering over the last stanza. He remembered the inflatable castle, the kids all screeching with joy as they bounced up and down together, hair flapping like wings. When had he told her about that? Feebly, he folded the poem into a square and stuffed it in his pocket. He could barely stand. He felt suddenly foolish. Misplaced—the way you feel when you wake up somewhere strange, a friend's couch, and don't know where you are. His head whistled with pain. If he returned home, if he climbed back into bed where he belonged, his mother would take care of him.

He left Raoul on Lyle's pillow. Training his eyes on the floor in front of him, he managed to shuffle down the hall and back to the empty living room, finding the door to the house. Hector closed it carefully behind him. For a second the twittering of birds made his head swim. Then he hunched down the Zillers' driveway to his truck, thinking vaguely—and just for a second—that there was something he'd forgotten.

CHAPTER 24

Warren pulled on his clothes, breath clouding in the brittle air, and hiked up the boulder to where the sun shone. The light warmed him immediately. It was like entering a different room. Below him, cocooned in sleeping bags, his family slept peacefully around the fire pit, a ring of question marks, their legs tucked up from the cold. There was something remarkable about seeing them in a circle. The shade in which they lay moved imperceptibly as Warren watched, shrinking like a tide and illuminating their faces one at a time, as if they were emerging from the deep.

He felt sluggish and happy. Last night, he and Camille had made love after the kids were asleep, slow as insects, their long johns shackling their ankles. He'd woken this morning with an afterglow of well-being. His family would be all right, so long as they stuck together and confided their failures. He felt this wholeheartedly but was afraid to move in case the feeling dissolved.

Later that afternoon, driving home, Warren gripped the wheel with two hands to keep the wind from yanking it sideways. Tumbleweeds bounced in front of the car. Jonas insisted on listening to a radio show called "The UFO Connection," which featured an interview with a "spirit photographer." *I asked the blue orbs for a little show,* the photographer said, *and they really hammed it up.*

"They should show a little dignity," Lyle said.

"What's a 'blue orb'?" Jonas asked.

"An orb that's having a bad day," Warren said, trying a joke.

No one laughed. Warren glanced in the rearview mirror at Dustin, who hadn't said a word since they'd stopped for lunch. The McDonald's straw he'd been chewing on was flat and mangled, sticking out of his teeth. If not an actual smile, Warren hoped to elicit an acknowledgment of some kind—a nod or a glance, something reminiscent of the camaraderie they'd had drinking beer together. Warren stared back at the highway. Ahead of them a gray cloud towered ominously, flickering with brilliant wishbones of lightning.

"How long have you known we were broke?" Dustin said from the backseat. His voice was slow and deliberate, as though he'd been preparing the question in his mind.

"Since January, probably. I don't know."

"What about UCLA?"

Warren avoided looking at him. "These tumbleweeds are out of hand. It's like an asteroid belt."

"Jesus, Dad. You haven't even talked to them, have you?"

"Let's talk about it later."

"We could have been applying for financial aid! Something! School starts in September."

Warren looked at Dustin: he was bolted to his seat, tense as a jack-in-the-box. The car thickened with the smell of rain, sweet and manurey and oddly singed. "I thought college was for 'capitalist sellouts.' You want to be a rock star."

Dustin's face clenched with rage. Warren shouldn't have said it. It was a stupid thing, a way of turning the tables. Rain began to hit the roof, a few lone smacks building into a torrential roar. He flipped on the wipers and then looked back at his son, hoping to apologize, but he'd strapped his headphones on and was glaring out the window, lost again to his music.

At home, Warren pulled into the driveway and waited for the stillness to catch up with his thoughts. The kids—Dustin included—were slumped sideways in the backseat, leaning together as if they were taking a hairpin turn. Even Camille had fallen asleep, her face mashed into the headrest. Warren sat there for a minute, not wanting to disturb his feeling that the world had stopped. Mr. Leonard snored geriatrically from the far back. Except for Mr. Leonard, for the ticking of the engine, there was no sound at all. A swallowtail landed on the hood for a moment and then flapped away. Dustin opened his eyes, yawning. The left side of his headphones had slid off and were wedged behind his ear like a hearing aid.

"We'll find a way to get you through school," Warren said.

"I promise." He glanced away from the mirror. "I did call them once, the aid office, but they never called back."

"Maybe you can steal enough wine to cover tuition."

Dustin got out of the car and walked toward the house, pausing for a moment to fish cigarettes from his pocket. The sun glinted off his hair. He was such a relentless boy, so unforgiving; why did Warren insist on trying to befriend him? It was like a sickness or a curse. He wondered what it would be like to stop trying. To give up completely and let Dustin set the rules, let his son's contempt seep into the ground between them.

It might be a relief, a great one, like sinking into bed after a long day of travel.

Camille was awake now, blinking at the windshield. Warren wanted to tell her that he'd mistaken fatherhood for true love, how sorry he was that he'd been fooled, but even as he thought this he knew it was a lie. He would seek Dustin's love at all costs, a hopeless search.

Warren watched his son walk toward the house, a cigarette dangling from his lips. Dustin stopped in the middle of the lawn and pulled out a lighter. For a moment, he seemed invincible. The birds seemed to stop chirping, as though in a trance, the air still as a question.

Then something strange: a whoosh, a gasp from the trees. It happened in an instant, but Warren saw the explosion unfold in a tranquil sequence of disasters. First the sound, this earth-sized whoosh. Then the house itself, a crumpling of wood and glass, like someone sucking the air out of a bag. The sky volcanic with fire. A hooflike clatter above him, the world outside the car swirling with debris.

His first thought was: *I'm free.*

Then he saw Dustin. He was writhing in the grass, trying to flap the fire from his arms. Warren grabbed a blanket from the backseat and bolted across the lawn and jumped on top of Dustin, hugging him with the blanket, his eyes shut to the smoke—to the sweet, bacony, gut-wrenching smell filling his nostrils—rolling through the grass with his burning son, clutching him with both arms, heaving him around and around until the blanket stopped feeling like a wild creature, aware of the awful smothered screaming only when it ended, his son alive and panting in his arms, quiet as a fish, and still Warren didn't move or speak or let go, ignoring the shouts of his family, the stink of burned wool and flesh, until finally he opened his eyes and saw the trail of scorched lawn and the black angel in the grass where his son had lain flapping, so small compared to the gorgeous disaster of his house, the kitchen and bedrooms and entryway transformed into a pyramid of fire, a tremendous rustling of heat, shirts rising from the popping windows like ghosts.

PART II

Summer 1986

CHAPTER 25

Lyle rolled down the window of the Renault, the desert air scorching her face. Her T-shirt stuck to her chest. Why the fuck hadn't she gotten the air-conditioning fixed? She'd replaced the muffler with her own money but had decided to skimp on the extras, forgetting that they lived in the Mojave desert. With coyotes and jackrabbits. Animals that dashed into the highway, hoping to be put out of their misery. Feeling faint, Lyle glanced in the rearview mirror and saw a hungry-looking vulture seesawing behind her, its red head hanging down like a trigger.

She hadn't been home in a month. It was a major topic of conversation, how little she visited. Last fall, when her parents had agreed to let her live with Bethany so she wouldn't have to commute four hours a day, they'd made it clear that they expected her to drive home every weekend. It hadn't occurred to Lyle that she wouldn't. At that point, Dustin was still wearing his pressure mask around and couldn't take a bath without someone's help. She'd actually *wanted* to come home. Bethany was her best friend, her parents very nice and generous, but she was also a person who equated combing the tangles from her hair with suffering. All she talked about was France and how much she missed the *tarte tatin*. The *tarte tatin* would make you cream your pants. If she wasn't talking about *tarte tatin,* she was cooing into the phone to her French boyfriend with the Dickensian teeth. It was a relief for Lyle to go home and face the gravity of her life, the irrefutable suffering of a crippled brother.

By spring, though, Lyle had stopped making the drive every weekend. There was the column she was writing for the newspaper—

"Severely Yours"—which took up a lot of time. There was all the work for her AP classes, and then studying for her achievement tests, and then of course finals, not to mention that she was working twenty hours a week at The Perfect Scoop. Did her parents think being manager was a walk in the park?

Now she'd quit her job and was returning home for summer vacation, the back of the Renault crammed with her things. "Vacation" implied some kind of holiday, but the thought of spending three months in the middle of the Mojave with her family alarmed Lyle deeply. As she exited the freeway, turning up the dirt road to Auburn Fields, the air began to take on the smell of rotten eggs and stewed cabbage, the putrid stench of home. It was like an enormous fart that never went away. She rolled up the window. To the left of her, dug into the earth and protected by a very tall fence, like a humongous footprint filled with rain, shone the dump. Its azure pool shimmered in the sun. A "sludge pond," they called it; what toxic things it retained, and why it was such a gorgeous, heartbreaking blue, Lyle could only imagine.

She followed the long dusty road to the entrance of Auburn Fields, which was not only fieldless but brown as a turd. The gate was open, as always. She waved at the defunct video camera in its little steel hut, to make it feel useful. Beyond the single block of empty homes sprawled a barren tract of desert. They had no neighbors: the last holdouts—the Jimenezes—had moved out in May. Driving up the block, Lyle always felt like the survivor of a nuclear war: she imagined the interiors of the other homes, each one a tableau of bodies, families slumped around the dinner table or huddled Pompeii-like in front of the TV.

She had to park on the road because a mail truck was blocking the driveway. She got out of the car and heaved her duffel bag from the trunk. The mailman, tan and colonial-looking in a pith helmet, stopped sorting the mail in his lap and looked at her from the driver's seat of his truck.

"Hello," Lyle said, smiling.

The mailman smiled back. Then—tenderly, as though holding out a present—he gave her the finger. Lyle thought she was seeing things, but the finger was still there after she blinked.

She schlepped her bag across the front yard—a crusty square of dirt—and plopped it inside the house. She peered into the little office where her dad liked to sit and do crosswords and saw a futon lying in the middle of the floor, her mother's shoes lined up against the wall. Sitting on the desk was a humidifier and her mom's makeup mirror spread open like a triptych. Lyle kept going, choosing to ignore this development. Her father was sitting by himself at the kitchen table. He was dressed in a shirt and tie, attacking a penny with a pair of scissors. Moons of sweat darkened his armpits.

"The mailman just gave me the finger," she said.

"Don't be too hard on him." Her father gave up on the penny and peered into the open case bristling with knives beside him. "We're ten miles off his route."

"He's never flipped me off before."

"Ten minutes each way. The stress of commuting. It accumulates."

Lyle waited for her dad to hug her or at least welcome her home. He returned his attention to the penny, squeezing the scissors with two hands and gritting his teeth.

"What are you doing?" she asked.

His face was red. "Trying to cut through this goddamned penny."

"Why?"

"For my pitch. It's supposed to, um, impress people." He gave up again on the penny, which seemed to have melded permanently to the hinge of the scissors. "The guy who does our training, Ted, cut one into a corkscrew. It was extremely righteous."

Lyle squeezed to the sink to get a glass of water, almost tripping over a hump of linoleum that had blistered from the floor. Ever since becoming a knife salesman, her dad had starting using words like "righteous" and "awesome." Lyle guessed they were sarcastic but wasn't a hundred percent sure. The kitchen sink was so full of dishes, some with whole servings of food on them, that she couldn't fit a glass under the faucet. She tried to use the water dispenser built into the fridge, but the lever had broken and the water dribbled out like a leak. While she was waiting to collect enough to drink, Jonas came through the sliding glass door that opened to the yardless desert, letting in a stink bomb of air. He was carrying a turtle. The turtle's head and legs were shrunk into its shell, which was divided into little trapezoidal sections. Jonas himself was tanned a reptilian brown. He'd been roaming happily around the desert even though this whole disaster was his fault. If he hadn't left the stove on for two days, if he hadn't been roasting marshmallows inside to begin with, the pilot wouldn't have blown out and choked the house with gas, and Dustin would be fine.

"Another turtle," her father said.

"It's not a turtle. It's a desert tortoise."

Lyle's mother came in from the hall, aghast. "Those are endangered!"

"Actually, they're only threatened," Jonas said.

"Please take it outside," she said quietly. She looked like she might cry.

"They'd be endangered, except they're good at relocating."

"Relocating! How would you feel if someone drove you from your bed?"

"Your mother would know," Lyle's dad said, grinning at her mom. It was not a pleasant grin but something you might give a little girl who'd trounced you at chess. Her mother scowled, refusing to meet his eyes. It occurred to Lyle that they could barely stand to be in the same room. Mr. Leonard hobbled in from the living room and peered at the tortoise shell with a look of undisguised longing. He was still alive, miraculously, which gave him a biblical sort of aura. Mr. Leonard began to sing to the shell, a lovelorn croon. The shell started to hiss.

"A duet," Lyle's father said.

"Jonas, take that outside this instant," her mother said. "I mean it. You didn't go near the dump, did you?"

Jonas shrugged. "What difference does it make? We're all going to die of leukemia, anyway."

"By the way," Lyle said, "I just drove an hour and a half with no air-conditioning."

"Welcome home," her mother said, hugging her.

"Where's Dustin?"

Her parents glanced at each other for the first time. "In his room, probably," her mom said. "Watching a movie."

Lyle walked back into the depressing living room, past the depressingly fake chandelier hanging in the foyer, and down the depressing hallway toward Dustin's room. It wasn't just the chintziness of the house that depressed her, but the fact that her father insisted on pretending it was as nice as their old one. Even the motel they'd stayed in those first couple months, when Dustin was in the hospital, was better than this: at least Lyle had had a bathroom in her room, with a shower that didn't have furry brown scorpions hiding in the drain, waiting to sting her feet. When she complained to her dad about the furry scorpions, or the rotten fart smell in her hair that she was afraid to wash out, he looked at her as though she were talking about a different house. It was the same one, ironically, that he'd tried to sell to Hector's mother. Lyle knew this because Hector had written her a letter a few months after the accident. Many letters, in fact. He had the address from the day they'd come to look at the house. Though she'd been too upset about Dustin to write back, Lyle had opened the letters immediately, hoping they'd live up to the buzzy, sexual thrill of seeing them in the mailbox. Instead, they were tame and disappointing, filled with a remorsefulness Lyle didn't understand. The hours she'd spent in the hospital, seeing her brother demented with pain, watching him weep and curse and howl without even knowing she was there, had shown her that she didn't really love Hector. Love was something that required you to be invisible. What she'd loved was Hector's attention: it had made her feel desired, which wasn't the same thing.

Lyle knocked on Dustin's door, wondering if he could hear anything over the sounds of mayhem rumbling from inside. Adding to the general tide of depressingness was the fact that he watched TV in his bedroom. It was one of the things on Lyle's list of THINGS YOU SHOULD AVOID DOING BEFORE YOU'RE FIFTY, right after *Go speed-walking with little arm weights*. Whenever she thought of her brother like this, holed up in his room all day watching movies, she felt forlorn and useless. She hesitated before turning the doorknob, dismayed to see that her hand was trembling.

"It's the best part," Dustin said, pointing at the screen. He was lying in bed, focused on Sylvester Stallone's shirtless body slumped in a helicopter. He liked movies with explosions in them: it wasn't ironic so much as a fuck-you to fate. "When Rambo hides the bazooka under his seat."

"Is that before or after he writes *A Season in Hell*?"

Dustin scowled, looking at her for the first time. It was always a shock to see him: the face not quite his, blotchy and discolored on one side, his cheek smudged into a purplish, rumpled bark. They'd rebuilt his eyelid, but it was still droopy and half-closed like a boxer's. It was supposed to gradually correct itself, but Lyle was having doubts. The lower lid had begun to sag, too, from the scars contracting on his cheek—you could see the inside of the lid, a dewy pocket of pink. Just a sliver, but it was enough to turn his eye from an ordinary thing into an eyeball. She went over and stopped the VCR just as Rambo was letting his bazooka loose on some astonished commies.

"Hey," Dustin said angrily, scratching at his elastic Jobst shirt. They'd measured him for the shirt at the hospital: it was meant to reduce scarring, though like the eye surgery it seemed a bit unambitious. Hard to believe a skintight shirt could do anything but make him feel more miserable. Along with the glove on his right hand, he was supposed to wear it twenty-three hours a day—his "second skin," the burn therapist had called it, though in reality it looked more like a scuba suit.

"Get your shoes on," Lyle said. "We're going to lunch."

"I'm not hungry."

"You can wear your, um, mask if you'd like."

She'd meant to be sensitive but realized by his face that she'd said the wrong thing. He raised his gloved hand off the bed. For dexterity, the fingers of the glove had been cut off at the tips. Lyle didn't know what was happening at first: she saw the fingers uncurling slowly, all together, Dustin grimacing in pain. Then the middle one inching higher, slow as a drawbridge. Less than thirty minutes she'd been home, and two people had flipped her off.

"I didn't know you could do that," Lyle said.

"I've been practicing."

Dustin insisted on going to Taco Bell, even though they had to drive an extra ten miles through Lancaster to get there, but Lyle was relieved she'd been able to coax him out of his room. It was like charming an animal out of its hole. He did not wear his mask, though he'd bought some mirrored sunglasses, huge and sparkling as a sheriff's, to cover up his eye. Lyle was surprised by how much better he looked. Still, when it was Dustin's turn to order, the cashier at Taco Bell turned to Lyle and asked in a quiet voice, "And what would your friend like?"

"I can't believe she asked me your order," Lyle said when they'd sat down. She was furious.

Dustin shrugged.

"It doesn't bother you?"

"At least she didn't point."

"People point?" she said quietly.

"Are you kidding? I've seen people back up their cars in the middle of the parking lot, just to get a better look." He took a bite of his Burrito Supreme, clutching it with his good hand. "Sometimes it's funny. *The Three Stooges.* The other day I was at the movies, buying a ticket, and a guy walked into a pole."

The air-conditioning was cranked so high that she was actually cold, her sweat-soaked T-shirt icy against her back. Dustin looked cold, too, even though he was wearing a sweater over his Jobst shirt. Lyle started to unwrap her taco and he flinched; she was always forgetting not to crinkle things.

"Sorry," she said.

"Don't apologize. It makes it worse."

She wanted to ask him how he could watch explosions all day long, then get mad at her for unwrapping a taco, but of course nothing about his accident made sense. At the next booth, a toddler in a pink dress had twisted around in her seat and was staring at Dustin with her fingers in her mouth. The toddler was nearly bald but had a giant bow stuck mysteriously to her head. Dustin was too absorbed in his burrito to notice.

"You never used to like Taco Bell," Lyle said. "Remember? You called it Taco Smell."

"That was you," he said.

"No, it wasn't."

"I always liked it."

"You hated it! We bought some tacos once and ended up giving them to Mr. Leonard."

Dustin looked up impatiently. "They have the Burrito Supreme now."

He sounded like Jonas. Lyle picked the tobacco-like shreds of lettuce from her taco, wishing she'd never come home. The excuses she'd been giving for not visiting every weekend were just that: *excuses.* She'd been avoiding Dustin's misery. Lyle watched him eat, succumbing to the silence until she couldn't bear it any longer.

"How's Toxic Shock Syndrome?"

He shrugged. "Fuck if I know."

"Aren't you still writing songs?"

"I sold my guitar."

"Dustin," she said. "You didn't."

He lifted his gloved hand, as though it belonged to somebody else. "What the fuck do you want me to do? Play with my teeth?"

"The OT said it might take a year. She wants you to practice."

"My amp's shot anyway. Smoke damage. Do you know how much a new one costs?"

"Mom and Dad would have helped you out, if you needed money."

He looked out the window. "Grow up, L. Dad's selling knives, for Christ's sake."

Stop feeling sorry for yourself, she wanted to say. But how could she? She didn't feel cold all the time, her face wasn't purple on one side, she hadn't been forced to give up college and work in a video store in the middle of nowhere. Lyle glanced at the next booth. The little bald girl with the bow was still staring, chewing on her fingers like a moron. Why the hell didn't her mother do something?

"What's up with Mom and Dad anyway?" she asked, changing the subject.

Dustin shoved his tray away. "Actually, they don't yell as much. Now that they've stopped sleeping in the same room."

"I saw the futon."

"They only talk to each other when they have to pay bills."

"Jesus."

"Anyway, she's never home. Dad does all the cooking."

"I can't believe she drives all that way to work. It took me an hour and a half, and it wasn't even rush hour."

Dustin frowned. "I never thought I'd miss Polynesian pork. Hector was over on Wednesday night, and Dad served us fried eggs for dinner."

"It's too weird," Lyle said, watching her reflection in his glasses. "You guys being friends."

"He's into pets. Makes perfect sense." Dustin laughed. "Anyway, he's the only person who doesn't pretend nothing's happened."

"What about Biesty?"

"*Mark,* you mean. He's in college now and too mature for nicknames. He's like a Moonie or something, always smiling at me and telling me how 'awesome' I look. Anyway, he's got his UCLA friends now."

Lyle watched her brother slurp the dregs from his Coke, wondering if there was an emotion besides bitterness lurking somewhere in his heart. Even though she'd returned none of Hector's letters, he'd driven out here to see Lyle in person and had ended up talking to Dustin in the kitchen for an hour. This was after she'd moved in with Bethany. For whatever reason, the two of them had hit it off. Maybe Dustin was right: there was something pet-like about him that appealed to Hector. With his crankiness, his precarious health issues, he was not unlike an exotic lizard. Like a lizard, too, he barely moved from his bed.

The little bald girl in the next booth was still staring at Dustin. Without warning, he whipped off his sunglasses and growled satanically at her, his teeth bared like a tiger's. The little girl burst into tears.

"What did you do?" Dustin asked the mother. "Krazy Glue that fucking bow on?"

"Dust, Jesus," Lyle said under her breath.

He turned back to his Coke. "One of our major pastimes around here. Scare the children."

On the way home, they didn't talk. Lyle squinted into the sun as she drove. They passed a Carl's Jr. on the outskirts of Lancaster, the last outpost of civilization; Dustin grimaced as if from a punch. It hadn't occurred to her that he'd insisted on going to Taco Bell out of fear, that the smell of broiled hamburgers was somehow distressing. She remembered when Dustin was in the hospital, that first week, the thick, Fourth of July smell of charred flesh seeping into her clothes. Zonked on morphine, he'd lain there in the sweltering room under a spiderweb of tubes. What she remembered most was how gigantic he looked: he'd blown up like the Michelin Man, bandaged from the waist up, his skinny legs sticking out as if he'd been crushed by a boulder. The nurse was worried about hypothermia and kept turning up the thermostat. Despite the nurse's warning, Lyle insisted on staying while she unwrapped Dustin's arm, stained black with chemicals. The stench was unspeakable. After washing his arm with sterile water, the nurse moistened a gauzy sponge and began to debride him, scrubbing his arm to loosen the skin, focusing on one spot at a time as though she were polishing a dresser, occasionally reaching down and picking some dead skin off with her fingers or using a scissors to snip it free before tossing everything—skin and sponge—into the hamper. It was something you could watch only by turning off your brain.

Near their house again, Lyle looked at the sun-choked buttes in the distance, which from this direction seemed to be covered in orange flowers. The poppy preserve. The blandness of the desert made the flowers stand out like a dream. Lyle was sure they hadn't been there a month ago. A strong wind buffeted the Renault; a minute later the whole hill seemed to stir, a great ripple of orange, like an insuck of breath.

"Has it been raining?" she asked Dustin, who was staring at the road.

"Beats me," he said.

CHAPTER 26

Dustin liked working at the video store, because he enjoyed the way people responded to his face. It gave him an excuse to hate them. Not that he needed an excuse: Lancaster was filled with people clamoring for his hatred. They had wraparound sunglasses and wore T-shirts that said TGIF: THANK GOD I'M FREE! or JESUSAVES or I'M ALL FOR GUN CONTROL . . . I USE BOTH HANDS. Most of the T-shirts had eagles on them. Dustin had begun asking these customers if they were bird-watchers. It was then that they'd get a clear look at his face. A sort of helpless double take, then a vague gastric wince they weren't aware of, then a polite glance away to pretend they hadn't seen anything. It was the glance away that made Dustin the maddest. Why didn't they have the fucking honesty to gawk?

"Rats, you just missed it," Dustin would say when someone asked why *Rambo: First Blood Part II* was still rented out.

He'd always wanted not to give a shit if people liked him. It was easy now, a reason to get up in the morning.

Dustin unzipped a sleeve of his Jobst shirt, scratching the itch that seemed to live inside his skin. It was deep and relentless. Beneath the welts from his nails, he could see the ghost of the skin they'd grafted on, a faint mesh stretching up his forearm, like fishnet. He preferred not to look at it. Since it was a slow Friday, there wasn't much to do but succumb to the itch and watch action movies on the mounted TV until his brain rotted. This afternoon, for a change, he was watching *Jaws*. Dustin liked that Brody wanted to blow up a shark with a scuba tank. It seemed creatively unsporting. Just as Brody was climbing the sinking ship's mast, preparing to take aim with his rifle, the phone rang.

"Do you have any adult films with little people in them?" a man's voice asked. It was hoarse and sniffly, as though he had a cold. Dustin hated it when people called pornos "films"; they were the only customers who didn't say "movie."

"Do you mean dwarves?"

"Yes. Adult films. With dwarves."

Dustin paused, and the man coughed. "What are you?" Dustin said. "Some kind of sicko?"

"Actually, I'm a dwarf," the man said indignantly before hanging up.

Dustin put the receiver back on its cradle, ashamed. The shame was mixed with a gratitude that dwarves existed. There were people more conspicuously out of whack than he was. He felt the same way when he went to outpatient rehab, glancing at people who'd lost their noses or had to have their jaws bolted through so they wouldn't melt into their necks. He tried not to think of the hospital, but the memory of those two awful months was there all the time, circling him like the unwearied shark in *Jaws*. Movies distracted him, but only for a while: sooner or later the memory returned, preying on his thoughts.

Luckily, he didn't remember anything from the first couple weeks. Just the nightmares, a parade of ghastly tortures: trapped in a burning leaf pile, skinned alive by demons. Then it was like a nightmare but he was awake, or at least conscious—floating on morphine. He'd pull in and out of sleep like a wave. When they told him he'd been burned, his first thought was World War III. The Russians must have attacked. He didn't remember the accident, but when they told him about it—the cigarette, the house exploding into flames—it seemed too ludicrous to be true.

It was Lyle who finally convinced him the human race was okay. She brought him an Egg McMuffin as proof: the ingenious hockey puck of egg and bed of yellow cheese, dog-eared over the side of the muffin. He couldn't do anything with it—he was still eating through a tube—but its perfection was indisputable.

Looking back, it was hard to believe how clueless he was. Dustin knew nothing about burn victims; aside from Freddy Krueger, he'd never even seen one. Those first weeks, before the nerve endings had grown back, he couldn't understand why they were keeping him there. He was upset about missing band practice. Mummified in bandages, his right arm suspended in a splint—but incredibly this was his biggest worry. Toxic Shock had a gig that weekend at a party in Redondo. (So he believed: actually, the gig was two weeks past.) He didn't understand that his life had ended.

When he tried to explain about the gig to his family, to the nurses and doctors—*I've got to go home and practice!*—they nodded kindly and smiled, as though he'd told them he had a date with Jesus Christ.

Finally, in despair, he yanked out all his tubes and made a break for the door, his splinted arm bouncing beside him like a wing. He knew his legs weren't burned, so it didn't surprise him at all that he could run. What surprised him was that a nurse no bigger than his grandmother could stop him at the door: she grabbed his arm, to catch him, and the pain was so bad, so spine-shriveling, that he shit in his hospital gown. Actually crapped down his leg. The same puny nurse had been holding his dick when he peed, but for some reason it took shitting himself from pain to drive home his helplessness.

Dustin remembered trying to escape only once. Apparently, though, he was a major tube puller. One day he woke up, paralyzed, his arms and legs strapped to the bed frame with plastic cable ties. He started to wail and curse. They were detaining him against his will, his father would sue them back to the Stone Age as soon as he found out. He'd call *60 Minutes;* the entire hospital would get shut down. Amazingly, though, when his dad saw Dustin tied up like a war prisoner, he did not offer to call the police. Instead he brought a mirror into the ward so Dustin could look at himself. Dustin had yet to see his face. He'd seen his arms, of course, but the silver nitrate stained them so brown it was hard to tell what they were like underneath. There were no mirrors in the ward, not even in the bathroom; it hadn't occurred to him before then that this was intentional.

The nurse took off his dressings, glancing at the mirror in his father's hand with an odd glint of fear in her eyes. His father had the same look, as though he was about to leap out of a plane, and Dustin started to get scared as well, his heart hammering in his chest. His father held up the mirror. Dustin focused on the person staring back at him. The person's right eyelid had crinkled up, revealing the sphere of the eyeball as it curved into the skull, the veins like tiny lightning bolts. A fish's eye. Beneath it, the cheek was rippled and blotchy, glazed like the frosting on a cake. The mouth drooped a little on one side. Dustin blinked his left eye and saw the monster in the mirror blink back.

His first thought was: *My face is dead.*

He did not try to escape after that.

Soon afterward, the pain began in earnest. It was fierce and unspeakable. The word "pain" didn't do it justice: there was nothing remotely analogous in the dictionary. The dressing changes were bad enough, but nothing compared to the tubbings. Just the sight of the hydro room would send Dustin into a spiraling, Paleolithic terror. He would tremble and get suicidal ideas. The burn tech, a Russian woman with glasses thick as ice, would lower him into the whirlpool bath and then begin to torture him, scrubbing his arm or chest with a washcloth and plucking the pieces of dead skin off with a tweezers. It felt like a cheese grater shredding his flesh. Dustin would take his suffering out on the tech. He screamed and called her a fucking bitch. He called her a fat ugly cunt. He reached into the darkest corners of his heart and pulled out names that didn't even make sense. *Fucking flabby-cunted cunt-face. Blind-as-shit fuck-eyed bitch. Gestapo Olga torture cunt.* He was ashamed of himself but couldn't help it. Sometimes he'd stick washcloths in his mouth—two or three of them—so that the burn ward wouldn't hear him scream like a baby.

Compared with the tubbings, the surgeries were a walk in the park. They'd put Dustin under and then he'd wake up with his back or ass stinging like a bitch where they'd harvested skin. That's what they called it: "harvesting." As if he were a plant. Once, walking back from the hydro room, he saw the machine they used for shaving off skin: a monstrous deli slicer sitting on a trolley. The worst was when they refused to dress his ass. More than once the nurse had to help Dustin peel his butt off the mattress, ripping him free like a Band-Aid. When he yelled at her, she said he should count his blessings, he was only 40 percent burned and had lots of good donor sites. They didn't have to use cadaver skin.

"What do I care?"

"You'd rather have someone else's skin?" the nurse said gently. "I bet your body feels differently."

"It's not my body," Dustin said. "Don't call it that."

"Well, whosever it is, it got off pretty lucky. There's a guy down the hall with eighty-five percent burns and no legs."

This wasn't the first time someone had used the word "lucky" to describe his accident. He was lucky to survive, lucky not to have been alone, lucky his eyesight wasn't damaged. It mystified Dustin. Wasn't it his *family* who was lucky? Or the trillions of people who went happily about their lives without ever catching on fire? Or the stupid fucking nurse telling him how lucky he was? If you couldn't hold your own dick, if doctors had to make you a new eyelid out of your ass, if you looked like half a zombie and couldn't blink one eye and had to wait a year or maybe longer before they could make you look partway human again—in what grievously fucked-up world were you lucky?

As soon as the grafts on his arm began to heal, the occupational therapist made him start doing things. He was supposed to put on his gown for her. The idea was that he'd slip it over his head himself, using the God-given power of his arms. Except they were no longer the ones God gave him. He couldn't raise them more than a foot without wilting from pain. His right hand was useless, too. His fingers seemed stiff and finlike, fused like a GI Joe's. It amazed him that he used to dress himself every day, without a thought. In the end, the OT adjusted Dustin's ADL rank and focused on "bathroom independence." This became the new goal: to wipe his ass on his own. It seemed a basic human right, to go into the bathroom by himself and return in a presentably shit-free state. When he tried it, though, Dustin found it was in reality a privilege. He could reach the toilet paper with his less-burned hand, could even tear a piece from the roll, but try as he might, he couldn't manage to lift the paper up to his ass and wipe. The pain in his arm was too great. He tried for fifteen minutes, sweat pouring down his face, until he finally—dejected, trembling with exhaustion—called to a nurse to help him.

Now, nine months later, Dustin watched the closing credits of *Jaws* at Mojave Video, waiting for the list of bit roles at the end. Often they stuck in his mind more than the movies themselves: *Ballistic Neighbor. Hooker with a Doughnut. Man Dodging Debris.* He liked this last one in particular. There was something inevitably misanthropic about him. If you were busy dodging bits of debris, how could you possibly care about anyone else? Dustin walked to the Comedy section to reshelve a video, trying to reach the top row to alphabetize it correctly. His arm quaked with pain. Sometimes it took him half a minute to reach the shelf. He hadn't been doing his ranges: What the hell difference did it make?

While he was ejecting the tape, a girl with a purple cast on her foot backed through the door on crutches. She pivoted around, surprising him with her beauty. Somehow, the cast and crutches made her seem even more beautiful. Instinctively, Dustin hid his face, pretending to count the money in the register. He could sense her glance at him absently before heading to New Releases. As often happened, Dustin's brain split in two, aware of what he might have done before the accident. He might have recommended a movie: *Repo Man*, say, or *An American Werewolf in London*. He might have flirted with her. When she chose a movie, crutching lazily to the counter, he might have said, "You're not watching this by yourself, are you?" But he didn't do these things. He counted the ones in the register. Thirteen. Then he ducked into the bathroom, pretending to wash his hands, and waited for her to leave.

CHAPTER 27

At the sales meeting, Ted, their regional team leader, went around the room and asked each team member to share an inspirational anecdote about his week. Warren was a bit fascinated by Ted. To begin with, he drove a Porsche 911 convertible that he referred to as "Baby." Once Warren had had an entire conversation with him about his weekend, believing Ted was talking about his girlfriend until he happened to mention that he'd replaced her ball joints. The convertible appeared to have no effect on Ted's hair, which was so sculpted with gel that you could balance an egg on it. The face under this helmet was improbably square. He looked less like someone on TV than the TV itself. What interested Warren the most, though, was the way he clapped after everything he said, expecting listeners to join in. This was amazingly effective. You could only watch a man applaud himself for so long before you started clapping, too, out of embarrassment and a sort of toddlerlike wish to please.

The other team members seemed less embarrassed. They sat in their plastic chairs like AA disciples, unbothered by the shabby, depressing office or the single poster on the wall that said BLADECO: A CUT ABOVE THE REST. They were all in college, which made Warren the oldest member by twenty-five years. He was older, in fact, than Ted, who liked to repeat evangelically that he was only twenty-nine and owned a $50,000 car and vacationed in Bermuda every Christmas. It seemed like a pretty humiliating position for Warren to be in, until you remembered that BladeCo was an equal-opportunity company that didn't believe in discrimination of any kind. They believed in sales. It didn't matter if you were old or leprous or missing several limbs, as long as you were raking in the dough.

"Thanks for that inspiring anecdote, Delio," Ted said, responding to a tedious story about convincing some woman with a walker to buy a Complete Kitchen Set by throwing in a free spatula. No one mentioned that the spatula would come out of Delio's commission. "And we should say, now's as good a time as any, that Delio was our top team member this month, making thirty-six appointments and earning a whopping six thousand twenty-eight dollars in sales. Which means, because BladeCo likes to reward its high fliers, he gets automatically entered into the statewide raffle to win a free trip to Cancún! What do you say to that, team?"

"Awesome!" everyone shouted on cue.

"Just awe*some*? Or awe-*much*?"

"Awe-much!"

Warren had stooped to many things, including selling knives to crippled old ladies, but he could not bring himself to say "awe-much." It was not a word he could say and look at himself in the mirror ever again. As a matter of fact, it was not a word at all. Ted had invented it because he felt that "awesome" failed to deliver the passionate encomium that BladeCo knives deserved.

"Warren," he said now, checking his name chart, "did I hear you say 'awe-much'?"

"No," Warren mumbled.

"Why not?"

"I'd rather not, if you don't mind."

Ted lost his smile for a second, like a waiter learning you'll only be drinking water. There was a whiff of desperation behind these pep talks that reminded Warren of his own sales approach. He guessed that Ted had some selling to do himself, to the higher-ups at BladeCo, and that Warren and the rest of the team were his product.

"Well, you *are* a member of this sales team, which leads me to believe that we're all in this *together*. And the definition of 'teamtastic'"—here Ted pointed at a homemade poster with TEAMTASTIC, another word he'd coined, written on it in capital letters—"correct me if I'm wrong, is that we're all equal. No better or worse than our teammates."

Warren could not possibly correct him, since Ted had made up the definition himself. "I'm sorry," Warren said, "I don't think I'm better."

Ted turned to Austin, a boy with blue novas of acne on each cheek. "Austin, do you have any objection to saying 'awe-much'?"

"No, sir. Awe-much."

"Shara, what about you?"

"Awe-much," Shara said, smiling.

"Carl?"

Carl, asleep with his eyes open, bolted upright in his seat. His tie was stained with coffee. "Yeah?"

"Does it affront you in some way to say 'awe-much'?"

"Huh?"

"If someone asked you to say 'awe-much,' in place of 'awe-some,' would you in any way object?"

"Awe-munch."

"Warren," Ted said, ignoring this, "I don't think your team members have any problem with it. Which means that you're letting them down. And if you're letting them down, *us,* how are we ever going to beat Quikcut's fiscal earnings—that's right, guys, *booo!*—for the second year in a row?"

"Come on, dude," the guy next to Warren said, clapping him on the back. "It's just a word."

Warren looked around helplessly. His teammates seemed to agree that the word was harmless. They were all waiting for him to say it—seemed, in fact, to share Ted's animosity toward Quikcut, the Darth Vader of cutlery, to the degree that they'd begun to eye Warren like a traitor. He wondered if losing your last shred of dignity in a place where no one was capable of perceiving its demise was like a tree falling in the forest.

"Awe-much," he said quietly.

"Thank you, Warren," Ted said, his smile deepening in a way that suggested genuine pleasure. "Let's show our support for team member Warren, who may—I'm just guessing, please correct me—need a bit of a boost today?"

After the meeting, Ted called him into his office and then made him wait there alone while he left to use the "crapper." Warren looked around the windowless room. Except for the framed picture of a bikini-clad girl on the desk, facing outward as if by accident, the office was as bare as a prison cell. Warren had a flashback to his day at the PV County Jail. That had been a humiliation, certainly—though after the degradations of BladeCo, it seemed like a prefatory glimpse. At least the Shackneys had dropped the charges after the accident; who was going to let him off the hook now? He was forty-five years old. No one wanted to hire someone his age, especially if they'd gone to law school and had nothing to show for it. He'd tried to get work in an office when they first moved to Auburn Fields, but after three months of sending him on interviews, the young woman at the employment agency had finally lost patience and said, not unkindly, "If you were younger, even by ten years, we'd be able to get you a job as a paralegal assistant." "Is that a paraparalegal?" he'd joked, but she hadn't laughed. That afternoon he'd seen the ad in the paper for BladeCo, asking him if he wanted to make "30K in 30 days." He didn't believe it, of course, but even 5K would be a nice start. He couldn't bear to work as a cashier somewhere: the idea of driving himself around, more or less his own boss, seemed less miserable. And at least there was the possibility of making a living.

Of course, to do that, he had to actually sell some knives.

"Are you having some trouble at home?" Ted asked when he returned, cocking his head in a way that resembled concern. Thank God for Camille's job. Warren often wondered what they would have done without it. Without her insurance, they would have been utterly destroyed.

"Why do you ask?" Warren said.

"Well, you've got the lowest numbers this week, only four appointments, and you didn't make a single sale. Plus the, um, *negativity* during the meeting." He waved his hand as though this were already forgiven.

"I've got some appointments lined up for Monday."

"So there's nothing upsetting your work?"

Warren stared at the girl on the desk, who was lowering a bikini strap while lifting her shoulder seductively. The picture—he now noticed—seemed to have been snipped from a magazine. "To be honest, yes, I'm having some trouble."

Ted nodded. "Is this a temporary matter? Or something . . . heavy-dutier?"

Warren could see that he wanted to fire him and was searching for a way to do it that would somehow preserve the image he'd cultivated as an inspiring guy who coined fun words. He was hoping the deed would somehow accomplish itself. Warren's only chance was to put him in a position where the deed and the image remained at odds. He told him about Dustin's accident, sick inside that he was using it as a guilt card—how his son refused to get out of bed some days or do the exercises that would keep his scars from contracting. They were thinking of sending him to a psychiatrist, but it wasn't covered under their insurance. In fact, they were still saddled with debt from Auburn Fields. The only reason the land hadn't been foreclosed yet was that it was worthless; no developer in their right mind would bid on it, given its proximity to the dump. When he finished, Ted seemed fidgety and uncomfortable, as though Warren had confessed to cheating on his wife.

"Wow," he said, shaking his head. "Well. That's a tragic thing, no doubt, but I've got a team to coach here, and if it's the first game of the season, which let's just suppose it is, you don't put in the cornerback whose mind isn't on the game. You put in the best tackler."

"Give me a week," Warren said, pleading. "I'll be the top seller."

On the way home, Warren tried to imagine how he would do this. He would have to be hardhearted and relentless. On Monday, he would show up at the Glazes', his first appointment, and refuse to leave until he'd sold everything in his case. He would exude positivity. If he had to use Dustin as blackmail, so be it. He'd tell the story of seeing his son in the warm room at the hospital for the first time, his head blown up like a pumpkin. He was still wearing the remains of his shirt, tatters of blackened cloth. His bandaged hand was large as a baseball mitt. The nurse began to dress his arm, sweating under the gigantic heat lamps pushed up to the bed, and Warren was surprised that they'd bandage him without taking his shirt off. Then it dawned on him that it was Dustin's skin he was seeing, hanging like a shredded sleeve down one arm. Warren stepped back. The boy sat up suddenly and reached toward him, red and gleaming and monstrous, his voice too garbled—too animal—to understand.

Save me, Warren believed he was saying. At least that's the way it sounded in his dreams.

Warren did his best to forget these memories, but they infested his sleep nonetheless. One in particular seemed to haunt him: Dustin on fire, Warren hugging the flames from his body as they rolled together in the grass. The strange smoke choking Warren's lungs. Of course, he would never be able to describe this to anyone. How could he hope to explain what it was like to choke on Dustin's flesh? To breathe it into his lungs? The blanket in his arms going still and quiet, panting on top of him, no other sound from inside except a faint, buttery, unforgettable sizzling? All that day and night, half-crazed at the hospital, Warren coughed up black gobs of smoke, spitting out mouthfuls of his son.

Warren passed through the permanently raised gate of Auburn Fields and pulled into its empty block, the same one he'd painstakingly planned with the architect in order to maximize its density while maintaining a sense of neighborly warmth. Just as Dante's sinners had their own punishments in hell, Warren had this putrid block of vacant homes. It was demonically tailored to his own sins. First he'd moved his family to California, to a house they couldn't afford. Even when he might have pulled out, he'd pushed through with the project anyway, investing money intended for his children's future. He'd lied to honest people about the dump. Now he'd gotten what he deserved, the same home he once tried to con others into buying.

Warren parked the Oldsmobile at the curb. He'd bought the car from some community college students for $500, when they—Warren's family—were still living at the motel. It was in surprisingly good condition, the only drawback being a gigantic sticker on the back window, a red, white, and blue skull bisected by a lightning bolt. The college kids had said it would be easy to scrape off, but Warren had not found this to be the case, giving up after ten minutes of negligible progress.

Warren waited in the car, preparing to face his hungry children. The desert trilled around him in an endless throb of static. With the two-hour commute, Camille rarely got home before eight. By then she was so exhausted, talking to her was like bleeding around a shark. Warren couldn't say hello without it turning into a fight. He'd been overwhelmed last summer when she'd seemed to forgive him; all their difficulties, their ingrown estrangement, had seemed to lift with the burden of his secret. But now Dustin's accident had shown this reprieve for what it was: a cruel joke. If Camille had not blamed him before, if forgiveness had seemed like the answer to their problems, this did not seem to be the case any longer. Warren couldn't look at her these days without feeling as if he'd lit Dustin on fire himself.

Inside the kitchen, Jonas was standing in front of the fridge, holding the door open as if to waste as much energy as he could. For a reason Warren couldn't comprehend, he was wearing ski goggles. Warren's toes curled. He knew that Jonas had left the stove on by mistake, but still he'd watch him stare into the open fridge, or forget to take his shoes off before tracking dirt all over the carpet, and his heart would clench with something close to loathing. It was wrong to feel this way, he knew it, but since Dustin's tragedy he'd given up caring why he favored one son over the other—it was a fact of life, as irreparable as what Jonas had done.

Lyle walked in and checked the cupboard above the stove. The laminate had started to unpeel from the corner of the cupboard door. Still sitting on top of the fridge, in a blanket of dust, was the dish towel bar that Warren had ripped from the wall a year ago.

"Where's Dustin?" he asked.

"Where do you think?" Lyle said. As if on cue, the sound of gunfire crackled from his bedroom. "What's for dinner?"

"There's a French bread pizza in the freezer, I think."

"We had pizza last night," Jonas said, "and the night before."

Lyle and Jonas looked at Warren as though this were his fault. At the grocery store, he let them buy whatever they wanted, partly so he wouldn't be held accountable. "What would you like instead?"

"Maybe some vegetables?" Lyle said.

"Have you ever heard of the food pyramid?" Jonas asked helpfully.

"Yes," Warren said. He turned to Lyle. "Why is your brother wearing ski goggles?"

"I was going to slice some onions," Jonas said, "for an omelet. But we don't have any eggs. So I decided to slice some onions anyway, hoping you'd sense it telepathically and bring some eggs home, sort of like a rain dance, but it didn't work."

Warren looked in the freezer. Besides the pizza, the only things left were a frosty bag of spinach, a carton of Chocolate Chocolate Chip ice cream, and something called Sizzlicious Pixie Crisps. "There's some frozen spinach."

"For a main course?" Lyle said.

"How about BLTs?" Warren said.

"We don't have any tomatoes. Or bacon."

"We have Bac-O-Bits," Jonas said.

Warren checked the cupboard. "There's a can of tomatoes! Right here."

"Those are *stewed*."

"Look, I'm trying my best. You'll have to be a little flexible."

Warren threw the spinach in the microwave and then drained the tomatoes, slicing them as best he could. Jonas and Lyle watched him without speaking. After making some toast, he scooped a seaweedy puddle of spinach onto a slice of bread and covered it with a few tomato globs, sprinkling the whole thing with Bac-O-Bits. He made three sandwiches this way. It was a figurative act of despair—he didn't expect his kids to eat them. When he was done, he carried two of the sandwiches over to the kitchen table, where Jonas began to devour his without complaint.

Lyle stared at her dinner. Then she fetched her camera from the other room and began to take pictures of the sandwich, snapping it from different angles. "Jesus, do you hear that?" she said, putting down her camera. The coyotes were at it again, *kiyi*-ing like crazy. "What do you think's wrong with them?"

"I'm sure they're just in heat or something," Warren muttered.

Lyle frowned. "Maybe they've gone, like, crazy from boredom."

Warren left the kitchen, carrying the third plate to Dustin's room. The room reeked of beer and musty sheets and something else—rotten banana peels—though Dustin himself smelled tropically feminine, perfumed with the moisturizer he went through like Budweiser. An old pizza box, open to reveal a single petrified slice, sat on top of the VCR. Warren's son glanced at him idly from the bed before returning his eyes to John Wayne inspecting a shish kebab of human scalps on TV. *The Searchers,* his new favorite. Before the accident, Warren had wondered whether Dustin should spend so much time reading about punk bands, poring over homemade-looking magazines called *SweatBomb* or *Narcoleptic Assassin*. Now Warren would have been delighted to see his son do anything but watch TV. At one point he'd thought about taking the television away, but didn't have the heart actually to do it.

Warren held the sandwich out for Dustin, who refused even to glance at it. For some reason, the droopy strangeness of his eye made the room seem stiller. Warren checked his watch: past six. They were supposed to be doing exercises. At the clinic, when the OT had helped them put together a rehab plan, she'd mentioned to Warren, privately, that there might be "some resistance." Warren remembered his naive response—"Nothing I can't handle"—with nostalgia. He had not anticipated the depth of his son's hatred of him, or the exhausting heartbreak of doing daily battle.

He got the handgrip from the basket of exercise equipment in the corner.

"Put an amen to it, Reverend," Dustin said. "Ain't no time for prayin'." He'd begun talking like this last week, as though he were John Wayne; Warren had the uncomfortable feeling he wasn't trying to be funny.

"Remember what the OT said? You're going to get contractures."

"Is she Comanche?"

Warren stared at him helplessly. "You want to play guitar again, don't you?"

"No, doc," he said melodramatically. "The didgeridoo. I want to didgeridoo one last time before I die."

Warren picked up his son's arm, slipping the handgrip into his fingers, but Dustin threw it on the floor as if he were a toddler. It was not unusual for him to behave this way. Warren retrieved the grip from the corner, a stab of pain twanging up his back.

"They'll have to cut your arm open," he said, "and do another graft. Is that what you want? Remember how fun that was?"

"I'm not having any more operations."

"Besides your face, you mean."

"No," Dustin said quietly. He grabbed the remote from the bedside table and turned up the TV. "I don't want any more surgery."

Warren's spine went cold. It was the same feeling he'd had when he saw Dustin at the hospital, putting a little peg into the hole of a baby's toy: the therapist had cheered as though it were the Olympics. He was scheduled to have a Z-plasty on his cheek next month, the first of several plastic surgeries. "We've been waiting this whole time for your scars to heal. They're going to fix up your face. Like normal."

"*Normal*," Dustin said. "You're the one who wants me to look normal so bad. It's all you fucking talk about."

"That's not true."

"You can't wait for me to look better again!"

"That's not true," Warren said. "I just want you to have the same opportunities as everyone else."

Dustin laughed. "What, so I can go to UCLA? You couldn't have sent me there anyway."

"We could save the money," Warren said quietly.

"Right. Maybe you can teach me how to sell knives."

Warren stepped back from the bed. He did not know what to do with this meanness: it was not the show-offy kind from before, dished out for the benefit of Dustin's friends, but a casual, remorseless hostility that seemed to trap him like a bug. "I'm trying to help, Dust. You might show a little bit of kindness."

"What have you done to help me?"

I saved your life, Warren wanted to say. Perhaps Dustin was able to read his thoughts, because he made a strange face at the TV. Or rather, he took his already strange face and tweaked it into something stranger, ghastly, a tightening of the skin that winged his nostrils. *If you'd wanted to help me,* the face said, *you would have let me burn.*

Warren left the room, carrying the sandwich out with him. He stopped in the hallway for no reason and stared at a large, fungus-shaped beetle crawling up the wall. He stood there for a long time. As always after visiting Dustin, he had to will his legs to work, focusing on each step as though he were climbing a ladder. In the kitchen, Jonas had his ski goggles back on and was slicing an onion into perfect, arboreal disks. Not for the first time, Warren wished it had been his youngest son who was injured. He would trade Jonas's life to get Dustin's back. Warren wanted to grab Jonas by the shirt, to shake this sacrifice somehow into being. Instead he sat down at the table and forced himself to eat the sandwich, which was soggy and disgusting. He almost gagged but took another bite, and another, his punishment for thinking such a thing.

CHAPTER 28

"We'll get fucked up and pretend to be Mormons," Biesty said, grinning. "Like old times."

"I don't remember that," Dustin lied.

He watched the shimmering green signs of the freeway pass overhead. They were headed to Manhattan Beach, where some of Biesty's rich UCLA friends had rented a house for the summer. Dustin hadn't been to a party since the accident, and Biesty had turned it into a Religious Event: he'd decided that Dustin needed to go, and there was no convincing him otherwise. He'd even driven all the way to Antelope Valley in his beat-up Karmann Ghia to pick him up. Dustin suspected he was feeling guilty, both for not visiting him very often and for going off to college while Dustin had to stay home and rot. Actually, rotting was one of Dustin's favorite activities, but the fight with his dad earlier had made him want to grab some fresh air.

"So the band's playing tonight," Biesty said, glancing at him before switching lanes.

"What?"

"Now a Major Motion Picture."

Dustin stared at him. "That was my fucking idea. The name."

"Was it?" Biesty smiled, unfazed. "As soon as your arm heals, you'll be playing lead guitar. That's why I wanted you to meet the guys."

He honked at a Mercedes that was trying to edge into their lane of traffic, flipping it off through the sunroof without losing his smile. This was part of his Moonie routine. If he stopped smiling, Dustin's face might catch him off guard and insert itself into their friendship, like an unwelcome girlfriend. Dustin pulled the eyedrops from his jeans and cocked his head back, lifting his sunglasses to drip some in. The lid graft was supposed to have fixed his tear ducts, that's what they'd told him in the hospital, but their promises weren't worth shit.

"Plus there's going to be a surprise tonight," Biesty said. "Something you'll like, I think."

"What?"

"If I told you, it wouldn't be a surprise."

Biesty slipped a tape into the stereo, a melodic crush of guitars. Dustin managed to eject it with his thumb.

"It's the new Hüsker Dü," Biesty said. "You don't like it?"

"No."

"It's a bit of a sellout, I guess." Biesty opened the glove compartment. "What do you want? I've got some X. *Wild Gift*."

"How about some silence for a change?"

Biesty glanced at him with his stupid smile before stretching to pick up some tapes that had slid into Dustin's lap. The truth was Dustin couldn't bear to listen to any of the music he used to like. Eventually they turned off the freeway and headed into Manhattan Beach, the streets narrowing into a warren of touristy, beach-flavored shops. Dustin felt a sudden rush of fear. It was still light at eight-thirty, though with his sunglasses on everything seemed strange. They passed a Jeep full of shirtless boys, surfboards jutting out the back, their leashes flapping like tentacles in the wind. It amazed him that people still drove around with hunks of foam, that they waxed them and floated on top of the ocean and stood up on waves. Downtown a few girls were walking around in their bathing suits, the tops of their bikinis showing through their T-shirts. Dustin's heart filled with sorrow. He stared at the surf shops and taquerias and tiki bars spilling with people. They seemed to belong to another world. He'd thought a lot about this world since the accident, but had failed to remember its sparkling invulnerability. It was like peering out of a spaceship: it was hard to imagine that he'd ever lived out there, sharing the same air.

They picked up some burritos at a taco stand and ate them in the parking lot. Dustin took a couple bites and then put his burrito back in the bag, too sick with fear to eat. At the party, he stayed in the car after Biesty climbed out, his hands clasped in his lap. The seat went back; he could stay there and maybe even sleep.

"Come on," Biesty said.

Dustin didn't move. Biesty leaned into the driver's-side window, still sporting his infuriating grin.

"What are you going to do? Sit in the car all night?"

"Yes," he whispered.

"Jesus," Biesty said, looking at him more closely. "Are you shaking?" He stopped smiling and got back into the car. "What is it? Your . . . face?" Dustin could tell he was embarrassed to talk about it. That was the worst thing, how this horrendously life-shattering thing could happen to you and it just ended up embarrassing people, like a fart. "Look, no one's going to care. We'll go and drink some twiggen. Like old times."

"Old times," Dustin said bitterly.

"How did we come up with that anyway? 'Twiggen'?"

"You mean because it's so stupid?"

Biesty looked at his lap. Dustin knew he was trying, but it wasn't enough. It would never be enough, because it implied someone could make things better. Casually, Biesty reached into the glove compartment and pulled out some sunglasses, a pair of fake Wayfarers with little silver flecks in the corners. He slipped them onto his face, prepared to go into the party like that. They'd both look like jackasses. Though he didn't admit it, Dustin was grateful.

The party was in someone's backyard. Longboards, in various states of disrepair, leaned against the fence. In one corner of the lawn, next to a garden gnome sodomizing a plastic deer, was a Jamaican flag nailed to a shed. Biesty introduced Dustin to the band, who shook his gloved hand carefully in a way that suggested they knew about his accident. The drummer was wearing a T-shirt that said UCLA: UNLIMITED COEDS OF LEGAL AGE. Dustin was relieved he didn't have to take them seriously. While Biesty helped set up the amps, he went to look for the keg, squeezing past some surfers smoking a joint on the patio steps. They gawked at him openly. Dustin went into the house, which through his sunglasses seemed dim as a church. A girl and a guy were making out in the middle of the hallway. You could see the guy's hard-on through his Jams; he was not embarrassed, flaunting it like a loud or wacky tie.

"Looking for something?" the guy said, eyeing Dustin's glove.

"The keg."

"Who invited Michael Jackson?" he said after Dustin had walked on, which made the girl giggle. Dustin found the keg under a card table stocked with plastic jugs of liquor. He grabbed a jug of vodka and then went into an empty bedroom, locking the door behind him. It was a guy's room, filled with guy things. There was a poster of a surfer getting tubed by a glassy wave, poised like a tap dancer at the end of his routine. By the bed, a topless *Sports Illustrated* model stared off the end of a dock, her ass seasoned carefully with sand. She pushed it toward the camera as though it were a gift to mankind. Dustin pulled the poster off the wall and crumpled it in his left hand as best he could. Then he sat on the bed and took some swigs from the jug of vodka, holding it with two hands because the weight hurt his arm. His skin itched like murder. He unzipped a sleeve of his Jobst shirt and scratched as hard as he could, digging his fingernails into the bone until blood seeped from the welts.

He stayed there for a long time, swigging from the jug. Outside the party grew louder: he could hear everyone getting drunk, laughing boisterously and bragging about how wasted they'd been the night before. How moronic they sounded. Dustin wondered if God ever eavesdropped on people's conversations and wished He had a machine gun. Someone rattled the bedroom door, banging on it with his fist. At one point Dustin heard his own name, Biesty's voice describing what he was wearing. It was like being invisible. In the corner of the room, snagged on some coral, was a lone seahorse floating in a fish tank. It was limp and dead-looking, swaying in the current like the lost half of a monogram. Dustin had always pictured seahorses as free and happy creatures—they were his favorite animal in second grade—but found the truth to be oddly gratifying.

After a while the band started. Drunkenly, Dustin walked to the window and parted the blinds, which afforded him a view over the patio to the crowded lawn below. He was shocked to see how many people had come. Biesty was crooning into the microphone, some song about a guy who removes his own brain and keeps it as a pet. He no longer stalked around like Iggy Pop but sang stiffly into the mike, his sunglasses sliding down his nose. The lyrics—if you could call them that—didn't make any sense at all. Plus the music wasn't punk. It was slow and melodic, the guitarist strumming his guitar like a folksinger. Dustin expected them to get booed offstage, pummeled by plastic cups. But the partiers seemed to be enjoying it. There were even some people—girls— who seemed to know the words, sloshing beer on themselves as they danced on the grass. The chorus came and the music suddenly erupted for no reason, a squall of arty feedback, Biesty screaming the words "Roll over, play dead!" while the crowd jumped up and down like Muppets. Dustin watched in disbelief. The next song was much the same, a piece of bubblegum pop that veered into a forced crescendo. He watched the whole set from the window, heart poised like an ax.

"There you are," Biesty said when Dustin found him during the break. He was sweaty and beaming, still giddy from being onstage. Dustin tried to focus on his stupid grin, though the blurriness of Biesty's face was making it difficult. Dustin bumped into a surfboard leaning against the fence and it knocked against two others, causing them to tip over like dominoes. "Jesus. Are you hammered?"

"I'm taking my brain for a walk," Dustin said.

Biesty stopped grinning. "You didn't like the music?"

"Oh, is that what that was?"

"I thought you'd be into it. It's like Bad Brains meets the Beatles."

"Fuck, that's good." Dustin laughed. "Don't you mean 'on acid'? Bad Brains meets the Beatles *on acid*?"

"The crowd seemed to like it," the guitarist said haughtily. He was wearing a T-shirt that said CONFUCIUS IS SEXY.

"Right. The Jimmy Buffett set. Sigma Chi Delta."

The guitarist's face hardened. On closer inspection, his shirt said CONFUSION IS SEX, a Sonic Youth LP. "Most of them aren't in sororities."

"Jesus Christ, I'm not talking to you. Why don't you go learn some more chords?"

Biesty took off his sunglasses and put them in his pocket. His face looked the same as it always had. "I thought maybe you'd forget to be an asshole tonight. That the band might even like you."

"'The *band*.' Listen to you. Are you on Casey Casey yet?"

"Casey *Casey*?" the guitarist said, smirking.

"Oh, and Toxic Shock was bound for stardom," Biesty said.

"Maybe if we'd had a decent singer."

Biesty laughed. "We're a hundred times better."

Dustin recognized this, suddenly, as the truth. It enraged him. He marched over to the Stratocaster leaning against its amp and slipped the strap over his shoulder, stumbling forward when he tried to turn up the volume and almost falling on his face. He couldn't hold a pick but began to play anyway, slamming his gloved fist into the strings and launching into the first delicious riff of "Los Angeles," his arm singing with pain. Dustin was dimly aware of how bad he sounded, just as he was aware that the partiers had stopped talking and were watching him. People yelled at him, demanding he put the guitar down. He approached the microphone, defiantly, but knocked it to the ground. A plastic cup bounced off his chest. Someone tried to pull him offstage and he fought him as best he could, punching at him with his left hand, which caused everyone to laugh—a chorus of jeers—until someone else surprised Dustin from behind and wrestled the guitar from his shoulders, slowly enough that Dustin turned and flailed at him too and got what he wanted, a bright burst of pain in his jaw, sharp and gratifying, and he stumbled backward through the grass, guitarless, the world tipping like a ship.

A sweet, mucky warmth entered Dustin's mouth. No one helped him up. He stumbled through the crowd—a sea of wheeling faces—until he found his way out of the party, collapsing on the curb under an arc lamp, his jaw throbbing to his pulse. He spat into the street: a gobbet of blood. The world seemed brighter somehow, more colorful, as though he'd stepped from a cave. He took off his glove and scratched at his hand. He didn't know how long he sat there; he could hear the band start up again, Biesty's peppy voice singing, *There's some integrity on my clothes, and I can't get it off.*

"That was quite a performance."

Dustin looked up to see two girls in front of him. The two girls merged into one, a fuzzy teenager in a Billabong sweatshirt and rubber thongs. Except for the beach clothes, and for the fact that her hair was blond, she looked suspiciously like Taz.

"You're not who I think," he said angrily.

"How do you know?"

"What happened to your wuzzit? Witch's forelock?"

"I dyed it."

He peered at her again, squinching his eyes to bring her into

focus. She seemed nervous, fingering the little mole on her lip
and trying not to stare at his face. Same as everyone. He realized
with dismay that his sunglasses were gone. Somewhere inside his
drunkenness Dustin felt a hopeless *poof!* In his fantasies, replayed
often in his mind, she'd looked him straight in the face and spoke
to him like she used to, insulting as ever, unashamed of his ugliness. He asked her what she was doing here.

"Mark called. He said you were coming."

"Biesty? You're pals now?"

"He called me out of the blue, pretending to be a youth minister. That's what he told my mom."

"You look like a cheerleader or something," Dustin said.

Taz frowned. "It was supposed to be a surprise. That I was
coming. He said you'd told him about us." She stared at her feet.
"He wanted me to see you."

"Well, here I am. How do I look?"

She shrugged miserably. "Honestly? I didn't recognize you."

Dustin frowned. He wanted the truth, and he didn't want it at
the same time. He was hoping Taz would go away, return to the
drunkenness she'd stepped out of, but she sat down on the curb
beside him. Her new hair made her seem bland and chirpy; she
looked like she'd maybe gained some weight. It was all fucked,
everything: nothing ever stayed the way you wanted it. He itched
so badly he wanted to cry. Then he did start to cry. He couldn't
help it. Taz stared at him finally, her eyes damp and serious. Dustin
wanted her pity at the same time that it infuriated him.

"Leave me alone," he said.

"Are you sure?"

"Fuck off! Do you need me to write it down?"

Taz stood up. Her rubber thongs slapped down the sidewalk,
in time with Biesty's music. Dustin wanted to call her back, to
apologize for his own misery, but couldn't bear the thought of her
watching him cry from one eye.

CHAPTER 29

Jonas could tell that his family hated him. They didn't mean to hate him, but the truth seeped out anyway. It was there in the mornings when Jonas ate his granola, his father eyeing him too long as he picked out the dates. It was there in the afternoons, leaking through Dustin's door like the sound of the TV. It was there in Lyle's never wanting to play Risk or Stratego with him even though she spent most of the time staring zombielike at the ceiling. It was there in the evenings, when Jonas's mother snapped at him for leaving the microwave open, weary and brittle-voiced and wishing he were a cigarette.

How different this voice was than the one in his head, playing over and over again even in his sleep. *Don't forget to turn off the stove.* He could hear them perfectly: his mom's garbled words, thick with marshmallow. Sometimes he could even see his fingers on the knob, turning it until the flame went out, clear as the image from a movie. He could remember doing this. But he hadn't, it was a lie, his brother's face was burned up. Your brain could convince you of anything.

Most days he spent roaming the desert. It was a relief to be free of school, that gloomy place where the teachers wore shorts and his locker was so hot he had to open it with a sock over his hand, where no one spoke to him except the garbled voice in his head and he'd somehow completed his transformation into a ghost. In the desert, at least, there were extraordinary things. There were scorpions eating each other. There were rats hopping around like kangaroos. There were wasps dragging tarantulas around by the leg. There were snake skins dried into paper, bird nests as small as contact lenses, lizard skeletons dangling from creosote bushes, delicate as ice. Once, not far from the house, he saw a roadrunner go after a rattlesnake, its right wing extended like a matador's cape. When the snake lunged, the roadrunner snapped up its tail and then cracked it like a whip, slamming its head against the ground—over and over—to bash its skull.

Jonas liked to stand as still as he could in the broiling sun, pretending to be a bush. He was a convincing plant. Maybe too convincing: one day a scarlet hummingbird flew right up to his face and fed out of the corner of his eye, its tiny tongue licking his eyeball. It felt pleasant and appalling at the same time. Afterward, Jonas couldn't shake the sensation that his eyes were flowers, in bloom fifteen hours a day.

"A hummingbird licked my eyeball," he told his sister later. She was sitting on the couch in the living room, reading a book called *The Spy Who Came in from the Cold*. Jonas tried to imagine a world in which it was colder outside the house than in. He'd found a rusty pair of roller skates in the desert and was strapping them onto his sneakers, amazed that they fit.

"Is that some kind of code?" Lyle asked.

"No."

"Does it mean, like, 'The East Germans have recovered the microfilm'?"

"It doesn't mean anything," Jonas said.

She returned to her book, her face slack with disappointment. It was the same look she always had, as if she were melting of boredom and you were somehow contributing to her liquefaction. Jonas roller-skated into the kitchen, where his mother was cleaning out the refrigerator. Even though it was Saturday, it was startling to see her home in the middle of the day. "A hummingbird licked my eyeball."

"That's nice, dear."

"I think it was after the salt."

She shook a carton of orange juice. "You're going to be licking each other's eyeballs, if your father can't find the precious time to buy a little food. And look at all this beer! How much beer does he want Dustin to drink?"

"I found some roller skates, too," Jonas said.

"Jonas, please go ask your father what he expects us to eat for dinner."

Jonas nodded. He skated down to his father's room, leaving little train tracks on the runner in the hallway. His father was lying in bed with a pen in his hand, a newspaper spread across his knees. He did his best to smile at Jonas when he stumped into his room. He hated Jonas even more than Dustin did, which was why he was always trying to smile at him.

"Outdoor youth counselor," his father said, shaking his head. "Three ads in a row. What the hell's an outdoor youth?"

"Mom wants to know what you expect us to eat for dinner, since all you buy is beer."

"Oh, is that what she said?"

Jonas nodded. He sometimes exaggerated his mom's messages: it made his father hang on his words in an appealing way. "A hummingbird licked my eyeball."

"Please go ask your mother if she's ever been in a burn unit with forty percent burns, and been in too much pain to hold her own penis, and then come home and wanted some beer at the supermarket, and then was her father—her own flesh and blood—petty enough after what she'd been through to deny her the chance to drink a measly goddamn Budweiser when she wanted to?"

Jonas skated back to the kitchen. Since his parents had stopped talking to each other, it was not unusual for them to communicate in this way. Jonas was happy enough to help—it made him feel needed—but recently the messages had become angrier and more difficult to remember. He relayed his dad's question as best he could, leaving out the part about Dustin's penis. His mother's face, still peering into the refrigerator, reddened. "If he's asking would I willingly turn myself into an alcoholic, on top of the rest of my problems, then the answer is no." She closed the fridge. "No milk even! Are you supposed to put beer in your granola?"

"The answer is no," Jonas reported to his father.

"No what?"

"She's not an alcoholic."

"What the hell is she talking about?"

"She's also wondering if you're giving me beer for breakfast."

"Yes! It's our major staple! Breakfast, lunch, and dinner!" He grabbed an open can of Budweiser off the bedside table and handed it to Jonas. "Do me a favor," his dad said. "Go in there and take a big swig in front of your mother. Chug the thing and lick your lips. Will you do that?"

Jonas skated back to the kitchen, some beer sloshing on his hand as he teetered off the runner. He had never drunk beer before and did not particularly want to try it, but felt he could not disappoint his father. He waited for his mom to look up and then lifted the Budweiser to his lips, closing his eyes in order to mask the flavor. It tasted so bad—tinny and bitter—that he almost gagged.

"Did your father put you up to that?" his mother said. She looked furious.

Jonas nodded. His mother began to say something but then stopped in midsentence, her eyes snagging on Jonas's roller skates. Her face softened suddenly, emerging from its frown. It was like seeing someone unzip from a costume. Silently, she took the can of beer from his hand and poured it down the drain, bent over the sink as though she didn't want to show Jonas her face.

He left the kitchen and skated past his father's room—his dad stood eagerly in the doorway, awaiting his mother's message—and headed out through the garage. The image of his dad's grimly hopeful face made Jonas wish he'd never come home. He knew that he was the cause of his parents' unhappiness. To distract himself, he unbuckled his roller skates and left them by his Schwinn Traveler in the driveway. The silver bell on the handlebar sparkled in the sun, too blinding to look at. It was a strange thing to have a bike in a place with only one block, because you could only ever ride it back and forth. The bell, too, was a bit of a conundrum. There were no pedestrians, the block was utterly, echoingly empty, so the bell's being there at all seemed like a philosophical question.

Sometimes Jonas would ring it anyway, feeling a forlorn *tringling* in his heart.

Gingerly, he climbed onto the scalding bike, tugging his shorts down to protect his thighs. The seat burned him even through his shorts. He stood up on the pedals, ringing the bell as he rode down the block. It echoed off the empty homes. He sometimes imagined that if he rang the bell loud enough, the front doors would fling open and the street would fill with children, an avenue of toys, Wiffle bats and skateboards and Big Wheels with rainbow-colored seaweed sprouting from the handles. But they didn't appear, and he felt more than ever like a ghost. Once he'd ridden up and down the block a hundred times, just for the hell of it, but there was no one to witness his accomplishment and he began to wonder if he'd really done it.

Jonas ditched his bike at the edge of the block and wandered back into the desert. He missed fencing practice. He missed watching videos with his family and throwing popcorn at the screen. He missed eating breakfast together in their old kitchen, missed playing Monopoly and Battleship and Connect Four, missed the way Lyle and Dustin laughed when he talked about the fast foods he was going to invent, like the Jelly Doughnut Dog. Mostly he missed his mother, who sometimes didn't get home until after his bedtime. There were days he didn't see her at all. But it was his fault she had to drive so far to work—his fault all these things were gone—so he deserved to roam the desert like an animal.

A hawk circled far above him, looking for food. Jonas was jealous that its wanderings had a purpose. He decided to pray to Mandy Rogers. He did not know when he'd started praying to her: last year sometime, after they'd found her cut up in pieces and planted in someone's garden. It was a creepy habit, but Jonas couldn't help it. Sometimes he imagined a garden of body parts sprouting from the earth, little toes and fists opening to the sun.

He wanted his family to stop hating him, so he prayed for something that would help them forgive him. Exactly what this would be, or where he might find it, Jonas could not imagine.

He roamed farther into the desert, treading softly so as not to scare anything off. Many strange things presented themselves— a lizard puffed up like a balloon, a heap of tiny ant wings—but nothing that seemed to answer his prayer.

For several days, returning home only for meals, Jonas searched. He had nothing else to do and remembered that Jesus had roamed the desert for forty nights. In a backpack, he carried water, Slim Jims, and a Swiss Army knife in case he got bitten by a snake. His lips chapped so badly they started to scab. He began to have trouble distinguishing between his thoughts and the hot breeze sipping at his ear. It wasn't like the loneliness he felt at home: it was large and breathable and seemed almost like companionship, since everything else was breathing it as well.

On the third day, he discovered a pile of trash out near the freeway. Jonas had come across these piles before, heaps of abandoned things: old TVs and car batteries and once a plastic Jacuzzi tub, sitting there as if dropped from a plane. This pile was different, however. There was something unsavory about it. There was a fish tank with some sizzled-looking plants inside, a tricycle with the price tag still attached to it, a dollhouse with a hunting knife sticking out of its roof. It looked like maybe whoever had dumped these things was not the true owner. Jonas found an acoustic guitar under the tricycle, its neck broken cleanly in two. The neck dangled by one string, like a trout. On the body of the guitar was a bumper sticker that said FINISH YOUR BEER: THERE'S SOBER KIDS IN INDIA.

Jonas rescued the broken guitar from the pile, wondering if Mandy Rogers had answered his prayer. He'd had something a bit more biblical in mind. Still, Dustin had sold his guitar; if Jonas could fix this one up, return it to good-enough shape, his brother might start playing again. He'd stop watching TV all the time, he'd join a band again, Jonas's family would rejoice. Anything was possible.

On his way home, passing the dump, Jonas peered through the fence and saw a coyote crouched on the embankment of the toxic pond, licking its own reflection. The coyote's ass was missing all its fur. It looked like a French poodle. It stopped drinking and gazed at Jonas for a minute, eyes crazed and bloodshot. Jonas held up the guitar, and the coyote seemed to approve. Then it ran at the fence and scaled it almost in a single leap, scrambling over the top and racing off into the desert.

CHAPTER 30

Ethan shot the dead Comanche's eyes out, which really put a scorpion up the reverend's ass. Everyone in *The Searchers* had a scorpion up their ass, which was why Dustin admired it. He rewound the tape and watched Ethan shoot the Comanche's eyes out again, impressed by the placidity of John Wayne's face.

"Why does he do that?" Hector asked, flinching.

"Weren't you listening?" Dustin said. "Comanches can't enter the spirit world without eyes. Now he has to wander between the winds."

"Wow. That's pretty harsh."

Dustin looked to see if Hector was joking. He was not used to this sort of sincerity, especially when it came to John Wayne movies. Lyle would have made some snide remark: *Between the winds? Isn't it warmer that way anyway?* It was one of the reasons he could stand being around Hector. The other was that he didn't try to sugarcoat Dustin's life; when Dustin described how miserable his arm was, how he just wanted to chop it off, Hector never did anything to suggest he was exaggerating but in fact looked as stricken as if it were his own arm being discussed. Unlike everyone else, he never acted as though Dustin was wrong to feel sorry for himself.

Hector was still wearing his Jungle of Pets uniform—green khakis and matching polo—which meant that he'd driven here straight from work. His devotion boggled Dustin: he'd never had a friend like Hector before. In fact, he'd never had a friend whose parents were Mexican, or who had to work in a pet store to pay his way through night school. If any boy at PV High had said he wanted to be a vet someday, he would have been jeered at in the halls. As Hector bent down to pick a tray of half-eaten breakfast off the floor, Dustin noticed something in his shirt pocket, a wad of fur. It looked alive. Dustin sat up in bed.

"What do you have in your pocket?"

"Ginger," Hector said. "She's a sugar glider."

"It's real?"

"Sort of like a flying squirrel." He continued to clear things from the floor, as if carrying animals in your shirt were perfectly normal. "They're marsupials."

Hector dumped some beer cans in the trash and pulled the tiny wad of fur out of his pocket with two fingers, like a dirty Kleenex. The wad of fur blinked. It seemed vaguely chipmunky at first, until you appreciated its striped head and gigantic eyes and uncannily human little fingers clutching Hector's thumb like a branch. It looked like what would happen if a bat and a possum could mate.

"They're nocturnal," Hector explained.

"Uh-huh," Dustin said. "Don't tell me you carry it around all day."

"I had one before, a male, but I didn't spend enough time with him. If they're too depressed, their hind legs get paralyzed. They can't move and they die." Hector stroked the thing's head. "They're illegal in California; this guy at Jungle of Pets—big-time gambler—got them for me in Vegas."

Dustin didn't ask him why he felt obliged to own an illegal animal in the first place. He seemed to like to make his life difficult. For some reason, the bug-eyed creature made Dustin thirsty. "How about a Budweiser," he said.

Hector slipped Ginger back into his pocket and went to get him a beer from the kitchen. In general, he did whatever was asked of him. Dustin had an image of himself as an exotic animal, his room a giant vivarium, Hector coming by to feed him and attend to his needs. He liked this fantasy and could find no problem with it.

Hector came back holding two beers poured into glasses. He didn't usually drink with Dustin before it was dark, but there was a first for everything. Maybe Dustin had driven him to it. "What's the occasion, Reverend?"

"My dad passed away today," Hector said, handing him a glass. "Four years ago, I mean."

Dustin stared at him. "You mean 'died'?"

Hector nodded.

"Say that then. I hate 'passed away.' It's like saying you have to 'go powder your nose.'"

Dustin found the remote and muted the TV. Sometimes his own callousness made him sick. Hector grabbed some Tabasco sauce from the tray of old food sitting on the desk and shook some into his beer, as if it were a steak.

"What are you doing?"

"My dad drank his beers this way. Ever heard of a *michelada*?"

"Your dad was crazy," Dustin said. He reached for his eye drops, making the movement seem more painful than it actually was. On cue, Hector rushed to do it himself, grabbing the little bottle from the bedside table and leaning over Dustin's face to squeeze a few drops into his eye before dabbing the tears with a Kleenex. "Dr. Akashi said three months. The lid's supposed to be shrinking back to normal. Does it look any better to you?"

Hector shook his head. "Not really. No."

"You're the only person I know who doesn't tell me how great I look," Dustin said gratefully.

Hector turned away, as though in pain. Any gratitude on Dustin's part seemed to make him miserable. Dustin had never met anyone with this particular quirk. He remembered the first time he'd seen Hector outside the house, parked by the curb in his pickup, his hands gripping the wheel as if he were stuck in traffic. He'd stayed there for nearly an hour. Dustin had enjoyed the spectacle at first, then finally took pity on him and went out to tell him that Lyle wasn't living with them anymore. He'd have to go stalk her in Palos Verdes. Hector had taken one look at Dustin and flinched, touching his own face without meaning to, as though he were looking into a mirror.

Dustin stared at the ceiling, where a bare lightbulb hung above his head. His father hadn't bothered to put the fitting back on; there was something wrong with the wiring and bulbs kept burning out after a week. "Taz called this morning."

"Your girlfriend's little sister?"

"Girlfriend, right. Who visited me exactly once in the hospital." Dustin took a swig of beer. "Anyway, Taz told me she has a new boyfriend. Some lacrosse player from Brentwood. Maybe her dad will finally have someone to talk sports with."

"Did he know Taz called you?"

"You kidding? He'd have driven out here personally to skin me alive." Dustin frowned. "She drives now, her parents' old Beemer. Can you believe that? She used to be all punk, and now she dresses like a Popsicle."

Hector, who was dressed like an asparagus, sat down. "People don't change that much underneath. I mean, maybe it doesn't matter that much what she looks like."

Dustin had to laugh. The idea that what was underneath mattered most, even to those who loved you, seemed hopelessly quaint. He'd read somewhere that ugly babies got yelled at ten times more than cute ones.

"Anyway," Hector said, "she seems interested in you."

"Right. As charity work."

"You think that's why she called?"

Dustin shrugged. "Honestly, I wish she'd fuck off and leave me alone."

More than anything, he did not want to become anyone's good deed. He put on his sunglasses, remembering how Taz could barely bring herself to look at him. On TV, Ethan and his adopted nephew were gathered around a campfire. Sometimes Dustin imagined their little heads bursting into flame, Technicolor faces melting like wax.

"How's everyone else?" Hector asked, changing the subject.

"Everyone else?"

"Your family, I guess."

"Who cares?" Dustin said. He suspected Hector wanted to ask about Lyle but was too embarrassed. "I wish you could trade in your family, like a used car. I'd start with Jonas. Shouldn't be too hard to trade up. 'Excuse me, do you have any kids who won't blow up your house?'"

"Maybe it wasn't his fault," Hector said quietly.

"Houses don't fucking explode for no reason."

"I'm just thinking of how . . . you know. Awful he must feel."

"Why shouldn't he feel awful? He ruined my life." Dustin drained the rest of his beer. "Besides, anyway, he's too much of a freak to care. We could all turn into brain-eating zombies and he wouldn't notice."

Dustin asked for another Budweiser. He decided to get drunk. Being drunk was almost as good as being asleep. For one thing, it helped out with the itching. Also, other people stopped having much significance. They went from being agents of pain or pleasure to harmless Hollywood props. If you were at Taco Bell, for example, chauffeured there by your sister's ex-boyfriend, you could bow to the couple in the next booth and say, *Grateful to the hospitality of your rocking chair, ma'am,* before sitting down. You could ask the cashier with a cold sore how he got an STD on his face.

"It's pretty dark in here," Dustin complained when Hector returned with a can of beer.

"Probably because you're wearing sunglasses."

"That's why I wear them. You can pretend it's night. Like you aren't one of those losers who gets fucked up in the afternoon."

Hector began to say something but then seemed to think better of it. He switched on the light—a flip of the finger, easy as pie—and the world exploded. A noise like a popped balloon. Something snowed on Dustin's face.

"Shhhh," Hector said. "It's all right." He grabbed the beer can from Dustin's hand. "The lightbulb exploded. Luckily you were wearing sunglasses."

"I wet my pants," Dustin mumbled, stiff with terror.

"No, you didn't. Just soaked yourself with beer."

He began to pick the glass bits from Dustin's face, one by one. His fingers were gentle as bugs. Dustin felt like a bomb being skillfully defused. In the middle of cleaning his face, as if remembering something, Hector reached into his shirt pocket and pulled out Ginger, who seemed to be trembling. He stroked her fur with his thumb until she'd calmed down and closed her eyes. How wonderful it would be to crawl up into his pocket and fall asleep.

Hector put the sugar glider to his ear. He let go and the animal clung there, like an earmuff. "Her only trick."

Dustin laughed. Hector grinned stupidly, the furry creature stuck to his ear, which made Dustin break up even harder. It was perilous laughter, shards of glass trickling from his Jobst shirt.

"You're my only friend," he said.

Hector stopped grinning and tucked Ginger back to bed in his pocket, his face as miserable as can be.

CHAPTER 31

Camille sat on the back deck, smoking a cigarette while the sun peeked over the desert. It was her favorite time of day, a moment's peace before she joined the endless caravan of traffic, before the smell of the dump had ripened in the heat. Below her, Mr. Leonard snooped around the dirt. The poor dog could barely walk. He could no longer climb the stairs to the deck; Camille had to carry him herself, his ribs pressing against her fingers like the springs of a mattress. Sometimes she felt closer to him than her own children. It was hard to explain, except that he preferred her arms and didn't want to be set down.

Now the old dog stopped at a creosote bush and stood there shivering, as though in pain. Camille realized that he couldn't lift his leg. Barefoot, she climbed off the porch and walked to his side, her toes turning brown as the desert. She knelt down in the dirt and lifted Mr. Leonard's leg as tenderly as she could. He wagged his tail, slow as a hymn. He'd long since given up marking his territory: the pee came out all at once, less of a hiss than a dribble. Camille held his leg while he finished, strangely moved. When he was done, she lowered his leg and watched him scratch confusedly at the dirt.

She wondered if they should put him to sleep. If possible, she would discuss the situation with Warren. They hadn't exchanged more than two sentences all week. At least when she'd suspected him of having an affair, there'd been something she could point to, a definable source. Now there was no beginning or end: Dustin's accident had robbed them of whys. Warren had turned old and strange and aimless, skittering around the house like a leaf. *Dev-*

astation. The word sounded like a place. A station for dried-up things. Camille imagined a deserted depot, rickety with breezes, the man she'd married abandoned there like a husk.

She was so angry sometimes she couldn't bear to look at him. He'd uprooted them all to pursue his idiotic dream and now here they were, in the middle of nowhere, prisoners of his folly. If it wasn't for him, they'd still be on the lake in Nashotah, worrying about acorns clogging the rain gutter. Dustin would still be a beautiful, music-crazed boy, sneaking girls down to the boathouse. How many times had she fantasized about quitting her job and returning to Wisconsin with the kids, leaving Warren out here to fend for himself? But of course she couldn't: they needed her insurance, needed to keep Dustin here for his surgeries.

Now she wondered if she could leave Warren for real. So much time had passed, nearly a year since the accident, that the idea had begun to seem possible. Wisconsin wasn't an option, but she could find an apartment somewhere near her office—Torrance, maybe, or San Pedro. Scrape by on her meager salary. She would of course take Jonas with her; Lyle could decide for herself. What terrified her more than anything was Dustin. No matter how miserable he was, Camille knew that he'd never consent to leave with her: it was too safe an island, this house in the desert. A refuge from the world. If Camille moved out, he would see it only as betrayal.

She did not know if she had the courage to do this, to leave behind her disfigured, frightened, TV-addicted son.

Inside, Camille washed her hands for a long time, letting the hot water scorch her fingers. Her feet were filthy, and she washed these awkwardly in the sink as well, using the little sprayer that had started working again for no reason. She remembered when Dustin was in the hospital, still drifting in and out of shock, the way the nurse had washed his feet with a spray bottle to keep them clean. Because she couldn't hold his hand, Camille would sit at the end of his bed and clutch his bare foot instead. Sometimes Warren or Lyle or even Jonas would hold the other foot as well, trying to soothe him in his panic, explaining where he was or why he was in pain. In some ways, that first endless month in the hospital, they'd never felt more like a family. They'd slept with their heads in each other's laps. They'd huddled together, choked with tears. They'd made a list of Dustin's favorite restaurants and driven miles across town for meals he wouldn't touch.

They'd combed a record store at Old Towne Mall for the posters Dustin used to have at home, curating the walls around his bed. Exhausted, giddy with grief, the stench of charred flesh and silver nitrate steamed into their clothes, they'd even had bouts of laughter, hysterical, table-pounding fits, making scenes at Denny's or Pizza Hut while Lyle did impressions of the nursing staff. What had happened? How had they unraveled again, worse than before? The mystery of life was not how it started, Camille thought. It was how people with every excuse to be close could grow distant as satellites.

Heating some oatmeal in the microwave, Camille turned on the portable TV over the sink and watched a commercial about a boy shaped like a cigarette. "Don't be a butthead," a man's voice intoned at the end. The commercial had the unintended effect of making her crave another smoke. She was pulling the pack out of her pocket when some footsteps behind her made her jump. Hector Granillo. He was cradling something in his shirt: a heap of beer cans, crushed into hockey pucks.

"You startled me," Camille said. She checked the clock: six-thirty in the morning. "You spent the night with Dustin?"

"On his floor. I'm just cleaning up a bit."

"Those aren't all Dustin's, are they?"

"I drank some, too," Hector said unconvincingly.

A slither of fear moved up Camille's back. The idea of his sleeping in her son's room made her oddly jealous. That this stranger had had sex with her daughter and now insinuated himself into Dustin's life seemed somehow outrageous. "If you're buying my son beer," she said angrily, "then I could have you arrested."

He looked mortified. "It was there already. In the fridge."

Hector stepped around Mr. Leonard's snoring body to dump the crushed cans in the trash. Camille felt bad for accusing him. Perhaps Warren was right to buy Dustin beer: anything to feel less helpless.

Timidly, Hector took a bag of cookies out of the cupboard. The bag was labeled HIGH PROTEIN MONKEY BISCUITS. "They're for lab monkeys," he explained.

"Oh."

"Ginger loves them."

"Ginger?"

"My pet sugar glider."

Camille, who'd been imagining a homeless girl with terrible breath, was too relieved to care what this was.

"She's asleep in Dustin's sock drawer."

"Wouldn't it be better off sleeping at home?" Camille asked.

"My mom won't let me leave any pets there unattended. I was keeping some Madagascar hissing roaches, you know, in a little terrarium, but I left the top off by accident one night and they escaped. Now they've bred and they're all over the house."

"Oh my God," Camille said.

"Luckily they only hiss when they're mad."

"Mad?"

He nodded. "Or frightened."

"Are they as big as regular cockroaches?"

"Bigger," Hector said. "More like mice."

Camille laughed. Once she got started, she couldn't stop. She bent over her bowl of oatmeal, eyes blurring with tears. Her nose was running, and she was having trouble catching her breath.

"Are you all right, Mrs. Ziller?"

"I don't know."

"Would you like some water?"

She nodded. Hector filled a glass in the sink and handed it to her.

"How's Dustin?" she asked.

"Asleep."

"No. I mean generally. Is he . . . okay?"

Hector looked at the floor. "He told me about a dream he had, on Monday night. He was lost somewhere and wandering around. He kept walking into different houses and trying to turn on their TVs, but couldn't find the on button. Finally one of the TVs woke up—an alien, I guess maybe—and said, 'This world is not your home.'"

"I'm going to be late for work," Camille said, glancing at the clock. She pulled the pack of cigarettes out of her pocket, unreasonably dejected to find it empty. "Damn it. I thought I had one left."

"Hold on," Hector said.

He went outside to his car and returned with a plastic grocery bag. He reached in and handed her a pack of Camel Lights, her favorite brand.

"I can't take your cigarettes," Camille said.

"I don't smoke," he said without smiling. "I bought some things for the house yesterday."

It took her a minute to realize he was talking about this house. He'd bought the cigarettes for her. There was something very strange about it—possibly even creepy. She did not want this twenty-year-old Dr. Dolittle sleeping in her house and buying her cigarettes. But what could she do? He was Dustin's only friend, the one person who didn't seem to find visiting a burden. Also, pursuing the matter would mean having to give back the cigarettes.

Camille got her things together for work, treading lightly so as not to wake up her family. Lyle. A husband she didn't speak to. Her tragically wounded son. She peered inside Jonas's room on her way to the garage, shocked to see him sleeping in bed with his clothes on. He hadn't even bothered to take off his shoes. Camille's throat swelled with guilt: for never being home, for stranding him out here in the desert, for being so stung by Lyle's hatred those months before the accident she'd all but forgotten he existed. Then there was the slight suspicion she had sometimes—more a tinge of uncertainty, something she worried like a tooth—that he'd burned down the house on purpose. To be noticed. An actual flare, impossible to ignore. Thinking such a thing—and the fact that she could barely look at him sometimes, her own son—made Camille sick to her stomach.

She entered Jonas's room and gently tugged off his shoes. His face, tan as a gypsy's, seemed inconceivably young. Camille went to the garage and lit a cigarette before backing the Volvo down the driveway. The glare of the sun made her squint. She shifted into drive and headed away from the house, filled with a mortifying sense of relief.

CHAPTER 32

Warren's heart sank as soon as he saw it. He'd tried selling knives in condos, apartments, even the army barracks in Lancaster—but never a trailer park. He pulled off the freeway and passed under the Mahogany Views sign, creeping past the ferocious, airborne barks of a rottweiler chained to someone's pickup. The name's similarity to Auburn Fields did not escape him. In better spirits, Warren might have savored the irony. The Librojos, the Szelaps, the Medinas—all of his appointments had come to nothing. Not so much as a nibble. This was his last chance, do or die, and so far it didn't look good.

Warren stopped the Oldsmobile in front of lot 27 and stared at the curtained windows of the trailer. A row of giant sunflowers, bowing under the heat so you couldn't see their petals, had been planted out front. He did not want to pester these people or enter their tidy, curtained lives. But the idea of returning to the house— where Dustin lay simmering with hatred, where the closed door of the office reminded Warren he no longer slept with his wife— appealed to him even less.

Glumly, he gathered his courage and knocked on the screen door of the trailer, mentally rehearsing his pitch. A woman cracked the door enough to peek out. Her face scowled through the crack, about as welcoming as a gun. Warren asked if Mr. Ingram was in.

"Taking a nap," she said.

"We're supposed to have an appointment."

"What kind of appointment?"

"I have some knives for him to look at."

"Christ. Last week it was Norman Rockwell plates. Limited

edition. He ordered twenty boxes on the phone." Warren's face must have betrayed something, because the woman looked at him carefully, opening the door a bit wider. She was wearing tight jeans and a T-shirt that said VIVA LAS VEGAS. "Was it a long drive?"

"Thirty minutes."

"You look thirsty."

"I am a bit, um, parched."

"Would you like some water?"

Warren nodded, following her into the kitchen. The Mr. Coffee had a measuring cup underneath it instead of a pot. The woman filled a glass from the sink and handed it to him, apologizing that the ice maker was broken. Her eyebrows, thick as caterpillars, were so at odds with the daintiness of her face that they seemed like the remnants of a disguise.

"Melody," she said, introducing herself. "La la la."

The woman watched him drink, as if she were waiting for him to leave. She was wearing something around her neck: a shard of broken pottery, white as bone. Warren looked closer and saw that it had the texture of bone as well, grainy and rugged. To avoid staring, he looked at a photo on the refrigerator, a shot of Jesus with His right hand poised in the sign of the cross. Someone had signed "Jesus Christ" at the bottom of the picture. Warren had seen all manner of Jesuses in the houses he'd entered, including a holo-graphic one that ascended from the cross—but never a photograph.

"That's my brother," Melody explained.

Warren nodded. He put the glass down on the counter.

"He's a Jesus impersonator," she said.

"A Jesus impersonator?"

"Parades, videos, that sort of thing."

"Wow," Warren said.

"He's in Salt Lake right now, doing a gig for the Latter-Day Saints." Melody nodded at the picture on the fridge. "That's a joke. Anyway, his idea of one. He doesn't really do glamour shots."

Warren might have laughed, but he was too dejected. Things were not looking promising. Nevertheless, he plunked his case on the kitchen table and began to unzip it.

"I'm sorry my dad got you all the way out here," Melody said casually. "But we don't need any knives."

"Do you mind if I just go through my pitch?"

"Won't do any good, I promise."

"This is my first day," he lied.

"I've got to fix the antenna before Dad wakes up. He can't get his shows."

"I could really use the practice."

She studied him resentfully and then sat down in a chair, fiddling with the shard of pottery dangling from her neck. Warren guessed she was in her mid-thirties, a pretty much hopeless demographic when it came to moving knives. The hopelessness was compounded by the fact that she still lived with her father. Warren tried to forget these things as he threw himself into his sales pitch, withdrawing a tomato knife from his case and describing the "patented edge" that never touched the cutting board, only the tomato, thereby requiring no sharpening at all. Contrary to popular opinion, dull knives were much more dangerous than sharp ones. "Did you know that more people lose their fingers every year from cooking with old knives than from working in factories?"

"All of them?"

"What?"

"'Fingers,' you said. I'm picturing someone with no digits."

Warren looked at her. "Fin*ger*. Sorry."

"Since you're practicing."

He passed her the knife so she could feel the patented, form-fitting grip for herself. She did not seem particularly impressed. He explained that BladeCo's patented handle was guaranteed to withstand temperatures of up to 850 degrees Fahrenheit, more than twice as hot as the average flame. It was the same material, in fact, that was developed for the space shuttle.

"Are you sure you want to mention the space shuttle?" she said.

"Why not?"

"I mean, it blew up."

"That's true, but the knives were in perfect condition." He took the tomato knife back, feeling the first flicker of a headache. "Sorry. A little joke."

"I don't think that's appropriate. To joke about a disaster like that. Personally, I'm not offended, but it's not going to endear you to the customer."

Who was this woman? She had something in her hair—a twig—

as though she'd just emerged from a tent. Warren wondered if she was insane. "What do you suggest I say instead?"

"You could mention a factoid."

"A factoid?"

"A factoid's a small, insignificant fact. Kind of like your thing about fingers. For instance, were you aware that bats always turn left when exiting a cave?"

Warren shook his head.

"I don't know how you could work that in—to your pitch, I mean—but it might liven things up."

Warren could see that the first-time angle wasn't working but did not know how to cut short his pitch. He found a cutting board by the sink and asked for something to chop. Melody brought him a carrot, which he began to slice into perfect orange poker chips. He'd practiced this many times and was secretly proud of his knifemanship. As he was blazing through the carrot, flourishing the knife like a chef—trying, for some odd reason, to impress her—the blade slipped and caught his finger. A deep gash, just above the joint. It closed up almost immediately before beginning to pool with blood.

Warren pressed the gash with his thumb, trying to staunch the flow. The amount of blood surprised him. He grabbed the cutting board with his uninjured hand, hoping to dump the bloodied carrot down the disposal.

"What is that?" Melody said from her chair.

"There must have been ketchup or something on the cutting board." Warren's finger had begun to throb, pulsing a half beat behind his heart. He wondered if he should go to the hospital.

"My father," she said, shaking her head. "You should see what he eats. He puts margarine *and* butter on his English muffins. I'm always, like, one's a butter substitute, it defeats the purpose, you can't substitute a butter that's already there! If you're coaching a basketball team, do you put in a player without taking one out? But he likes the taste." She leaned forward, squinting at Warren's hand. "Hey, look. There's blood running down your wrist."

"It's nothing," he said.

"Did you know that Attila the Hun died from a nosebleed, on his wedding night?"

Warren pressed his tie against the wound, hoping the absorbency would help. The blue tie bloomed purple, a broad stain creeping upward like a thermometer.

"Wow, that's nastier than I thought," Melody said. "Sit down. I'll get the first aid kit."

Warren did as he was told, slumping into a chair. He was feeling a bit woozy. When Dustin was a kid, he'd get excited over the smallest bruise or scratch, barging into the house and demanding a Band-Aid like a biker ordering a drink. Warren could picture the euphoric swagger of his walk. Returning to the kitchen, Melody unbuckled an old tackle box and pulled out a gauze pad and pressed it to his finger hard enough to hurt. She lifted his arm above his heart, to "elevate the wound." Despite the twig in her hair, she seemed to know what she was doing. The shard of pottery around her neck dangled near Warren's face.

"What's on your necklace?" he couldn't help asking.

"My skull. A piece of it, I mean. The doctor asked if I wanted to keep it, you know, for a memento."

"Doctor?"

"Surgeon, actually."

"You had an operation?"

"Craniotomy." She glanced at him for a second, as if he might challenge this. "Brain tumor."

Warren felt a vague tug of hope. "My father had a brain tumor," he said.

"Was it benign?"

"No. I don't think so. He died when I was seven."

"Probably an astrocytoma," Melody said. "Actually, there are no benign ones. They just call them that, to classify them, but they can still kill you." She looked down at her necklace. "I just wear it to remind me, you know, where I've been."

Warren peered at the shard of skull. There was an intimacy about it that seemed somehow comforting. Something about the way she was holding him, cradling his elbow and gripping his index finger like a baby, compounded this feeling.

"I lied," he said. "This isn't my first day on the job."

"I know," Melody said.

"You do? Why were you critiquing my pitch?"

She shrugged. "You don't often get the opportunity," she said thoughtfully. "Oh, great. Dad's up. I just heard his door."

A man with bushy eyebrows entered the kitchen, wearing pajamas and no teeth. You could see Melody's face in him like a dirty joke. She introduced Warren, explaining why he was there. The man's eyes took in the scene in front of him—Melody holding Warren's arm over his head, the first aid kit open on the table—before moving to Warren's shirt, which was covered extravagantly in blood.

"Make sure you get the free spatula," he said before leaving the kitchen.

"I wish all my customers were like that," Warren said.

"He'll buy anything," Melody said, "so long as he gets something free."

Warren laughed. The noise—his own laughter—sounded foreign to him. "Has it stopped bleeding?" he said, looking at his finger. His whole arm was asleep.

"Oh yeah. A while ago." She blushed. "Not sure why I'm holding it."

CHAPTER 33

Lyle was bored bored bored bored bored bored bored. She tried to imagine that the boredom itself might be interesting, or even have some sort of artistic significance, but after taking eleven photos of her big toe exhibiting a range of human feelings—sleepy, awestruck, etc.—she decided that being bored out of her mind was not leading to greatness. It was leading to mental dysfunction. Whoever said that only boring people get bored should be whacked on the head with a bat. Obviously, the person had never lived on an abandoned block in the middle of the desert, a place so hot and miserable the mailman flipped them off every afternoon and the nearest library was thirty miles away, stocked with the complete works of Robert Ludlum but not a single immortal novel by George Eliot or Charles Dickens.

The thought of the library in Palos Verdes, with its luscious rows of books, made her head swim. The coolness between the stacks. The smell of perfume and beanbag chairs and hot Xeroxed paper. She missed the place like a lover. She could be there right now, reading to her heart's content, if her dad hadn't lost all their money and condemned them to a living death.

She glanced at the copy of *Ulysses* sitting on her bedside table. A glass of water was perched on top of it, staining the cover. The book had been there for two weeks, gathering rings inside rings, like a mass of dividing eggs. Lyle felt she'd better read it, especially if she was going to go to Columbia next year—her dearest fantasy—but for whatever reason couldn't bring herself to crack the cover.

To keep herself from taking any more pictures of her feet, Lyle rolled out of bed and got dressed for work at The Pumpkin Patch. She'd found the job in the paper two weeks ago. It was her father, in fact, who'd shown her the ad. *Servers needed: seeking naturally gifted team members who were "born to serve."* Though she'd wondered who exactly was born to serve—oxen?—she'd been intrigued by the idea of using her natural gifts. As it turned out, this meant unbuttoning her shirt to a nebulous point that maximized her tips but was not obscene enough to offend people. In the year since Dustin's accident, something had happened to Lyle's body. Or rather, something had happened to her *perception* of it, which amounted to the same thing. Mainly, she was no longer completely disgusted by it. She could look at herself in the mirror and not want to crawl under the bed. In fact, she'd begun to realize that she might actually attract a certain species of male: she'd heard boys use the term "stacked" before, whistling with a jokey sort of reverence, but was only beginning to realize she fell into this category.

Pow, they said, cupping their hands in front of their chests, as though they were firing weapons.

Stripping out of her T-shirt, Lyle pulled a white oxford from the closet and buttoned it to the top of her bra, revealing a pale chink of cleavage. It was hard to imagine this had any power over men's hearts. Since Hector, she'd slept with several boys from school, mustacheless kids who'd asked her out to the movies during lunch or had caught up with her in the parking lot, staring at the ground in embarrassment—boring, fidgety, half-popular boys, the kind who listened to U2 with their eyes closed and wore concert T-shirts the day after they'd seen a show. They were in bad cover bands called The Rhythm Method or Möbius Striptease. She felt nothing for these boys but was too flattered to resist: the way they trembled before unbuttoning her shirt, their hands clumsy as a toddler's, made her feel like Shannon Jarrell. *Expensive.* Like that day at The Perfect Scoop, watching Hector suffer through his ice cream. Afterward, it was always the same: they'd climb off of her with a gentle push and she'd feel beyond miserable, not just cheap again but disgustingly buglike, paralyzed with shame, as if she couldn't bear to crawl out of the backseat or turn on the lights.

She'd confided this last April to Bethany, who'd suggested her sleeping around might have something to do with guilt. The worst part wasn't even that she'd said "sleeping around"; it was the reason she gave for Lyle's supposedly feeling guilty. After all, wasn't Lyle living there, in Bethany's house, while Dustin was stuck out in the desert? And—*Please don't take this the wrong way, I'm not saying you're a pervert or anything*—but didn't the three boys she'd slept with even look a little like her brother? Brown hair, and weren't they, like, musicians, too? It was so ridiculous Lyle had laughed in her face. She'd ended up insulting Bethany's boyfriend, calling him a scrawny little two-timer, even though he wrote her every week from France and was coming to visit later in the summer. She may even have said something about his teeth. The argument just about ruined their friendship, though in truth living together all spring had already pulled it to the snapping point.

Now, stranded out in the desert like her brother, Lyle stared at herself in the mirror until she couldn't bear to anymore and then wandered off to find Hector, who was visiting Dustin for the third time that week. She was bored enough to see what effect she might have. She didn't want to get back together with him—she had a hard time believing they'd ever dated—but she liked to tempt his unrequited love for her, drifting in and out of range like a song.

Lyle found him in the kitchen, stooped in front of the cabinet with a tube of something in his hand. At the sound of his name, Hector spun around quickly, the creepy rodent he went around with peeking out of the pocket of his T-shirt. Lyle found the animal profoundly unnerving—what a rat might look like in the afterlife. Neither Hector nor the creature so much as glanced at her breasts.

"What are you doing?" she asked.

"Putting on contact cement. The laminate's coming off."

"It's been like that for months!"

Hector shrugged.

"We don't fix things around here," Lyle explained. She pointed at the sink. "The sprayer's been busted since January."

"I fixed it a while ago. Just needed a new nozzle head."

He turned around again and began to fiddle with the tube, shaking it with one hand. Lyle stood there for a while longer, bending over conspicuously to pet Mr. Leonard, but Hector failed to appreciate her presence. Why the hell was her ex-boyfriend—who lived in Wilmington—doing handiwork on their house? There was something going on here that she didn't understand. Maybe the toxic fumes were making everyone insane.

She wondered, a bit morosely, if he was no longer in love with her.

Since it was Saturday, Lyle stopped by her mother's room to verify that she actually existed. Sure enough, she was kneeling on the lumpy futon she slept on, taking shirts from a laundry basket and sorting them into towers. A surprising number of the shirts were gray or black. Lyle didn't know why her parents had decided to sleep in different rooms but blamed it entirely on her mother. It was another example of her deranged behavior. Having a mother who chain-smoked was not at all as wonderful as Lyle had expected. She missed her old mother, the one who spoke Spanish and wore pink cardigans and didn't think she was too good for Lyle's dad.

Her mom looked up from the laundry she was folding and stared at Lyle's clothes, eyes resting on her unbuttoned shirt. Something old and lonely drifted into her face. Having your mother look at your tits was a bit like hearing your own voice on a tape recorder trying to sound sexy.

"What are you doing after work?" Lyle's mom said. "I thought we might drive into Lancaster and see a matinee."

"Can't," Lyle said, relieved not to have to lie. The idea of sitting in a dark movie theater with her mom, possibly enduring a sex scene, was more than she could handle. "I've got to go to the library and research volunteer opportunities."

Her mother sighed. "Don't you think you've got enough going on at home?"

"What am I going to write my college essay about? A day in the life of a desert tortoise? Mrs. Silverberg says I need some more extracurricular interests, to distinguish me from the pack." Mrs. Silverberg was her college adviser.

"Tortoises might be interesting, actually."

"Right. Just what Columbia's looking for."

Her mother stopped a shirt in midfold. It was uncanny: just say "Columbia" and she froze like a statue. "We still need to talk about this. I mean, have you even thought about how much a school like that costs?"

"Dad says I can get a scholarship. Or loans."

"Loans! Your father isn't living in the real world, if you haven't noticed. He still thinks we'll be able to move back to Palos Verdes." Lyle's mother frowned. Annoyingly, you couldn't dismiss her opinion the way you used to be able to—not like when Lyle's dad made all the money and she was merely embarrassing. She folded the sleeves she was still holding, crossing them like a dead person's arms. "Anyway, didn't Mrs. Silverberg say something about Columbia being a long shot?"

"I signed up for an SAT course. It starts next week."

"I suppose your dad will take out a loan for that as well?"

Lyle scowled. "I'm a professional waitress," she said. "I paid for it myself."

She undid another button of her shirt, belligerently, before backing out of the room. Her mother wanted her to rot out here forever. In fact, it was her mom's fault that Lyle had screwed up her SATs last spring. She'd insisted she come home for the weekend, for Jonas's birthday, meaning that Lyle had to get up at 5:00 a.m. and drive an hour and a half to get to the testing center in time. She'd spent the four hours in a daze, filling in bubbles randomly when she ran out of time.

Lyle peeked into Dustin's room, hoping to gripe about their mother, but he was watching *The Searchers* for the hundredth time. "That'll be the day," he said to the TV. Lyle couldn't be sure he was reciting a line from the script and not having an actual conversation.

"Why's Hector repairing our kitchen?" she said, interrupting him.

"Beats me."

"Don't you think it's weird he's over here all the time?"

Dustin looked at her for the first time, his droopy eye lingering on her shirt. She fumbled at the button she'd undone. "No weirder than your trying to seduce him all the time."

"Jesus. I'm not trying to seduce him. Is that what he thinks?"

He shrugged and went back to his movie.

"Maybe he wishes," Lyle said.

Dustin laughed. "He's been over you for months."

This was so obviously true that Lyle looked down at her feet. "Anyway," she said, "I'm just saying it's weird. He's always bringing you things."

"Somebody needs to open my beers," he said.

"You talk like he's your personal assistant."

Dustin frowned, turning up the volume with his remote. "Can I go back to my movie? Or did you come in here for a reason?"

"Maybe I should just kill you and put you out of your misery," she said.

It was too late to take back. Dustin's face turned into a hideous smirk. Lyle left the room and went to gather her things for work. She should have known better than to try to talk to him; all they ever did was argue. A year ago, if someone had told her that her handsome older brother would be injured beyond belief, that he'd need to be cared for like an invalid, it would have seemed like a fantasy: a chance to recover what they'd had as kids. She would never have imagined that she'd be applying to a college in New York, more desperate than ever to get away, or that Hector would be the one taking care of him.

Just picturing Dustin in his bed, so bitter and self-pitying and remote, made her want to shake him. It was infuriating. Still, she hadn't meant to say what she did.

Driving to work, Lyle tried not to let the monotonous brown vistas lull her into a coma. She distracted herself by touching the Columbia bumper sticker on the dashboard. She made an effort to touch it whenever she could, so that its Ivy League juju would enter her fingers and climb upward to her brain, transforming her into the perfect applicant. She liked to fantasize that she was the only one to get a sticker in the mail: so eager was Columbia to have her as a student, they'd slipped it into her application materials like Willy Wonka's golden ticket. Lyle had stuck it on the dashboard to remind herself—while she was driving through the barren, dream-sucking desert—that she wouldn't be living out here forever.

At The Pumpkin Patch, Lyle's boredom grew even worse. In retaliation, she sighed murderously and stared out the window while people ordered and gave the general impression that she'd rather be nailing tacks into her eyeballs. It occurred to her, not without shame, that she was behaving like Shannon Jarrell. Of course, Shannon Jarrell would never consent to work at The Pumpkin Patch. You had to actually *do* something, though it would have been hard to guess that from today's shift. Lyle had only four tables, all of them female except for a group of old men accompanied by an oxygen tank. She wondered if there was any way to turn her job at a crappy chain restaurant into a college essay. She could call it "Serving Others: Finding Myself in The Pumpkin Patch." Perhaps someone would come in off the street—a homeless person, say—and dispense some poignant, hard-won advice, teaching her the true meaning of nourishment.

She was hopeful when a girl in a wheelchair came in, pushed by her mother, though these hopes were dashed when she got a good look at the kid's face. The girl wouldn't be dispensing any advice. Her head sagged listlessly to one side, her hands curled in like tarantulas. Her mouth gaped open in a permanent yawn. Lyle had never thought of a mouth being "ajar" before, but that seemed like the right word to describe it. In general, she looked like she might be better off dead. With mounting dread, Lyle watched the hostess lead them to a table in her section and prop a menu resourcefully in the girl's lap.

"You know, it's not nice to stare," the woman said when Lyle approached to take their order. She wore heavy mascara that made her eyes seem like they might flap away.

"I wasn't staring."

"Yes, you were. You've been watching us since we came in." The woman unfolded her napkin and wiped some drool from the girl's chin. "How do you think it feels to be stared at all the time?"

"You should ask my brother," Lyle said softly.

The woman's face changed. "Does he have CP?"

"He was burned last summer. He almost died."

The girl in the wheelchair laughed, a wheezy, elaborate production. Why did Lyle care what this woman thought of her? Her daughter, too, made her feel ashamed. She tried to take their orders, but the woman seemed uninterested in letting her escape.

"You're in high school?"

"College," Lyle said, not sure why.

"Nearby?"

"Back East. I live in New York."

"So you came back here to take care of your brother." Lyle did not deny this. The woman put her hand on Lyle's elbow. "You won't regret it," she said warmly. "He may not always see it, but the real gifts in life aren't always visible."

The woman smiled at her daughter, who strained her head in the woman's direction for a few seconds before collapsing again like a marionette. It was a gesture of such onerous affection that Lyle felt dizzy.

"Are you all right?" the woman asked.

Lyle shook her head.

"He's lucky to have you. You should see how many kids with disabilities get dumped in homes. If I'd listened to Jaynee's father—God knows, I don't think she'd be alive right now."

Lyle took their orders—"french fries," the girl said passionately, startling Lyle with the lusty warble of her voice—and then went to the waiter station to type in the codes. She stared out the back window at the parking lot. Someone had traced some extra letters on the door of the Renault, running a finger through the filth, so that it read LE CARCASS. She thought of the Columbia sticker on the dashboard. Dustin had ridden in the front seat with her several times. What must he have thought? Not just that she wanted to abandon him: *she couldn't fucking wait.*

Lyle buttoned up her shirt. She tended to other customers, avoiding the mother and her atrocious daughter as much as she could. She was startled, after they'd left, to find a 25 percent tip. The money made Lyle feel even more despicable. At one point a guy in mirrored sunglasses walked into the restaurant: Lyle's heart leaped, but his face was smiling, handsome, not a thing like her brother's.

CHAPTER 34

"How can you stand the smell?" Taz said, holding her nose. There was something heartbreaking about her face—some change in its appearance—that Dustin couldn't put into words.

"You get used to it," he said.

"It's like something died. But in a sauna."

They were walking around the desert because there was nothing else to do. Taz had driven all the way out in her car, the white BMW she'd inherited from her parents, telling them she was going to Venice Beach with some friends. Dustin didn't understand her desire to visit him but had decided to tell her not to do it again. The sight of her made his soul hurt. He was disappointed in the BMW. He was disappointed in her hair. He was disappointed that she hadn't sprouted a tail and avoided the unadventurous fate of being a teenager. Everyone was a letdown; the trick was to escape before they could squash your image of them completely.

Taz's mascara had begun to melt down her cheeks. She was wearing a giant Hanes T-shirt, stirrup pants, and Jelly shoes. He wondered if the clothes were really what they pretended to be, a sign of recovery, or further proof of how unstable she was. To keep his scars out of the sun, Dustin had on a cowboy hat he'd found in the Dumpster behind the video store; he'd taken to wearing it around Lancaster and calling people "Boss" or "Missy." Taz kicked over a rock with her shoe, revealing a pocket of darker soil.

"Watch out for rattlesnakes," he said.

"Do you always have to wear that thing?" she said, looking at his Jobst shirt.

"Why?"

"I'm just wondering. It must get hot."

"At least I don't fucking wear Madonna bracelets."

She glanced at the rubber bracelet around her wrist and then stared at her feet. "It's from Teen-to-Teen," she mumbled. "My support group."

"Support group?" he said, laughing. It was easier to hurt her feelings than to explain his disappointment.

"It's supposed to remind us not to do things. 'Self-injurious behavior.'"

"Like swallowing glass?"

She didn't answer him. "There's a girl in my group, Kendall, who broke her own arm. Stuck it in a vise and then tightened it till her bone crunched."

"Jesus," he said.

"Sounds lame, I know. My parents are making me go."

Dustin tried to picture Taz crushing her own arm. It occurred to him that what he'd thought was romantically deviant in her character—screwing her big sister's boyfriend, for example—might to other people look like despair. "They tried to get me to go to a support group," he said. "At Torrance Memorial. I told them they'd have to tie me to a bed again and wheel me in there." A breeze wafted from the direction of the dump, and Taz winced. "Think this smells bad, wait till you spend some time in a burn unit."

"I know," she said.

"What do you mean?"

"I came to visit you. At the hospital." She kicked over another rock, and a lizard slithered away from her foot. "I snuck out and took the bus."

Dustin looked at her in amazement.

"You were all strapped down," she said, "zonked on morphine. I remember how hot it was, all those lights around your bed. The nurse called them french fry lamps."

"When was this? Right after the accident?"

"I told them I was your sister."

The felt inside Dustin's hat was spongy with sweat. He remembered that night at Breakfast's party, when he'd thought he was dying and Taz had looked at him as if she were in love with him but would rather kill them both than admit it. Now she'd told him, of her own free will, that she'd visited him in the hospital.

She'd sneaked out of the house when her dad was at his most murderous. She could tell him now, unsmirkingly, because there was nothing at stake. He was safe and unlovable.

That was the heartbreaking change, Dustin realized. She no longer smirked at him but smiled almost with approval.

At the dump, Taz stopped in front of a Joshua tree tall as an oak. A rabbit dangled by its armpits from one of the forked branches, maybe eight feet off the ground, its hind legs crossed dapperly at the ankles. Where its eyes had been were two empty holes, bubbling with flies.

"Did it jump up there itself?" Taz asked.

"Maybe a hawk dropped it," Dustin said.

"Dazed by the smell, I bet."

They peered through the chain-link fence surrounding the dump. In the unspeakable heat the reservoir looked beautiful, its spotless water opaque as a mirror, a movie of clouds. It was the kind of blue you might see in a lagoon. It was hard to match it with the stench, so powerful it made Dustin's eye water.

"What's the pond for?" Taz asked.

Dustin shrugged. "The sludge settles to the bottom, I think."

Taz wiped the sweat from her face. "All I can say is, it looks pretty inviting."

"Yeah. Right."

"I'm serious. Don't you sort of want to take a dip?"

"No thanks."

"We'll keep our mouths closed," she said. "Come on, let's hop the fence."

She's still crazy, Dustin thought with relief. He pointed at his arm and reminded her how long it took him just to hang up his hat. She frowned, unable to conceal her disappointment.

"I'll just cool off for a second and come right out."

Taz gripped the fence and began to scale it like a burglar, easing herself over the top. There was no barbwire, which surprised Dustin until he remembered they were in the middle of the desert. Anyway, who in their right mind would sneak over the fence for a dip? Nimbly, Taz leapt down and walked around to the far side of the reservoir and then took off her shirt and pants and underwear, reaching behind with two hands to undo her bra, until she was standing there in only her Jelly shoes. She looked ridiculous that way and somehow more naked. On her arm, like a smudge of charcoal, was the botched tattoo she'd gotten at Breakfast's party.

She wandered down the tarp-covered embankment that sloped to the reservoir. He could see the veins in her breasts, faint as the ones in a leaf. The pond reflected even the veins. She peeled off one shoe, hopping to keep her balance, and dipped her foot in the gorgeous blue water.

"Wow," she said. "Your foot just, um, disappears."

He felt suddenly frightened. "I wouldn't go in there."

"Why not?"

"What if you . . . I don't know. Die?"

"I'm not going to *die*. Not right away, at least."

She peeled off her other shoe, leaving it on the embankment. Then she dove into her own reflection, a four-legged creature folding up like a card. Dustin waited for her to come up for air. A breeze rippled the water, erasing any evidence of her splash. The fear in Dustin's throat froze into an icy dread. Maybe the toxins had dissolved her like a pill. Insects droned all around him; the effect was to make the silence seem even greater. As he was beginning to panic, wondering if he should run to the highway for help, Taz's head broke through the water and she came up in the middle of the pond, gasping for breath.

Smiling, she swam back to the embankment and pulled herself out, her scarless body dripping in the sun. She got dressed and scaled the fence again and jumped partway to the dirt. Her hair was dark from the water. Dustin couldn't help feeling there was something enchanted about her, as if she'd just returned from another world. He had the odd sensation that he shouldn't look at her too closely.

"You smell terrible," Dustin said.

"How many years did I shave off my life?"

He shrugged. "Five?"

"Let's keep track. I want to die at twenty-five."

Dustin noticed that her left ear was stippled with tiny scabs, just as he remembered. He wondered what he could possibly offer this sixteen-year-old girl, or why on earth she would want to visit him. He felt barely alive himself. Starting back, they passed the dead rabbit swaying gently in the breeze. Its face was aswarm with flies. The shape of it kept changing, a black mask simmering in the sun. Dustin found it almost beautiful, this face that wouldn't stop moving, but decided not to mention this to Taz.

CHAPTER 35

At work, Mikolaj was premiering his video about reproduction, *Even Educated Fleas.* Camille had suggested calling it *Conception Is FUNdamental,* a far better title, but he'd either forgotten her suggestion or ignored it on purpose. As for the video itself, Camille had watched a few minutes of it in the editing room: a little redheaded boy with a lisp talking about his "penith." She felt bad for Mikolaj, of course, but some wicked part of her looked forward to the advisory committee's verdict. He believed he could make a better video than hers; he'd have to learn the hard way, as Camille had, how unforgiving they were.

At least she'd bear no responsibility for it. They'd moved her out of visual media last September, after she'd returned from her month off tending to Dustin. It had been packaged as a promotion—senior text editor—but in hindsight she suspected it was because of the debacle with *Earth to My Body: What's Happening?* It was hard to be too offended at the time, what with Dustin so much on her mind. And she had to admit she was good at her new job: in particular there was something about putting together the newsletter, assembling the jigsaw puzzle of graphics and text, that appealed to her. It was only recently, when they'd asked Mikolaj to direct something, that she'd started to feel betrayed. It wasn't only his newfound competence that annoyed her. He was always stomping down the halls in that ridiculous ponytail, dropping names of directors she'd never heard of, as if he were God's gift to the production department. He'd taken to wearing sunglasses on his way to the parking lot. He had an especially annoying habit of jotting ideas down on his hands, sometimes when you were speaking to him, so by the end of the day they were tattooed with words.

Seeing Mikolaj before the screening, however, pacing nervously in front of the auditorium in a brown suit and enormous wingtips, probably secondhand, Camille felt a stab of compassion. His eyes were bleary, as if he hadn't slept well the night before. Camille missed the old Mikolaj, his puppyish ineptitude and disdain for small talk: these days he tended to talk about AA meetings and his "personal struggle."

She offered him a cigarette, but he shook his head. "I'm trying to quit. It goes to set wrong example."

"Right," Camille said, lighting a Camel. Somehow, giving up drinking had made his English worse. She noticed that his hands were clean, scrubbed of ideas.

"I look to you nervous?" he said.

"The committee can be a bit petty. Just remember not to take it personally."

Mikolaj nodded. It amazed Camille that she'd kissed this sleepless-looking man standing in front of her. If Warren hadn't called her from jail that night, they might have done even more. After Dustin's accident, in the frantic, heartsick months that followed, Mikolaj and their spur-of-the-moment kiss had been the furthest things from her mind. Neither of them had mentioned it again. In the meantime, he'd become sober, capable, a changed man. *Uninteresting.*

Now, as Camille took a seat among the board members and listened to their poised-for-battle voices, watching Mikolaj fiddle with the video projector stationed over the front row, she felt an old flicker of attraction. The feeling grew when she saw him sit down to collect his thoughts on his way to the podium, his sideburns dark with sweat, studying a yellow notepad in his lap. In his brown suit and gigantic shoes, he looked like a duck. A sitting duck. It took her a minute to realize it wasn't *him* she was attracted to but the certainty of his doom.

"Thank you for come to see my new film," Mikolaj announced to the room, "*Even Educated Fleas.*" Silence. He cleared his throat. "Do you have any brief questions before the premiere?"

Rabbi Silverberg raised his hand. "I don't get the title."

"Please, we have the time only for questions," Mikolaj said, scanning the room.

"I don't get the title?" Rabbi Silverberg asked.

"It's from your American Songbook, by Cole Porter. We're using it as a sound track. '*Birds do it, bees do it, even educated fleas do it.*'" This last part Mikolaj actually sang. He had a suave, angelic, unaccented voice, so incongruous with his appearance that the audience was momentarily struck dumb. Perhaps they'd ask Camille to take her old job back. Eventually Father Gladstone raised his hand, breaking the spell.

"Wasn't Cole Porter homosexual?" he asked.

"What does that have to do with anything?" said Wendy Felsher of Planned Parenthood. She was sitting—deliberately, Camille suspected—in the same row as Father Gladstone. A large pin on her sweater said KEEP ABORTION LEGAL.

"Well, I don't think we should be endorsing his lifestyle."

"Are you suggesting he's referring to male fleas?"

"Actually, some water fleas don't mate at all," said Lane Mazerra, who taught science at Laguna Elementary. "They reproduce asexually."

Carl Boufis turned around in his chair. "By themselves?"

"Yes. They basically self-clone."

"This is very stimulating discussion," Mikolaj said, "and I would like to continue about flea sex at a later date. The film, in fact, is about human beings. Boys and girls of America talking about the fact of life."

"You don't worry it's a bit dumbed-down?" Rabbi Silverberg said.

"Dumb down?"

"*Dumbed.* To the kids' level. We don't want a repeat of last year."

There was an awkward silence. Several of the committee members glanced in Camille's direction. Mikolaj leaned into the podium, narrowing his eyes. "You use this expression because I am Polish?"

"No," Rabbi Silverberg said. He looked stricken. "I wasn't . . . I didn't mean anything like that."

Mikolaj smiled, and Rabbi Silverberg flushed with relief. "I kid with you. You should see a mirror. Anyway, Polish people *are* dumb. They put up with Soviet communist for forty-four years. But we are dumbing up, I think."

The audience laughed. Camille was amazed; it never would

have occurred to her to make a joke at Rabbi Silverberg's expense. Before the good cheer had evaporated, Mikolaj dimmed the lights and began his movie: a little girl, maybe six years old, talking about where her baby sister had come from. Sighing, as if addressing a roomful of half-wits, she declaimed with perfect conviction that Daddy had planted a seed in Mommy's belly button. What followed were kids of all ages discussing where babies came from, some of whom—like the chubby five-year-old who claimed he'd been fed by "an extension cord" and delivered through his mother's "potty hole"—rocked the board members with laughter. But it wasn't a silly film. It was good. Very good. There was no voiceover, but Mikolaj had edited the interviews artfully enough that the more enlightened children—the ones he'd enlisted to educate the viewers, some with pictures they'd drawn themselves—were clearly in the know. The film was funny and entertaining and trusted the intelligence of its audience. It felt like a real documentary, something you might see in a theater. And the fact that there was no script to speak of, that the kids themselves were doing all the talking, virtually ensured that the board would find nothing to object to.

Nonetheless, the warmth of their response astonished Camille. They crowded around Mikolaj, shaking his hand and describing their favorite scenes. Camille tried to congratulate him, too, but couldn't get close enough to catch his attention. At one point he looked up and met her eyes; perhaps she imagined the look of triumph—the shyly delighted grin—on his face.

The rest of the day she spent holed up in her office, darting past Mikolaj's cubicle on her way to the bathroom. At one point he knocked on her door, calling her name in his Polish accent; she pretended not to be there, holding her breath until he'd left. Back home again, she dragged herself from the Volvo, trying to shake the stiffness from her legs. She wondered if spending so much time in the car was crippling her joints. No one met her at the door or took her bag or asked her about her day at work. The house smelled like a microwave, muggy with Chinese takeout. Camille wandered down the hall and glanced into her daughter's room: Lyle was sitting on her bed, reading a book called *The Icarus Agenda*. She'd scratched out the word "agenda" on the cover and written "pudenda."

"Shouldn't you be at your SAT class?" Camille said.

"I didn't feel like it."

"I thought you had to pay for the whole course!"

Lyle looked up from her book begrudgingly. "It's *my* money, right?"

Camille felt guilty enough for making Lyle pay for classes, without her missing them. She bent down and picked up a Snickers wrapper sitting at her feet. "But you have to take the test again in October. It's your last chance."

"I'll just use my first score. From the spring."

"You need a fourteen hundred. Isn't that what the counselor said? You won't get into Columbia."

"Oh well," Lyle said, staring at her book.

Camille blinked at her. "So you've decided to apply to UC schools," she said, relieved.

"Actually, I was thinking of taking the year off. Staying out here and helping out."

She seemed to be serious. It was Camille's own fault, probably, for trying to dissuade her from Columbia. Now that she seemed to have given up on the idea, Camille was in the sudden, inarguable position of wanting her to go.

Camille left the room and knocked on Dustin's door, hoping to at least converse with him once before bed. Surprisingly, he was not watching *The Searchers* but something else: a spaghetti Western, Henry Fonda wearing a black hat and looking archetypically murderous. The words were too loud for the actors' lips. Camille moved an empty plate off the foot of the bed and sat next to Dustin's feet. She'd begun watching movies with him sometimes, expecting nothing in return. His bitterness did not seem to preclude this intrusion. It was the only time they ever spent together and made her feel like she was doing something, however small, to stage a resistance.

"How can you trust a man that wears both a belt and suspenders?" Henry Fonda sneered to a guy on TV. "Man can't even trust his own pants." Camille glanced at Dustin: he was beaming rapturously at the screen, the way a mother might at a newborn. At least there was something that seemed to bring him joy. She waited until Henry Fonda was offscreen before braving an interruption.

"I realized something today," she said.

Dustin looked at her, his droopy eye still managing to startle her. "What?"

"The movies I made. The videos." She paused. "It wasn't just the fertilization one. They were all pretty bad. Terrible, actually."

He did not dispute this. She was less upset, surprisingly, than grateful. "That's okay," Dustin said. "It's the same with Toxic Shock Syndrome."

"Your band?" she said, taken aback.

"Yeah."

"I thought people loved you."

"We were a joke," he said.

"I'm sure that's not true."

"We were terrible. The songs were all rip-offs. Even the name was moronic."

Dustin turned back to the TV. Camille reached out and touched his foot, gripping it as she used to do in the hospital. She didn't squeeze or anything, simply held it with her fingers. Dustin did not look at her. Camille waited for some sign of encouragement, a flex of the toes even, anything to nourish her hunger. She could feed on so little. But the foot only sat in her hand, still as a statue's.

She left Dustin's room and headed into the kitchen, grabbing a Diet Coke from the fridge. Outside, beyond the deck, Warren was walking Mr. Leonard in the last light of evening, the tops of the Joshua trees eerily aglow. He still had his tie on, perhaps to prove he'd been working. Something about the way her husband crept along at Mr. Leonard's gait, following him laboriously from bush to bush, filled Camille with an excruciating tenderness. She did not understand this tenderness or why it had come on so suddenly. She thought of the alien in Dustin's nightmare, its grouchy rebuke: *This world is not your home.*

It was only when she looked away, safe from Warren's image, that she realized she'd come to a decision. She would leave him. Free herself from his misery. Not right away, but she would. She tried to pin herself down, before her resolve could falter, and decided she would move out as soon as Mr. Leonard died.

It didn't make sense, to choose such a random date. But what in this life made the slightest bit of sense?

The doors slid open eventually and Warren walked into the kitchen, carrying Mr. Leonard like a baby. The old dog whimpered when he put him down. Camille looked at Warren as if to greet him but he avoided her eyes, awkward with something other than dislike, an odd skittishness like guilt. There was a Band-Aid around his finger, and she remembered that time on the tennis court when he'd nearly cut off his pinkie. He'd been opening a can of balls and sliced it on the edge of the metal top, down near the base, so deeply that you could see a frail twig of bone. She'd driven him to the emergency room in her bra, his hand swaddled in her shirt because she didn't dare take off his own. But it wasn't the terror she'd felt at her reddening shirt, or even the embarrassment of running into the hospital half-naked, that she remembered now. It was the pride—majesty, even—she'd felt when everyone stared at them from the waiting room. Shirtless, hugging Warren's waist, she'd felt the greedy omnipotence of love. Now his eyes met hers finally: his tie was covered in dog hair. They had been married for twenty years. She turned to the sink to hide her face.

"Mr. Leonard's going to be all right," he said softly, as if to console her.

CHAPTER 36

Lyle surveyed the room of drunk-looking UCLA students. A college party, her first. She'd been anticipating it all week—so bored out in the desert she thought her brain would die, would actually drain out of her ear like sap—and now she was here. At an apartment in Culver City. With actual undergrads. In her tedium-fueled fantasies, she'd imagined skinny men in vintage shirts, their legs crossed at the knees, listening to squawky jazz and firing off bon mots. She had not imagined a group of overgrown boys throwing a Ping-Pong ball into one another's beer. But this was what was happening in the living room, to the strains of "Addicted to Love." The boys stood at opposite ends of a table, adorned in baseball caps, kissing a plastic ball with their eyes closed before lobbing it at a triangle of cups. As she watched the triumphant stupidity of their faces, any second thoughts she'd had about dropping her SAT class were gratifyingly squashed.

"Beer Pong," Shannon Jarrell explained. She'd been here for a while and was already drunk, a beige barrette snagged in her hair like a moth. It was Shannon who'd told Lyle about the party, claiming it would make high school ones look like *Romper Room*. Lyle had promised to meet her here. She'd convinced Bethany and her French boyfriend, Gérard, to come along as well. He was visiting for a month, starved no doubt for a bit of culture. Shannon turned to him helpfully. "If it lands in one of the cups, you have to chugalug."

"Chugalug?" Gérard asked.

"Drink. Slam. Down the snatch."

"You mean 'hatch,'" Lyle said.

"Right," she said. She turned to Gérard. "'Snatch' means vagina."

Gérard nodded thoughtfully. This was his first time in America. "If they are so wanting to drink, why they don't just chugalug the beer instead?"

Shannon looked at Bethany with compassion. Lyle had not understood how plain her best friend was—the peculiarity of her face, with its long chin and faint nests of fuzz under her ears—until she'd seen her beside Shannon. "Doesn't he like sports?"

"Actually," Bethany said, "he's *very* athletic."

"He does look a bit like a jockey," Shannon said. She put her bottle of Miller Genuine Draft down on the mantel, where it promptly tipped over. "Fuck me! Shit! Pardon my French."

Bethany smirked and whispered something to Gérard. Lyle was beginning to regret the whole evening. She'd invited Bethany because she hadn't wanted to show up alone, but now she saw that this was clearly a mistake. Bethany did not understand her persistent friendship with Shannon. Lyle had tried to explain it, but the truth is she did not understand it herself. It had something to do with Shannon's beauty. Not just the long, flattering, irresistible shadow it cast, but the loneliness hidden inside it like a pearl.

Bethany and Gérard began to speak French, as if to exclude her and Shannon from the conversation. Gérard said, "Pardon my English," and they both laughed. He did look a bit like a jockey, with his large ears and Gaulishly tight pants. Lyle might have felt guilty thinking this if Bethany hadn't pretty much deserted her since he'd arrived, leaving her in the desert to rot.

"What do you think of that one?" Shannon said to Lyle, nodding at one of the Beer Pongers. He was wearing sunglasses on top of his cap. "He keeps looking at me."

"I don't know," Lyle said. "Kind of a douche bag."

"I know," she said enthusiastically.

"How many beers have you had?" Lyle asked.

Shannon shrugged. "Five or six."

At the far end of the table, a bearded guy leaned backward to chug a beer, exposing a dark-haired sag of belly. He looked like one of those football players whose popularity hinged on their willingness to eat strange things. He slammed the empty cup down, his beard glistening with beer. "What about that one?" Shannon said. "With the beard?"

"Are you serious?"

"He's kind of cute, in a *Where the Wild Things Are* sort of way."

Lyle did not know what to say. It heartened her somehow that Shannon could find him attractive.

"Just *joking*," Shannon said, laughing. "Jesus. I'm not into crossbreeding."

The guy with the sunglasses on his cap said something to Shannon, inviting her to play, and she moseyed over to join the table. No one invited Lyle. She was relieved and also offended. Failing to get Gérard's and Bethany's attention, she left the living room and went out the kitchen door to a courtyard surrounded by identical apartments, where a string of guests stood drinking around a dingy-looking pool. The pool was littered with cups and beer cans and an array of half-submerged garments, indistinguishable in its debris from the few high school parties she'd been to in ninth grade.

Lyle closed her eyes and let the breezy Pacific air remind her what it felt like to be cold. In less than an hour, she'd gone from being giddy with excitement to woozily depressed. A guy in a shirt that said CANCÚN PARTY PATROL on it wobbled up to her and began telling her a racist joke featuring the Queen of England. Excusing herself, Lyle rounded the pool and ran into a handsomely disheveled boy sitting all alone by the deep end. Mark Biesterman. She hadn't recognized him in the dark. His professorial glasses were gone, and he'd grown his hair into a tangle of Byronesque curls. He was about to scootch his chair back to let Lyle by when he saw who she was, almost spilling his beer in surprise.

"What are you doing here?" he asked.

She shrugged. "Discussing the British monarchy."

He put his beer down on the deck, as if he'd been doing something wrong. He did not appear to be having much fun either. Overhead, a police helicopter roamed the starless smog, its spotlight twitching back and forth like an antenna.

"Is this what college parties are like?" she asked, sitting next to him.

"Not really," Biesty said, relaxing. "Usually there are Jell-O shots and more people going *wooooh*!"

He took a sip of his beer and watched the pool, avoiding her eyes. On the other side of the deck, a girl kicked her high heels into the shallow end, one at a time, like a stripper. A boy in a tank top began to yell at her, grabbing a net from the bushes to fish them out.

"How's Dustin doing?"

Lyle shrugged. "Do you want the honest answer?"

"I don't know."

"He never leaves his room. The only people he'll talk to are Hector and John Wayne."

"Who's Hector?" Biesty asked.

"His best friend." She glanced at Biesty. "I mean, now that you're in college."

He stared into his cup, as though something had caught his attention there. A bug paddling its last. "I tried taking him to a party, to hear my new band. He put on quite an act."

"You should call him," she said angrily.

"Didn't he want to come out tonight?"

"I don't know."

"You didn't invite him?"

Lyle stared at the deck. It hadn't even occurred to her. "He wouldn't have come anyway," she mumbled, tossing a bottle cap into the pool.

Biesty's face softened. He seemed sad and lonely and perhaps not as happy at UCLA as he'd led Dustin to believe. He put his beer down and it wobbled a bit before he could rescue it, his eyes catching for a moment on Lyle's leg. She realized for the first time that he was drunk.

"We used to make fun of you sometimes," he said, "me and the band. When you weren't around. We called you the She-Yeti. And Dustin would always get mad at us and stick up for you. He said you were smarter than all of us combined."

Lyle felt sick. She slid her leg over, letting it rest against Biesty's. She watched herself do this, mysteriously, as though in a dream. She was not the agent of her leg but a helpless onlooker. Biesty flinched away and sat up in his chair.

"What are you doing?"

"I don't know." She felt like crying.

"Whoa. Perfect. Just what I need." He threw his empty cup into the pool, where it floated toward a raft of other cups flot-samed in the corner. "Everything that seems cool and momentous when you're a kid is a load of crap. You'll understand when you get to college."

"I'm not going to college," she said quietly.

"What do you mean?"

"We can't all, like, grow our hair out and go to frat parties."

Biesty did not tell her what a noble sacrifice this was or that she was a wonderful sister for doing it. She got up without saying good-bye and went back inside the party, wading through a crowd of people dancing to "Takin' Care of Business" by Bachman-Turner Overdrive. The puritanical work ethic espoused by the lyrics seemed deeply at odds with the dancers themselves, one of whom was wearing a box on his head that said NATURAL LIGHT. The words on the box struck Lyle as forlornly beautiful. When the singer of the song got to the part about "working overtime," the crowd erupted in cheers.

Lyle went down the hallway in search of a bathroom, stepping over a guy in madras shorts passed out on the floor. He smelled unpleasant, and Lyle wondered if he'd shit his pants. She tried a door that turned out to be a garage before finding one off the living room that looked promising. She knocked loudly. When no one answered, she cracked the door and was astonished to see Shannon Jarrell praying on the floor, kneeling by a sink with her head bowed. Her face was hidden behind a curtain of hair. Lyle felt a queer zag of joy. Quietly, she opened the door farther and saw a boy standing in front of Shannon with his arms akimbo, head tossed back as if he were admiring a cathedral. His jeans were at his ankles, exposing his hairy ass to the mirror. The burly guy with the beard.

Lyle closed the door and went back down the hall and left the party, squatting in the bushes behind the parking lot before climbing into the Renault. She felt dizzy. She forgot to switch on her headlights in the unfamiliar glow of streetlamps until someone honked at her from the other lane. It wasn't until she'd turned off the freeway and seen the lone light of her house in the distance that she remembered Bethany and Gérard, that she'd stranded them at the party. Somehow she did not regret this.

She might have run over Jonas in the garage if he hadn't stood up at the last minute. An acoustic guitar lay on some newspapers at his feet. She left the Renault in the driveway and got out.

"The coyotes have gone crazy," he said. "They're killing their own young."

"I don't want to hear about it," Lyle said.

"I found the remains of one out by the dump today, torn to shreds."

"What's wrong with you? Are you deaf?" She looked at the can of spray paint in Jonas's hand, wondering if he'd turned into some kind of aerosol huffer. Given how little she knew of his life, it wouldn't have shocked her. "What on earth are you doing?"

"Repairing this guitar. For Dustin."

"At twelve-thirty in the morning?"

"It's a surprise," he said. "I don't want him to find out." He jiggled the spray can. "I'm stenciling the name of his band on it. Toxic Shock Syndrome. Do you think he'll like it?"

"You're ruining Dad's scissors," Lyle mumbled, bending down to pick up the BladeCo scissors, freckled with orange paint, that were sitting on the floor. She walked inside and wandered down the hall toward the kitchen, pausing at Dustin's door. The TV murmured from inside; he often fell asleep with it on. She turned the knob gently and stepped into the room. Dustin was sitting up with a beer in his hand, the murky light of the TV flickering over his face. In the corner of the room, surrounding the wastebasket, lay a solar system of empty cans.

"Have you come to kill me?" he asked, eyeing the scissors in her hands.

"No."

"Damn."

Lyle put the scissors on the bedside table and got into bed and lay down beside him. He didn't object. She pulled an empty beer can from under her back and tossed it at the wastebasket, where it joined the other cans.

"I went to a party," she said.

He frowned. "Did you party till you dropped?"

"No. I left early. It was beyond depressing."

Dustin looked at her. His breath smelled like beer, warm and bean-sprouty. "What happened?"

"I don't know. They were playing Beer Pong. And I saw this drunk girl giving some football player a blowjob."

"Party head."

"What?"

"That's what you call those chicks. If you play Beer Pong. Party head."

Lyle stared at the ceiling. She could feel his misery coming off him like a vapor. It fogged up the room and made it hard to think.

"Biesty was there, too," she said.

"Goody gumdrops."

"He misses you a lot. He told me he'd written you some letters, but was too embarrassed to send them."

Dustin's face brightened for a second, despite himself. It was worth the lie. On TV, Leonard Nimoy was pondering the existence of Bigfoot, analyzing the blurry footage of a man in a gorilla suit. The gravity of his voice was so at odds with the subject matter that it made Lyle angry: somehow, it summed up everything that was wrong with the world, its continual misadvertisement.

"I want life to be as interesting as it is in books," Lyle said. "That's my problem."

"Everyone's got some problem like that. A glitch. Something they can't fix." Dustin put his hand on her head, as if to suck out the problem. He was drunk.

"I thought you didn't like me anymore," Lyle said.

"I don't." He rolled over, facing the wall. "That's *my* glitch. I don't like . . . anyone."

"What about Taz?"

"I used to," he said. "Now I just want her to go away."

Lyle didn't move. It had never occurred to her that he *wanted* to like people but couldn't. Those lists she'd kept of people she hated: it made her ashamed now, all that righteous, delectable loathing.

"Can I sleep in here tonight?"

He didn't say no. The TV went newsy with voices and Dustin sat up to turn it off, the room going dark as a closet. Lyle kicked off her shoes. Some coyotes were howling in the distance. They sounded as if they were not only killing their young for the fun of it but frolicking in their blood.

"I'm not going to college next year," she said. "I'm going to stay here."

"Why?"

"To be around. Help out."

Dustin didn't respond. What she'd meant to say was: *Ask me to stay.* Her brother's breathing thickened in the dark, steady as a pulse. Lyle wondered if he'd fallen asleep. As a kid, he'd kick her by accident sometimes as he was drifting off, jerking for no reason, sometimes two or three times in a row. She lay there with her eyes open, waiting to feel his helpless blows.

"Don't be a moron," he said.

CHAPTER 37

"Did you know that Leonardo da Vinci could write with one hand and draw with the other at the same time?"

"Where do you get this stuff?"

Melody shrugged. "It's important to exercise your brain."

They were lying in Melody's room, the blinds parted just enough that Warren could see the small, penned-in yard of the trailer next door, her neighbor's pet pig lolling in the dirt. Warren had taken an irrational dislike to the pig, whose name was Twinkle. It was always lying around in the middle of the day and reminding him of himself. Like himself, too, it was unemployed and relied on the charity of others. It wasn't even a real pig but a miniature one, roughly the size of a rottweiler. For a week or so, Warren had been watching to see if it ever raised its head; Melody had told him that it was physically impossible for pigs to look at the sky.

He was learning things from her. For example, on average twelve newborns are given to the wrong parents every day. Also, India is the only country with a bill of rights for cows. It was a relief to fill his head with useless knowledge. Melody's body was completely different from Camille's: brown as an Eskimo's, with a cozy plumpness that made him think of colder climes. He liked to nestle into her soft skin and imagine they were in Alaska, where the sun didn't buckle the roads. She always let him lie on the left side of the bed. In fact, she insisted upon it. She couldn't hear out of her right ear, one of the effects of the tumor, so it was the only way they could talk.

"Here," she said now, taking Warren's hand. "You can feel

where they left the window in my skull. For brain swelling. There's a little soft spot."

She showed him where they'd made the hole, running his fingers over the tender, dime-sized divot above her ear. He imagined there was still a window. Sitting up a bit, he made a little spyglass with his hand and cupped it to her head, pretending he was peering into her brain.

"What do you see?" Melody asked.

"Filing cabinets. Filled with trivia."

She laughed. "Is there one marked Warren Ziller?"

"Actually, a whole special wing."

"Don't flatter yourself," she said.

Twinkle stood up suddenly and wandered over to the other side of its pen, making Warren feel guilty. He didn't like it when the ugly creature seemed more industrious than he was. Camille and the kids believed he was spending his afternoons looking for work, something more dependable than selling knives, going to interviews and temp agencies all over the valley. He was choked with guilt as soon as he got home, but here the world seemed to have pardoned him in advance. Melody *wanted* him to do nothing. Even Melody's father, who spent most of his time copying phone numbers from the TV, had never asked him why he didn't have a job, or what he was doing lying in bed in the middle of the afternoon. It was as though he'd stumbled across a refuge in the maze, some secret corner where the shifty-eyed monsters couldn't find him.

The TV murmured from the next room; as usual, Melody's father had left it on before making his daily trip to Denny's. Warren touched the shard of skull hanging from Melody's neck; he liked that she refused to take it off, even during sex. It didn't seem to bother her to lie in bed all day, either. She was still living off the disability from her old job, as the receptionist in a dental office. Playfully, she rolled her fingers into a spyglass and stuck them against Warren's head, as though she could spy into his brain as well. "Aren't you going to ask me what I see?"

"No," Warren said.

"No interest at all?"

He turned away, staring at the blinds. He was suddenly frightened. "What do you see?"

"Miserable things. Now you don't have to talk about them."

She smiled. "My ex-husband needs to talk about everything. People think that's what all women want, Phil Donahue, but it isn't true. Getting your brain opened up helps you appreciate the right to remain silent."

Warren was deeply grateful. He did not want to ruin these afternoons with intimacy. Melody got out of bed, slipping on the pink robe that hung from the doorknob.

"Anyway, I have a theory about Phil Donahue," she said from the bathroom. "I think he's a reincarnated sheepdog. I mean, he's so big and shaggy. Also, he runs around inside. Dogs do that. Personally, I don't think people should run around inside, it's unseemly."

"Why do you do this?" Warren asked.

"Do what?"

"I don't know. Let me come over like this."

She stepped out of the bathroom, suddenly serious. Her bushy eyebrows looked stranger from across the room, less native to her face. "When you're sick, you're everyone else's problem. It's like you've turned into a helpless baby. I guess I'm attracted to being the solution for a change."

While she showered, Warren put on his khakis and slipped out of the trailer, squinting in the ridiculous heat. Clouds littered the sky like shreds of Kleenex. It was only when he was alone that he felt truly disgraceful. The miniature pig watched him from the edge of its pen, oblivious to the sky's presence. Perhaps it didn't even know it existed. Warren walked up to the pig and clapped directly over its head, several times, but the miserable creature didn't look up.

That night at home, watching Lyle and Jonas gather around the table, their hungry faces sinking at the sight of the chili he'd reheated for the third night in a row, Warren found he could not look them in the eye. The kitchen smelled bad, like rotten onions. Probably no one had bothered to take out the garbage.

"Did you find any jobs today?" Lyle asked, worrying a kidney bean with her spoon.

Warren felt sick to his stomach. "We'll see. Maybe. I had an interview with a company."

"Where? In Lancaster?"

"Yeah."

"What kind of company was it?"

He thought of an ad he'd seen in the classifieds. "Actually it was a mortuary. Administrative assistant."

Jonas looked up from his chili. "Do you get unlimited free coffins?"

"No. I don't think so." Warren stared into his bowl. "Anyway, it didn't sound promising. I think they're looking for someone with more experience."

"You're looking, Dad," Lyle said. "That's the important thing."

Warren excused himself before the kids were done and went to the bathroom. He missed the old Lyle, her bratty insolence; this new version was impossible to look at. He heard the TV going in Dustin's room and forced himself to knock on the door. At least he knew he wouldn't be met by kindness. The room smelled considerably worse than the kitchen. In the corner, collecting dust, was the basket of exercise equipment; Warren had long ago stopped trying to get Dustin to follow his rehab plan.

On TV, a man—Henry Fonda, it looked like—was holding someone hostage in a prison yard, sticking a gun into his back. "What are you watching now?" Warren asked.

"*You Only Live Once.*"

"Sounds like a soap opera."

"It's a film noir," Dustin said irritably. He was balancing a beer on his stomach. "By Fritz Lang."

Warren nodded. "You really love Henry Fonda."

"That's right. I want to do him up the ass."

On-screen, a man in a clerical collar grabbed a telegram from somebody and rushed into the prison yard, pleading through the fog to Henry Fonda, who fired his gun at him. Dustin burst out laughing. Warren realized that he was drunk. Camille was right: he'd turned their son into an alcoholic. He felt suddenly like he might throw up.

"Atta boy," Dustin said, toasting the TV. "Picking off a priest."

"Dust."

His son looked at him, but Warren didn't know what to say. At one point, he'd been brave enough to hold up a mirror and show him his face. Dustin turned back to the TV. "Close the door when you leave," he said.

Later that evening, hearing Camille pull up the driveway after her grueling twelve-hour day and stagger into the kitchen, too exhausted to heat up her chili before eating it, Warren vowed he would not go back to Melody's trailer. He was not a religious man but promised this with the soul-nursed conviction of the saved. Despite this moment of clarity, he returned the next day, and the next. Just the sight of the RV park from the road, a Christmasy sparkle of antenna, flooded him with gratitude and relief. On Thursday, napping in the swamp-cooled haven of Melody's room, he woke up alone with the covers at his feet, the odd tang of salt in his nose. He'd been dreaming about Dustin, a favorite nightmare. This time, though, when he'd unrolled Dustin from the blanket, braving the awful stink of his flesh, his son had become twelve years old, gawky and beautiful and unscathed, his smile as big as a harmonica. Jonas's age. *You only live once,* the boy said. Warren sat up in bed, the salt in his nose leaking down his throat. It wasn't until he touched his face, feeling the dampness there, that he realized he'd been crying in his sleep.

Naked, Warren parted the blinds and saw someone besides the pig, a shirtless man who was the spitting image of Jesus Christ, sitting in the gravel that bordered the neighbor's lot. He had long blond hair and a beard and a luminous, underfed look. Warren thought maybe he was deranged. The man lay back in the gravel with his hands on his hips, holding his legs in the air and scissoring them back and forth.

Warren slipped into his clothes and roamed the trailer in search of Melody, who'd disappeared. He went outside, where pig and man were still lying on the ground.

"You must be Warren," the man said, standing up. He offered Warren a gravelly hand and introduced himself as Melody's little brother. His name was Kenny. "Melody told me about you."

"Do you know where she went?"

"She and Pop went to buy an antenna. End of the free world, he can't get his channel anymore. She told me to tell you she'd be back." He looked at his dirty palms and then wiped them on his shorts. "Sorry, long drive. Got to keep my abs in shape. Do you want a beer?"

Dustin had the night shift at the video store; another hour or so and Warren wouldn't have to face him. He followed Melody's brother into the kitchen, wondering if a Jesus impersonator would dread returning to his own house so much he'd start an affair. Kenny handed him a Bud Light from the fridge and then chugged his own in what seemed like several gulps. Warren asked him how his trip was, remembering the video shoot in Salt Lake City.

"Those Momos are real slave drivers. Had me up on a cross for two hours. I mean, they wanted some Method acting up there. The bad part is your neck. They're all like, 'Your head isn't sagging!' Do you know what that does to your splenius muscle?" Kenny shook his head. "Kirk used to be Mormon, Melody's husband, and even he thinks they're greedy."

"You mean ex-husband."

He seemed embarrassed. "Well, I guess technically they're still married. I don't know about the terminology."

Later, Warren helped Kenny put the new antenna on the roof, which meant crouching on the marshmallowy tar and handing him screws when he needed them. He felt uncharacteristically useful. Melody and her father watched from below, the antenna box discarded at their feet. She looked different in her sunglasses, younger and almost beautiful. The shard of skull dangling from her neck glimmered in the sun. Her dad squinted at the long-haired man fiddling with an antenna, his half-naked son, telling him how to install it. What an odd thing a family was, Warren thought. The permutations, like the patterns of a chess game, seemed endless.

The installation was harder than it looked. Kenny began to curse under his breath, his bare back glazed with sweat.

"Put it where it won't get hit by lightning," the old man said.

"Don't give me any ideas," Kenny muttered.

"That's what happened to the old one. It got hit by lightning. It messed up the signal."

"That's *not* what happened," Kenny said. "Lightning wouldn't mess up the signal."

"I don't know," Melody said thoughtfully. "Animals in Africa won't attack another creature that's been hit by a lightning strike."

"Excellent point," Kenny said.

A boy in jungle-print sneakers began to antagonize the miniature pig next door. Warren could see him from the roof. The boy had a slingshot and was zinging gravel through the fence at the pig, which squealed when it was hit and gimped around its pen. Kenny stood up on the roof and raised an arm theatrically over his head, as if he were giving the Sermon on the Mount.

"How many days will it take the devil's minions to tear off your flesh?"

The boy stared up at him, startled. "Huh?"

"Wrong! You can't measure it in days!"

The boy ran off, spraying gravel. Kenny knelt down again and finished with the antenna. Following him down the ladder again, Warren slipped off the last rung and turned his foot on the ground, his ankle flaring with pain. It swelled up immediately. Melody jogged into the trailer to get some ice, her necklace clinking against the buttons of her shirt. Warren wondered if it was true what she'd said about animals being struck by lightning. Perhaps it was the smell that warned other creatures away. How lonely you would be, tottering around the Serengeti, smelling like bad luck. But you'd be safe as well—an accidental blessing. He started to get up but Melody had already come back with a bag of ice, tender with concern, pressing it to his ankle to numb the pain.

CHAPTER 38

Taz climbed out of the water in the moonlight, naked except for her high-tops. She'd taken her clothes off first before climbing over. Scaling the top of the fence, wet hair dangling in her face, she looked like a little girl. Dustin turned away, studying the rabbit enshrined in its tree. Its skeleton had been picked clean, a ghoulish Christmas ornament.

"What are we down to now?" Taz asked, catching her breath. Her wet hair, pasted to her head, made her seem even nakeder. This was the second time she'd visited since the day they'd found the rabbit; as before, she'd asked to go down to the dump, insisting on an "after-dinner swim."

"Sixty-five," he said. "You've got, like, forty more years to shave off."

"I don't feel any different. I hope it's working."

She plucked her bra from the Joshua tree and slipped it on, reaching behind her back with two hands to clip it together. There were two types of girls: those who waited to dry off before putting on their clothes, and those who didn't. Dustin had forgotten which kind he preferred. He took a swig from his beer, unable to taste a thing over the smell of the dump.

"I watched a video at the store today," he said. "*Faces of Death*."

"What is it?"

"A bunch of people dying. Real ones. There's this one part where some waiters bring out a screaming monkey to some people at a restaurant and stick it through a hole in the table, like from underneath so you can only see its head. Then the diners beat it to death with hammers and eat its brain right out of its skull."

"Christ," she said.

"It made me sick."

"But you didn't turn it off."

Dustin shook his head. He took another swig of beer. The stars were getting fuzzy around the edges, fat as snowflakes.

"Are you going to work there, like, forever?" Taz said.

"Where?"

"At the video store."

He bristled. "Why not?"

Taz shrugged. "It's just that you were all set with college. UCLA."

"That's just what I need. To hang out with a bunch of assholes in Calvin and Hobbes T-shirts."

"They're not all like that."

"I went to a party with Biesty, and everyone was doing beer bongs."

"There are some cool people at UCLA."

Dustin glared at her. "What the hell do you know about it?"

"I was *there,* remember? At the party."

"You're sixteen!" he said.

She scowled, wringing some toxic water from her hair. Her T-shirt was stuck to her back, a shoal of pink. "Must be hard, being so old and mature."

He stood up angrily, searching through his backpack to see if there was any beer left. She didn't know anything. Actually, growing older was a breeze; it was just a matter of getting in touch with your inner creep. When you were in high school, you had certain ideas about creepiness and the sorts of things you would never in a million years be caught doing. For example, getting drunk by yourself. Or watching *Faces of Death* all alone in a video store in the middle of the day. And then you were doing the thing, and you realized it was no big deal.

"Sometimes I wonder why I even come out here," Taz said. It looked like she might start crying.

"Why do you?"

"I don't know. That night at the party . . . I have this idea, maybe, that we're kind of the same."

"We're *not* the same."

"No," she said. "You're much more of an asshole."

This wasn't a joke. She rummaged in the backpack and pulled

out a beer for herself. A shooting star flared over the poppy preserve to the west. Dustin had never thought about the word before,
"poppy," but being out in the desert did this to him. Words stood
up from their sentences and waved at him. It was all the emptiness, with no TV around to distract him.

"When I first started doing shit," Taz said quietly, "my parents
sent me to this therapist, Dr. Feferman, who used to show me
pictures of things, dead birds or people kneeling in graveyards or
yelling at each other, whatever, and ask me which one described
the way I felt. But none did."

"Why are you telling me this?"

She sipped her beer. "I don't know."

Dustin felt something unspool inside him. He wondered if his
face was the picture she was looking for. Surprisingly, this did
not infuriate him. Another star streaked into oblivion, silent as
a thought. He told Taz about how when he was little, he used to
believe that meteor showers were things scientists used to clean
off meteors. "I had this whole idea in my head about what they
looked like. Sort of like a car wash, but with a conveyor belt."

She laughed. "I had this thing about gold bullion. I heard the
name somewhere, and all I knew is that my mom had bouillon
cubes in the cupboard. I thought it was a kind of soup made out
of gold. I used to look for it whenever we went out to eat, gold
bullion, under the appetizers." She frowned. "For years, I had this
vision of a beautiful, expensive soup, totally delicious."

Dustin chugged his beer, actual gulps. It enraged him that there
was no such thing as gold soup. He would add this to his list of
injustices.

"You shouldn't drink so much," Taz said.

"So my mom tells me."

"She knows about your drinking?"

He shrugged. "Like my parents are going to kick me out, a
scarred-up cripple." Dustin chucked the empty can with his left
hand, awkward as a girl. "Anyway, it makes me itch less. It's
medicinal."

Just saying the word "itch" made his arm prickle all over. He
scratched at his Jobst shirt, wishing he could dig into the flesh.
Sometimes he had dreams of this sort: he scratched and scratched
and scratched, until he'd dug through the skin and was scraping
marvelously at bone.

"Can you take that thing off?" Taz said.

"My Jobst?"

"I could scratch you. If you want."

Dustin blushed. He tried to remember if there was any more beer hiding in the fridge. "We should head back."

"Are you embarrassed?"

"No. I'm just supposed to keep it on all the time."

Taz laughed. "Come on. You shower, right? I don't think ten minutes will matter."

He could have refused to sit down with her, but he didn't. When he was still in the hospital, he often thought about what it would be like to have a girl touch him. The idea had seemed preposterous. Who would ever want to lay a finger on him? At the time, he couldn't even touch himself. In the night, haunted by dreams, he was his former, naked, unrepulsive self, girls from his past sucking him or riding him or fondling him in twos until he stained his sheets. Waking up was like the end of life, a loss that made him gasp. Now a girl wanted to scratch him, nothing more, and he couldn't move from fear.

"Could you, um, take it off yourself?"

Gingerly, Taz unzipped the arms of his Jobst shirt before *scrutch*ing open the Velcro that fastened around his chest. Dustin couldn't look at her. Her hair smelled like rotten eggs. There was a moment, after she'd slid the shirt down his arms, when he thought she was too horrified to speak.

"You can't even see them," Taz said. "The scars."

"It's nighttime."

"The moon's pretty bright." She looked away from him. "Anyway, I lied. You *can* see them."

"So you're saying they're ugly," Dustin said, trying to laugh.

"A little bit."

She asked for his hand and then took off the Isotoner glove, peeling it inside out until all his burns were visible. If he were still in love with her, he could never have done this. Slowly, as if it were a doctor's order, she began to scratch him. She held his fingertips in one hand and raked her nails up and down his arm, all the way to the shoulder, digging hard enough that it hurt, leaving a trail of sting that lingered wonderfully until the nails returned. The relief was incredible. He could scratch himself raw, but it was like the difference between jerking off and getting laid. Taz moved up to his chest and began to scratch him in circles, swirling her nails around, soothing a misery he'd forgotten was there. Dustin closed his eyes and tried not to think about how he looked, picturing himself as he used to be.

Later, he felt strangely bereft. It was only 10:45. She hadn't done anything, really, only scratched him, but it was like waking up from one of his dreams. The throb of loneliness surprised him. He knew she had to be home by midnight, her parents would find out where she was—still, he couldn't help wondering if she'd left before she had to. He couldn't blame her, that was the worst part. Would he have wanted to touch a girl who looked like him?

Dustin put on *The Searchers* to distract himself. Ethan was jabbing the dirt with his knife, having just found Lucy's ravaged body in the pass. Tonight he seemed less dumbly iconic than just plain dumb. Why didn't he go home and leave everyone alone? What the hell was his problem? And why, of all movies, had this become Dustin's favorite? He was just about to stop the VCR when someone knocked on the door, a gentle tap, as if Taz had decided to screw her parents and spend the night.

It was Jonas. Dustin couldn't hide his disappointment. He was holding a guitar, a bottom-of-the-line Yamaha. He handed the guitar to Dustin: the neck had been duct-taped, and there was something funny about the strings. It took Dustin a second to realize they'd been strung in reverse order, with the low E at the bottom.

"What is this?" he said. "A joke?"

"I had to tape it, because the glue wouldn't hold."

Jonas stood by the bed, as if waiting for him to do something. Dustin looked at the soundboard, which had the words TOXIC SHOCK SYNDROM spray-painted on it. There must have been no room for the *E*. He strummed the strings to see if he could and the neck broke, springing up like a catapult.

"Jesus Christ," he said, handing the thing back to Jonas. "Who sold you this piece of shit?"

Jonas held the broken guitar in his arms for a minute without moving. His lips were so chapped they looked like beef jerky. Cradling the instrument gently, as though it might wake up, he walked out of the room. Dustin overheard his father scolding him in the hallway. *What on earth was he doing, bringing a guitar into the house? Didn't he know better?* It was only then that

Dustin realized Jonas had brought the guitar to him as a gift. He felt a thickness in his throat. The feeling persisted until he remembered that Jonas didn't seem remorseful for ruining his life. Did he really think a guitar, one Dustin couldn't even fucking play, would help?

On TV, John Wayne spat charismatically, on his way to kill his own niece. Dustin found the remote control and switched him off.

CHAPTER 39

Jonas sat in the front seat of the truck, which was so tall he could only see the roofs of cars as they passed, like clouds from an airplane. Occasionally someone with a sunroof would drive by, a hole in the clouds. Jonas's backpack trembled at his feet. Among the items in his pack were a water bottle, a map of California, two bologna sandwiches, and a pack of cigarettes he'd stolen from his mother. He figured he might use the cigarettes as a way of extorting favors, since it seemed that people were often desperate to have them.

Another truck pulled beside them, trying to pass. It took a long time getting by, close enough to touch through the window. A sticker on its bumper said WE HIRE ONLY SAFE AND COURTEOUS DRIVERS.

"Fucking Freightliner," Jonas's driver said. "He got a custom-curved bumper, that's how safe he is." He glanced at Jonas and frowned. "Pardon the language."

"Okay," Jonas said.

The driver's face lit up. "Look her there."

He pointed at a humongous miniature golf course to one side of the interstate, a sprawl of frosting green fairways crowned by waterfalls and windmills and a rainbow-colored dragon with smoke pluming out of its mouth. It looked like what a freeway might dream about eating for dessert. Behind it stood a giant castle with a banner draped between its turrets that read GRAND OPENING. "They just put that up. There's an arcade inside with video games. Everyone dresses like jesters and stuff, all middle-evil."

"It's very beautiful," Jonas said. He would have liked the world much better if everything were in miniature, particularly if it were a series of elemental tests that involved no personal risk.

"You're a weird kid, you know that?"

"Thank you."

The driver scowled. His face was a little bit like Jonas's father's, except that it was meatier and more crinkled and his beard seemed like part of his job rather than a sign of not having one. He looked like he'd have no trouble at all cutting a penny in half. Jonas had packed his backpack earlier that afternoon, worried that perhaps his dad would come home while he was making sandwiches. But he hadn't come home. No one had. After wrapping each sandwich in tinfoil, Jonas wrote a note and left it on the kitchen table. He tried to be brief but also to avoid contractions since it might be the last thing he ever wrote:

> *Dear family,*
>
> *I have decided to leave and not return any time soon. I am sorry for blowing up the house and ruining Dustin's life. I know you want me never to have done this, but there is nothing I can think of that will fix it. I will write to you in exactly one year, August 3, 1987, so please don't worry about me getting killed or chopped into pieces unless there is nothing in your mailbox.*
>
> *Love,*
> *Jonas Ziller*

This last part seemed a bit dramatic, but Jonas liked thinking about his family's faces when they read the "unless." Before leaving, filled with a chewy, appealing sadness, he fed Mr. Leonard a piece of baloney and watched the old dog wolf it down whole. Then he strapped on his backpack and made the long trek to the freeway, sweating through his freshly washed Izod. It was close to an hour before the truck pulled over. The driver said he could take him as far as Ventura; Jonas had no destination in mind and in fact did not know where Ventura was. Since then the driver had made several attempts at conversation, seeming more angry and upset after each one. This was peculiar, since he really seemed to want to talk.

"Do you have any questions about being a truck driver?" the man asked now. The shadow of a giant daddy longlegs covered the dashboard, cast by a knot in the windshield where a rock had hit it.

"Like what?"

"Like how many gears this puppy has."

"Not really," Jonas said.

The driver leaned toward him, winking. "What if I told you it was thirteen speed, with three-point-three-six rear and a three-stage Jake? Do you know what that is? A Jake brake?"

Jonas shook his head. The man began to explain what a Jake brake was, pointing at some of the gauges on his dashboard, but Jonas found it difficult to listen. His stomach was grumbling too hard. He decided it was okay to have half a sandwich, since he hadn't eaten anything for lunch.

"What's that?" the man asked, cutting short his explanation.

"Bologna."

"I don't think I've had one of those since I was a kid."

"My dad buys it," Jonas said. "For dinner."

The driver leaned over to get a better look. "Can I see that? I just want to smell it for a second."

Jonas handed him the sandwich. The man held it to his nose and sniffed it like a flower. He asked for a nibble and then took a bite before Jonas could answer him, chewing with his eyes closed.

"Jesus Chrysler, that's good."

"I only brought two," Jonas explained.

"I shouldn't eat this. It gives me gastritis."

Jonas watched the man finish his sandwich. It did not take long. By the way he started eyeing Jonas's backpack, failing to stay interested in the road, Jonas knew he would have to come up with a question or he would lose the other sandwich as well.

"Have you ever been in an accident?" he asked.

"No," the man said proudly.

"You've never jackknifed on the freeway, killing an innocent family on their way to the beach?"

The truck driver glanced at him. "What's wrong with you?"

Jonas shrugged. He deeply resented this man for eating his sandwich and had decided to annoy him. "Is that how you'd want to die? Behind the wheel of your semi?"

"I don't intend to jackknife or crash or do anything that'll unperil my life in any way."

"You could have a myocardial rupture. It's when your heart explodes out of the blue."

"Hey now, little buddy. I've got half a mind to dump you at the next exit." The driver scowled, lips disappearing into his beard. "Anyway, I'm straight now. A clean liver."

"What's that?"

"I used to be a swirl in the devil's fingerprint. I couldn't see it was the devil's, or even that I was a swirl to begin with."

Jonas giggled.

"Think that's funny, huh? How old are you, anyway? Fifteen?"

"Twelve."

"Twelve!" He seemed suddenly nervous. "What the hell are you doing in my truck?"

"My family hates me."

"No shit," the driver said. "I can see why. They're probably drinking champagne right now."

"They didn't used to hate me," Jonas said defensively.

"Actually, I'm betting they always did."

"My brother wrote a special song about me, for his band."

"Probably he hated you just as much and you were too young to notice."

The driver got off at the next exit and pulled beside a Wendy's and told Jonas to get out, staring antagonistically at the windshield. He did not offer to repay him for the sandwich. Jonas climbed out of the cab, slipping his backpack over both shoulders for fear of being mugged. The parking lot was nearly empty. The truck rumbled back into gear and drove away, smoke chugging out of its metal chimney as it climbed the on-ramp back to the freeway.

It was starting to get dark. As far as Jonas could tell, he was nowhere near Ventura. He went into the Wendy's and sat in a booth with bacon bits stuck to the table. In his wallet were exactly twelve dollars, which he'd stolen from his mother's purse. He wondered if he should save the money or buy a Classic Double with Cheese Combo. Outside the cars had begun to realize it was nighttime, switching on their lights as they nosed out of Carl's Jr. across the street. Jonas began to shiver. The reality of what he'd done—run away from home, forgetting even to bring a jacket—began to sink in. Something about the bacon bits boogered to the table filled him with homesickness. He was cold and alone and scared of using the bathroom, which had a yellow CAUTION sign in front of it with a person slipping on his back. He did not want to break his back, no matter how remorseful it would make his family when they discovered what had happened.

He left Wendy's without buying dinner. After peeing in the hedges, he crossed the parking lot and walked through a smelly concrete place with Dumpsters and broken glass and found himself behind the Happy Trails Inn, in reality a row of sad-looking doors with numbers painted on them. There were cars pulled up to some of the doors, and he could see TVs flickering in the windows. Jonas knew he didn't have enough money for a room—the sign said $39.00/NIGHT—but didn't know where else to go and was too scared to hitchhike after dark. He decided to wait and see if anyone came out. If he kept his mouth shut and didn't make them mad, they might let him sleep in their room. He sat on the opposite curb beside a motor home, an old, beat-up truck with a white shell melting like marshmallow over its roof.

He ate the second bologna sandwich and immediately regretted it, wishing he'd saved it. It began to drizzle. He clutched his backpack to stay warm. After what seemed like an hour, a woman emerged from one of the rooms, barefoot despite the broken glass, her hair braided with beads so that you could see white lines of scalp. She walked up to the motor home and began to fumble with the door, dropping her keys twice on the pavement. Rings gleamed from her toes, like a practical joke. Jonas cleared his throat, loudly, but she failed to notice him. She got the door open finally but then seemed to forget something, blinking into the RV before heading back to the motel without bothering to close up.

Jonas yawned nervously, the taste of bologna burping into his mouth. He sneaked inside the RV. He did not have a plan but decided it would be a better place to spend the night than outside in the rain. Crouching in the half dark, he picked his way through stray clothes and beer cans and at least one hula hoop, almost tripping over some hiking boots stationed near the sink. The place stank of dirty laundry and wet towels. He climbed up the little ladder to the sleeping compartment over the front seats. The sheets were tangled into a wad at the foot of the bed, next to a stuffed gorilla with what looked like a firecracker sticking out of its nose.

Jonas took off his backpack and pulled the sheets over his body and lay there at the edge of the clammy mattress so he could spy on the door. Before long, the woman returned, the beads in her hair clicking as she ducked inside. She flipped on a light and searched the mess at her feet before rooting impatiently around the RV, picking things up and tossing them around. Jonas worried she might climb up the ladder. Instead she pulled a glass from the sink, her face slackening with relief. The glass was tall and had a sticker of some bears on it kicking their legs like Rockettes. A bong, like the one Dustin used to hide in his closet. Collapsing in a chair, the woman took a plastic bag from her pocket, did something to the bottom of the bong, and then jammed her lips inside it as though trying to suck herself in like a genie. After a long time, she unsucked her face and raised it to the ceiling, blowing out a stupendous cloud of smoke.

She did this five or six times, the RV filling with a smoggy haze that seemed to hang from the roof. Jonas's throat began to itch. The itch grew into a ticklish burr, making his eyes water. He tried to keep it down but couldn't. He coughed. Once he'd started, he couldn't stop. Incredibly, the woman didn't seem to notice, staring at the clothes by her feet. Jonas clapped his hands. She didn't look up. He said, "I'm right up here, you stupid idiot." Nothing. After a while the woman's hands began to move around, not slowly but quickly, spastic as birds, touching her face and filling the space in front of her with nimble, twittery forms. It was only when a strange sound came out of her, like someone yelling from the inside of a coffin, that he realized she was deaf. The signs began to repeat themselves, whole strings of them, and he understood that she was singing some kind of song. Jonas watched in amazement. His brain felt gooey and undercooked. He closed his eyes but could still see the woman's hands in front of him, dancing their silent dance, singing him to sleep.

He roamed the house, calling for his father. It was their old house, but this didn't impress him any more than the fact that he was wearing a backpack indoors. His voice echoed through the empty rooms. Finally he opened the kitchen cabinet: his dad's face was trapped inside a glass, staring at him from the middle shelf. Jonas opened the other door of the cabinet. His whole family peered back at him, sucked into glasses. They looked scared and unhappy. What power he had over them! He knew the secret genie words to release them. When he said them, they'd bloom forth from their tragic prisons, grateful as flowers.

When Jonas woke up, the RV was moving. Driving. There was real music playing, a fidgety song about someone's uncle and their band. The roof bounced above his face, pinging up and down. He could see the deaf woman from last night: she was swiveling her seat like a girl, sucking on a Tootsie Roll pop. A man's voice, gleefully off-key, rose from the driver's seat below him. Jonas rolled over quietly and looked out the long, skinny window facing the road, hoping to tell which direction they were going, but he didn't recognize the signs.

CHAPTER 40

Camille followed Warren in the breathtaking heat, trying to keep up with him. His steps were long and aimless, turning abruptly for no reason, beelining through scraggly pieces of brush. The lack of direction infuriated her. She wanted to tackle him, make him walk in a straight line. They'd been over the same area last night, all four of them, combing the desert with flashlights and calling Jonas's name until they'd lost their voices. Back home again they could only whisper, their house as solemn as a library. Camille hadn't slept a wink. Every creak, every snort and rustle from Mr. Leonard's bed, was Jonas at the door. This morning, she'd agreed to come with Warren only because she couldn't stand to sit around and wait.

The police were conducting their own search, supposedly, but God knows how long it would take them. Jonas knew no one nearby; they lived in the middle of nowhere; there was no place for him to go.

"Have you contacted the neighbors?" the policeman had said, filling out a missing persons report. It was a myth that you had to wait seventy-two hours. Just say "runaway kid" on the phone, 105-degree heat, and they zipped right over.

"We don't have any neighbors," Warren had said absently. Jonas's disappearance seemed to have sunk him into a deeper trance. The policeman had glanced out the window at the darkening saltbush, as if to confirm this.

"Any trouble at home? Marital problems?"

Warren and Camille looked at each other. For a second, she wondered if they'd admit the truth about their marriage. It would be like coming up for air. Instead, Warren got the note from the kitchen counter and showed it to the cop, explaining everything that had happened. As he read the note, the cop's eyes widened a bit.

"Has he ever exhibited suicidal behavior?"

"He's not suicidal!" Camille said.

"The note raises some concerns."

"Jonas is perfectly normal," Warren said.

"I see," the policeman said, returning to his checklist. "Right now I'm doing a risk assessment. Standard procedure."

The cop asked for a recent photograph. Camille got their albums from the bookshelf in the living room and began hunting through them. It occurred to her that, since the accident, neither of them had taken a single picture. The most recent one she could find was from last year, a picture of Jonas at fencing practice. He was posing in the en garde position, pointing the twiggy sword at the camera, his arm raised in a right angle behind him. The expression on his face was comically fierce. Camille remembered that day last summer, when she'd forgotten to pick him up from practice and he'd walked home in his gear, two miles uphill. She had to sit down by herself for a second, the wind knocked out of her like a blow, before handing the picture to the policeman.

She followed the zigzag of Warren's footprints, the sun scorching her bare arms enough to give her goose bumps. She glanced back at the house now and then for signs of life; Lyle and Dustin had driven to Lancaster, combing the streets in search of their brother. Camille stopped and fished the crumpled pack of cigarettes from her pocket. Only two left.

"Do you have to smoke at a time like this?" Warren asked, stopping to wait for her. His new beard glistened with sweat.

"What difference does it make?"

"Our son has disappeared."

"So I shouldn't smoke," she said, scowling.

"Jesus, Camille. Our fucking house burned down. What do you think it does to Dustin, to see you lighting up all the time?" Warren closed his eyes suddenly and clapped his hand to his chest. His face seemed to go still and careful, focused on the air right in front of it, as though he were walking through a cobweb.

"Are you all right?"

"Fine," he said, wincing. "Just heartburn."

Camille had a moment's fantasy that he'd drop dead. That she'd wished this, even for a second, shocked her deeply. She sat down in the dirt. They had not brought water or even hats. Her throat was so parched she couldn't swallow. Warren dropped his hand from his chest, slowly, and came over and sat beside her. He was wearing the same clothes as yesterday, his T-shirt splotched with grease. His breath reeked of coffee. She remembered the times they used to go camping in Wisconsin when they were first married, how she would use Warren's long underwear top as a pillow, dizzy with the miracle of his scent.

"It's my fault," he said finally.

"No, it isn't. I blamed him, too." Camille started to cry.

"Everything will be fine. He'll come back by tomorrow."

She could not tell whether he actually believed this. If he wasn't as hope-dead as he seemed, there might be some way to love him. A tiny feather was stuck in his beard; it touched her strangely. She picked it out, her stomach growling. Warren reached into his pocket and pulled out a piece of string cheese still wrapped in plastic. He peeled open the plastic and tore the cheese down the middle, offering a droopy white stalk to Camille.

"Where did you get this?"

"From the fridge. Jonas insisted on buying it."

The cheese tasted like rubber. Camille devoured it.

"Remember when we lived in Chicago?" he said. "Living off frozen moose meat?"

She didn't say anything.

"We made up those jingles, remember?"

"Don't," Camille said.

Need a last meal? Date with the chair all booked? Ask for Moose Helper, and your moose is cooked!

He wasn't smiling. If anything, he looked a bit crazed. It was as impossible to imagine them like that, goofy with love, as it was for their younger selves to have imagined this: sitting in the blistering desert, eating their missing son's cheese.

Later, without admitting to giving up, they drifted back toward the house, Camille leading the way in her sandals. A hawk circled overhead, coasting on black-fingered wings. Camille turned to look behind her: Warren's strides, so big and unstoppable before, had slowed to a limp.

"What's wrong?"

"I twisted my ankle. Rushing to an interview." He looked at the dirt. "I had the wrong address, which is why I was late."

There was that strange blush again, the eagerness to explain. Camille remembered how insane she'd been last summer, suspecting him of having an affair. She'd dumped urine in his coffee. Now, watching his blush deepen under her gaze, suddenly positive that he was seeing somebody else—her delusion made real—she found that she didn't care. Their son was gone. They made it to the back deck and Warren paused, staring at the steps.

"I need your help," he said quietly.

Camille put her arm around him and helped him up the stairs, surprised by the flabbiness at his waist. He leaned into her like an old man. They reached the top of the steps, sharing his weight, but he didn't let go right away. She allowed this to happen—invited it, in fact. She'd failed Jonas as much as Warren had; they had this at least in common. She looked at the sky, but the hawk had already captured its prey or given up looking. There was nothing but blue.

CHAPTER 41

Hector stared at the walls of his room, the same ones he'd stared at since he was seven, blank except for the hardened pieces of Blu-Tack stuck everywhere like gum. At night he could hear giant roaches climb up the walls and nibble at the tack, a peaceful rustling. He'd taken all the chameleon posters down, sometime last year, and had never bothered to put anything else up. He was not a seven-year-old. He was a grown man, the manager of a pet store. He was supposed to be at the store right now, not staring at the walls, but his stomach hurt so badly that he'd called sick. Probably it was a lie for him to say he was ill, though he couldn't imagine going to work.

He'd called Dustin that morning, to check in, and his mother had answered on the second ring, breathless from running. She'd seemed angry that it was Hector. That's when he'd learned about Jonas. Missing, no word at all, for three days. The stomachache had begun soon afterward, like an allergic reaction.

Eventually he got out of bed and padded barefoot into the living room, making sure there were no Madagascar hissing roaches under his feet. He'd spent over a week's wages on an exterminator, not to mention $64 on a motel room for his mom and grandmother, but the fumigation hadn't worked. The roaches were still around. The exterminator, an old man with thirty years in the business, had jumped when Hector showed him one of the roaches climbing the window, which should have tipped him off from the beginning.

"We're still infested," his mother said now, addressing him in Spanish. She'd gotten fatter recently: the bracelets on her arm no longer clinked. "Fourteen years in this house, I never had a single cockroach problem!"

"I'll find a different exterminator," Hector said. "Today."

"How much did he cost, the first man?"

"I'll pay for it, Mama. I already said I would."

"With what? Your Jungle of Pets salary?" She looked down at the floor. "You're never here anymore. I looked at your Visa bill yesterday . . . where on earth are you going, to spend all that money on gas?"

He shrugged. "Wandering between the winds," he said in English.

"What?"

"Out. In the desert."

Hector walked into the kitchen to fill up Ginger's water bottle, clutching his stomach. The last thing he needed right now was a lecture. His grandmother was squatting in the middle of the room, hissing at the plastic cutting board on the counter. A giant cockroach sat there quietly, refusing to hiss back or even raise its head, its mahogany abdomen large as a toe.

"He's back!" his mother said, following Hector into the kitchen. "That's the one that lives under the toaster."

"Actually, it's a female. Males have little horns."

"I don't care!"

"I'm just telling you." He pointed at the roach's abdomen. "See, her egg sack's about to burst."

His mother put her hand to her mouth. Hector turned on the sink and filled up Ginger's water bottle, which caused his grandmother to mysteriously stop hissing.

"Do you love me, *mijo*?" his mother said.

"Yes, Mama," he said seriously. "I do. I'm sorry."

"Then come home."

"I am home. I'm right here in the kitchen."

"That's not what I mean."

The stomachache was still there as he sneaked out to his pickup. The sky was so smoggy he could barely see the refinery, its flames hovering magically in the distance; the on-ramp, even as he approached, was sponged out by the haze. He did not know why he gravitated to the Zillers like this, as if by some invincible force—or rather, he knew why, but the guilt was so constant, such a permanent part of his being, that it seemed somehow instinctive. Last year, when Hector first found out about the accident, he'd felt a shiver of revenge. Hadn't they gotten what they deserved? Then all at once he'd remembered the stove, the water on for tea—it was like waking up suddenly and recalling a crime. It was when he saw Dustin's face, the day he drove out there to find Lyle, that he began to lose sleep at night, the guilt spreading malevolently into his dreams. Dustin in flames, screaming like an animal. His burning face crumpling to ash or clothespinned bizarrely to a line. Hector couldn't shake the awful visions from his head. A year later they haunted him still, waking him with a jolt that startled Ginger in her cage.

The descent into Antelope Valley was windier than usual, the big rigs rattling like train cars when Hector passed. The pain in his stomach tightened. The image of Jonas—hungry, trembling, sleeping behind a Dumpster or worse—kept invading his thoughts. He fantasized about finding the boy on the side of the highway and returning him safely to the Zillers. They would embrace Hector, transported by gratitude. Lyle would explain that she was in love with him, even now, and he would have the precious burden of breaking her heart. A stupid fantasy that made him feel even worse. It was only when he saw the Auburn Fields sign up ahead, its curlicue lettering and gold-spoked sun peeking over the N, that he realized why his stomach was cramping. He'd decided to confess once and for all. Tell the Zillers who was really to blame. They might attack him, strangle him, charge him with arson. But what a relief it would be, to free himself of Dustin's face.

Hector pulled off at the exit and followed the dusty, familiar road to the open gate of Auburn Fields. Jonas's bike lay by the curb near the gate, cooking in the sun; perhaps they couldn't bear to bring it into the garage. Hector drove through the gate. No sooner had he turned up the block of identical homes, singling out the Zillers' by the potted cactus on their porch, than the door opened and Mrs. Ziller rushed out into the front yard, her bearded husband squinting behind her, Dustin and Lyle joining them in the dirt. At first Hector believed they were excited to see him. Then he realized they'd mistaken him for someone else, someone with news about their son. As he drove closer, their shoulders seemed to droop. Mrs. Ziller sat down in the dirt. One by one, like children—first Mr. Ziller and then Lyle and then Dustin—the others sat down with her. Hector could feel his nerve beginning to cave. He stared at them helplessly: the only people for miles, dazed with grief, sitting in the dirt that should have been a lawn.

CHAPTER 42

Jonas had to pee so badly he couldn't think. He moaned under his breath, clutching his khakis. It had been two hours, maybe more, since he woke up in the RV. In his catalog of painful deaths, he'd never considered dying from an exploded bladder. He could see the open bathroom from the sleeping loft, beckoning him like paradise. The deaf woman with beaded hair sat beside it, drinking Diet Cokes and playing solitaire on a little fold-out tray. Twice, suffering terribly, Jonas had watched her get up and use the toilet without closing the door.

There were two other people as well, men, riding up front. Jonas could hear their voices now and then, talking over the docile, boinky guitar solos on the stereo.

Jonas decided to wet his pants. There was no other alternative. He wondered with dread if he wouldn't be able to, but then the slow hiss began in his crotch, more a feeling than an actual noise, his khakis pooling with a sickening warmth that seeped down his thighs. Carefully, so as not to alert the deaf woman, he peeled his smelly pants and BVDs down his legs, trying to kick the heavy, pee-logged clothes over his sneakers. In the struggle, one of the sneakers popped off and tumbled out of the sleeping loft, crashing into the sink. The deaf woman looked up from her solitaire game. So lovely was the sound she made, low and mermaidy and obscene, that it took Jonas a second to realize she was screaming.

"What in the monkey's ass is going on?" a guy in a ponytail said, ducking into view. He saw Jonas in the sleeping loft and startled, grabbing onto the ladder. Jonas kept his mouth shut, deciding the best strategy would be to pretend he didn't speak English.

"Pull over, Captain," the guy said to the driver. "There's a half-naked boy in the loft."

"What?"

"A boy with no pants."

The RV slowed and they pulled to a stop. The air smelled like salt; from the sound of mewling seagulls, Jonas guessed they were near the beach. The driver emerged from the front seat, his face dripping with a straggly red beard. Jonas began to get frightened. The beard looked like something you were supposed to clean off a shellfish. Also, though Halloween was two months away, he was wearing a glove on one hand made to resemble a werewolf's paw.

"Who is he?" the driver said. He put the hairy paw to his forehead and squinted at Jonas.

"An angel?"

"A guardian angel," the driver said optimistically. He looked at the khakis wadded at Jonas's feet. "I think he wet his pants."

"Typical, really. Just our luck."

The driver stuck out his hairy paw, introducing himself as Captain Lobo. "This is Major Meltdown. Over there, sitting in the chair, is Miss Anthropy. Known to acquaintances by her first name, Griselda."

"He's not being cruel," the guy with the ponytail said, folding a piece of gum into his mouth. "That's her real name."

The woman came over to where they were standing, her hands fluttering in front of her face. Jonas was not embarrassed to be naked. He felt as if it gave him a tactical advantage. Also, the woman had no qualms about flinging her hands about.

"She's asking do you have any parents," the guy with the ponytail said, snapping a bubble.

Jonas shook his head.

"An orphan troll child."

"Looking, no doubt, for a home."

"Nevertheless," the guy with the werewolf paw said, "this recreational vehicle only sleeps three *adults*. My italics."

The other man yawned. "We can't let him out on the street half-naked."

"Why not?"

"There are perverts. Unitalicized."

The driver nodded. "And yet somehow he makes his way, without pants."

"I see what you mean. It's inspirational."

"Raped repeatedly, and yet he goes on to prominence. Founds a program for the abused."

The way the men talked intrigued Jonas: it was real and not real at the same time, as if the words were presents waiting to be unwrapped. Inside each wrapping was an empty box. The deaf woman reached up and touched Jonas's hair, combing it behind his ear while speaking in her vowelly voice. He didn't understand a word.

"She's asking if you listen to the Dead."

Jonas didn't know what to say. "Sometimes I feel like one myself."

"What?"

"A dead person."

The guy with the ponytail laughed. "Welcome to the club."

"What club?" Jonas asked politely.

"The dead people. You found us."

He took the gum from his mouth and placed it in Jonas's hair, like a benediction. Jonas could feel its secret weight in his bangs.

"What's that for?" he asked.

"You're a kid. You're supposed to have gum in your hair."

The first thing they did was get Jonas some pants. "The living demand it," Captain Lobo said, driving into a neighborhood of skinny houses with old couches on the porches and garage doors you had to tug down with a rope. Without warning, he screeched to a stop, dashed over to a clothesline in someone's yard, and stole a pair of blue jeans, replacing them with Jonas's pee-stained khakis. The jeans, crisp as a leaf, had flowers on them and little zippers at the bottoms of the legs. Jonas decided not to complain, even when he found an old Jolly Rancher gluing the front pocket together.

"What's it today?" Major Meltdown asked later, sitting in the back next to Jonas. He had a bad cold but seemed uninterested in wiping his nose; his face was half covered in snot, as if he'd just plopped out of a cow. "American Foundation for the Deaf?"

"Negatory," Captain Lobo said from behind the wheel. "Ran out of stationery last week."

"Roof repair?"

"Are you forgetting one of us left the fold-out ladder in Colorado Springs?"

Major Meltdown scowled. "I thought we agreed to take collective responsibility."

"Excuse me. Are *we* forgetting." Captain Lobo glanced back at them, smiling his planktony grin. His mouth was a museum of gunk. Jonas liked him because he spoke like one of Lyle's T-shirts, behaving as though he made perfect sense. *Don't feed the spectators,* he'd say, or *It's the logicians versus the magicians.* He was fond of this last saying and had already repeated it twice while they were driving. "Anyway, we've got the changeling. Commercially untapped."

Griselda stopped her chair in midswivel, patting her knee and snapping her fingers as though she were calling a dog.

"A brilliant idea!" Captain Lobo said.

Before long they turned down a side street and parked in front of a quiet house with plastic animals grazing in the yard. Jonas had no idea where he was. He didn't mind not knowing and in fact preferred being lost. Amazingly, neither Captain Lobo nor Major Meltdown had asked him anything about his family. He'd woken up in their bed, a possible criminal, and they'd anointed him with a piece of gum.

None of them had called him "weird" even once or blamed him for their problems. If they had problems, they did not seem to care what they were.

Captain Lobo got out of the RV, grabbing an old leash from the back, and the three of them walked with him around the corner and stopped behind a pickup truck with a bumper sticker that said IF THESE ARE MY GOLDEN YEARS I AM SOOOO FUCKED. Jonas noticed that Captain Lobo was no longer wearing his werewolf paw. He squinted at an old woman at the end of the block. She was sitting in a lawn chair, smoking a cigarette while a tractor sprinkler battered her window, its wheels stuck in the grass. Captain Lobo squatted to Jonas's height and asked if he'd like to partake in a theatrical improvisation.

"You've lost a puppy," he explained, "so your principal function is to look sad."

Jonas squinched up his eyes and did his best to look miserable. While Griselda and Major Meltdown waited behind the pickup, Captain Lobo grabbed Jonas's hand and walked him down the block to the old woman smoking in a lawn chair. She was wearing a red bathing suit with a little skirt attached. Her naked arms, sagging in folds, made Jonas think of scrambled eggs. Captain Lobo greeted her kindly and explained that their puppy had run away. "A little black Lab," he said, lifting the leash. "Randy here says he saw it run into your backyard."

"I've been lying here like a dog myself. Getting my daily vitamins." She took off her sunglasses and peered at Jonas strangely, eyeing the gum in his hair. He was aware of the purple flowers embroidering his jeans. "Does your son need to use the bathroom?"

"No, no. He's just upset." Captain Lobo glanced at the screen door of the house. "Your husband? Might he have seen him?"

"Stanley passed last June. Pancreatic cancer."

"I'm sorry."

"It'll be a year this Sunday."

The woman screwed her cigarette into the arm of the chair and began to cough, losing herself to a fit of hacking. By the time she'd recovered, her face was red as the bathing suit. Captain Lobo asked if anyone else lived at home and she shook her head like a lament. She leaned toward Jonas.

"What's your puppy's name, sweetheart?"

"Stanley," Jonas said.

The woman recoiled. "Same as my husband's?"

He nodded. Captain Lobo led them around the side of the house and into the backyard, a small tidy lawn bordered by a wall of hydrangea shrubs. Jonas wished he hadn't said "Stanley," but he couldn't think of anything else and it was the first name that had come to mind. Draping the leash around his neck, Captain Lobo waded into the shrubs at the back of the lawn, yelling the dog's name as though he enjoyed the ambiguity. Jonas had no choice but to help out. The woman failed to join in the search and stood there on the lawn, her face growing more and more distressed. Jonas waited for the game to be over, wanting to leave the old woman alone, but Captain Lobo tramped farther into the bushes.

"Must have run off," the woman said, glancing at her watch. "Your Labrador."

"Poodle, you mean," Captain Lobo said.

She looked at Jonas for a second. "You called it a Labrador before. I'm certain of it. I remember because of Blackie, our old Lab in Port Townsend."

"Perhaps you're right then," Captain Lobo said. "To be honest, we're none too impressed by Stanley's pedigree. Among other things, he licks his own balls."

The woman stepped back. "I don't know who you are, but I've had just about enough of this. You're trampling my hydrangeas."

"Where are you going?"

"If you're not gone in two minutes I'm phoning the police."

She started up the stairs to the deck. Captain Lobo came out of the bushes and jogged over and grabbed the woman by the elbow, yanking her off the steps. It was like someone picking something from their soup. The woman leaned over and began to hack, dangling by one arm. She coughed so hard her teeth shot out of her mouth. Captain Lobo let go and she sat down on the lawn next to them, her legs splayed like a marionette's.

"I wish it wasn't like this," he explained to her, brushing the hair out of her face, "but increasingly it is."

He told Jonas to make sure she didn't move and then disappeared into the back door of the house. The old woman began to cry. Jonas did not know what to do. A yellow jacket landed on her head, its tiny butt twitching, but she did not move and only whimpered to herself like a prayer. "Stan," she seemed to be saying, though he couldn't be sure. Jonas picked the woman's dentures off the lawn, thinking he might put them back into her mouth, but she did not seem to care one way or another.

When Captain Lobo came back to retrieve him, he was carrying a piggy bank under one arm like a football. Griselda and Major Meltdown were already in the RV, sweaty and excited, the backpack sitting beside them on the couch. It was stuffed so full the zipper wouldn't close. They screeched out of the neighborhood and back onto a bigger street, driving some time before pulling behind a deserted-looking church with a sign in changeable letters that said THE ONLY VITAMIN FOR CHRISTIANZ IS B1. Griselda unzipped the backpack and dumped out a pile of stuff, necklaces and earrings and a big book that looked like a photo album filled with strange silver coins.

"Fuckin' A," Captain Lobo said. "Stanley the manly."

"Please watch your language," Major Meltdown said, pointing at the sign. "We're at a house of God."

"For an avenger of the poor, he's sure got a lot of houses."

Captain Lobo glanced at Jonas. "You're not experiencing some remorse for the logicians, are you? Just remember we're dead."

Jonas didn't know what he was experiencing. He kept thinking of the woman's teeth on the lawn, her mouth sucked in and punched-looking. He squeezed his eyes tight and curled up into a ball on the sofa, wishing he really were dead.

"Meltdown," Captain Lobo said.

"At your service."

"No, I think the boy's having one."

Griselda wrapped him in a dusty blanket and enclosed him in her arms. She smelled like a cave: dank and pleasant and gleaming with secret drips. Captain Lobo and Major Meltdown leaned down, too, and the three of them hugged him, smooshing him into the couch. Jonas felt squished and valuable. They hugged him for a long time. Griselda leaned back and signed something with her hands, wiggling a downturned finger as if she were trying to pet a fly in midair.

"She's saying we need you," Captain Lobo said, kissing his forehead. "The trolls can't have you back."

That night in the smoke-filled RV Jonas couldn't sleep. His thoughts turned thick and gooey again, refusing to cook into words. Eventually, after the moaning below had stopped, he climbed down from the loft and crept past the naked, snoring bodies in bed and stepped out into a campground packed with RVs. The sky was slathered with stars. Wandering the row of motor homes, thirsty and goose-pimpled, Jonas realized he was wearing a stranger's pants and nothing else. His teeth began to chatter. The RVs were all dark except for one parked next to a junky playground, flickering like a candle. From inside rumbled the muffled din of explosions. Jonas peered through the window and could see a family arrayed in chairs, watching TV in the dark and passing around a bag of popcorn. A girl in plaid pajamas was sitting on the floor just below him. She ate some popcorn from the center of her hand and then licked her palm. If the window were open, he could have reached through and touched her. Jonas sat down in the dirt and put his ear against the side of the RV, hugging himself for warmth, listening to the cozy booms exploding in his head.

CHAPTER 43

Warren touched the place where his heart hurt. A gentle clawing weight, as though a kitten were sitting on his chest. He'd been having the pains since Jonas ran away. By now, the sixth day of his disappearance, they'd become a familiar occurrence, enough to make him stop what he was doing. Warren stared through the windshield at one of Melody's neighbors sitting on his roof; he was kicked back in a La-Z-Boy, fiddling with a Rubik's Cube. Warren tried to imagine how he'd gotten the La-Z-Boy onto the roof. The world, full of casual mysteries, made the pain in Warren's chest seem less troubling.

When the pain subsided, he got out of the Oldsmobile and walked through the dust to Melody's trailer. He hadn't seen or called her since the day with the antenna. In truth, Jonas's disappearance had startled him from a kind of daze. He felt like Rip Van Winkle, waking up after twenty years and returning to his ruined life. This was ironic, since he hadn't slept for days.

Warren knocked on the screen door, startled by its noisy rattle. It was only now that he noticed the motorcycle in Melody's front yard. It had a leather seat with little springs under it, the whole thing painted a military green. The gas tank was emblazoned with a star, like the prop from an old war movie.

"How can I help you?"

A strange man was eyeing him suspiciously through the closed door, his face pitted with tiny commas. Warren might have considered him ugly before Dustin's accident. "Is Melody home?"

"At the hospital," the man said.

Warren stared at him. "She's . . . okay?"

"Her dad's got pneumonia. Coughing so hard he busted a rib."

Warren stepped back from the door. It amazed him that other people had problems.

"Whom shall I say has graced us with his charms?" the man asked. He was not smiling.

"Warren. We're friends."

"Right. Stupid me. The knife salesman." The man leaned close to the screen, poking his finger into it as if trying to break through the mesh. "Did you know, Warren, that more people are killed annually by donkeys than die in plane crashes?"

Warren headed back to his car, taking the long way around the trailer to avoid the man's eyes. Ducking under the men's T-shirts fluttering on the clothesline, he caught the familiar scent of Melody's detergent. The neighbors' pig was gone from its pen, which had been cleaned up and raked free of shit. He'd never cared much for the pig, but its absence unnerved him. He thought of Jonas and the way they'd cleaned his room impeccably for his return.

Melody's brother was doing chin-ups from the sun visor above the kitchen window. Warren tried to sneak by, but his shoes crunched on the gravel and caught Kenny's attention. He was wearing shorts and aviator sunglasses, his long hair matted with sweat. Warren felt his heart stop and catch, like a bike changing gears. It had been doing this lately as well. Kenny dropped to the ground and asked if everything was all right.

"There's a man inside," Warren managed.

"Roland," Kenny said. "Melody's husband."

"I thought they hated each other."

"They get along much better now that they're separated." He laughed. "Anyway, he's just staying here for support while Dad's in Lancaster. Or so he claims, when he's not dropping factoids."

Kenny caught Warren staring at the zinc oxide on his chest, explaining that he couldn't afford to get too tan or no one would hire him. People liked their Jesuses white. He went on to talk about a Nicaraguan Jesus he'd met in L.A. and Warren tried to follow what he was saying, but his words began to melt together, a puddle of gibberish.

Kenny lifted his sunglasses. "Are you sick?"

"Why?"

"You're shaking."

Warren looked at his hands. Certainly he felt unwell. He wasn't sure if this was the same as being sick. "I do feel cold," he said, surprised. "What's the temperature?"

"One hundred and four."

Kenny put his arm around his shoulders and led him into the narrow strip of shade under the window awning, clearing some broken glass away with his flip-flop. He sat down with Warren in the dirt, still hugging him with one arm. It was nice to be held. The sunglasses, the lotiony, tropical smell, were just like Dustin's. The chill in Warren's body retreated into his bones.

"My twelve-year-old son's gone. He ran away." Warren didn't know why he was telling him this. "It's my fault."

"Probably not," Kenny said.

"Something bad happened to his older brother, an accident, and I used to wish it was him instead. All the time. I couldn't stand to look at him."

Kenny nodded. He did not seem shocked by this.

"I had a gig once at this evangelical church," Kenny said finally. "They hired me to stand there during Sunday service and help people pray. You know, one by one. I put my hand on their heads and they prayed for whatever they wanted." He let go of Warren and flipped his hair back, plucking a sweaty hank from his eyes. "Would you like to pray for your son?"

"I don't believe in God," Warren said.

"That's okay. I work for myself."

Warren looked at him. He seemed to be serious. Kenny knelt in front of him and laid a hand on Warren's head. His sunglasses reflected Warren's face, turning it moosey and distorted. Warren closed his eyes. He did not know how to ration his prayer. There were so many things he could ask forgiveness for: for loving Jonas least of his children; for giving up on life; for being here at all, in grease-stained khakis, at a strange woman's trailer. Once, as a boy, Warren had asked his mother if animals ever prayed to God; she'd told him that they didn't need to, that God heard them through their suffering. The *thwup*s of a hammer echoed nearby, fading into the relentless buzz of cicadas.

"Please," he said, "bring Jonas home."

Something touched his ear, gently, but it was only a trickle of sweat. Kenny nodded and stood up, his right knee cribbled from the gravel. There was nothing left to say. The sun shone, the bugs bugged, his son was still missing. Warren thanked the freelance

Jesus in front of him and headed back to the car. As if remembering something, Kenny popped into the trailer for a minute and
then caught up with Warren, holding a sheaf of papers.

"It's a petition," he said. "We're getting as many sponsors as
we can. They want to raze this whole place and put in a gated
community."

"Here?"

"Fucking developers. Dad's lived here for thirteen years. They
think because it's a trailer park, no one's going to raise a stink."

Warren almost laughed. Using Kenny's back, he signed the petition and wrote his address in. The man in the La-Z-Boy was still
fiddling with his Rubik's Cube, wearing an enormous sombrero to
protect himself from the sun. Warren wanted to ask Kenny how
his father had come to feel at home in such a place.

"What happened to the neighbor's pig?" he said instead. He
pointed at the empty pen, raked clean as a baseball diamond.

"Bacon."

"What?"

Kenny dragged his finger across his throat. "You can smell it
in the morning."

CHAPTER 44

Lyle sat in the backseat of Taz's car with Hector, who looked as miserable as you could look while eating a bag of Funyuns. In Hector's case, this was profoundly miserable. He hadn't said a word since they'd left the house. He'd insisted on coming along and helping them look for Jonas—there was no convincing him otherwise.

"Are you sure you want to do this?" Lyle asked Dustin.

"Why not?"

"I guess because you still flinch when I unwrap a hamburger."

"No, he doesn't," Taz said from the driver's seat. She was wearing a Dead Kennedys T-shirt, which seemed—given that she was driving a BMW—a contradiction at best. Lyle wanted to say, *He's my brother, what the fuck do you know about him?* But she didn't. For one thing, they needed Taz's car to get inside Herradura Estates. For another, she might have been right: Lyle hadn't been out to eat with him since the beginning of the summer.

"It's the only place we haven't checked," Dustin said. "For all we know, he might be camping in the backyard."

They were going to their old house in search of Jonas. Or rather, the place where their house used to be. The idea—Dustin's—was that Jonas might have gravitated there instinctively, like a sea turtle. It seemed like a desperate hope. Frankly, Lyle had not wanted to come at all, but her mom and dad were at the police station again and she hadn't wanted to stay home alone. The idea of waiting around helplessly for Jonas to show up made her sick with dread.

Taz put her hand on Dustin's leg, resting it there while she drove. When she'd met them at a pay phone down the road, pulling up in her car with little windshield wipers on the headlights, Dustin's face had actually brightened. Something had happened between them, a shift. Lyle did not want to begrudge her brother his little bit of daylight—you couldn't call it happiness—but she didn't like Taz's face when they were together. There was a touch of pride in it, as if she were showing off a tattoo. She was younger than Lyle, a spoiled little girl, which made it all the more irritating. Before summer started, Lyle used to see her hanging out sometimes at school, talking to her new tenth-grade friends—girls in lip gloss and stirrup pants—but Lyle had never approached to say hi. Anyway, what would she have said? *I heard my older brother was fucking you.*

At the gate, Taz stopped at the guardhouse and waved at Bud, who'd lost the "male pattern" from his baldness and was now more or less without hair. He peered into the car and seemed to recognize Hector, his face going slack with amazement. Lyle was amazed as well—less that she'd lost her virginity in this glorified closet and more by the fact that the deflowerer was sitting beside her, holding a half-eaten U of Funyun, a flying rodent asleep in his pocket. They had held each other while the trees outside swooned in the wind. The fact that you could know someone almost intimately and then a year later not know him at all seemed to be at the heart of everything sad and fucked-up in the world. Bud opened the gate and let them pass.

"They replaced the clock," she whispered to Hector. She felt strangely desperate.

"What?"

"The clock," she said. "The one that fell on the floor."

Hector seemed to have no idea what she was talking about. Since Jonas had disappeared he'd been at the house every day, arriving unannounced, a look of irritating exhaustion on his face. It was as though he'd lost his own brother. Even Dustin was beginning to dislike him. The more irritated Lyle or Dustin got, ignoring his stricken-looking silence, the more Hector insisted on helping them.

They drove along John's Canyon Road, past old stables and flowering bougainvillea and trees cotton-candied by webworms, skirting the horse trail where Lyle's mother used to honk people into the bushes. Nothing had changed. The lawns were green as golf courses and smelled of rain. Wands of water moved across them in lazy arcs, silent under the *chk chk chk* of sprinklers.

"I can't believe we used to live here," Lyle said.

"Why not?" Dustin said.

"I just mean, it smells so nice. Like spring."

Dustin glanced at the backseat. "You used to call it Hairy Turd Estates."

"Personally, I like it where you guys live," Taz said. "It doesn't feel like Never Never Land."

Lyle waited for Dustin to pounce; if Lyle had said such a ridiculous thing, there would have been little mercy. Instead he took his sunglasses off and squeezed some drops into his eye. She remembered Cats vs. Dogs, the game they used to play when they were kids, choosing one thing or another to zap into extinction. Lyle wondered who Dustin would pick now, her or Taz. They drove by the Wongs' and the Dunkirks' and the Starchilds', the houses as remote and familiar to her as the faces in a dream.

"Remember at the Starchilds' barbecue, when Mr. Leonard ate their Amazon parrot? It cost Mom and Dad seven hundred dollars."

"He wouldn't even eat his kibbles this morning," Dustin said. "I think he's dying."

Lyle frowned. "He's not dying. He's just arthritic."

"He hasn't moved from his bed in two days." Dustin put his sunglasses back on. "Ask Hector. He's the animal expert."

Hector glanced over uncomfortably, prepared to answer, but Lyle didn't want to hear his opinion. They'd been through enough. Somehow, if Mr. Leonard was dying, it meant that Jonas might actually have disappeared. They turned onto High Street and then followed the snaking, tree-tunneled road until they reached their old driveway, where Taz parked at the curb like a chauffeur. Remarkably, their old mailbox was still there: THE ZILLER FAMILY, a cardinal sitting atop the words as if perched on a branch. They had not bothered—or perhaps not had the courage—to take it with them. Facing them from the other side of the driveway was a backhoe, its hood carpeted in red berries.

"Our home on High," Lyle said.

Dustin didn't respond. She got out of the car by herself and walked up the driveway to where she could see the construction. The remains of their old house were gone, replaced by a half-built frame. A mansion, flowering into a corolla of rooms. Birds flitted in the joists, chirping like crazy. Lyle wondered where the workers were until she remembered it was Sunday. The yard itself, where they'd played torturous, Dad-driven rounds of croquet and boccie and horseshoes—where Dustin had rolled across the grass, coiled in flames—was gone as well, turned into dirt.

When she was little, Lyle used to think that the frames of houses being built were models. You practiced with the model first and then put up the real thing. The idea that a pile of sticks could shelter anyone, could protect them from the dangers of the world, seemed preposterous.

She glanced behind her, but there was no one in sight. Lyle went back down the driveway to where the BMW was parked. Taz and Hector were standing by the open door of the passenger seat, peering inside at Dustin, who sat in the car without moving. His back was hunched like an old lady's.

"I thought we were going to look for Jonas," Lyle said.

"He's not here," Dustin said. "It was a stupid idea."

"Now you tell us."

"What do you think? He's camping in the yard and no one's seen him?"

"We came all the way out here," Lyle said. "We should at least *look*."

"Can't you see he's petrified?" Taz said angrily, glaring at her.

It was true. Dustin's face had gone rigid, his arms tucked in as if he were bracing against a wind. He would not move his eyes from the dashboard.

"I'll go help Lyle look," Hector said. "We'll find Jonas if he's here."

Dustin snapped toward him. "What the fuck's wrong with you? My little brother's disappeared, maybe dead, and you're acting like he's your own fucking relative!"

Hector took a step backward. He looked pale, as though he might throw up.

"Why don't you go *home* for once? *H-O-M-E*. We have a fucking pet already."

"Dust," Lyle said.

"All he does is stand around looking miserable!"

"I'm the one who did it," Hector said quietly.

Lyle looked at him. "What are you talking about?"

"The stove. I left it on by accident. I broke into your house because I was mad at Lyle." He caught his breath, staring at the curb. "I blew up your house."

Lyle was suddenly scared. A peacock cried from somewhere below, the call echoing down the canyon.

"It's my fault. I was sick . . . I left some water on the stove."

Hector started to cry. For some reason, Lyle remembered letting him eat that pistachio ice cream cone the day he'd wandered into The Perfect Scoop, the way he'd closed his eyes to swallow, hunched over to mask his suffering. Dustin got out of the car suddenly: his face was so awful, so red and still and strange, that Lyle wondered if he would strangle Hector with his bare hands. Instead he reached into Hector's shirt pocket and pulled out the sugar glider, gripping the furry creature in his glove. Hector shook his head, eyes wide with fright. Dustin turned and crossed the street toward the Constables' house, holding the tiny animal in front of him like a grenade. He strode swiftly, as if he were carrying an actual bomb. When he reached the Constables', he walked down the sidewalk to where you could see the blue glimmer of their swimming pool through the bushes. The deep end was a stone's throw from the street. He was going to heave the thing into the Constables' pool and watch it drown.

Lyle rushed across the street but he'd already cocked his arm, his bad one, letting it fly. She waited for a glimpse of fur, for the hurled creature to open in midair—a puny flying carpet—before gliding into the pool with a splash. Nothing happened. When she reached Dustin, he was standing on the sidewalk, clutching his arm. His sunglasses lay at his feet. He opened his fist and the remarkable creature was still there, panting like a heart.

"You couldn't kill it," Lyle said.

"I would have. It stuck to my glove."

The animal's claws were still dug into the leather, eyes big as marbles. Even scared out of its wits, it was infuriatingly cute. Taz and Hector watched from the car, frozen like statues. Zap, Lyle thought. Us vs. them. She glanced back at her brother, who was staring at the scrub oak across the street.

"Jesus," he said.

Caught high in the branches, where the leaves were spotted from blight, was one of Lyle's old T-shirts. It was ratty and yellow, but filling in some letters she could still make out the slogan: MURDER IS A FAUX PAS. It must have escaped the fire only to get stuck in a tree. Once she'd walked around with jokes on her chest, believing herself to be unhappy. The shirt flapped in the breeze, like a kite she couldn't get back.

CHAPTER 45

People. Jonas had never seen so many in one place before. Smoking pipes by their cars or dancing like noodles to noodley music or playing Hacky Sack as though they were learning a Russian dance. Blasts of mossy perfume made his eyes water. On the roof of a van, a woman was swaying in a circle, a hula hoop spinning around her neck. "Steal your face?" a man asked Jonas. He held up a T-shirt with a skull on it. Jonas hurried past. This was the third time someone had asked if they could have his face. He did not know what they planned on doing with it. Perhaps they were unhappy with their own faces, which were gaunt and hairy and sometimes even missing teeth.

The parking lot went on forever, bristling with cars and vans and motorcycles. Jonas entered a maze of vendors selling jewelry and skateboards and T-shirts with teddy bears on them like the ones on Griselda's bong. He stopped in the narrow shade behind a booth, wondering what to do. He did not know where Major Meltdown and Griselda were. He'd gone with Captain Lobo to sell the tickets they'd picked up from the stationery store, the ones they'd had copied onto special cardboard and cut out carefully with scissors, making sure the little skeleton doffing its hat didn't get snipped off at the top. People had bought these tickets believing they were real. Captain Lobo had not felt bad about this: he called them Trustafarians. Trustafarians were from Trustafaria, a very rich planet. They did not deserve their money, and therefore it belonged to the "mendicants of Earth." Explaining this to Jonas, he'd smiled to show off the gunk in his teeth, as though it were proof of his impoverishment.

Captain Lobo had seemed less happy when three of the Trusta-farians had found him behind a porta-potty and demanded their money back, waving their fake tickets in his face. When he claimed not to know who they were, they tackled him all at once, punching him in the face while he screamed and cried for help. Jonas had run away as fast as he could, ignoring the panicked yelp of his name.

Now he was lost and frightened, a haze of smoke stinging his eyes. Where had they parked the RV? He ventured into the hot sun again, searching for the flutter of Griselda's hands. His stomach growled. He hadn't eaten anything all day, unless you counted the day-old maple bar he'd had for lunch. He dreamed about calling his family—as he had a hundred times before—but he could not bear to spoil their relief. Sometimes he'd trick himself into believing they missed him, that they maybe even wanted him back, but then he would remember Dustin's face and what he'd done and how his dad or mom or brother looked at him some-times as if they wished it were him. The truck driver had said they were probably drinking champagne.

Jonas froze. Up ahead, near the wiggly heat from a grill, several people were squatting in a circle and tending to a man who was jerking comically on the ground, his bare feet pointed like a bal-lerina's. A guy ran up with an Evian bottle and poured some water on the man's face. Jonas backed into a van, which came alive and touched his shoulders. A beautiful woman with tufts of hair in her armpits. He had never seen anyone with this particular deformity. Her breasts, naked under her dress, were lower than they should have been.

"It's all right," the woman said. "Got dosed, probably. Bad news." She looked down at Jonas's pants—his filthy, flowered jeans—and her eyes sparked with interest. "All by your lonesome today?"

Jonas nodded, worried that she might know about Captain Lobo and have him arrested. The woman's face softened. She put an arm around his shoulders and led him over to a VW bus twinkling with music. A group of people—two shirtless men with ponytails and a girl not much older than Lyle—were sitting in foldout chairs behind it. The girl was holding a baby, her top pulled down on one side so that it could suck at her breast.

"Guess what I turned up," the woman with hairy armpits said, showing Jonas off.

One of the shirtless men opened his eyes. He seemed disappointed. There was a jean jacket draped over his lap, a skeleton smoking a cigarette painted on the back. "It's boob o'clock," he said. "Come and get it."

The girl with the baby didn't laugh. The other man put down the Dr Pepper he was holding and leaned forward, as if he needed two hands to steady himself. He reached up to touch the gum still tangled in Jonas's hair. Painted on his stomach, which was large and flabby, were the words THE FAT MAN ROCKS.

"Whoa, dude. Kid's been roading it for months."

"Would you like a sandwich?" the girl said.

Jonas was too hungry to say no. The woman with hairy armpits opened the cooler and handed him a sandwich on crumbling brown bread: peanut butter and jelly. It tasted better than french fries.

"Dr Pepper?" she asked.

"If there's any left," the man with the jacket said irritably.

The fat man held up his can. "This is my fourth appointment with the doctor today," he said proudly.

"What's your favorite song?" the girl with the baby asked, ignoring them.

Jonas could not think of one. In general, music did not interest him as much as its baffling significance to people. "Mr. Frog Went A-Courtin'," he said finally. It had been his favorite song when he was a little kid, mostly due to Miss Mousie's tragic death.

"No shit," the guy with the jacket said. "They do that?"

"Cal Expo. Eighty-four, I think. Phil pulled it out of his ass."

"You're high, dude."

"I've got it all right here!" the fat one said, tapping his head.

"Try, like, your own ass."

The fat man frowned. "At least I don't have a goofy jacket," he said quietly.

"What are you talking about?"

"All the album covers out there, and you pick *Skeletons from the Closet*?"

"What's wrong with that?"

"It's a greatest hits album!"

The guy with the jacket blushed. "I like the visuals. They're really kinetic."

"You guys are like a broken record," the girl said. "Blah blah blah."

She leaned down and kissed the baby, which was smooshed against her breast but no longer sucking. She stood up slow as a grandmother and leaned into the back of the VW, laying it gingerly on a sleeping bag surrounded by pillows.

"Put her on her stomach," the guy with the jacket said. "She sleeps better."

"How many times do I have to tell you? She'll die of SIDS!"

The guy flicked something off his shoulder. "You're so, like, negative. It's bringing me down."

"What's SIDS?" Jonas asked politely. He was hoping they'd offer him another sandwich or at least remember about the Dr Pepper.

"Sudden infant death syndrome," the girl said, glaring at the guy with the jacket. "Babies stop breathing for no reason."

"See what I mean?" the guy said unhappily.

The music was loud enough, blaring out of the bus, that Jonas wondered how anyone could sleep. But the baby seemed to be used to it. Perhaps it was deaf already. The fat man saw someone he recognized and jumped out of his chair, his stomach bouncing as he ran off. He came back, panting for breath, and explained that someone in B6 had backstage passes. The catch was he was only giving them away to girls. Excitedly, the woman with hairy armpits squatted in front of the side mirror of the bus and began to fix her hair with two hands.

"I'll take Eva along," the other girl said.

"Are you whacked?" the fat man said. "He won't give them to us if you've got a baby."

The girl peered nervously into the bus, her top still hanging down on one side. The sight of her naked breast depressed Jonas, as if he'd seen through a magic trick. "Don't leave the car," she said to the guy with the jacket. "Or I swear to God."

"What am I supposed to do?"

"Keep our hungry bro company," the fat one said. "He's in need of some calories."

The guy with the jacket protested, complaining about being stuck with Jonas, but they were already gone. The guy sat down mopily in his chair. Jonas waited for another sandwich before finally getting one out of the cooler himself. He was hoping he would see Griselda or Major Meltdown walk by. They'd spot him from far away and then run over to meet him, smothering him the way they had that night in the van. He tried not to give in to the other fantasy, the less reasonable one, but as usual it was too glamorous to resist: his mother, clean and beautiful and smelling of cigarettes, swooping out of the crowd of grubby people to take him home.

"Man, there are some biscuits here," the guy said, watching a girl walk by in cutoff jeans and a bikini top. He shook his head. "I'm telling you, everything changes when you have a kid. It's like maximum security. Enjoy your freedom while it lasts, bro. Before the warden gets you." He looked at his lap. "What do you think of this jacket?"

Jonas could tell he wanted him to compliment it. "It's very attractive."

"Fucking believe it. Cost me sixty dollars. You see tons of *Shakedown Streets*. Or *American Beauty*, how obvious can you get!" He got up and leaned his head into the back of the bus, a yellowed band of underwear peeking above his jeans. He told Jonas he had to take a leak. "Don't move. Baby's out like a light, but just in case. I'll be back in five."

Jonas watched him vanish into the labyrinth of booths. The sun was very hot. Sweating, Jonas ate his third sandwich, chewing it extra slowly in order to make it last until the man came back from the bathroom. He did not return. Jonas wondered whether he'd said he would be back *at* five, not "in." Eventually an ambulance wailed into view, blaring its siren and nosing through the crowd. Jonas plugged his ears. People gawked at the ambulance as it passed, shambling out of its path.

The baby started to cry. Jonas poked his head inside the bus: its little limbs flailed around, jerking like a puppet's. The crying got louder and more frantic. Jonas could see all the way down its throat, its tiny uvula switching up and down. He started to worry. The baby wouldn't make any noise at all for about five or six seconds, its face darkening to a grapey purple—a screamless scream, strange and terrible and frozen—before catching its breath finally and letting one fly. It was like playing with the mute button on a TV. The screamless screams began to get longer. The baby was dying. Clearly, it couldn't breathe. If it was SIDS, the girl had not mentioned any way to stop it.

Jonas lifted the screaming baby out of the van and held it to his chest. It seemed as fragile as a kitten. Its heartbeat raced under his thumb, a spastic flutter, like something in the throes of death.

He would go find the baby's mother. She'd know what to do. B6, they'd said. Jonas scanned the parking lot for a sign before spotting one right above his head. R11. How big could the parking lot be? Even if he couldn't find the baby's mother, he was bound to run across the ambulance. Jonas rushed into the throng of people crowding the booths, hoping he was heading in the right direction. Strangers stared at him as he passed. He imagined that someone might grab the baby from him, so obvious were the symptoms of SIDS, but instead they dodged out of his way without blinking.

The baby stopped screaming, burrowing into Jonas's chest like a mole. The silence frightened him. He shook the baby, and it began to scream again. He'd read somewhere that you should keep people awake if you thought they might die. He passed a row of motorcycles; some men with long, Moses-y beards pointed at him and laughed. Jonas hurried on, the muscles in his arms beginning to burn. The baby sputtered and gasped, as if it were choking. Near the entrance to the arena, where people were waiting to get in, he saw a woman with a plastic chair strapped to her back, a baby in a floppy bonnet enthroned there like a queen. Jonas ran up to the woman, thrusting the baby in his hands at her and telling her it was sick.

The woman recoiled, reaching back to shield her daughter's face.

Jonas kept going, entering a more deserted stretch of parking lot. The baby had not stopped screaming since he'd shaken it. He was starting to wish it would hurry up and die. Breathless, he stopped at a lamppost and checked the bolted sign to see where he was: V10. He hadn't even reached the end of the alphabet. Fatigue swamped his legs, weighing them to the asphalt. He tried to recall where he'd started from. Was it R or T? He couldn't remember. The number, too, had vanished from his head. The lot stretched on forever, scattered with identical buses.

Jonas contemplated leaving the baby under someone's car. He was only a kid; who would suspect him?

He sat down next to a filthy-looking pickup truck, the heat of the asphalt oozing through his jeans. The baby's screams had gone strange and croaky. Jonas had a weird sensation. The sensation was that the baby in his hands was himself. He—Jonas—had been sent from the future to dispose of it. That way he could undo his brother's accident. If the baby died, Jonas would vanish from the face of the earth. Different from dying: he would have never existed.

His family would want this to happen, if they only knew how.

Jonas settled back against the wheel of the truck, waiting for the baby to die. He closed his eyes. Beyond the dying gasps of the baby, he heard a distant sound like a roll of thunder. A roar of cheering voices. He imagined that the voices were greeting him. These were the unborn souls, the ones who'd somehow reversed themselves from existence. It wasn't until the voices swelled into music that he realized the baby had stopped screaming. It was still and damp and silent. He waited for something to happen, now that the baby was dead, but nothing presented itself.

He opened his eyes. The baby was sleeping, its tiny back moving up and down. Its fingers, balled into a fist, were clutching Jonas's shirt. The fist was no bigger than the head of a spoon. Jonas cupped a hand over the sleeping baby to shield it from the sun. It would grow up and have any life it wanted. He stood up gingerly. In the distance, gathered in front of a white tent, was a crowd of busy-looking people; Jonas headed in their direction, hoping to find the ambulance nearby.

CHAPTER 46

As always, they were stuck in traffic. It was the one constant in their lives, Dustin thought—the only thing they could count on from week to week. He sat in the backseat of the Volvo with Lyle, listening to his father honk at the convertible in front of him. They were going to pick up Jonas from the police station. Some paramedics had found him at a Dead concert in Irvine, carrying a baby, and had handed him over to the cops. Dustin's relief at the news had quickly reverted into guilt. He kept thinking about the time when Jonas was four or five, suffering from night terrors, and he'd come into Dustin's room in the middle of the night, babbling about the Muzwald sitting at the foot of his bed. The Muzwald was a giant vulture with the head of an old lady and a long lizardlike tongue. It sat at the foot of Jonas's bed all night and cleaned its eyeballs with its tongue. Dustin had gone into his room to kill it with a Swiss Army knife. Entering Jonas's room, he could almost see it as well, licking its own eyes, a horrible hag that devoured children. For several weeks that winter it became a secret ritual: Dustin visiting Jonas's room with his knife, killing the monster on his bed until it returned the next evening, summoned fiendishly back to life. Night after night he sent the invisible creature to its grave. Only gradually did he realize what was really going on, that Jonas seemed disappointed when Dustin slit its throat and returned to his own room.

Dustin hadn't thought of the Muzwald for years until recently, plagued by similar visions himself. The truth was, he'd grown impatient after a month and insisted he'd killed the Muzwald for good. He'd ignored Jonas's protests, tiptoeing past his room every night so he wouldn't call out to him.

The car stank of BO and cigarettes. Dustin wondered how long it had been since any of them had showered. Like Lyle, he'd insisted on coming along with his parents. He'd called in sick at the video store. It was important to him, important in a way he couldn't remember feeling in a long time.

"I forgot to fill Mr. Leonard's bowl," Dustin's mother said, the first time anyone had spoken since they left the house. Her hair was silken with grease. Perhaps, as a form of punishment, they were all turning into Deadheads. "It's almost his dinnertime."

"He's not eating anyway," his dad said.

"Even if he's got cancer, we still have to feed him."

"Who says he has cancer?" Lyle said crossly.

His mother gazed out the window. "Hector. He told me last week he thinks he has lymphoma."

The car hummed in the silence that followed Hector's name. When Dustin had first told his parents the truth, that Hector had caused the fire that ruined his life, his father had gone out onto the back deck with one of Dustin's beers and bent over in plain view, hanging his head between his legs as if to catch his breath. *We'll send him away,* he'd said, returning with the unopened beer. He had not mentioned it since then, but there was something in his face now—a harshness as he tried to nudge into the right lane—that spoke to what he'd do if Hector was dumb enough to show his face.

"Where are you going?" Dustin's mom asked. His father had pulled out of the traffic and was zooming down an exit ramp.

"I need to make a pit stop."

They pulled into a gas station, his dad straddling two spaces as if he didn't have time to park properly. Painted on the front window of the mini-mart were the words MAKE YOURSELF AT HOME. After a minute, Dustin followed his dad inside; he couldn't bear to sit in the car while the three of them choked on their guilt. Heading for the coffee machine, he noticed his father standing in front of the microwave. His eyes were closed in a stoned-looking way. It was the dreamy tenderness of his smile, more than his standing there with his hand to his chest, that frightened Dustin.

"Dad, are you all right?"

His father looked at him for a second, as though he didn't remember who he was. He was breathing quickly. "Heartburn," he said.

"Do you want to sit down?"

He nodded. Dustin walked him over to a plastic chair pushed against the door marked EMPLOYEES ONLY. His father sat down in it. He had always seemed ageless to Dustin, unchangingly dadlike, but now he saw in the harsh light of the store that he was growing old. His eyebrows were getting thick and unruly, sticking up over the frame of his glasses. A freckle on his forehead had darkened, black as an age spot. Breathless, still smiling, his dad took off his glasses and tried to clean them with his T-shirt. One of the metal arms came off in his hand. His father stared at it in betrayal. Dustin went over to the register and found one of those miniature eyeglass repair kits, which he bought from the obese kid behind the register. He asked his dad for the glasses and then squatted beside him, trying with his good hand to poke one of the tiny screws into the end piece. It was like doing surgery on an ant. The little screwdriver kept slipping, sending everything to the floor. A radio behind the register piped out "Girls Just Want to Have Fun." Dustin took off his sunglasses so he could see better, placing them on the microwave counter. Even using his good hand, pinching the tiny handle with three fingers, his eyes teared with pain. When he was done, he handed the eyeglasses to his father, who put them on without speaking.

"What did you buy?" Lyle said when they got back to the car. His dad had lost the smile and was breathing again like his normal self.

"Stuff for Jonas. We thought he might be hungry."

"I hope the police fed him something," his mother said.

"This isn't 'something,'" Dustin said. He reached into the bag in his lap and pulled out the snacks they'd bought, displaying them one at a time. Rainbow Sprinkle Pop-Tarts. Cool Ranch Doritos. Abba-Zaba. "We tried to find some Ring Dings, but they didn't have any."

"You couldn't have bought him *anything* nutritious?" This sounded so much like his old mom that Dustin checked for her cigarettes on the dash.

"We got him some Raisin Bran," his father said. "Show her, Dust."

Dustin pulled out the tiny box of Raisin Bran and showed it to his mother. Lyle took the box from Dustin's hand and opened it before he could stop her, reaching in with her fingers.

"What are you doing?"

"Picking out the raisins for him," Lyle said. "As long as we're stuck in traffic."

There was nowhere to put them. Dustin held out his hand, and she placed them one by one in the palm of his glove.

"Remember when we got that croquet set for Christmas," Lyle said, "and Jonas insisted on wearing his bike helmet? He thought we might hit him in the head with a mallet by mistake. Probably he's the only person in the history of the sport to wear a helmet."

"What made you think of that?" Camille asked.

"I don't know." Lyle closed up the cereal box. "Just that image of him in his helmet."

"He used to wear one when we went sledding, too," Warren said. "In Wisconsin. Plus he refused to go straight downhill. He'd turn the thing back and forth so that he was barely moving." Warren began to swerve the car, to demonstrate.

"Learn to drive, asshole!" someone shouted from a Civic in the next lane. The man's face was contorted with fury. He glanced at Dustin and his face changed, eyes shifting back to the road.

"You're not wearing your sunglasses," Lyle said, looking at Dustin.

He touched his face. It was true; he'd left them in the minimart. He hadn't even noticed. He rolled up his window, catching only the murky shadow of a reflection.

Jonas waited in the police station, sitting by himself in the corner and listening to the noisy smacks of a policeman sucking on a cough drop at his desk. Earlier the guy had shown Jonas his gun. It was the third one he'd been asked to admire that day. "Wow," Jonas had said, because the man so clearly wanted him to say this. He'd asked the guy if he was ever tempted to turn the gun on himself, since police officers had the third-highest suicide rate of any profession. The policeman frowned and moved to the other side of the office, where he'd remained for the past hour in a suicidal funk.

"Want a croissandwich?" the man's partner said now, hoisting a greasy bag in one hand. He was less suicidal and even seemed to enjoy his job. You could tell they were partners because one was black and the other white.

"What's a croissandwich?" Jonas asked.

"It's a croissant and a sandwich combined. They eat them in France."

"Okay," Jonas said. He took the croissandwich from the policeman's hand. "Is my dad still coming?"

"Probably stuck in traffic."

"He might have decided not to come."

The policeman looked at him carefully. "Believe me, he's coming. I talked to him myself. Bet your family hasn't slept in a week."

"Actually, they sort of wish I was dead."

The two policemen glanced at each other. The happier one checked his watch, a cloud of worry spreading over his face. Jonas wiped his fingers on his embroidered jeans. He was sure, now that he'd run away and stolen a baby, that his family hated him even more than they used to. He wondered if the policemen were hiding something from him. Perhaps they knew about the fake tickets, or the coins, or his tricking that poor old woman into searching for his puppy. He thought he was too young to be put in jail, but he wasn't a hundred percent sure.

Either way his dad would be furious. Jonas imagined him showing up at the police station, too mad to speak, his eyes narrowed into slits.

After what seemed like forever, Jonas having long since finished his dinner and given up hope of anyone's taking him home—after the reality of his future had sunk in, a life of hunger and scabby feet and crack houses with no plumbing—there was a call from the reception area. His father was here. Jonas's heart stopped. One of his feet was asleep, and he found himself limping down the hall to greet his punishment. When he rounded the corner to the reception area, still limping, he was surprised to see his entire family waiting for him, a group of disheveled people with greasy hair. His dad in sweatpants. His freckled, exhausted-looking mom, a pack of cigarettes bulging from her pocket. His newly pretty sister and now-ugly brother, lopsided without sunglasses, like a snowman just beginning to melt. They were lined up beside a plastic fern, as if posing for a picture. Beneath his joy at seeing them, his relief and pride and wonderment, Jonas felt obscurely disappointed that they were only themselves.

Jonas's mother rushed over and hugged him, holding him so tightly he thought he might suffocate. She was crying. When she was done, his dad approached without smiling but then hugged him, too, smooshing Jonas's face into his belly. It smelled like rotten leaves. His dad's hands unflexed but seemed to have trouble letting go.

While his father talked to the police, signing papers, the rest of them sat on a bench next to the plastic fern. A fly crawled up the window and then daredeviled down again, like a skier. Dustin and Lyle started pulling things out of a plastic bag, Pop-Tarts and Doritos and candy bars, shoving them in Jonas's direction.

"You're not starving?" Lyle asked.

"I had a croissandwich."

Dustin opened his hand, revealing a sweet-smelling mush. "So I can get rid of these raisins?"

By the time they got back on the road, it was nearly dark. There were still patches of traffic, but Warren did not nudge his way into a faster lane. He was not in a rush to get home. Partly he was happy to have the family together: he couldn't remember the last time they'd all been in the car at the same time. Even with everything that had happened, there was this absurd and stubborn joy. Perhaps, in the end, it was all you could hope for: to get your family together in one car, once or twice a year now that they were older—now that you were going gray yourself—and feel the precious weight of their presence.

He tried not to think of Hector, worried about what it might do to his heart.

Warren glanced in the rearview mirror at Jonas. He was sandwiched between his brother and sister, staring into a bag of Doritos. Warren blamed his spaciness on everything that had happened. And what *had* happened? As far as the cops could tell, there were no indications of abuse or maltreatment. When Warren had tried to find out the details, probing Jonas at the police station, he'd ignored the question completely, fiddling with the gum in his hair.

"Are you feeling up to it now?" Warren asked, glancing backward.

Jonas seemed startled. "Up to what?"

"Filling us in. On your adventures."

Jonas handed the bag of Doritos to Lyle.

"We'd just like to know that no one hurt you," Camille said.

"A deaf woman took care of me. Griselda. She drove me to her house and let me sleep in her bed. Sometimes she took me around in her van. She was a magician. We helped an old lady find her dog."

"She was deaf? How did you communicate?"

"She taught me sign language."

"Are those her daughter's jeans?" Lyle asked.

Jonas nodded. "She was murdered last year. Griselda gave me all her clothes to wear. She brushed my hair and taught me magic tricks and made me eggs Benedict every morning, because that was her daughter's favorite."

Camille turned toward the window. Warren wanted this implausible story to be true: the idea of Jonas making it up on purpose was too much to bear. Perhaps they'd never know what happened. It would remain a mystery, like the gum tangled in his hair.

As darkness fell, the brake lights in front of them began to pulse more brightly in the stop-and-go traffic. Warren turned on the radio. Some pundits were talking about the USSR and the threat of global annihilation. Strangely, it didn't darken his mood. If anything, the dire forecast of the world's future consoled him. Everyone was in the same boat, their hopes equally benighted. What difference did it make if he pretended, too?

He took Camille's hand, which was resting on her seat. She didn't respond, but didn't remove her hand either. Given the state of things, it seemed like a blessing.

By the time they got home, past ten, Jonas was asleep. Warren carried him into the house, cradling his head on one shoulder as he had when Jonas was a baby. The boy was filthy, his nails black with dirt. In bed, arms flopped out and motionless, he looked even more babylike. Warren grabbed some scissors from Jonas's desk and cut the gum out of his hair. He put the hairy piece of gum in the trash. Then he had second thoughts and dug it out again, slipping it—why, he couldn't say—into the pocket of his sweats.

In the kitchen, Camille and Lyle and Dustin were sitting on the linoleum beside Mr. Leonard's bed. The old dog whimpered softly, his breathing swift and shallow. Warren knelt down to touch him, but he didn't lift his head or open his eyes.

"He's dying," Camille said.

"There's an animal hospital in Lancaster," Lyle said.

"No," Camille said, almost angrily. "We should let him die in peace."

She put her hand on Mr. Leonard's ribs. Her fingers moved up and down, bobbing with his breath.

"You three should go to bed," she said.

Lyle shook her head. "I want to stay up."

"Me too," Dustin said.

Camille looked at them, her eyes damp.

"I'll make some coffee," Warren said.

He spooned some Chock Full o'Nuts into a filter and filled the coffeemaker with water. Turning from the sink, he bumped a glass off the counter and it shattered on the floor. Mr. Leonard didn't flinch. As Warren was sweeping up, Lyle went out through the sliding glass door and reappeared with something in her hands. A rock. It was the size of the garden stones they used to have in Herradura Estates. She laid it by Mr. Leonard's head, where he could see it if he opened his eyes.

His breathing grew shallower, more and more labored. It was like watching a fish on a dock. Warren joined his wife and children on the floor. They sat there silently, drinking their coffee, waiting for Mr. Leonard to open his eyes and notice the rock.

"If he'd only eat something," Lyle said.

"What's his favorite food?" Dustin said.

"Steak."

"Has he ever had it?"

"Don't you remember on the Fourth of July, when he ate the steaks off the grill? He kept going back there every night, like to pray."

"There's some London broil in the fridge," Warren said. "I was going to cook it tonight."

He'd picked the steaks up yesterday, perhaps as a way of atoning for his sins. Warren got up now and placed one of them in a pan, turning the stove on high. Before long the kitchen filled with a dinery smell, as unfamiliar as the joy he'd felt earlier. Mr. Leonard didn't stir or look up. Warren cut the steak into little pieces and put them in his bowl, moving the rock away so he could place it under the dog's nose.

Mr. Leonard opened his eyes for a second, a dreamy, indifferent glance. His entire life he'd been trying to eat the meat off their plates. Camille got up suddenly, grabbed the pan from the stove, and brought it over to where Mr. Leonard was lying. She dipped her finger in the grease at the bottom of the pan and painted Mr. Leonard's lips with it, making sure to cover every inch, as if smearing them with ChapStick.

Mr. Leonard opened his eyes again, licking the grease from his lips. He roused himself enough to sniff the bowl. Shyly, he managed to lift his head and take a bite, gulping down several pieces of London broil.

"He's okay," Lyle said, laughing.

"He's going to expect this from now on," Dustin said. "Filet mignon."

Eventually he began to wheeze. It was a horrible sound, undoglike and mechanical, as though his insides were being sucked out by a machine. It was too awful to acknowledge. They sat there for a long time, unable to look at one another. Finally Lyle got up and left, and then Dustin, and then Warren stood up slowly, leaving Camille on the floor by herself. He knew better than to ask her to leave her post. Alone, he took off his clothes without brushing his teeth and climbed into bed, the stars swarming outside his window. The wheezing was loud enough to travel down the hall. He couldn't remember feeling this tired since Dustin was in the hospital: the bed like something you'd forgotten about, a long-lost embrace. Stars pulsed at the window. His wife began to sing from the kitchen. It was the lullaby from *Mary Poppins,* the one she used to sing to the children when they were little.

> *Stay awake, don't rest your head*
> *Don't lie down upon your bed*
> *While the moon drifts in the skies*
> *Stay awake, don't close your eyes*

Perhaps Warren drifted off himself, because the next thing he knew the house was silent. There was no light from the hallway. He moved over to touch Camille, to comfort her, but of course she wasn't there.

PART III

Winter 1986

CHAPTER 47

In the land of underwater birds, everything is reverse. For example: Fish fly through the sky and make their homes in trees. Skunks smell like flowers. When they're getting married, people say *I hate you*. The minister says, *You may now punch the bride*. Girls go to the bathroom standing up. Also, in the land of underwater birds, you win the Olympics by running slowest. Childhood is the worst time; you get happy when you're older. Also, people go to heaven before they're born. They hand out cigars when someone dies. In the land of underwater birds, they say *There are a million places like home*.

Lyle's dad fiddled with his tie, hiding the skinny end by tucking it into his shirt. Ever since Lyle's parents had separated, her father had begun dressing up for visits. Lyle found the whole thing depressing, all the more because Jonas and her mother were wearing sweatpants.

"Enjoying the beach?" her dad asked. As usual, he and Lyle's mother were sitting on opposite ends of the couch. Jonas lounged near her mom's feet, playing a video game. The demonic music bleating from the TV set made the room seem even smaller than it was.

"It's the middle of winter," Lyle said. "Anyway, I hate the beach. Thank God we're nowhere near it."

Her dad smiled politely, glancing toward the kitchen. "Well, it must be nice to see the harbor at least."

"The balcony faces the freeway. All you can see are cars."

He seemed disappointed. Why he wanted to romanticize their

life—their small, dark, brown-carpeted apartment—was a mystery to Lyle. The three of them had moved out in August. It seemed like Dustin and her dad had vanished overnight, left behind in Auburn Fields. Seeing as how she'd been dying to return to civilization, Lyle was surprised by the fact that she missed them so much. She'd be waiting for the phone to ring, or watching TV with Jonas, and an emptiness would fill her like a breath.

Lyle's father stared at his lap, fidgeting with his wedding ring.

"You shaved your beard," Lyle's mom said, watching him.

"What?"

"In October, you still had it."

"That's what I wanted to tell you," her father said. "I'm back, um, selling knives."

"You *are*?"

"Last week I was top seller. Beat the Gold Blade of the Month."

He said this ironically, though not without a sparkle of pride. If he was trying to impress Lyle's mom, it was a lost cause: she'd told Lyle several times that they were not getting back together. "We have different goals for ourselves" was how she'd put it. Lyle had almost smirked, this sounded so much like her old mom—except that her old mom would never have left.

On TV, a jouster sitting atop a flying ostrich was battling some red knights mounted on buzzards, who had the unseemly habit of laying eggs as soon as they were killed. Since Jonas had run away, Lyle's mom had bought him a pogo stick, a Mongoose dirt bike, and an Atari 7800. Lyle was beginning to worry about Christmas, only a week and a half away.

"Is there an object to this game?" her dad asked.

"Yes and no," Jonas answered without glancing from the screen. "You're supposed to kill the enemy knights with your lance and then squash their eggs before they hatch. If you fly too close to the lava, the lava troll will pull you under."

"The lava troll."

"You have to flap with the button. It's very lifelike."

"What do you get if you kill all the knights?"

Jonas seemed nonplussed by this question. "Nothing. Another wave of them come out."

"I see what you mean," Lyle's father said, nodding.

Lyle wandered into the kitchen, where Dustin was stirring a gigantic soup pot with a spoon. He was cooking a birthday

lunch for Taz, who was due to arrive any minute. He was host-
ing the lunch here so she wouldn't have to drive all the way out
to Auburn Fields and concoct a lie for her parents. That's what
Dustin had said, but Lyle suspected there was another reason, too:
he wanted them all together, a family, so he could show Taz off.
He would never admit this, but there was something in him that
craved their approval. When they first moved to California, before
Lyle or Dustin had friends, he used to stop by her room with his
unplugged guitar and sing her the songs he'd written, blushing as
he waited for her verdict. Now it was rare for him to visit at all.
Lyle saw him more than her father—once or twice a month—but
not enough.

Dustin looked up from the pot, his face flushed from cooking. The surgeries—Z-plasty, and something to release the tugging under his eye—had been called a great success. In truth,
they hadn't made him look better so much as different. In some
ways he looked even stranger: the lopsidedness was mostly fixed,
so you had to look even closer to see what was wrong, how
the two halves of his face failed to match up. Even with more
surgery, the hard truth was he was never going to look normal.
There'd always be something off about him, an ugliness posing
as a riddle.

Except for Dustin, they'd all been deceiving themselves.

"It's taking forever to boil," he said.

"It's electric. The stove. Mom's always complaining about it."

Dustin knew this, of course; he wouldn't be cooking otherwise. Certain things—gas flames, the crinkle of tinfoil—still upset
him. He covered the pot and then squeezed past her to get to the
sink. It was a tiny kitchen, barely big enough to cook in, but there
was relief in its cabinet-like functionality. Their old life had happened almost entirely in kitchens, and look what had happened
to them.

"Mom told me you got in early to Columbia," he said, washing his hands. "I forgot to congratulate you."

"I was sure I wouldn't get in."

"I knew you would. You're the smartest person I know."

Lyle blushed. She'd been too nervous to tell him herself,
convinced he'd despise her. The phone rang on the windowsill;
Dustin picked it up and fell immediately into a crouch, cupping
the receiver with both hands, his voice shrinking to a murmur.

Taz. Lyle left him alone and went into her room, unable to bear the awkwardness of the living room. The shag carpet felt cold between her toes. The rug was hideous, brown as a turd, but she loved it. When she'd gotten the letter from Columbia, she'd lain in its plush woolen grass and stared at the ceiling for an hour, grinning like an idiot. It was hard not to feel a sort of postcoital glow over the whole thing. Back in October, working on her essay, she'd had the strange, vaguely titillating feeling that she was trying to coax Columbia into bed. Even the term "early action" seemed to imply she was trying to get into its pants. In the end it was her mother who'd helped her, filling out the financial aid forms and proofreading her essay for the millionth time. The essay had made her mother cry. Lyle knew this because she'd spied on her from the balcony, hidden behind the ficus tree that was supposed to block their view of the Harbor Freeway. When her mom had looked up from the table, face wet with tears, Lyle had felt a jolt of astonished pride.

In gratitude, perhaps, Lyle had decided to help her stop smoking. Whenever her mom got the urge, Lyle would fix her a Coke. Actually, what she fixed her was the Platonic ideal of Cokeness: a tall, fizzing, ice-packed glass, the kind that tickles your nose when you drink it. The first time she'd tried it, Lyle's mom had closed her eyes between sips, dazed and speechless, like someone savoring a joint. "Sheez," she'd said, staring into the glass. Recently they'd begun watching TV together after Jonas had gone to bed, drinking Classic Coke on the sofa and taking in *Moonlighting* or *Miami Vice*. Sometimes Lyle's mom would drink four or five glasses.

Now, in her room, Lyle opened her desk and found what she was looking for, the thing she wanted to show Dustin. From the kitchen she heard him raise his voice, yelling something into the phone. Eventually the receiver clattered back onto the wall. When she emerged from her room, he was sitting out on the balcony off the kitchen, half-hidden behind the ficus plant. Because he was her brother, and because she didn't know how to ever really leave him alone, she went out on the balcony, too.

"Is Taz coming?" she asked timidly.

"I don't know."

"She didn't say?"

Dustin scratched his arm. He'd stopped wearing his Jobst shirt and glove in July; Lyle was still getting used to the nakedness of his arm, brown and plastery with scars, like a wall that had been sloppily repaired. "She hung up on me."

"You haven't been getting along?"

"Less and less."

Lyle surprised herself by not feeling pleased about this. She sat down in a deck chair, watching the river-slow current of cars in the sun, the shush of traffic as soothing in its way as waves on a beach. Bordering the freeway was the refinery she used to see driving to Wilmington: the row of giant tanks and Erector-set towers and chimneys burning like candles or sending up speech bubbles of smoke in the wind. Hector's house—its weight bench in the driveway, covered in plastic—was just on the other side. Lyle hadn't seen him since the week of Jonas's disappearance; none of them had. He'd become another cruddy twist of fate, an event they never talked about.

"Look," she said, handing Dustin the homemade book in her hand. "I dug this up when we moved."

"What is it?"

"The Land of Underwater Birds."

It was in surprisingly good shape, staples lining one side like a column of ants. Dustin stared at the cover. Painstakingly drawn in colored pencil was an underwater vista of strange-looking birds, strings of bubbles rising from their beaks. They swam on outstretched wings, gliding like manta rays, floating peacefully or bringing worms to nests sitting in the seaweed. You could tell which ones were Dustin's because of the blobs of bird shit sinking from their tails. Lyle's birds tended to have lipstick and long eyelashes. In the sky, more indifferently drawn, were fish: a shark with saw-blade teeth, an octopus lounging on a cloud. The octopus had on a name tag that said CLAUDE.

"This made it through the fire?" Dustin said, amazed. At the bottom of the page, in different-colored letters, were their names: DUSTIN AND DELILAH ZILLER.

"It was in the garage, I guess. With the other junk that survived. I didn't even know till I found it in storage."

Dustin flipped through the pages, sending up an acrid must of smoke. It amazed Lyle how much they'd written. How they'd looked forward to it, rushing upstairs after day camp or swim lessons to sit in the closet and dream up more details. *It snows when it's hot outside. Caterpillars are more beautiful than butterflies. Also, movie stars have terrible faces.* When Dustin reached the drawing for this—an acne-riddled man with a long, bulbous nose, bumpy as a pickle—he stopped smiling, staring at the man's face.

"Did I draw that?" he said.

Lyle nodded. The cars on the freeway had begun to move in starts, bunching and unbunching like a snake. Dustin closed the book and handed it back to her.

"Mom sent me a copy of your college essay," he said finally.

Her heart sank. "She *did*?"

"At first I was pissed. 'My Brother's Life Is Fucked, I'm Not Going to Fuck Over Mine.'"

"It was about all of us."

"I know. You told the truth." He looked off at the refinery. Lyle wondered which part of the essay he was talking about: the bit about seeing him in the burn unit for the first time, how some teensy part of her had been happy he wasn't more beautiful than her anymore? "Will you write me from Columbia?" he asked.

She had to clear her throat to speak. "Yes. Every week."

"You'll forget to. But that's okay. It's enough that, you know, you think you're going to right now."

Lyle wanted to assure him she wouldn't forget, that she would write him every day if that's what he needed, but somewhere inside the unkempt crannies of her mind she knew he was right. She would get pulled into a new life, frantic with friends and classes. It occurred to her that her brother would never apply to college; he was too frightened to leave his hideout in the desert. He'd end up working somewhere like Mojave Video for the rest of his life, the strangeness in his face seeming less and less like an accident. At some point he'd become one of those men who look older than their bodies, trolling the supermarket with a cart full of frozen steaks. *In the land of underwater birds, they say good-bye for hello.* Lyle's stomach growled so fiercely that Dustin heard it over the traffic, looking at her in surprise.

"I forgot to have breakfast," she said. Maybe she was wrong; maybe Dustin would do something great with his life, as unexpected in its way as what had already happened to him. She tried her best to convince herself of this.

"We should eat," he said, frowning. "Taz can fucking celebrate with her friends."

In the bathroom, Camille washed her hands, fighting the urge to smoke the cigarette hidden in her pocket. She'd had to escape the awkwardness of the living room. In the mirror, the face peering back at her seemed pale and tired, tiny wrinkles creping the skin above her lip. The lines around her neck seemed deeper than usual. She reached into her pocket and touched the Camel Light. It was the only one she had; she didn't dare smoke it yet, so early in the evening, no matter how much she wanted to.

She began to organize Lyle's and Jonas's things, putting the cap back on some deodorant and collecting a stray Q-tip that had dropped on the floor. She'd done what she had to do; she'd left Warren in the desert to nurse his failure, to watch over their poor, bitter, sick-hearted son. So why did she feel so wretched? Perhaps it was having Warren in the apartment with his wedding ring. Her own was in a drawer, tucked inside an old prescription bottle. Running the sink to seem busy, she wondered if she'd made a mistake in leaving him. At the time it had been a matter of survival. She could forgive him for moving them out to California, perhaps, for bankrupting them in pursuit of some fantasy of wealth, for falling victim to a malady of shame he could never pay off—she could forgive Warren these things, but this was different from getting over them. In the end it was her disappointment in him that had proved toxic. He'd squandered the life they might have had together, the one he'd promised her those moose-eating days in Chicago before they were married. After Dustin's accident, he'd given up completely, in love with his own misery. Or so she'd thought. Now that she'd left, she could see him more clearly: a broken man, well-meaning but not as brave as life required, who'd become something he'd never imagined.

But perhaps you could never imagine it. She'd wanted to be someone else, a glamorous woman in black. But she wasn't. She was a woman who assembled newsletters, who looked better in pastels, who'd found a small, fragile, unexpected peace with her daughter.

Camille turned off the sink and stepped out of the bathroom, where Warren was standing in the hall. She wondered if he'd been waiting for her. In his hand was a present, a Bullock's box wrapped up in a bow. Camille felt suddenly ashamed; she hadn't thought to buy Taz anything for her birthday.

"That's thoughtful," she said. "I should have gotten something, too."

Warren held the present out to her. "It's for you."

"What?"

"I wrapped it myself," he joked. His hand—the whole present—was trembling. He could barely look at her. Camille took the present from him, as much to relieve her own discomfort as his.

"Warren," she said helplessly.

"An early Christmas present." He laughed. "Anyway, I'm not used to having an income. I don't know what to do with my money."

Camille looked at the ribboned box in her hand. She knew he couldn't afford his own health insurance, let alone a gratuitous gift from Bullock's. Still, she had no choice but to open it. Folded ineptly inside some tissue was a black stole with a viney pattern woven around the edge. Possibly it was cashmere. For a second something caught in her chest. She pictured Warren taking the stole out of the box at home, making sure there was nothing wrong with it before folding it up again as best he could.

"It sort of reminded me of that shawl you used to have. The Western one? But, you know, without the fringes."

"It's beautiful. Warren, it is. But I'm not moving back to Antelope Valley."

"It's only a present," he said.

"I just got Jonas enrolled back in school here. And what about Lyle?"

He frowned, gazing at the ribbon she'd handed him. "I'm not saying right now. Maybe when the school year's over." He gestured vaguely at the hallway. "You can't stay in this tiny place forever. You don't even have room for a Christmas tree."

"I haven't had time to pick one up."

Warren avoided her eyes. "Anyway, I found a big one. A tree. You can spend the night at the house."

"Maybe the kids," she said, shaking her head.

Looking at her husband's face, its chronic, communicable unhappiness, Camille knew she hadn't made a mistake. She'd escaped for a reason. When she'd first moved out and found the apartment, Warren had seemed to think it was worse than their place in Auburn Fields: "dark as a forest," he'd called it. He seemed to hold himself responsible for its gloominess. Of course, it would never occur to him that she loved it. The tiny kitchen whose windows fogged up when she cooked. The shag carpet that harbored old coins, causing a racket when she vacuumed. The wallpaper in the living room that Lyle called "inkblot beige" because of its tacky Rorschach blobs. Even the sound of the freeway at night, steady as a waterfall, a mindless roar that helped Camille sleep. It might seem cramped to anyone else, even cavelike, but mostly what she felt was *space*: the freedom to be happy if she wanted to.

She walked back into the living room, where Jonas was playing his video game. There was a stillness in his face that frightened her. She saw it at times like this, when he didn't know she was watching: something like sorrow, a mortal wound. Camille watched him from the doorway. For so long, well before Dustin's accident, she'd been dissatisfied with who she was. She'd wanted to surprise people, to be the person who wasn't afraid of doing the wrong thing. A different kind of mother. Well, just look at how she'd succeeded.

She bent down and kissed Jonas's head, hoping he'd look up from his game. She knew he wouldn't, but her heart waited nonetheless. Dustin called from the kitchen that lunch was ready. She told Jonas to switch off his game and he did, jumping up like any other kid, shocking her with his gawky height. He's going to be fine, Camille thought—and then said it again to herself before leaving the room.

After lunch, they all drove out to Herradura Estates to see the new house that had been built where their old one had been. Jonas thought it was strange that this would interest his family, since the place was no longer theirs, though in his experience grown-ups were often interested in things that no longer existed. Not just coins: old things that had happened to them. It was like a disease. He hoped there was a way to avoid getting it, but figured it must be something inevitable like hemorrhoids.

It had been Dustin's idea to go look at the house, but now it looked like maybe he was having second thoughts, his leg jerking up and down as they drove up Crenshaw toward the gate. Jonas wondered if they'd still be making the trip if he'd actually blown up the house. He doubted it. Since they'd found out it was Hector's fault, his family had been doing a constant sort of egg-and-spoon walk in which he was the egg. They were always hugging him out of the blue or offering to fix him his favorite dinner or buying him something no one else at school had. His mom, especially. It was like living with Santa Claus. If he told her that he wanted a torpedo, right that second, she'd probably stop the car and drive them all to Submarines-R-Us.

Still, there was something missing. Would they be buying him all this stuff, showering him with hugs, even if he *had* blown up the house? That was the question that nagged him while he brushed his teeth or waited for a Pop-Tart to pop. Would they have loved him anyway? Probably it was one of those things you could never know.

They had no trouble getting past the gate, Jonas's mom being old pals with Herman the guard, who put a finger to his lips before waving them through. The new house looked nothing like their old one. It was much bigger, for starters. Plus it had two stories and a little castle wall like the teeth of a jack-o'-lantern sticking over the top and a giant arch where the front door was supposed to be. Heaped in the muddy yard was a pile of scrap, materials enough for another house. Jonas's mom parked at the curb since the driveway was mud. They stayed there in the car looking at the house. A girl on a horse stared at them as she rode by, stiff as a pole, her head turning slowly as if she were one of those mechanical dolls at Disneyland.

"Our mailbox is gone," Lyle said.

"Maybe they've moved in," Jonas's mom said.

"Unlikely," his father said. "There aren't any windows." He turned to the backseat. "Well? Should we head back?"

"No," Dustin said. "I want to check it out."

He climbed out of the Volvo and tromped up the muddy slope toward the house, leaning into each step, as if he were walking into a wind. Jonas's parents waited until he'd gone into the house and then got out of the car and then Jonas and Lyle did, too, following Dustin through the giant archway into the doorless vestibule curtained with plastic. Inside there were no walls, only wood studs like bones marking where they'd go. Pipes snaked up to the ceiling or jutted toward invisible sinks. The skeleton of a staircase, tall and banisterless, rose up to a hole in the second floor.

Jonas followed his family through the half-built house, watching for nails and leaving scattered footprints in the sawdust. Dustin was nowhere to be found. They wandered from room to room, stepping through the walls like ghosts.

"This must have been where the sports closet was," Jonas's dad said. He was standing in the middle of a large room, next to a tall pile of Sheetrock.

"How do you know?" his mom asked.

He shrugged. "It's in my head. Like a map."

"Where am I?" Lyle asked.

"In the laundry room. In front of the dryer."

They called Dustin's name, but no one answered. In the corner of the next room, beside a wall stuffed with pink insulation, Jonas found a party-sized bag of M&M's sitting in a hardhat. He and Lyle sat down on the unfinished floor, feasting on M&M's. The orange ones embarrassed Jonas and he didn't eat them.

"Was this the kitchen?"

Jonas's dad nodded. He sat down with them, slow as an old man, and then his mom did, too, the four of them passing the hat around. The room smelled like pee.

"I hope Dustin's all right," Lyle said.

"Probably he just wants to be by himself," Jonas's mother said.

"Remember when Mr. Leonard ate all those espresso beans?"

"God. Right. He didn't sleep for days."

Jonas's dad shook his head, his mouth stuffed with M&M's. "I wish he could be here with us."

"*Here?*" Lyle said. "Why?"

"I don't know. Isn't that what you're supposed to say?"

There was a noise behind the wall, a doglike rustle. The rustling grew louder, moving in their direction. Jonas's mom grabbed his father's arm. A peacock emerged from the wall, a wisp of insulation sticking from its beak like cotton candy.

"Our famous garbage eater," his mom said, dropping her hand. "You can tell by the crest."

While his family finished the M&M's, Jonas went upstairs to look around. There was no ceiling, only a tunnel of triangles holding up the roof. He peered behind a stack of Sheetrock and found his brother sitting by himself on an Igloo cooler. He looked carefully at Jonas, his leg still bouncing up and down. He was holding an X-Acto knife. Jonas had the eerie impression that he'd been sitting there for months.

"Want to write something?" Dustin asked.

Jonas looked at the stud in front of his brother's face. He'd carved something into the wood, in mismatched letters. THE ZILLERS WERE HERE. It would be inside the walls forever. Jonas took the knife but couldn't think of anything to add.

Eventually they all went out to look at the backyard, where the people moving in were building a swimming pool. Jonas walked up to the edge. He'd always wanted a swimming pool but didn't like seeing a big muddy pit where he'd once practiced his fencing moves. A brown puddle of rain moldered in the deep end. Aside from some pipes sticking out here and there, a steel fence holding up the taller walls, the thing was pretty much indistinguishable from a ditch. For some reason, it filled him with a cold and spooky feeling, as though he were peering into a humongous grave.

He told himself it was just a hole, a big fat ditch, but the feeling wouldn't go away.

Jonas glanced behind him. His mom and dad, Lyle and Dustin—they were staring at something on the other side of the yard, bunched together and talking as a family. They seemed to have forgotten about him. In a second he felt his trust suck away. What happened next, whether it was an accident or not, Jonas couldn't say. What he remembered was stepping right to the muddy lip of the hole, the feeling of *presto!* as the mud collapsed under his feet. A scuffle of shouts. His dad dropping next to him in the shallow end, splashing up mud, flushed with concern though he'd only fallen a few feet. Dustin and Lyle and his mother gathered at the edge.

"Are you all right?" his father asked, breathless.

Jonas looked at the mud. His family waited for an answer, as though they could help.

CHAPTER 48

Dustin got off the elevator and walked through the doors of the burn unit, wondering at what point the smell of charred flesh had ceased to be remarkable. It had become just another thing, like the picture—hanging in the nurses' lounge, part of a before-and-after sequence—of an Afghani girl's cheeks melted into her shoulders. He remembered the shock he'd felt when he first saw it, as though something had unzipped his brain and stepped out of it. Now, staring at the picture from the hall, the coniferous shape of the girl's face, he felt only mild revulsion. It amazed him that you could pretty much adapt to anything. He walked past the ICU rooms, the thick, porky smell filling his nostrils. Once, during rehab, one of the other outpatients had told him that the word for human among cannibals in the Pacific Islands was "long pig." He'd said this not as a joke but as a way of introducing himself.

Just last week Dustin had gone to Carl's Jr. and eaten a Western Bacon Cheeseburger, his first since the accident. It had tasted ghastly and delicious.

The support group had already begun. Dustin sat down at the conference table without speaking, embarrassed by the smallness of the group. In the middle of the table, partly blocking his view, was a tray of bologna sandwiches stacked into a Mayan pyramid. Dustin wasn't sure who all these sandwiches were intended for. Aside from the two burn counselors, he was one of only five people who'd shown up.

"I'm surprised to see you," said the counselor he recognized. Jane, Janice, something like that. "How long has it been?"

Dustin shrugged. He was as surprised as she was. "I don't know."

"A year at least. Maybe more. I remember seeing you a couple times in rehab."

Dustin nodded. He squinted at the woman's name tag: JAMIE. A burn victim herself. She was missing both forearms and navigated the world with prosthetic hooks, which tended to give her the edge in the self-pity department. Her face, too, was worse off than Dustin's, a mask of barklike skin caked with cosmetics. She used to bug him all the time in the ward, trying to get him to come to meetings, insisting how important it was to talk to fellow "burn survivors." The insistence on "survivor" had made him laugh. The last thing he'd wanted was to hang out with a bunch of pathetic freaks talking about how grateful they were to be alive. Now here he was, confronting a tray of sandwiches. Jamie introduced the woman beside her, a pretty counselor-in-training named Angela; the girl glanced at her lap, ashamed perhaps that she wasn't disfigured.

They went around in a circle, introducing their burns to the group. A guy with one arm, Dustin's age, who'd been charred to cinders when someone threw a firebomb into his bedroom; a man with 65 percent burns who'd put gasoline on his carpet to eat away the glue, intending to strip it; a woman in a plastic mask whose face had caught fire at a restaurant, ignited by a flaming drink. Walter, a burly guy in a wheelchair, talked about the destruction of his legs after his motorcycle exploded on the freeway. When the nurses unwrapped him for the first time, he'd seen something crawling from his leg, a gleaming white snake; he'd screamed for the nurses to get it off, but it had turned out to be a tendon.

Dustin had the rare feeling he'd gotten off lucky. There were two planets: the one where unburned people lived, filled with music and light and strolls on the beach, and the other one, where tendons fell out of your leg and people's faces caught fire during dinner. For the first time, it made sense to Dustin to want to hang out with people from the same planet. What would he possibly have to say to anyone else?

"Is there a reason you've decided to visit us now?" Jamie asked him, after he'd introduced himself. For some reason, Dustin found her face less startling than the watch strapped to her prosthetic arm.

He shrugged. "It's my day off work."

"Did you have a Z-plasty?"

She was looking at his face. Did she remember what he'd looked like? "Two months ago," Dustin said quietly.

"And a graft, too, looks like."

He nodded, embarrassed.

"Looks terrific," the pretty counselor-in-training said.

The others chimed in, too, a chorus of compliments. A year or even six months ago, he would have told them all to fuck off. Now, barraged by their compliments, Dustin realized that he'd driven all the way out here—fifty miles—to show off his new face. To have some perfect strangers lie to him. He felt queasy, partly because the lies made him feel better.

"And your hand," Jamie said, nodding at it, "does it hurt?"

"When it's cold," he said.

"You're exercising it—to help the banding?"

Dustin nodded. He didn't tell her he had to keep his thumb stretched up like Fonzie when he drove; otherwise, he'd lose the movement in it altogether and it would stay bent into a hook for the rest of the day. Down the hall, a boy was screaming at the top of his lungs, upset about getting his dressings changed. It sounded like he was being savaged by bears. Even for a burn unit, the screams were impressive.

"Eight years old," Jamie explained, "and hasn't had a single visitor in a month. His mother calls once a week and says she's coming over, but never shows up."

"What happened to him?" Walter asked.

"Do you want the *official* story? The official story's some kids threw gasoline on his legs and lit him on fire. This is in Jordan Downs, mind you. The projects. Of course, it's the father who brought him in and told us the story." The anger in her voice, so incongruous with the clown-thick makeup on her face, startled Dustin. "His whole family came to see him once, after he was admitted, and stole a VCR from the waiting room. Everyone but the mom's been barred from the hospital."

They went on with the meeting, trying to ignore the unholy screams. Dustin's heart seemed to curl up like a pill bug, poked into a ball. It was news to him that there was anything much to poke. Angela, the counselor-in-training, must have seen something in his face, because she leaned over to him while they were eating sandwiches. "Would you like to stop by the boy's room? I'm going to visit him after the meeting."

"For some reason, I'm scary," Jamie explained, raising her metal hooks.

After the meeting, Dustin found himself trailing Angela down the hall. The boy had stopped screaming a while ago, but the silence, after such an unearthly racket, made Dustin nervous. He followed Angela inside the room and stopped at the foot of the bed. The boy, burned from the waist down, seemed to be asleep, legs and feet bandaged into elephant-sized stumps. There was nothing extraordinary about his burns—percentage-wise, he was fairly well-off—but something about the room, its complete lack of cards and flowers and proof of visitors, took Dustin off guard. He remembered the way his family had visited him constantly on the ward, those first weeks when he was out of it on morphine, confused and miserable and assaulted by nightmares, devil men with long, fiddlehead noses trying to skin him alive or set him on fire—how his dad had written the day of the week on a big sheet of paper and hung it in front of him, taped to the heat shield, so that Dustin would see it whenever he woke up and know what day it was. His mother had held his foot like a hand, squeezing it gently to say hello. Looking at the abandoned boy in his room, Dustin felt petty and ridiculous, ashamed for taking his misery out on his family.

"Someone's come to see you," Angela said, leaning over the bed.

The boy opened his eyes, flinching in terror. "Mommy?" he said, trying to sit up. When he saw who it was, his face fell so completely that Dustin wanted more than anything to be his mother.

He began to visit the boy every week, driving out to Torrance Memorial on one of his days off work. The boy never seemed particularly pleased or unpleased to see him. Even when Dustin brought him something—a GI Joe, a Matchbox car—he would clutch the toy to his chest without taking it out of the package, refusing to talk. To fill the silence, Dustin would tell him about his own burns and how pissed off they'd made him, how sometimes he'd wanted to kill himself instead of going through another day. He still felt this way occasionally, when the itching wouldn't stop or when he made the mistake of looking at old pictures that had been salvaged from the fire. Except for a tightness in his brow, the boy's face gave no indication he was listening. It was a handsome face with miniature, doll-sized ears and eyes that ticked like a watch when he blinked. His eyelashes were unnaturally long, curled at the tips like a camel's. Dustin wanted to clean the goop from them, but didn't dare try for fear of making him scream.

It wasn't until he started bringing him food, smelly bags of Wendy's or McDonald's, that the kid began to brighten when he entered. His favorite were vanilla shakes. Dustin made sure to pick up one for each of them. The kid would slurp at his shake ferociously until it was gone, his cheeks sucked in like an old man's. When he could slurp no more, Dustin would give him what was left of his.

One day, after finishing both their shakes, the boy stared at him instead of the TV, as if working up the courage to speak. "Does my face look like you?" he asked finally. Dustin's heart plummeted. He'd fooled himself into believing he looked unremarkable.

"No," he said softly. "You look normal."

The boy frowned, as if he didn't believe him; the kid had no idea that his burns were confined to his legs. Dustin left the room and went to talk to a nurse, who gave him a hand mirror. It was the same one his father had held up to his face after the accident. On his way back, Dustin stopped for a second and leaned against the wall to catch his breath. He brought the mirror to the room and held it in front of the boy, who studied it fearfully before easing into a grin. This is what had been worrying him the whole time: the idea that they looked alike.

Later, as he was leaving, the boy met Dustin's eyes: a look of such fierce attachment that Dustin almost flinched.

Outside the hospital, in the parking garage, he grabbed the hand putty from the passenger seat and kneaded the pain from his fingers. He still had an hour before he was supposed to meet Taz. More and more, it was his decision to visit; he couldn't remember the last time she'd driven out to Auburn Fields. It should have been humiliating, this crawling after her, but then when he actually saw Taz in person—standing there all tan and friendly and contrite—he forgot the grievance he'd been nursing or whatever they'd been arguing about on the phone and felt only the frantic stage fright of losing her completely. Dustin tried to think when this fear had begun in earnest. Her birthday, probably. He couldn't even remember what they'd fought about; what he remembered, clearly, was returning to his mom's place with muddy shoes and seeing Taz waiting at the door, damp-eyed and apologetic, newly seventeen, and the flood of happiness in his chest giving way to a sort of panic. Lately she'd begun backing out of dates at the last minute, calling him to say she wasn't feeling well or that her dad was getting too suspicious. He couldn't be sure, but Dustin suspected she was actually going out with friends her own age. Yesterday he'd called her line at home and it had been busy for over an hour; when Taz answered, on the tenth try, she claimed she'd left the phone off the hook by mistake.

In these desperate moments he still missed the old Taz, the one who'd hugged him so hard she'd left bruises. He was afraid of her confidence. But it was also what attracted him: now that he was a freak, an outcast himself, he'd stopped glamorizing the freaky and unpopular. He needed someone who didn't eat glass to like him.

Dustin slipped the Dart into reverse and headed back toward Hawthorne Boulevard, making sure to keep his thumb up in the air so it wouldn't cramp. Last week, drawn by some irresistible force, he'd stopped by Jungle of Pets. He'd parked in front of the store and waited in the car, nervous as a child, unsure if Hector still worked there until he saw him appear in the window. Here was the person who'd ruined his life, dressed in a green polo shirt and matching khakis. Hector bent down to show something to a customer, and Dustin could see Ginger, the sugar glider, nestled in the pocket of his shirt. Amazing that the tiny creature was still alive. He wanted to feel angry, but what he felt at the moment was wonderment. This strange man who carried animals around in his pocket: he hadn't intended to destroy Dustin's life, and yet he had, thoughtlessly, without even meaning to. Now he seemed to have returned to his life as though nothing had changed. Dustin imagined that if he came here every day, if he parked in the same spot and spied on Hector, tracking his every move like a scientist—if he did this, something might be revealed to him, a deeper meaning; the reason behind this obscene cosmic joke would present itself.

Hector bowed his head as he talked to the customer, dispensing some sort of advice, his tall shoulders stooped like a vulture's. The truth was, Dustin missed his companionship. He had no other friends; often, if he wasn't working, he went to the movies by himself. He waited for Hector to look up and see him through the window, knowing that he would not have the courage to come back, but Hector had turned his head and walked the customer to the front of the store.

Now Dustin drove through Palos Verdes on his way to Rat Beach, where he was meeting Taz. It was ridiculously warm for February; the sun glinted off the cars in the parking lot and hurt his eyes. He put on his cowboy hat and walked down the dirt path to the water, wearing a long-sleeve shirt to protect his scars. It was the first time he'd been back to his old surfing spot since the accident. The waves were small and mushy, four-foot cappers that foamed off on the sand; a few kooks in wetsuits did their best to ride them, spilling off their boards as though yanked by a cane. Dustin was relieved not to see any of his old friends out on the water before remembering they were all in college. It amazed him that he used to call this his life.

How long ago—centuries, it seemed—that he'd come down here with Jonas to meet Kira.

He found Taz near the first lifeguard stand, talking to several teenage girls in sweatshirts hanging to their knees. Even from a distance she looked poised and Kira-like, flinging her hair back when she laughed. She'd stopped dyeing it a while ago; her witch's forelock shone in the sun. Taz reached up to touch her earlobe—just a touch, but Dustin could see the effort it took to keep herself from picking at it. The secret struggle gave him hope. She peeled away from her friends without waving at Dustin and wandered over to greet him.

"Who was that?" he asked.

"Some girls from school," she said, refusing to glance their way. "They're playing hooky, too."

She looked at his cowboy hat, furtively, and the embarrassment in her face made him heartsick. He wondered if she'd chosen this time to meet him—three on a Wednesday afternoon—because she'd thought no one would be here to see them. He took off his hat and tossed it in the sand, knowing how burned he'd get even in February. The sun on his face felt like a long-lost friend.

They spread a blanket out on the sand, each of them taking two corners and tugging it flat. Dustin had brought some wine in his backpack and they uncorked it with his Swiss Army knife. Passing the bottle back and forth, Taz seemed to lose her embarrassment, her voice low and affectionate. She leaned her head on his shoulder. She was like this lately, as unpredictable as a cat. He couldn't help wondering if her tenderness was part of a good-bye she'd already enacted in her own mind.

He told Taz about seeing the boy in the burn unit, how his face had seemed so dejected when he left.

"I never would have pegged you for a dad," Taz said.

"Me neither," Dustin said. "Maybe it's all those toxic fumes."

"I'm starting to get a little jealous. You see him more than me."

"That's not true," he said, taking a swig. "Anyway, whose fault is that?"

She lifted her head from his shoulder. "What do you mean?"

"It's hard enough to get you on the phone. It's like you don't want to talk to me."

"Don't be stupid."

He watched a longboard wash up on the beach, an old man in a wetsuit wading through the foam to retrieve it. The man's face was gouged with wrinkles.

"Maybe we should go on a trip together," Dustin said desperately. "Drive down to Mexico or something."

"Yeah, right," she said, looking away.

"Why not?"

"Maybe because my dad would charge you with rape."

"He can't charge me with rape. There's got to be a three-year age gap."

"Anyway, I've got, like, a year left to live, remember? From swimming in the dump. I might as well be ninety."

"You always joke," Dustin said quietly.

She frowned and stood up, as though to end the discussion. He knew going to Mexico was a ridiculous idea—she'd miss school, for starters—but he wanted to at least indulge the fantasy like they used to. Taz kicked at the sand, her face hidden behind her hair.

"Do you think . . . I mean, are you going to live out in the desert forever?"

"Why not?"

"I don't know." She shrugged uncomfortably. "Maybe you should go to college or something. Like Lyle."

"Okay," Dustin said. "I'll just move into her dorm."

It wasn't meant to be funny, and Taz didn't laugh. She began to dig a hole in the sand with her foot, as if she were burying a bone.

"So that's what you want?" Dustin said. "Me to ship off to New York like Lyle?"

"It doesn't have to be Harvard."

"*Columbia*. For Christ's sake, Harvard's in Cambridge."

Taz looked up from the sand. Perhaps she'd made him angry on purpose; it would make breaking up with him easier. The truth was, he sometimes fantasized about going to New York with Lyle, the two of them renting an apartment somewhere near CBGB and riding the subway around like the Ramones. A ridiculous fantasy. He could work at a video store, a *real* one where customers had heard of John Ford. They'd fix breakfast together in the mornings, before Lyle had to go to class, joking around like they used to do as kids. How much fun they'd had, making up Tom Swifties to lob over their mother's head. *I'll give you a thousand bucks for that piano, she said grandly.* When he looked back at his former life, it was these moments that he missed most of all: not writing songs with Biesty and the band or even surfing a perfect break at the Cove, but the ordinary moments he'd always thought he was tolerating, the meals and camping trips and Monopoly games—the slow, jokey, unrehearsed vaudeville of being a Ziller.

"I thought Cambridge was a school," Taz said.

Dustin laughed—more meanly than he'd intended. "That's Cambridge *University*. Different continent. This is the United States."

Taz's face darkened. "Oh, Mr. Fucking Genius. Just because you got burned. It's like you know everything now."

He knew the day would come eventually when his tragedy would no longer be sacred. Nothing stayed sacred very long: disfigurement, unspeakable pain, it would be used against you eventually. People grew bored with it, and then angry that they were bored.

Weirdly, Dustin felt a lifting in his heart, like a release.

Though it was the middle of February, Taz began to undress, tugging off her dress and stripping down to a black bikini. It hadn't occurred to him that she might actually go swimming. She left him sitting there and walked down to the water, passing a few hard-core sunbathers basking on their towels; her body was softer than these girls', slightly chunky at the waist, but she seemed utterly unself-conscious. Dustin had only a faint recollection of what this must be like. A cloud moved across the sun, dimming the ocean. Walking down the mostly deserted beach, taking her poised, sweet, oblivious time, Taz seemed like an alien species. She splashed into the water and then dove headfirst into a wave, disappearing from sight before popping up again as if from a toaster.

She was all that he had; he would not have her much longer. Dustin double-checked to make sure nobody he knew was around, then slipped out of his pants and shoes and socks. He saved his shirt for last, yanking it quickly over his head. He'd imagined it might be a liberating moment, but what he felt was ugliness and shame, the scars magnifying in his mind because he refused to look. They embarrassed him much more than the fact that he was standing on a public beach in his boxers. He walked down to the ocean, forcing himself not to rush, all the while imagining the disgust—the shrinking—he was causing in people's hearts. The sun reappeared from its cloud; his new body had never been touched by it. Dustin waded knee-deep into the foam and then dove into the icy water, surfacing from the shock, suddenly alive and gasping.

CHAPTER 49

Warren parked the Oldsmobile a block away from the Tremors' address and then straightened his tie and name tag in the rearview mirror. The name tags were a new development, designed to make the BladeCo team look more professional. They were instructed to wear them at all times. They were also instructed to park a block away from the house, so that no one would see their cars through the window and make a snap judgment about their character. Snap judgments did not tend to sell knives. Neither did '79 Oldsmobiles with giant skulls on the back window. What sold knives was the sort of cockiness—bullying, effervescent—that did not permit the existence of '79 Oldsmobiles in the world.

Even under the tutelage of Ted, his team leader, it had taken Warren a while to learn this. But he had. Last month alone, Warren had sold six Ultimate Entertainer Sets at $1,899 a pop. Ted had given him a gift certificate to an Italian restaurant in Lancaster: a reward, for him and the "lovely lady." The certificate was still there on his refrigerator, waiting to be redeemed.

Warren opened the case beside him and did a quick inventory of his knives. As he was hiking the steep hill to the Tremors' house, lugging the briefcase along with him, his chest locked with a familiar pain. He sat down on the curb. The pain deepened into a physical weight, dense as quicksand, before spreading up his neck. A thawlike warmth. He closed his eyes, waiting for the weight to dissolve. This one took its time: even after the pain had faded, the quicksand seemed to remain where it was, lodged firmly in his chest.

He sat there for a long time, catching his breath. The episodes were getting worse. He'd seen a doctor finally last week, a cardiologist, who'd made him run on a treadmill until he dropped. He had an abnormal EKG—nothing off the charts, but nonetheless "a concern." Warren was supposed to call the hospital to schedule a follow-up test, something to do with injecting dye into his blood vessels, but for some reason he kept finding excuses to put it off.

One of these days, perhaps, he wouldn't get off the curb at all. He'd collapse out here in the desert. How long would it be before anyone found him?

He got up from the curb and walked through the sun to the Tremors' house. A young woman in a headband answered the door, her red hair crimped like a rag doll's. Warren asked her if her mother was home.

"I'm Mindy Tremor," the woman said. "We talked on the phone. I was just on the Exercycle."

Warren apologized and followed the woman into the kitchen, surprised to find a boy only a few years younger than Jonas sitting at the table. A girl was there, too, bony and beautiful, peeling some cellophane from a Fruit Roll-Up. She looked about fourteen. Warren felt impossibly old. Mindy Tremor drifted over to the corner of the room, where an Exercycle stood in perhaps symbolic proximity to the refrigerator.

"You don't mind if I hop on while you talk? I was just finishing my miles."

Warren had done whole demonstrations to people who were drunk, senile, terminally ill; he could make his pitch to someone on a bicycle. He opened his case on the table and began humbly, inquiringly, as if he were skeptical himself. *Why does a knife go dull? Any guesses?* He was careful to make eye contact, to treat the boy's dim-witted answers with respect. Once he'd earned the family's trust—he was a father himself, not some weirdo off the street—he turned to Mindy Tremor atop her Exercycle and preyed gently on her maternal fears, talking about the danger inherent in a dull blade, citing statistics he made up on the spot, asking how long it had been since she'd sharpened her favorite knife. When she objected to the idea of a metal spatula because it would scratch her nonstick pans, he pulled an article from his pocket—Xeroxed from *The New England Journal of Medicine*—which claimed that Teflon might cause Alzheimer's. Mindy Tremor stopped pedaling to look at the article. Patiently, Warren moved on to the convenient features unique to BladeCo, touching on the lifetime guarantee, the patented ergonomic handle, the notch on the top of the tomato knife that prevented juice from running down your arm. He asked the boy to get a tomato from the fridge and then sliced it speedily into disks, pretending that Jonas and Lyle and Camille were watching him. He was making a pitch to them as well, the family he'd lost. It was not the words themselves that mattered but the fact that he was making them. He was doing something for a change. In the end, if it was a good-enough pitch, his family might even buy what he had to offer. They would say, *It's not too late, you've actually learned something, your life hasn't been entirely hapless and for naught.*

"And I don't know if you're like me, sick of wimpy scissors that won't cut anything but hair, but we've got a special offer right now if you order any BladeCo set and knife block. I'll throw in these sixty-dollar Super Shears, guaranteed to be the sharpest on the planet. Would you have a penny on you, by any chance?"

Mindy Tremor got off her Exercycle and fished one from her purse. Brandishing it between two fingers, like a magician, Warren slipped the penny into the hinge of the scissors and then snipped it effortlessly in half. Mindy Tremor actually gasped. Her daughter smirked, but oddly he did not feel humiliated. He had not felt humiliated for some time. All the shame he'd felt over his failure— losing his money, letting down his family—seemed ridiculous to him now. Or not ridiculous: *immaterial.* It was as if it had happened to someone else.

"That's what I mean when I say BladeCo products speak for themselves."

"Hey, that's pretty awesome," the boy said.

"Not just awe*some,*" Warren said, handing him a new penny from his pocket. "Awe-*much.*"

Later, driving home, Warren passed the exit that led to Melody's trailer park. The sign for Mahogany Views was still there, advertising ANNUAL EASE ONLY. A couple weeks ago, he'd stopped by on his way back from an appointment in Rosamond, not knowing what he would say if Melody was home. He hadn't wanted to seem overly pitiful; nor, if it turned out that her husband had moved back in, did he want to cause trouble. He wasn't sure if he'd be greeted with a kiss or a punch. In any case, the problem failed to present itself. The trailer park was gone. Vanished. Instead of rows of tidy, sun-bleached trailers, Warren was confronted with a bulldozer sending up a great pillar of dust, digging up some broken concrete and shoveling the giant slabs into a dump truck. They were breaking ground for a subdivision.

Warren sat there in his car for a long time, watching them work. He wanted to laugh at the developer's hubris but did not feel at all confident that the project would fail. There were developments springing up all around them, from Palmdale to the 405, dotting the Mojave with miraculous three-story homes.

Except in the vicinity of the dump, of course. Cancer Corridor, they called it on the news. That was a wasteland, Warren's own.

Today, instead of heading right home, he stopped by Mojave Video. He'd gotten into the habit of doing this; it was right off the freeway, and he enjoyed having Dustin pick out a video for him to watch at home. Now that they were the only ones there, he had nothing else to do at night.

"You look like a Mormon," Dustin said, glancing at Warren's name tag, which he'd forgotten to take off. As always, the inside of the store—its aisles of dusty tapes, TV flickering in the corner—made him comfortably depressed. A woman in fatigues opened the door, looked at the two of them, and then left, checking her watch as if she'd forgotten something. "See there? You're driving away customers."

"That was a coincidence," Warren said.

Dustin began sorting through some videotapes by the register, logging their titles into a notebook. "Actually, she's a pain in the ass. I don't even know her name. Rents *The Deer Hunter* like three times a week, just so she can hang around and talk."

"Maybe she's attracted to you."

Dustin looked away without saying anything. Even Warren had to admit this was unlikely. Last week, Warren had seen a mother—a woman with flabby, sunburned arms—whisper to her toddler before approaching the counter. Dustin had either given up caring or was too distracted to notice. Since he'd stopped seeing Taz, he'd been more out of it than usual. Warren felt bad for him, of course, but, selfishly, he couldn't help thinking of it as a blessing, too: without Taz, he and Dustin had been spending more time together, sometimes even driving into town to grab lunch.

He started to ask for a recommendation but Dustin hushed him, turning his attention to the TV. On the screen, a man with a blue-painted face was wrapping himself in dynamite; he lit the fuse but then changed his mind at the last minute, saying, *"Merde!"* and trying to put the flame out with his hand. The dynamite exploded anyway. Unconcerned, the camera panned out to the ocean, the word FIN appearing divinely in the sky. It was so awful Warren had to laugh.

"What on earth was that?" he asked.

"Godard. The New Wave."

"I thought you hated New Wave."

"That's *music*. Jesus." Dustin turned around, fiddling with the VCR behind the register. "Two completely different things."

Somehow they'd come full circle: Warren staring at his son's back, facing the brunt of his disdain. At least they were talking, though. He asked Dustin if he could rent the New Wave movie.

"They talk to the camera and stuff. It's weird. I don't think you'll like it."

"I like weird," Warren said. "Plus I'm into explosions."

Dustin didn't laugh. Still, the fact that Warren could make a crack like this at all—without incurring his wrath—seemed like progress. To be honest, he was surprised that Dustin had wanted to live with him instead of his mother. *He'll sit around watching movies all day,* Camille had warned. If Warren were a better man, perhaps, he would have insisted Dustin move out and face the world, but he was too grateful to make him leave.

Dustin slipped a different tape into the VCR, another French film with the same riveting, boxer-faced actor who had blown himself up. The owner had put Dustin in charge of stocking the foreign film section, and he was doing his best to fill it with movies no one would rent. For the first time, it occurred to Warren that his son *liked* working in a video store. The place was cool and peaceful, the buzz of a trapped fly mixing with the melodious breeze of French from the TV. What was wrong with watching movies all day? As a man you were so conditioned to believe that ambition was important, that without it you were lost—but what did it matter in the end? Certainly there was little evidence that it made you happy.

"This reminds me a bit of your mom's videos," Warren said. "The same sort of non sequiturs."

"He smokes about as much as Mom did, too."

Warren nodded, pretending to watch the movie. "What do you want for dinner tonight? I was thinking of making veal parmigiana."

"I might go out with Osman," Dustin said. "There's a movie he wants to see. I haven't decided."

"Who's Osmond?"

"*Osman*. He works the weekend shift with me."

"I'll make dinner anyway," Warren said, trying to hide his disappointment. "You can eat it tomorrow, if you decide to go out."

At home, Warren stripped off his coat and tie and filled the bathtub with steaming water. He'd never taken baths when Camille lived here, not wanting to hog the bathroom. Now that she'd left, he had the freedom to do other things as well. He could leave his shoes in the bathroom overnight. He could play the stereo as loud as Dustin's. He could call tank tops "wife beaters" without being scolded. He could leave the newspaper any way he wanted, sections folded this way and that, not having to reassemble each one primly like a gift. Generally, though, these freedoms paled in comparison to what he'd lost. The loneliness mired everything, like a swamp. It was huge and unnavigable. Sometimes he missed Camille so much he felt like he couldn't walk. Though they hadn't shared a bed in months, he'd gravitated back to his old side of the mattress, perched at the edge as if making room for her restless limbs, the only way he could sleep.

He tried not to think about Dustin moving out. He knew the boy would eventually find his own place, perhaps even make a life for himself. The idea of living in an empty house, waiting for the bank to kick him out, filled Warren with dread.

He got out of the bath and changed into sweats. On his way to the kitchen, he heard a car outside the house, pulling up to the curb. Warren's heart leapt. He rushed to the window but it was only the mailman, brown and sun-wizened, his pith helmet slipping forward as he leaned out of the truck. Surprisingly, the man failed to flip off the house or even glower in its direction. He seemed to have accepted his mail route at last, resigned to a fate he couldn't control.

Warren went out to get the mail after he'd gone, the evening sun on his shoulders gentle as a hand. The smell of the dump still had the power to turn his stomach, though there was something consoling, too, about its unwavering stink, a feeling he'd come to associate with home. Curled inside the mailbox, sand-wiched between the phone bill and a Sharper Image catalog, was an eleven-by-fourteen envelope. Warren opened the envelope and pulled out a glossy photograph of Jesus Christ in a hooded robe, clutching a shepherd's staff and staring majestically into the distance, presumably at His flock. It took Warren a second to recognize the face. At the bottom, just above Christ's bold and splashy signature, were the words *Keep on keepin' on.* Warren laughed. He started to throw the picture in the trash can, but some unnegotiable force caused him to hold on to it.

Back inside, he began to get dinner on, pulling *The Joy of Cooking* down from the shelf and flipping to the recipe for veal parmigiana. It was Dustin's favorite dish; he'd loved it since he was a little boy, four or five, ordering veal pajama at restaurants because he couldn't pronounce the name. Warren took the cutlets from the fridge and began to pound them thin as pancakes. He didn't know when he'd begun to like cooking; it had happened after Camille left, a way to fill the hour before dark. It wasn't the cooking itself he liked so much as the idea that Dustin would eat it. Up until now, everything Warren had done for his son—buying him beer, breaking into the Shackneys' house, even saving his life on the lawn—had failed to make Dustin happy. In his own peculiar way, Warren had devoted his life to helping him. But perhaps he'd needed something else, a devotion strong enough to refuse him.

Warren would do what he could to let Dustin live. Surely, though, it was still his duty—a father's one true job—to feed him.

He mixed up some bread crumbs and Parmesan and then began the sauce, chopping an onion on the counter. He'd become so expert at the task that it annoyed him when his eyes burned. He opened the window. The air was turning cold and breezy, hoarse with insects, the desert beginning to take on the otherworldly glow that happened before dusk. The Joshua trees, dwarfed by their own shadows, moved him strangely. Lately, the smallest things had the power to crush or elate him. Except for the freeway in the distance, there was no one for miles. Warren had the shivery, unsettling feeling that he was the last person on earth. Millions of years ago, this was the bottom of the sea, a place of gigantic sharks and four-legged fish.

He set the table for dinner, inspecting the knives for stray bits of food. The clock over the sink said 6:43. Dustin would be home in a few minutes or not at all.

The tomato sauce simmered on the stove, fogging Warren's glasses when he bent down to stir it. He set the timer for ten minutes and then sat down to wait. *You've got your whole life ahead of you,* people liked to say. In truth there was not much time, a blip, and most of what you did was a mistake. You were lucky to find a safe and proper home. In the end, even the world cast you out, withdrawing its welcome.

The kitchen darkened slowly, dimming imperceptibly as a cave. Warren remembered being sick as a boy, too flu-ridden to go to school, how he used to lie in bed as the windows grew dark and wait for his mother to get home from her interminable shift at the gas station, the walls of his room disappearing bit by bit before his eyes. The boredom would merge with his sickness until he couldn't tell them apart. How desperate he'd felt! He could have switched on the light but out of some childish perversity refused to get out of bed. Lying there in the dark, damp with sweat, Warren would imagine his mother's face with the studious precision of a dream, perfecting every last detail in his mind, from the tiny pores in her nose to the mysterious, slept-on crease of her earlobe. Only a perfect likeness would bring her to his door. And somehow it worked: she would show up after what seemed like years and flip on the lights of his room and touch his forehead with a rough, slender, gas-smelling hand, which wouldn't shame him in the privacy of their own home but feel like all he'd been waiting for, the purest of joys. It startled Warren now to think of it. Was that really all there was to love? Darkness undone, a hand on your forehead. In the meantime all you could do was wait—tired, alone, the minutes as long or short as a lifetime—for the face in your dream to appear.

ACKNOWLEDGMENTS

I would like to thank the Stanford Creative Writing Program and the National Endowment for the Arts for their generous support in helping me write this book. I am deeply grateful to Andrew Altschul, Scott Hutchins, Dorian Karchmar, Greg Martin, Samantha Martin, and Tom McNeely for the extraordinary time and effort they put into this book and for their invaluable insights and suggestions. I am indebted to Dr. Gordon Noel for his medical expertise and to Alison Florance, Hunter Johnson, Margaret W. Noel, and Bruce Snider for their advice on professions not my own. I am also indebted to the following authors and books: Barbara Ravage, *Burn Unit: Saving Lives After the Flames;* Andrew M. Munster, MD, *Severe Burns: A Family Guide to Medical and Emotional Recovery;* Dennis J. Stouffer, *Journeys through Hell: Stories of Burn Survivors' Reconstruction of Self and Identity;* John Stauber and Sheldon Rampton, *Toxic Sludge Is Good for You: Lies, Damn Lies and the Public Relations Industry.* My wife, Katharine Noel, helped me more than I can possibly express—for her patience, encouragement, and abundant wisdom, I am profoundly grateful.

ABOUT THE AUTHOR

Eric Puchner is an assistant professor of literature at Claremont McKenna College. He has received a Pushcart Prize and a National Endowment for the Arts grant. His short story collection, *Music Through the Floor,* was a finalist for the New York Public Library's Young Lions Award. He lives in Los Angeles with his wife, novelist Katharine Noel, and their two children.

A SCRIBNER
READING GROUP GUIDE

MODEL HOME

QUESTIONS FOR DISCUSSION

1. *Model Home* is told in chapters from alternating points of view. Did this allow you to get a full view of the Zillers? Was there any character you wanted to hear from more or less? Until late in the novel, we see Jonas through other people's eyes, but don't hear his point of view. Did his perspective surprise you?

2. Was there a character you found yourself most identifying with? Did you relate most to the one closest to you in terms of age and gender, or another one entirely? Why?

3. At the beginning of the novel, Dustin is popular and eternally optimistic while Lyle is an angry outcast, making lists of people and things she hates. At the end of the novel Dustin and Lyle seem to have reversed roles as Lyle becomes more outgoing and Dustin retreats. Why do you think the author positions them as foils to each other? Do their differences make them seem more extreme?

4. One of the major themes of *Model Home* is that of being an outsider: in life, at school, in one's own family. In what ways is each character on the outside looking in?

5. Although Dustin is likable and friendly, he has "a different vision of himself. In this vision . . . he was strange and spontaneous and did charismatically delinquent things" (p. 26). After the accident, he becomes angry, withdrawn, and often cruel. Do you think this latter version of Dustin is his true self, which he allows to come out once he's no longer concerned about people liking him? Or is it just a show to keep everyone at bay?

6. Did Jonas's quirks make him more or less likable to you? Dustin states that Jonas's "life would be an endless trial of humiliations that he was too . . . clueless to avoid" (p. 29). Do you agree with that statement, or do you think it's a stage he'll outgrow?

7. There are many moments in the novel when the characters are mistaken about the facts or about one another's motives, but the reader can see the whole picture. How did this affect your reading experience?

8. Dustin seems to have the perfect girlfriend in Kira, who is beautiful and supportive and believes in his talent, but he is drawn to her troubled younger sister, Taz. What is he drawn to in Taz? Once she's no longer acting out against herself, does he feel differently about her?

9. Although Lyle is sleeping with Hector, she won't tell her family about him, and when she sees him in public she pretends not to know him. Does Lyle want to be with Hector, or does she just want to be wanted? Is she upset after their breakup because she misses him, or because she doesn't want to be alone?

10. When Warren finally tells Camille the truth about their finances, "there was a release to it, the words tumbling free. He waited for the reckoning to begin" (p. 158). Many of the characters in *Model Home* are carrying heavy secrets. At what points in the novel do the characters confess secrets or choose to continue to hold them? Do they release them for the sake of others, or are their motives selfish?

11. Camille knows that Warren is keeping something from her, and suspects him of having an affair. Is the truth more or less of a betrayal? At the end of the novel, is Camille disappointed in Warren, or in the way her life has turned out?

12. After Jonas is reunited with his family, he makes up an idyllic story about where he's been and what happened to him. Why do you think he chooses not to tell them the truth? Are his parents right or wrong not to push him for an answer? Is this willingness to accept a lie, however obvious, indicative of how they react to one another in general?

13. When Warren is driving home from picking up Jonas, he muses that, "Perhaps, in the end, it was all you could hope for: to get your family together in one car . . . and feel the precious weight of their presence" (p. 325). Does Warren find redemption in his family? Ultimately, what does the novel say about family?

1. When Jonas runs away, the experience is very different from what he expected. Have the members of your book club discuss, if they were to "run away from home," what that ideal experience would be like, and what they think they would miss the most from their own lives.

2. *Model Home* is filled with such rich language and dialogue. There are many points where the author seems to capture whole scenes or tell whole stories with one sentence. As they read, have the members of your club keep track of their favorite passages or quotes to share during your discussion.

3. Have the members of your club visit the author's website, EricPuchner.com, to read some of his short stories and nonfiction essays, or read his short story collection *Music Through the Floor*. Discuss how his writing style varies across genres.